STREETWHYS

STREET WHYS

STREETWHYS

a Dickie Cornish mystery

Christopher Chambers

THREE ROOMS PRESS
New York, NY

StreetWhys
A DICKIE CORNISH MYSTERY BY Christopher Chambers

ISBN 978-1-953103-55-0 (trade paperback)
ISBN 978-1-953103-56-7 (Epub)
Library of Congress Control Number: 2024950071

TRP-116

Pub Date: April 15, 2025
First edition

BISAC category code
FIC049050 FICTION / African American / Mystery & Detective
FIC049070 FICTION / African American / Urban
FIC022010 FICTION / Mystery & Detective / Hard-Boiled
FIC050000 FICTION / Crime

COVER AND INTERIOR DESIGN:
KG Design International: www.katgeorges.com

DISTRIBUTED IN THE U.S. AND INTERNATIONALLY BY:
Ingram/Publishers Group West: www.pgw.com

Three Rooms Press
New York, NY
www.threeroomspress.com
info@threeroomspress.com

*To my family, those side by side with me,
and those unseen but having my back.*

STREETWHYS

CHAPTER ONE

Mexican White, Esmeralda's Red

FUNNY, IN THAT INSTANT I KNEW I'd moved up in the world.

I'm catching a beating from United States Marshals.

In the E. Barrett Prettyman Federal Courthouse, during lunch hour. Couple blocks from the U.S. Capitol. See, that also means some honcho who doesn't answer to nobody has green-lit my misery.

Uh-huh. I came to do my civic duty. Now my civic duty's doin' me.

Accordingly . . .

"Stay down, Pops!" Equal Protection growls.

"Lurch-lookin' mutha-fff . . ." Due Process huffs. He's an old fart like me so kicking at my kidneys while I'm doubled over from Equal Protection's fists has got him a bit winded.

Back in the day, I'd be so zooted on the Kush or boat that I'd rupture myself jumping the turnstile at Metro Center dead to midnight . . . and the WMATA cops'd wail on my big ass and toss me out onto Thirteenth Street . . . just in time for an MPD unit to come rolling up. I'd be all mumbles and stumbles . . . tore-up trousers wet with piss, toenails all ursine and poking through the sneaker canvas . . . throwing down a beat-feet to whatever Rare Essence bounce was playing in my head, and then I'd do a *Gladiator* yell to the jakes: "Are you not entertained?"

Nah. They weren't. And after they'd get their licks in, they'd leave me bloody on a bus shelter bench in Silver Spring or across the Potomac in a parking lot with the admonishment not to return to the District.

But I'd always come back. I'm a native. Hail to Redskins with mambo sauce, moe.

And nothing short of that hotshot of horse and China White . . . what regular folk and docs call fentanyl . . . would keep me from my appointed rounds as a fucking bum. Sorry . . . *unhoused.*

Now, back to the beating at hand . . .

. . . and stamp, in their navy blazers and gray slacks, these two gorilla-looking fools looming above me resemble ghetto prep schoolers held back twenty years. And here I am in my best gray suit from the Central Mission "unhoused men's clothing exchange." Shirt and necktie . . . brown gators with tassels . . . from Macy's and the Goodwill store, thank you.

Now, the red foam on my lips and stabbing pain in my gut tells me I'll see redder in my toilet if they ever let me out of this broom closet . . . uh-huh, a broom closet . . . there in the basement of ugliest building in Judiciary Square, like titan's tot with greasy fingers stacked some gargantuan white Lego blocks. Pretty words cut in stone above the lobby, though. Yep, Equal Protection. Due Process of Law.

So I roll onto my haunches, yank a wadded handkerchief from my trouser pocket to wipe my nose and mouth.

"Y'all meet me outside . . ." I mutter with a cough, ". . . with no badges—this won't be a one-way beatdown."

Equal Protection grunts and give an evil smirk before he tells me, "Your old ass's goin' catch more hands if you don't behave y'self, hear me? Lady want ta axe you some questions."

I watch Due Process tugging at his starched white shirt cuffs, straighten his tie as he cosigns, "My nigga here was all-conference defensive end at Morgan State. Clown again like you did when they brought that witness off the elevator and he'll clown on that ass."

Can hear my joints crackle as they hoist me to my feet. Can't let that diss go, however.

"I-I was All-American . . . tight end . . ." I stammer, breathless, ". . . and we used to come up to Baltimore and crumble y'all Morgan pussies like your big momma's stale biscuits . . ."

I'm certain they're about to kirk me, round two, when suddenly there's static and a beep from Due Process' waist and he's yanking the radio off his belt. Dig it, here and over at the Moultrie Courthouse, U.S. Marshals double as bailiffs—and they aren't the overweight nepotism hires you see in these dismal county courthouses in Virginia and Maryland, as my body can attest . . .

. . . and so it's now a female voice prompting one of my tormentors. That white chick . . . the other Marshal upstairs. The one who escorted *her* off the elevator.

Yeah, her. The reason I freaked out . . .

"Ten-four," Due Process acknowledges. "Comin' up. Move Esmeralda Rubio to conference room seven. They goin' do it in there." Can't make out what the response is but it's vexing him judging from the grimace. "I know it's 'irregular' but *you* goin' tell *her* no? I like my paycheck and my pension."

Meantime Equal Protection's looking me up and down to make sure no more blood's visible and my clothing ruffled not ripped.

"Was up wid you an' that ole rolla *Miz* Rubio, Pops?" he presses. "Geekin' like a mug."

"Nothing. And she's no rolla." Why am I defending her?

He keeps bluffin' on me. "Looks fine and phat in that red dress. Mexican, like black, don't crack, eh?"

Due Process opens the closet door, clocks the checkboard-tiled hallway. Not a soul. Justice ain't busy today. He adds his two cents. "She what the white boys call a MILF. Shit . . . a GILF—I saw the briefing memo . . . she like, fiddy, goin' on eiddy, like your ole ass, Cornish?"

"No," I whisper . . . really to myself. "She's a ghost."

They toss me into the same elevator that brought me down to perdition. It smells of defendants soiling their orange jumps . . . snot and vomit blown all over the insides of their spit-guards. Clearly not the lift used by proper white-collar scum, including friends and allies of the former President of this US of A.

Elevator doors slide open and the Marshals flank me and link my arms. You know it takes a lot to scare me; well . . . now the bile's rising into my mouth and there's no sound but our shoes tapping the tile, echoing through the corridor . . .

Equal Protection swipes a card key at a lacquered wooden door close to a stairwell. No tile or marble this time under-foot, just dingy federal blue carpet. Room's got a rear hall closed off by a smoked glass door but otherwise no windows, bare white walls, another door to the rear. Empty swivel chairs are on either side of a metal table. The table's too rusty and dented for this jont . . . like someone moved it in to make the place more fucked up and scary.

The Marshals leave me in there. No lunchin'—just some weird silent reverence as if I'm a temple sacrifice.

"Hello?" I call out once they shut the door but I can sense them posted just outside.

That back glass door opens with it comes a nostril-full of Esmeralda's south-of-the-border scent—Coqui Coqui—as jungle-pungent and floral-sweet as the day she turned me out in my dorm decades ago. Yeah, after the sex . . . and I almost lost my sense of smell or taste from her sherm sticks, graduating to the puffs on the rock pipe chased by a shot of tequila as she chanted her fucking *bruja* spells. What a show. I grit my teeth, await her presence . . .

. . . only it's not Esme, abundant flesh spilling from that red dress.

This sister could be Verna but for the plainness of the white blouse, short gray skirt . . . and she's tinier, despite the inches added by serious stiletto heels on those black shoes. Big almond-shaped eyes behind round glasses hit me next; they seem so oversized it's like she's a cartoon character or doll. She's got a short page boy hair cut like Halle Berry's back in the day and doll or not, this girl's no youngin'. See, the skin's flawless smooth bronze till I see up close it's mostly Maybelline or whatever hiding the blemishes, and the hair's flecked with gray, unlike Esme's Cruella De Ville ribbon.

She takes a seat. Sets one of those mini tablet computers in front of her along her phone. Gestures me to sit—no words coming from her pert lips.

I could Frankenstein her little ass easy, hit that back door. But hey, I've done nothing wrong but show up to court to see justice done, show-out with my new ends, necktie and gators, flash my new PI-license.

"Please sir," this little honcho finally says in a frosty, high-pitch voice. "*Sit.*" No heat or officious toadies as back-up. Just those big eyes, confidently staring.

"Ma'am, I know my rights. I'll stand so I can get up outta here."

She lifts a painted-on brow. "*Ma'am?* Mr. Cornish, I had imagined years on the street, in and out of shelters, jail cells and rehab and such surely stripped away your home-training. I was wrong."

She pauses because she damn sure clocks the *are fucking joanin' me?* look in my eyes.

"Who are you?"

That knocks her back a bit. "I take it you don't watch or read the news . . ."

"Been busy. Thanks to you Feds. You are a Fed, right?"

"*Oh yes.*"

"Whatever I did, I plead the Fifth Amendment."

Still, no reaction. Same stare until she says, also monotoned, "You made quite a scene when you saw Ms. Rubio being escorted from the elevator to the Magistrate's chambers. You assaulted court personnel."

"I-I didn't."

She studies my face, my swaying stance. "Maybe the Marshals went too far in . . . pacifying you."

"Is that a joke?"

"I wanted to meet you."

"Am I under arrest?"

"Feel free to call an attorney."

Yeah, I sit my ass down with that one remark. And she doesn't need to ask me if I want water, or first aid. I know how this goes. I decide to be the gentle giant, feel her out.

"I-I was here . . ." I'm studying the table now, not her, ". . . cause my friends were testifying in front the same grand jury downstairs that subpoenaed me back in August. *The* Chief of the Metropolitan Police Department . . . Linda Figgis and her

Amazons in blue—heard of them? Stealing children and selling them up for adoption by 'proper' people. On the other side, there's Deputy Chief Dante Antonelli . . ."

"A bad apple."

"A dead one, and I'm happy. His officers were waxing black men like this was Mississippi, robbing the pluggers, taxing corner stores . . . making women in shelters turn tricks like we're in Russia, feel me, Miss? See, *then* his goons covered for the those crackers running amok in the Capitol Building . . . the January Sixth shit . . ."

Now she's clocking me like she's that mean little blue chickenhawk from Bugs Bunny and I'm Foghorn Leghorn. After a few unblinking, discomfiting seconds she finally says, "I was with the FBI for many years. I saw . . . terrible things. *Terrible* things." Suddenly I'm feeling what—a thaw? "Eventually I went to Georgetown University Law Center on Uncle Sam's dime." I spy a ring on one of her slender fingers and thanks to another one of my afflictions, fixations, peculiarities, I know it's not it's not a Hoya piece of jewelry.

"Y-You HU Bison?"

She nods.

I say, "I am . . . I mean, I was—"

"Number Eighty-Eight," she cuts me off.

"Kill . . . who . . . who are you?"

"My sorors and I saw you break records at that Morehouse Homecoming game, a lifetime ago. Only fun thing the big sisters allowed my line to do that Fall."

Brain's probably one half Swiss cheese now but I'm running the catalog of faces, voices . . .

"One hundred thirty-three yard's receiving in that game," she recites. "Would have been MEAC MVP four years in a row had you not . . . *quit.*" And all this time, no smile, just a deadpan like mine . . . and now I'm thinking she's got the same affliction *you* tried to beat out of *me*, Daddy. "Three TDs—two from passes and one when you were blocking on a sweep and the halfback fumbled and—"

". . . the ball just bounced into my arms." I twitch a grin. "You were always following me and my O-line boys around Founders when we were tryna study . . . well, when I was cramming, and they were plagiarizing my shit. Always asking questions; they thought you were a freshman groupie. But nah, you even asked me why I turned down the Naval Academy and Ivies for HU."

"Recall what you said?"

I nod. " 'To honor my mother, to piss off that motherfucker called Daddy.' *Lil' Angie.*"

Finally, she extends her small hand. Even smaller in my big mitt. "Yes. Angela Bivens. I am not one of the U.S. Attorneys. I am *the* Deputy Attorney General of the United States—at least so long as we have a working democracy. For the next few months, at least. Good to see you, Richard."

"Call me Dickie."

"Dickie . . . I'll get to the point. I knew you'd be in the courthouse today. This coincides with our recission of Ms. Esmeralda Rubio's deportation. We have unfinished business regarding Mr. Jaime Bracht. You remember Mr. Bracht, right?"

With Bracht's name leaving her lips I release her hand. No more twitched grins, just twitches.

"Bracht's . . . Bracht's dead. And Esme . . . she's a dope fiend, a phony-ass trick . . . rich-bitch . . . with that deluded peasant conjure woman bullshit act."

Little gal's still unfazed no matter how unhinged I sound. "Be that as it may . . ."

"I'm . . . sorry."

"It's okay. Again, let me get back on track here. You ever hear of 'Mexican White?'"

Out of the fucking blue? I dip my head and correct her. "*China* White."

"Mexican White now. Chinese fentanyl is being processed in Mexico, then secreted across the border under the eyes of corrupted Federal patrol agents and local law enforcement, or by migrants used as mules under pain of death. There're rumors that fentanyl precursor materials like NPP are now coming up through the Sonoran Desert and into San Diego, then sent east where it's cooked into the final product. We've even tested other imported synthetics like Adderall: every batch adulterated by Mexican White. But it gets worse."

Gotten. Gotten worse. Takes these people a year to catch-up to death's head start.

"What's that got to do with me?"

"Do you know what xylazine is?"

"Not really." Of course I do. Back in the day the D.C. fiends called it horse aspirin.

"The dealers are getting a version of xylazine cut with the fentanyl . . . it's either injected . . . or pill form. So my question is have you heard of some new variants hitting the east coast, particularly here in the nation's capital as a . . . test market. 'Apache Tranq' or 'Zombie Tranq?' Doesn't ring a bell?"

"No."

"*Hmmm . . .*"

"I'm clean."

"You have no opinion, as a former *fiend*, recently 'unhoused?'"

"I'm clean."

She leans in again, as if she's six-three and I'm the littl'in. "You're telling me that with your knowledge of the street you have no clue what this Zombie Tranq or Apache is . . . the ulcers and sores? How some people would rather die than endure rehab's pain?"

I'm buttoned up.

"Is it true the supplies of crack rock, loveboat, meth, smack—all're dried up? Even the weed that's illegal—the 'Za' you all call it—is adulterated with this mess like an invasive species, right?"

I bite my lip, shift, do anything but look at her. "I-I guess."

Those big cartoon eyes of hers narrow.

"Then allow me to enlighten you, Dickie, as best I can. The Zombie, the Apache—it's like a stool with three legs. One leg is the street dealers—or pluggers as you native Washingtonians call them. MPD has no clue who these people are. They don't operate out of traditional traphouses."

Fuck's she doing? "Angie—"

"Miss Bivens will do," she corrects, curtly. "But not *Ma'am*."

"Miss Bivens, don't the FBI and DEA work for you?"

"May I finish? The next leg is the guarantor, sort of an ombudsman or troubleshooter who backs the plugger financially . . . we're guessing it's someone the cartel trusts . . ."

Ombudsman. *Ha*! On the street that's the shot-caller, at least that was the term back in the sweet ole rock and heroin days.

"So I'm guessing MPD hasn't been helpful."

Her deep sigh belies another thaw, another glimpse there's a person under that ice veneer.

"At MPD Deputy Chief Dante Antonelli was in charge of that intel. And he sabotaged it, with you giving the reason yourself. You see, Dickie, the third leg is the supplier. Now here, I have the great fortune and misfortune of knowing exactly who I'm dealing with. The supplier imports the fentanyl or fentanyl precursors, obtains the xylazine, finances the operations. Jaime Bracht's private equity fund headquartered in Virginia . . . whose assets we seized . . . was inextricably meshed with China's pharma sector. Ironic—considering the former Administration's position on the Chinese, come the pandemic . . ."

"He was only in the in the Cabinet for a minute . . .

"Commerce Secretary. That's even more ironic given what I'm going to share. At the time of his . . . *death* . . . Bracht still had significant holdings in Texas and Mexico. Enough to allow Esmeralda Rubio to live comfortably and openly. His family trust wasn't touched by DOJ and it remains connected to billionaires . . . extremists, white supremacists."

"He is . . . was . . . Mexican American. The whiter kind."

"Texas-sized self-hatred and racism toward indigenous peoples. Nothing new."

"And?"

"The President and my boss the Attorney General are old white men . . . boomers who still believe there are patriots out there playing by the rules, adhering to a higher calling, vested in a system. You and I, we've seen horror. We know the reality—the filth. Bracht's rich country-club *friends* are the suppliers, Dickie, I am sure of it. I can't prove who, not yet, I am on the cusp. But I will. I *must*, before Election Day.

They are in league with underground Chinese pharmas, Mexican cartels. Their cronies are people like Dante Antonelli, their allies are members of Congress and they are big donors to our orange-haired former President's campaign. Yes, my big prize defendant. In fact, some of them are on Fox News and Twitter . . . sorry, 'X' . . . at this very second, demonizing *me*. They're killing people with fentanyl. Full stop . . ."

So the little chickenhawk's not even blinking, eyes locked right on mine.

And I don't give a fuck. With the Donald's return at least the folk trying to end me'll be in my face, not behind my back . . .

"You strofin' if you think I'm going to help you."

"What you did say?"

"You heard me."

Thusly my nutsack's somewhat re-descended. Half expecting her to call in those two gorillas outside the door.

Nah. Her little face's getting all plumy, tight.

"Was I weak when I was in school?" she whispers, and I swear it's as if she's talking inwardly. "A little fool?"

"Pardon?"

For a second she just stares as she tries to steel herself. Sure enough, the ice's returning slowly, and so does the robotic tapping on the screen.

"This is bullshit," I get the balls to huff. "So let me go, or arrest me . . . but I swear if you let those niggas lay another on finger me . . ."

She's on that tablet, tapping and reading as if I'm a goonish afterthought. "As stated, feel free to call a lawyer." She halts, looks up. "You can even use my mobile. But we're not done yet."

Stamp, my mouth's wide damn open now, like some caught fish.

"You almost died of from fentanyl," she continues in the monotone. "Ten, eleven years ago, correct?"

Jesus, Mary and Joseph. "Uh . . . It was—"

"A hot dose," she cuts me off. "Smack and fentanyl? Until then it was fortified wine . . . get high on Kush, crush a deck of Xanax. Why a hot dose, Dickie?"

Neither the ceiling nor the desk, or the blue carpet offer quarter. "You . . . you're *wrong* . . ."

"Ms. Rubio . . . *Esmeralda* . . . she says . . . it was because you had a broken heart. I understand she was on methodone . . . then abandoned you. Yet she was the one who turned you out, correct—on campus, so long ago."

Now I'm looking at her dead-ass earnest face . . . through my fingers. This was the chick who used to puppy dog me in Founders, simpering?

"I'm leaving," I whisper.

"Again, technically you're not under arrest or in custody or sworn. Technically. But you'd be wise to stay seated. Street-wise." She closes the cover on her tablet abruptly. "Dickie, Ms. Rubio isn't here to just to give testimony on one leg of this Tranq business triangle. Ms. Rubio is prepared to sign a statement that you killed Jaime Bracht—the man who engaged you to locate her owing to your . . . street-wise skills . . ."

Didn't take my bladder pill. So all I can do squirm to keep piss from leaking onto my trousers.

"You killed him with a shotgun at his hunting lodge in Pennsylvania . . ."

I hear you laughing, Daddy.

". . . you departed with an infant birthed by an underaged undocumented teen killed by . . . MS-13 members, under Bracht's employ? I believe the young woman and the baby were the subjects Bracht truly wanted you to locate."

I'm slumping in the chair now, eyes shut. You stay down in there Daddy, down in my bowels . . . toiled too long and bled much to put you there, keep you there . . .

"The child's been adopted, through Mr. Bracht's former corporate attorney . . . whom you've somehow kept a sort of relationship with, correct?"

"N-No."

"When he got his law license reinstated he seemed to have only one paying client, in cash—regarding this child. The IRS and Bureau said a large amount of cash was never recovered, a sum Mr. Bracht was using for pay-offs."

I swallow the bile, the bad—and toss her as tough a look as I can muster. "Why don't ask Esme, la bruja, the witch? Now—can I go?"

This time, I'm giving her neither a leer or snarl. Just as prosaic a face as she's been assaulting me with, huh?

Well, I guess she's prepped to smack me right back. "Or maybe we can ask Verna Leggett?"

"Nah . . . stop."

"Did she take that money? You live in what—an SRO on Georgia Avenue, correct?"

"First, leave Verna be. Second, I'm no thief. Third . . . I'm no damn hobo. Not anymore. It's . . . it's a real apartment . . ."

"How'd you qualify for it?"

"Huh?"

"Seems to have been a quid pro quo with the city, my predecessors, perhaps? It's not like you've filed a tax return . . . last year for the first time in two decades, claiming various credits even though you don't seem to be enjoying much income in your chosen profession as a . . . gumshoe? You employed an undocumented habitual offender named Ernesto Rivas?"

"Uh-huh. He was murdered by the police."

She takes a breath like she's a bored rehab counselor at the VA, ". . . in essence you learned how to be a private detective when you were unhoused . . . on the job, through Bracht and his stooge . . ."

"Burton Sugars, Yes. And I was training . . . Ernesto. Stripe. That was his street name. We used YouTube videos, stuff I sent away for in the mail . . . they'd grade it for you for a fee."

"How'd you obtain a provisional PI license, then sit for the exam? You got past the background check and bond requirement. Former D.C. Chief of Police Linda Figgis?"

"Yes."

She clasps her little hands, leans forward. "So one could say that your current vocation, which has done so much good for you, has in fact come from the largesse of evil people?"

"Yes."

She leans back. Nods.

And finally smiles.

"This . . . is why I wanted to see you again. Five years ago you were an unhoused addict, a drunk—and yet you've brought down one of the wealthiest scumbags north or south of the Border, shaken corrupt or extremist elements from the police department of nation's capital and exposed the one of the biggest cold case frauds in the history of that department. Bravo, Number Eighty-Eight."

"There's the rub . . ."

"Yes, as Mr. Shakespeare wrote. Here's the point."

"No, Miss Bivens. Hamlet didn't mean here's the point. He meant there's the bullshit. Are you done torturing me now?"

"Just one more thing."

My nostrils fill with Coqui Coqui. I catch a blur of red . . . fire fucking engine red.

Damn, she's still luscious even with the streak of gray, the little lines at her eyes . . . those tits and those hips now pushed with the aid of whatever elastic's under that tight dress.

"*Lo sciento, Ricardo,*" Esme says.

CHAPTER TWO

Scream for Ice Cream

BACK IN DAY I'D THROW UP and not give a damn how it looked, smelled . . . tasted.

Ain't back in the day no more, huh? Soon as the Marshals showed me the door I hit the bathroom and puked. Don't think I got all the fear and smallness and pain flushed. And I can still taste it, over the dried blood from the pounding those motherfuckers gave me, and sniff it, over the Coqui Coqui . . .

Now comes the game of playing all that off because I'm a suit, a solid citizen? Ha! Only thing that hasn't changed are the eyes on me. Or the weight. LaKeisha, Katie . . . Croc, there in his new wheelchair, looking like a hood Professor X from the *X-Men* . . . they all still look, they all still lean.

Yet for all their digging and picking and biting as to where I disappeared to for an hour, why I look crazy as fuck, when we come out of that courthouse to trash-strewn curb at the corner of Constitution and Third, quickly they melt into their own shit. Croc, calling on Melvin the Henchman to pick us up in whatever whip Croc's put in his niece's name, LaKeisha and Katie prattling about God knows.

Got to get this taste banished. Got to distract myself from those gorillas putting their hands on me . . . from Lil' Angie shoving her fingers in my dome seemingly for an offense I never knew was given?

And from Esme.

"Y'all, anyone want some ice cream?"

They're running their mouths—okay Katie at least, and Croc's on his phone—so I repeat the proffer and again it's ignored.

My eye catches the animation screen on the bus shelter walls: breaking news. See, they put these up in the shelters before COVID, back when folk were using the damn bus. In the tonier, leafier or high-rise glass environs, where the riders were white collar colonizers or blue-collar folk from east and south of Rock Creek Park, the screens remained pristine, even watched. In other spots, the screens were smashed every other weekend, or tagged so badly they looked like glowing Jackson Pollock knockoffs. This one here just has a few renderings of genitalia. An erect dick is superimposed over the face of a pretty news anchor with long black hair like Esme's. If you squint, she looks like an elephant, trumpeting . . .

"*. . . this marks the fifth violent carjacking in the District in twenty-four hours. The latest victim is a grandmother loading groceries into her SUV at a Giant off Riggs Road, Northeast. She's remains in critical condition at Medstar after the tragic shooting. The suspects are described as three males and one female in so-called 'shiesty' masks, one of the males is possibly a juvenile, all armed with pistols . . ."*

Is there a non-tragic shooting?

"*Frightened D.C. residents are asking themselves if they should buy a firearm for protection, or is this vigilantism, in light of the shooting weeks ago of two black Deanwood teens, allegedly attempting to rob a young white ex-Capitol Hill staffer in Adams Morgan. The shooter,*

Dean Scholtz, a native of Ohio, was arraigned last week on charges of reckless homicide and depraved heart murder." She continues, trunk still proud and turgid, *"There has been no statement yet from the Mayor's Office, or interim Chief of Police Buster Patterson . . . ."*

Croc, off his call, nudges my leg with his chair wheel. "Kill, moe . . . stop lunchin'. We gots a problem, fam'ly."

Inside the courthouse, he played a meek and proper diabetic old fart; now he's popping the gold fronts back onto his choppers, doffing his version of an Aussie slouch cap adorned with faux reptile skin.

Apparently, Melvin the Henchman has gone AWOL and the rest of us depending on Croc for a free ride home are SOL. Listen, when Croc's parents ruled a portion of the town during the Marion Barry days, a shirker like Melvin would've been found in a Dumpster in Maryland with two in the head. Nowadays, his punishment's likely the joy of emptying Croc's catheter.

Ole Croc. My boy since Catholic school. Gray slacks, maroon sweater-vests, zits. Confession on Wednesday morning after assembly, Vespers each Thursday before football practice. *Mater Maria.*

"Ain't this a bitch," I hear Croc grumble. "Shit's a plague. See this mug?"

He's pointing across Constitution toward a vignette just below the "birthday cake with a bell on top"—what I called the Capitol when I was a little boy and Daddy was a Gunney, on his first tour at the Eighth and E Street Barracks.

It's Coats. And Coats his waving from the sidewalk. Barechested. Covered in dry sores. White woman with him's pacing aimlessly. She's barefoot.

"Good news, Rick!" he shouts at me, all toothless. Don't know why he calls me "Rick" but folks call him "Coats" because he has a moveable shelter there on the concrete, fashioned from high end men's trenchcoasts and such some Youngs housed in a smash-n-grab couple weeks ago from some designer Italian jont at City Centre. Heard through grapevine he, in turn, housed their larder from an old Verizon junction box so he's not long for this world when they catch up with him. "Me an' my lady, we quit the her-ron!" he announces.

"That so." I try to smile to keep from wincing.

"A-pache be the Za now!" He whoops like a brave in a cowboy movie. "A-*woo-woo-woo-woo-woo*. Don' ask the street why, Rick!"

The Tranq. Yeah, all Lil' Angie has to do is look out the window.

Katie's shrill musings to LaKeisha shake me out of my sad trance.

"Keesh, all these folks out here runnin' their motherfuckin' mouths just to hurt people . . . and here we are dragged into this damn place!" Sounds inapt coming from the thin lips and pie-shaped Irish face, but the Northern Virginia suburbs spat miss thing onto the street with us negroes long ago for the dire crimes of addiction and bankruptcy, so we cut her a break . . .

"But we're helping people," LaKeisha replies. LaKeisha had been her usual silent or mumbling self since we walked out the courthouse door. Like me, probably time to re-up happy meds. Real talk though, I think she's on edge because D.C. Child and Family Services—or what's left of it after my grand jury testimony—may let her see her kids again. But that's contingent on a job. And both hers and Katie's are dependent on Miss Verna Leggett, also the subject of grand jury scrutiny from her dealings with former Chief Linda Figgis, in their bullshit fiefdom's war with the late Dante Antonelli.

"Verna . . . she might be going to jail, Keesh. We gotta wake up to that."

For an instant the sun disappears behind this dark, amoebic cloud as if there's sci-fi movie eclipse underway. No cap it's still hot as fuck in the D-M-V as we hit autumn today and the temp will sure enough see-saw till Halloween. But that cold wind . . . Jesus, Mary and Joseph . . . is more bad *juju*.

"*Dickie*," Katie suddenly prods, pudgy little fist on her hip like she's an honorary sista, "Am I hearin' correctly that your gangsta friend's fittin' ta leave us!" I note the wind's put a blush back into Katie's fat pink cheeks. Not that cold bothers her, by the way. Hell, I've seen her in nasty busted Birkenstocks in knee-deep snow. Figure she's got four toes left between two feet and doesn't complain.

"Ice cream. Let's get some ice cream. I got a cab voucher. Croc's getting his own ride."

"Jon Snow, Lord Commander of the Night's Watch," LaKeisha says to me, and I hate that cray TV shit she reruns on she and Katie's busted screen in the halfway house. She'd read the novels in her down time after skin-popping in a lady's room stall, there in the Shaw Public Library. At least she's not calling herself the dragon-mother anymore . . . that chick, pale and white-haired? Poor LaKeisha's black as coal, buggy eyes beneath Coke-bottle glasses. "Fell deeds in the grand jury room of King's Landing, Jon Snow. Made worse because you disappeared. I'm scared they'll indict Verna for helping that evil Chief of Police."

"Keesh I'm sorry I was late . . . they . . . the U.S. Attorneys and stuff . . . made me go to another floor while you were waiting on Verna's case . . ."

Croc's replacement ride, an Uber, Lincoln Navigator, rumbles to the curb.

"Look at this muv . . . ," Katie mumbles as the driver jumps out to help Croc to his swollen feet.

"Quash it," I say to her. And to Croc, "Stamp . . . got to talk to you . . . in private. Stuff that went in there." I motion back toward the courthouse with my head.

"Whatchew got to worry 'bout, fam'ly," Croc says, chuckling and grunting his way onto backseat. The driver folds his wheelchair into the trunk. "You and the Vice President of the *U*-nited States was what again—in some seminar back at Howard? *Ha*! Call *her* if folks be fuckin' with you. Call her soon, though. If the gubmint don't make these traitor cases on Agent Orange and gangsta-ass Re-pubs she an' Grandpa Joe goin' be left on the sidewalk like y'all. *Peace*." Just before the driver shuts Croc's door Croc gives a lean, whispers, "If you need Valium, 'nother clip a ammo for the three-eighty . . . jus' use Imani's number to get me. Ain't comin' back to court, moe."

The Navigator careens away in a wide U-turn . . . just as the sun returns, warming the pavement and our faces. Finally, Katie's piggily nose wriggles a bit and she says, "I think you mentioned ice cream, Big Daddy?"

I nod.

"M'Lord," LaKeisha perks up. "We Valeryians do not patronize a mere Mr. Frosty truck."

"If I'm your liege-lord," I play along, "my demeanor is to be unquestioned. Got a *migraine* is all, and ice cream'll calm it. No Mr. Frosty: Jubilee or Jeni's?"

"And I shall follow in the footsteps of your loyal *esquire*, Ser Ernesto Rivas . . ."

"*Stripe*," I whisper.

I see Stripe a lot . . . you know, right in front of me yet not truly there. *Grinning and gung ho*, as Daddy used to say. Christ, with that mohawk, piranha teeth like the thing in the *Gremlins* movie . . .

. . . and hear him calling "*Oye, Rain Man*," as I flail for any red cab to stop.

The second one coming on the opposite side of Constitution busts a U-turn right there, cutting into an angry tide of cars, Metrobuses, electric scooters and rental bikes. Oh yes, there was a time when hacks would likely run the three of us down rather than stop. Hey I'm in a suit and Katie's a chunky white woman who's always smiling when she's not in tears. LaKeisha's squat and timid; she features her hostility inwardly. The hack frowns a bit when he gets a closer look at us but we bum-rush the doors and off we go. He's a bit more relaxed when I tell him to drop us at 14th and T, Northwest rather than a spot with no whitefolks in proximity.

"Yo, any of you all know about this woman, big in government—Angela Bivens?" Indeed, as we pass Franklin Square Park, across from the Babylonian ziggurat-looking *Washington Post* HQ, normally repressed and reticent LaKeisha can't stop babbling about what a superhero that little chick is, as if she's the first wave in from "Wakanda" to set shit right.

"So Keesh, this lady's *jhi*-Coca Cola, huh?"

"Affirmative. Brienne of Tarth's strength and prowess, with Tywin's intellect . . . and height . . . and Danearys's beauty and resolve to break wheels all at once."

I turn and face her from the front seat. "Damn girl, someone's been watching *Face the Nation* lately, huh?"

The hack's back to a frown then full-on scowl by the time we reach the ice cream jont. Guess he doesn't like our lower-class banter. Dude's black as pitch tar but when you immigrate from some spot with *juntas* in charge and no running water or Netflix, American poor folk must sound like whining brats. After he dumps us, I watch the scowl immediately transmogrify into a toothy, obsequious grin toward the white people in cargo shorts and peasanty sundresses hailing him on 14th.

Quickly the gossip starts.

"You know about Kenny, right?" Katie says as she eyes the menu on the outdoor placard. "Raping people under the K Street Bridge before the City got rid of the tents."

"Look, Kenny's got eyes-on, stays hid. Helped me with the Acevedo case . . . dude's wife was right where he said she was, when Keesh, your laptop said she was still down to the Audi Stadium watching his soccer jont."

"Tech's not infallible, m'lord," LaKeisha grumbles. "I want a salted caramel shake."

"A nasty rapist," Katie snears. "Oh, um . . . a Marionberry cone, double scoop. And I hear he's been pushin' on up on your girl Peach, down at 7th and Florida. Your backyard. And I hear they closed the CVS, all them robberies and light-fingering Tide and Advil? Bet Kenny and them fiends he knows, and them kids are behind that."

"I'm not the CEO of CVS."

"You spose to be Batman there, Dickie. You slippin'."

"Ain't in the mood, Katie . . ."

They're soon quiet but for the slurping, and brain freeze is better than brain fog owing to Esme or Bivens or those fucking marshals. That is, until LaKeisha sucks down dregs of her shake and informs me, "Federal and Superior Court want *you*."

"Pardon?"

"Are you Dothraki or something? I taught you how to check emails, m'lord. Did you not see that stuff from the Federal Public Defender and the D.C. Public Defender's Service?"

Katie adds, "Probably looking for private detectives to use as investigators."

"Paid work, remember?" LaKeisha huffs. "Like what *us two* need to keep. Halfway house funding's for pandemic's going away. Medicaid and stuff's only going to make up a little. And Jon Snow—your voucher's not made out of Valeryian steel, either. You'd be back out on the street, too."

I know I sound weary, gruff. "Got paid work. Next Friday at Club Midtown . . . Ivy City, New York Avenue . . . celebrity DJ . . . need me for bouncer work, checking out the street vibe for any troublemakers."

I see Katie's jowly face contorting and it isn't from the last drops of Marionberry in the cone. "And?"

"*And* . . . Mr. Echevarria got me on two bills retainer to see if he's being cucked, plus an extra hunned to do security at his daughter's *quinceañera* on Sunday. Stripe brought him in as a loyal client. Anyway, I don't wanna talk about this no more . . ."

"Why you all jankty an' shit, Dick? *Damn*." She gestures to LaKeisha. "Keesh, my phone says the Number Seventy-two bus's coming. Let's just get away from Mr. Morose here, acting all *new and snippy*."

I offer an extra cab voucher, but they are both now waxing agitated and suspicious with me pretty much up in my feelings. Katie rations a single kiss on my forehead of ever retreating salt and pepper curls. LaKeisha's always shrank at such physical contact even before COVID so she just exacts a fist-pound. I watch them limp and waddle toward 14th's bustle. Yeah, I figure I'll grab a pint to go, to be consumed in private. A cold, creamy balm in Gilead . . .

"Shorty's right," I muse aloud as I pick my overpriced diabetes booster. Gooning work ain't *detective* work. But who in the government's going to hire me, when I dropped a dime on the government, and the government's just beat the shit out of me, and the government's brought Esme back to torment me?

My landlords, or more accurately the jerks who take the City's rental assistance checks for whatever program they got me under, are whiteboys in their yellow Jeep and dark Wayfarers and pale khakis. They had long papered my crib's brick façade and indeed the whole damn block with realtor and "re-development" notices, and yet have nothing to show for it but for a sketchy neon-aglow weed shop run by dudes I used smoke K2 with, and pre-paid wireless store. Both occupy the space where Pilar's Salvadoran Carry-out used to be.

I miss Boston's wiry purplish arms welcoming me with a plea for a can of beer from Chuck & Billy's down the way. He died a couple of weeks ago. Old school tuberculosis, which is why they wrapped him up like contaminated meat, burned him.

I suppose this jont's made me less of a damn hermit, though. Different sort of human company: Latin dudes upping their minutes, all five feet-five inches tall wearing hardhats and on break from the endless road-carving PEPCO's been doing, black moms wearing all manner of uniforms from desk security to shuttle bus driver . . . peeping the cheap phones for them and their kids. Got another iPhone—bricked and legit "previously-owned"—on 7th Street and LaKeisha worked her magic and Verizon was none the wiser. Problem is, assorted mangy motherfucking thieves think this jont's a fence for heisted phones. Their predatory loitering, plus the line of Peruvians with green in their pockets have brought the cluckers, too.

And on cue, here come Patsy and Wilhelmina, who today are featuring stained bloomer-looking pajama bottoms and tank tops, fuzzy bedroom slippers. From the customers going *in* the shop, they beg for change. For the customers coming out they hype their fellatio skills and intercourse acrobatics.

"Dickie you my Tree-top sexy man," Wilhelmina indeed tickles as I search my pocket for my key. "Need five for the K-two cause y'all know I be renouncing the demon rock."

"No Tranq neither!" Patsy cosigns, reclipping a hair track. "All kinda stanky muvfukkahs goin' ova North'eas. Get that devil Apache. But not me!"

"Haven't heard of no Tranq over there, girl," I say. "Just Tina and Za. Um, grocery list? Lipstick . . . cinnamon for you, cherry for you, Willy. Rubbing alcohol, cortisone cream, Funions, Oreos, Fanta . . ."

"No Fanta!" Patsy hollers. "Thas a Nazi soda—they invented it when they couldn't get no Coke or Dr. Pepper."

Another reminder that we were all someone real, before this . . .

"Rock Creek," Wilhelmina orders.

"Rock Creek it is. Mother's milk, baby. But uh . . . gimme some time. Shit's come up."

Wilhelmina stops me before I go in. "You wrong 'bout dat Apache. It eatin' folk alive cros't the river. My sista say they be livin' in tents and boxes from MLK ta Seat Pleasant now, all covered in red cherry sores an' shit so she say keep yo' chickenhead ass ova here."

"I'll get y'all's stuff. Stay outta trouble."

Grunting, cooing—nasty noises like that assault my ears suddenly, and they're coming from steps down to the boarded-over basement apartment.

"Dickie why can't you kick Simon's ass outchere?" Patsy presses.

Boston's heir is Simon . . . and now I catch a better view of him in a grimy Washington Wizards tee shirt, rolling and writhing on the steps in utter ecstasy . . . one hand down the front of muddy jeans, the other digging in his ass like he's prospecting for gold. Like the cluckers, Simon used to be someone. A manager at the old JCPenney's out on Colesville Road, I heard.

"Tell whiteboys to handle it," I huff.

McDonald's wrappers, some beer cans—even a small open tin of cheap catfood—greet me on the first floor inside. Squatters are back, this time with pets. Only constant: the top floor landing's still broiling hot no matter the season . . . same swinging bulb.

But I got a new door, the replacement for the one MPD smashed in before I became a grand jury asset. Once I jiggle the key and walk in I immediately sniff the remains of yesterday's Chinese in my sink, lorded over by my own six-legged pets. Never get the motherfuckers when I cook, however. They don't seem to appreciate my prison pizza and buck-fifty ramen!

Dishes can wait; roaches scatter. I shove the ice cream pint in a freezer that can barely solidify a tray of ice cubes. I strip down to my beater and draws and pull my chair up to the laptop.

Let's see about these "opportunities." *United States Department of Justice Grant for D.C.-based investigators: D.C. Superior Court and U.S. District Court for the District of Columbia.* Shit—response to RFP due . . . in an hour?

Fuck that, but . . .

. . . Federal Public Defender stuff's sweet and Uncle Sam probably pays more but no, I don't like that address. I was just beaten there. Plus the Feds ask for too many references.

Public Defender Service . . . yeah, that's D.C. local shit. One page application, it figures. I call them.

What sounds like dude answers and says, *"Okay, uh, yeah the proposals're open till five p.m. but Attorney Yi's out if you gotta question."*

"Can I leave Attorney Yi a message?"

"She in court . . . she ain't got time for calls then she goin' home."

"Can I leave her a message, please?"

I hear a huff, then a sharp, *"Hold on for her voicemail."*

After a molasses-slow recorded voice prompts me, I start unpacking. Yeah, a freight car of unpacking . . .

"My name is Richard E Cornish, Jr. and I was just sworn in for my PI license this morning down on 4th Street, Northwest. I used to be homeless . . . um . . . I mean unhoused, I've been incarcerated, I was an addict and an alcoholic. B-But I am a college graduate, I mean sort of . . . I was a football player and I was also on the Deans List but that was a long time ago 'cause my dad wanted to me to go to Annapolis and be a Marine officer and athlete, see, but, ah . . . I had to join the Air Force when I left school and then got discharged . . . and twenty years on the street . . . wow . . . I've overstayed my welcome on Earth . . . because I was taken out of the St. Jude's Men's Shelter to find a missing person and instead I uncovered human trafficking and some bad things that MS-13 did and then I was hired by MPD, but I said fuck that . . . sorry didn't mean to be coarse . . . I meant no way, 'cause that was through the old chief of police, Linda Figgis, who you know doubt have seen on TV now. Uncovered her sham that was the old K'ymira Thomas kidnapping, remember that? And I ended up messing around with deputy chief Antonelli. But he . . . he killed my friend and he was like my sidekick because he wanted to train to be a private detective with me to keep him out of jail, being deported. His name was Ernesto, but everybody called him Stripe . . . and his name, I would really like to help defendants even though I know everybody's pretty much guilty of something 'cause I know I certainly was. *Ha!* But . . . everybody needs a chance because the cops are wrong or lazy . . . and one bad choice by a good person then you're marked with the truly bad people and—" Mercifully, I get the beep and prompt to wrap this mess up. "Um . . . sorry for the long message. Here's my number . . . I'll work for whatever you can pay me."

Guh . . . the dishes still got to be washed. Let me get a little nap first, just twenty minutes . . .

. . . and I wake up in my narrow rack. Phone screen says 2:23 a.m. and the darkness is so palpable and shadowless in that little stinking room that I'm now molding it in my fingers. Don't reach out too far, though. Something might snatch me. The alley streetlamp below my lone window's been out a few months, so there I am, like I'm dead myself . . .

. . . and deadfolk got me gutted with their mute stares. Forever in limbo, their eyes pleading why they deserve better . . .

. . . there's the *pop-pop-pop* of rounds in the distance—likely over a petty beef. A full-bodied firetruck siren on Georgia Avenue. A cat new mewling beyond my front door. All of it means the nightmares are on pause. So I'm praying as the nuns and priests taught me. "*Sancte Michael Archangele, defende nos in proelio, contra nequitiam et insidias diaboli esto praesidium . . .*"

St. Michael answers me by keeping me alive to endure. He's got wings, I don't, so I can't go nowhere except to the fridge.

I snatch that pint from the freezer. With dim light from the open freezer door I find a clean spoon. I'm eating all that damn ice cream and the kitty's now scratching rather than begging. Must belong to the squatters.

"You scream for ice cream, too?" I call out. "Can't let you in for a melted dish. Then you'll want to stay. Everything close to me gets hurt."

My belly's bloating-up with nascent farts from that damn pint of ice cream as I lay back down. But see, I like this feeling. Being full of something sweet. And I'm grateful for the *-itis* consuming me now, making my eyelids heavy, making me forget about the previous day . . .

. . . and I'm at that Morehouse game . . . spiking that fucking ball in the endzone . . . the stands vibrate with stomping feet, the cheerleaders are jumping the horns are blaring, the air's full of clamor . . .

. . . but there's Lil' Angie. Seated, silently digging into a cup of stadium ice cream.

I shout up at her from the sidelines, "*Street wise*, yeah . . . I'll outlast you, too. That's how I win."

Because winning looks like this two room shithole with a single bunk and a dresser and rusted tub and leaky crapper.

Empty pint container of ice cream by the sink, ready to receive the next wave of roaches . . .

. . . and I'm thinking they feasted fine for breakfast while the kitty starved because my phone's been blowing up and finally my head rises from the my pillow . . . and the time of day kirks me more than the name on the caller ID:

1:24p.m. D.C. Public Defender Service.

"Hello, this is Helen Yi. Is this Richard E. Cornish, Jr?"

I'm jumping off my rack like you're in the room for devil dog morning inspection, Daddy. My nuts are in my throat. "Y-Yes . . . hello?"

Her voice is very low, deep and almost a whisper. *"The proposals . . . they were due yesterday, no exception."*

"Oh . . . yeah . . ." What lie do I tell LaKeisha and Katie?

"But . . . given the message you left—I wanted to call you personally."

I search my gnarled toes, trying not to yawn. "Well, maybe . . . you got an investigator who can kick me some sub-contract biz, like for security, um . . . I'm available."

"We do have a few PI's on retainer: we call it our CJA panel. It's a rotating roster of work and you are paid through the panel. Things were difficult during and immediately after the pandemic and we are praying that the DOJ grant can make up for the losses."

"Yep . . . uh-huh."

"Mr. Cornish have you heard of Gerard Porter? Big name in your gumshoe circles."

"Um yes." Never heard of the dude. I'm about to politely end the call and make coffee.

"Apparently he had bypass surgery before Labor Day . . . he's also in a side business writing bail bonds in PG County and well, he

hadn't disclosed that, either . . . therefore he's been put on indefinite leave from the panel . . ." I'm hearing a deep inhale. *"Accordingly, uh . . . there's an opening."*

"Ma'am . . . is this for real?" I can't believe I just said that . . .

"Ah . . ." She pauses, oddly. *"I'm . . . I'm sorry."* Puts me on hold. Fuck's this? Then . . . *"Hello, Mr. Cornish, I'm back."*

And now she's spilling stuff yet I'm not really paying attention because my feet are flush with warm blood and now they are pushing around the room in the afternoon light, diffused by my gauzy curtains as if Chuck Brown's in my ear with that D.C. swing . . .

"Can you come in tomorrow at eight-thirty a.m.?"

"Ma'am, I can be in your office in an hour if you want."

Shit, she's cool with it!

And so I resolve to rinse out the pint container of sticky ice cream leavings in the kitchen sink before I rinse myself.

Caught one of my six-legged roommates flailing in the drain's whirlpool. That's not going to me, ever again.

CHAPTER THREE
Very Troubling Case

THIS LADY YI'S WALLED HERSELF OFF behind two ginor-
mous desktop computer screen and lots of framed pics of pink
hairless cats—facing outward, toward me. And she's nodding
along, slowly, like I'm a kindergartner recounting a play-
ground spat. The first thing I noticed about her *wasn't* that
she's stringbean thin, and with that same sort of page-boy,
man-cut hair style as Bivens'.

It's her skin.

Translucent and fissured as pale rice paper. Even on her
face, behind tea saucer-sized tortoise shell glasses—I swear I
can see blood pumping through capillaries. Extra dabs of
peach blush and lipstick, some definition for her eyes and
lashes don't help. Thought I was going to break her hand
when I shook it, even gingerly.

"Sorry I was late . . . big problem on the Green Line."

Her voice and her movements are somnambulistic, like a
pervert slipped a cloudy into her vodka tonic at the club and
it's the morning after. "Um . . . again, Mr. Cornish . . . you
could have come in tomorrow morning. So the hold-up was
turnstile jumpers?"

"Uh-huh . . . Twelve . . . I mean, WMATA police, were going
hard on some kids."

She starts writing on a pad. "Despicable. This was supposed to be decriminalized."

"Shame on them. Yet . . . too pretty a day to be underground, huh?" My white-collar chit chat game still sucks. "What we used to call 'Indian Summer.'"

"It's a very offensive term. As for the weather, I have a condition . . . I avoid . . . a lot of direct sun."

Chick's bizarre. But the prospect of steady work makes this is a trillion times better than sitting across from Angela Bivens. Shit, imagine what being in a room with Yi, the chickenhawk and Esme would be like? *Nah.*

Anyhow, I guess I'm no a prize for the eyes or ears either. I'm hoarse, got on my same suit from the beatdown, just hung while I showered to keep it from looking champ. Blue shirt sprayed a bit with Lysol at the armpits; I'm wearing my second of two neckties. Hair's greasy but shit, given the old baseline was the Frederick Douglass tip, guess I'm good. Pretty sure my eyes are hooped and drooped and no, I didn't shave so there's gray stubble stippling my dry face.

"There's a three hundred case backlog in D.C. Superior and Federal court," Yi redirects. "This matter is one of the seventeen that have been fast-tracked."

Since she's having a hard time maintaining anything close to eye contact with me as she speaks, I'm clocking the cubicle farm beyond the corridor to her office and it's almost empty of folks. A little ironic considering the big poster of their logo hanging conspicuously over the desks: a mounted paladin knight facing a star. Or is it Don Quixote, self-deluded.

"Budget cuts hit that bad?"

"We aren't forcing our staffers with families to come back full time from COVID. But they meet their court appearances, be assured."

"Things're full time down at the CDF and Fed lock-up, ma'am."

She seems a more miffed at my euphemism for the D.C. Jail than my dig at the empty digs. I learned from my vagrancy busts that you're *not* supposed to say *Central Detention Facility* because D.C. Jail implies Black Hole of Calcutta, and the PDs and community activist types love pushing that horror show narrative. Not saying it *ain't*. Just for me, it was worth the sadistic hacks and nutty jailbirds just to dry out, get free meds, three hots and cot.

"Do you want this legal pad for notes?" she adds.

"No. I'm good." Another affliction that geeked Daddy to no end. "I remember things. Short term, pretty photographically. Long term, not . . . not so much."

"Well, um . . . it's been over about a month since the shooting and the arrest. We've had the arraignment . . . the boys names are Diamante Diggs and Arthur Sellers. Ages sixteen and seventeen, respectively."

"Your clients . . . defendants?"

Her eyes get every big behind those big ass frames. "No Mr. Cornish. *Victims*."

"I was bit . . . *preoccupied* in August . . ."

"The shooting occurred in Adams Morgan."

The bus shelter screen news . . .

"*Our* client is charged with second-degree murder, depraved indifference, fleeing the scene of a felony . . . twenty-five years to life. The U.S. Attorney and MPD say he gunned the boys down on a crowded sidewalk on Eighteenth Street near the intersection with Columbia Road, around two-forty a.m., just as the bars and clubs were letting out. Witness say the boys appeared to threaten . . . strike that, *threatened* to . . . rob our client at knifepoint, and a knife was recovered from Arthur Sellers' body. We are developing a self-defense strategy for the not-guilty plea."

"Kill, you represent . . . *the white guy*? Scholtz?"

She nods.

"S-So I'd be helping?"

She nods again.

"Aw man . . . I bet there was a good deal floated, huh?"

"He doesn't want a deal."

"*Mater Maria* . . ."

She comes back with, "Are you Roman Catholic, Mr. Cornish?"

Weird thing to ask. So I hit her with a weird answer.

"Attorney Yi, I once saw Jesus plain as day . . . nude on Georgia Avenue but-for a hospital gown . . . absconded from the rehab ward, shunt still dripping his holy blood. I once saw Lucifer in the glow of the Washington Monument one night . . . near beating a man to death for deck of Xanax and the man's French fries fished out of a garbage can on 17th Street . . ."

Wonder what she'd think if I told her both were me?

Well, this wraith, like Bivens, is utterly unfazed.

"Mr. Cornish, I know you've had difficulties in your past, but your background makes you, well . . . *uniquely situated* to aid in our client's defense."

"How so?"

"I'm a bit maladroit around people, but in the law's *minutae*, in a courtroom, I'm very different. Likewise, you seem—if I may say . . . ill at ease in normal contexts. But I've heard you *fear nothing* out on the street . . . can find anyone."

"Heard from who?"

She doesn't answer. Instead, she hands me an old school manila folder and inside is something from Pretrial Services. I recite it. "Dean Scholtz, age twenny-five . . . Cincinnati, Ohio . . . victims are from Ward Seven . . . Nannie Helen Burroughs Avenue and Gault Place Northeast . . . Diamante Diggs DOA . . . Arthur Sellers is at Medstar . . . prognosis isn't good. Ventilator's keeping him alive. *Jesus.*"

Ye joins in with, "My client . . . *our* client . . . Mr. Scholtz graduated from Princeton University but not without some . . . clouds . . . on his record. Worked on the Hill . . . some political organizations, media . . . it's all there. Highly . . . partisan . . . conservative Republican causes I might add. Very much in support of the former president Mr. Trump."

Outwardly I'm still featuring the deadpan, muttering the monotone. Yet inward . . . *goddamn* . . . and now my mind's ticking back to those St. Albans, Georgetown Prep, Holton, Madeira, Landon, Sidwell assholes and flat-assed cheerleaders Croc used to hook up with weed, pills, and blow when we were teenagers. They'd call them "party favors" on their ski jaunts or Delaware beach safaris; lot of future hedge fund bros, senators, media moguls and supreme court justices in that bunch . . . and my sister clamored to join in. First time away from home and those animals hurt her bad.

Of course, Daddy—he had have his turn to "fix" her. Croc and I didn't make it any better. We didn't think about her, just revenge. So she fixed herself, with a bottle of pills.

Yi breaks me from my grim funk. "If you have a bias due to injustice and abuse by whites, you should tell me now." It was black Marshals who beat me up in the courthouse, but hey. "P-Please understand . . . it's been hard for staff to accept this client . . . but this young man's penniless . . . fired from his job, parents refuse to help, fiancée disavowed him, he's been ostracized . . ."

"Ostracized by who? Lotta whitefolk would consider him a hero like the kid who murked the BLM protesters. And I suppose the prosecutor's let the boys' mamas do their tears and teeth gnashing thing on TV . . ."

"That's very cynical, Mr. Cornish."

"Attorney Li I've seen it all."

She gets this pained look, and it's not from the dry skin. "I . . . I really think you should read on. See, neither is true. He's no hero to extremists—that we're representing him should have been your clue. Concurrently, however there's been a loud call for justice, some demonstrations that sadly are getting out of hand, aimed at Mr. Scholtz . . . yet . . . little if anything from the victim's families in support. Indeed, the U.S. Attorney's been struggling to get any assistance or info out of next of kin."

"Maybe the government doesn't need the families if it thinks it's a slam-dunk and Scholtz is being tried in the news media. I mean . . . he's—"

Yi interrupts me. "A perfect white villain, to distract from the more mundane young black male 'thug' villains, out of control? This is a very troubling case . . ."

No shit. "It says here he's ROR with an ankle monitor? He's *not* in jail?"

"Pretrial Services uses some sort of algorithm now to streamline cases. Scholtz fit whatever was programmed—like some of those January Sixth defendants who claimed indigency used our services. We had a *sympathetic* judge at arraignment. He usually holds a grave dislike for our office and positions on over-policing and mass incarceration. As I stated . . . a very troubling case."

I'm clocking her translucent shell pulse like she's ready to molt. She mentions something about a password to their paperless reporting and billing system and access to their research library, blah blah; I strofe like a mug and assure her my "IT system" is secure. I watch her peel off a green Post-it, fill it with ink.

"As noted, he's on a PSA GPS ankle bracelet. Here's the address. It's known only to us, and law enforcement."

"For his own safety, huh?"

"Yes," she says, handing the Post-it to me. The address is scribed in perfect cursive. "There's a docket call next week and the A-USA, Jacob Markowitz, is readying a show-cause motion to get him off ROR and into a jail cell. "Optics" . . . *politics* . . . has enhanced the explosive atmosphere your police corruption matter in front of these grand juries has created."

"And on top of that," I muse, "you're gonna want me to help you smear these boys, eh?"

She shrugs. "Refresh yourself with the crime scene and eye-witness statements, initial police report. Nothing else."

Some dude named David will process my paperwork, she says. Five hundred dollars to start, then another five. Expenses are capped at two hundred with an Uber voucher and Metro card.

"I-I'm sorry about the . . . laughable . . . amounts compared to the private sector."

Fuck do I know about private sector cash? "I'll do some prelims. If it smells, I'm out and I keep the balance of the first payment."

"That's not in our standard panel agreement . . . but . . . I can waive a refund."

I hold up my finger; the Post-it's stuck to the tip. "I'm a professional, an expert."

David smells like he makes more trips to a Sephora than his boss; guess he missed the HR training where you don't refer to contractors or visitors as "Big Papa." Hell, I'd've kissed him after handing over the W-9 if he'd given me five cees rather than a paper check.

Still, I put my ride voucher to use. Don't want to waste any time, and so here I am, in the leafy, ivy-covered old brick part of town. Good ole venerable Capitol Hill . . .

. . . and the car puts me off at 8th and Independence, not too far from the yuppie craft-fair and craft-food paradise of Eastern Market . . . never been down here much except when I was little and it was a *bona fide* greengrocer for we natives, with Daddy at the Barracks down 8th.

Wouldn't have savvied this dude Scholtz for this spot. I mean first, he's supposed to be "penniless." These are the federal-style tidy brick rowhouses that rival the stooped brownstone stuff up in New York. Some with cupolas and cornices, some squat and colorful, camouflaged by the last greenery or yellow hydrangea of the season. And all around, the oaks, maples, elms providing shade. In other words—perfect for whitefolk with older sensibilities. Doesn't go with white boys in our Chocolate City. They opt for the flashier roof-deck condos around 14th and U Street or Union Market, or up with the Birkenstock types in Columbia Heights, or the beer gardens around the baseball stadium at the Navy Yard.

I ring the bell. I hear a dog barking and instantly I grit my choppers. Dogs. The other yuppie accoutrement.

Okay, the door parts and this red-haired, freckled chick . . . Irish or Scottish stereotype, textbook . . . appears. Pretty brown eyes yet full lips like she could be mixed, no lie. I see the rest of her: all cutey in a Ohio State Buckeyes sweatshirt and shorty-shorts, flip-flops. She's got the chain still engaged—not as a barrier to the big scary black man but to protect the big scary black man from the scarier rover what looks like a cross between a slim wolf and furry torpedo. She's throwing embarrassed smiles as the dog lunges and barks.

"Woody *stop*-it! I'm *sooooo* sorry, sir. The lawyer said you might be by."

Sir? Nice. "I-I'm Richard E. Cornish, Junior . . . private investigator hired by the PD's office. Representing Dean . . . Dean Scholtz?" I pass her the crumpled temporary ID sheet; "Woody" almost rips it from her hand.

"Dean!" And then a labored, "H-Hi . . . I'm Aidy. *Dean come get Woody puh-lease!*"

I spy more movement behind the canine . . . hear the smack of bigger flip flops or sandals on parquet. Woody's woofing is suddenly muted by a "*Calm down, shut-up!*" How brave.

The latch comes off. Dog's still snarling and straining, but this time it's man's hand gripping the collar. Uh-huh, not pulling the damn thing away, mind you. Just holding it in place, just beyond snapping distance.

Damn skippy I got one eye on that wolf while I try to peep this guy.

"Dean Sholtz?"

"Yeah? You're Cornish? Cool."

Half expected a version of the vacant face and muscle-headed affectations teammates featured decades ago. That recipe doesn't change if it's a whiteboy: just take away a pinch of swagger and add a pound of utter insouciant privilege.

Instead, *this* motherfucker facing me, barely restraining the beast, doesn't quite come up to my chin. He's almost as pale as Yi and just as stringy . . . sunken chest under a black tee shirt with "Princeton Squash" imprinted in orange thereon. Short brown hair, tousled at the top, faded on the sides like a little boy's. Maybe a little chin and side burn stubble. Antique-y Harry S. Truman-looking spectacles frame his narrow face. I mean an otter or weasel-like narrow goddamn face.

And the eyes. Woody doesn't distract me from those eyes.

Gem-like blue, like Chief Linda Figgis'. Except his are beads, hers are marbles. Whitefolks with eyes like that probably were burned at the stake back in whitefolks' good ole days. Completing the look—the kid's got on those goofy shower slides on unusually wide hairy hobbit feet. And there's the clunky PSA ankle bracelet.

Stamp, got to *stop* thinking of him as a kid. His victims were kids. Then again, how could a callow dipshit like this wax two human beings?

"*Dude*," this guy gushes in a bass voice bigger than his body. "Don't be scared. If you're gonna be part of the team, he's gotta get used to you."

Right. Woody's still in a lather. I've squared off against every canine out there but he's my first . . . okay what is he?

"Belgian Malinois," the guy says, chuckling as the dog strains on the collar. "Like a small German Shepherd who gives zero fucks."

Eyes on the animal—the four legged one this time—I squat, trying not wince as my bones creak. "Good boy . . . you're a good boy." Then I look away. Sometimes that works.

Learned that on the street. Sometimes it doesn't—and they tear in that ass anyway.

He sniffs me, whines. Growls. Woody either wants to know me better, or wants to gnaw me better.

Suddenly the ginger reappears all cute, perky, cheery. Grabs the collar.

"Sweetie," she coos to Woody. "The nice man's here to help Dean!" Whereupon she tosses me a weird wink, plants a juicy one on the whiteboy's pale cheek with those thick lips and pulls the dog down a hallway, chirping, "I'll back with some lemonade, 'kay?"

The guy's all peacocked and proud at his girl because clearly he's outkicked the coverage. "Helen said we'd get a new investigator when the old Morgan Freeman-looking guy crapped out." He offers his hand. I shake it non-ethnically. His skin's soft but that grip is real live.

"You can call me Dickie. Um . . . is Aidy your fiancée?" Clearly he ain't broke or dumped.

"Nope she's just Aidy," he remarks with that snicker again. "C'mon in."

God I suffocate in these houses—everything in place, including succulents, leafy fucking plants, nothing askew. Scented candles . . .

"Yeah so that's Aidan Bertina Voss," he schools me. "This is her house, had roommates but all alone now. Works for friggin' *Biden* but hey, all the cute girls are libs, ain't that something?"

"Aidan? That's a boy's name . . ."

"Oh, let's not be a gender bigot, Mr. Cornish!" he says in mock offense.

The chick skitters back with a tray of three glasses, grinning and apologizing for a perceived lack of hospitality. Ushers us to a parlor room: bare but for a hassock, a long tan leather sofa, a tree-size sort of palm in a huge ceramic vase and a small round table painted in garish colors, with the pretense of being "ethnic" no doubt. There's a TV the size one of my apartment's walls.

I bend achingly to situate myself on that little hassock; they tuck themselves into the sofa, all-cushy. It's hot for September so I chug the lemonade and watch, smiling. I set the glass down on a tiny round table next to a stack of oldfashioned U.S. mail. Looks like bills and looks like someone forget the fine use of a letter opener because the outer envelopes are shredded open. Medical bills. Past due?

They are whispering blather and sweet nothings while I'm nosy as hell, until the ginger says with a chuckle, "Dean's my project, sort of."

"I see."

"And that doggo's 'Woody,' for Woody Hayes, my uncle and grand-dad's favorite football coach. My grand-dad gave Dean's dad his first job back in Cinci. Woody is *not* racist. Malinoises are just that way with everyone."

Jesus they act like I'm here selling yacht vacations to Jamaica.

"Miss . . . Voss? Um, some I need to talk to Mr. Scholtz about some . . . tough matters . . . shooting of two boys . . ."

Scholtz suddenly sneers, "They're *both* my height so that automatically means they aren't 'boys!'"

I'm looking right at him and he glances away.

"*Weren't* boys . . . not present tense. Anyway, Miss Voss . . ."

"I-I understand Mr. Cornish," she whispers. " *Ahhh*, there's a room on this floor—"

He cuts her off. "She was using it as a home office during the so-called pandemic, a.k.a Wuhan Flu, a.k.a Biden's Chinese bullshit. Got her bikes, hiking gear, skis in there. I'd vape in there but Pretrial'd gets a hornet up its ass."

He catches me peeping his state property anklet and gives me this sheepish, slouchy grin.

Yet, as the ginger wriggles past me down the hallway toward what must the kitchen door to greet a restive Woody, the grin disappears.

He's squinty. Drawing heavy breaths. Beads of sweat blossom on his forehead, his cheeks flush pink . . .

"You okay, Mr. Scholtz?" I have to repeat it because the whiteboy's truly lunchin' now.

He groans, "*I'm no fucking midwestern rube, okay man?*"

Okay then, bye Jekyll. Welcome aboard Mr. Hyde.

Then again . . . I've seen this type of sudden labored breathing, the two-second mood shift before. Yeah, featured it myself, and he is swaying a little as he leads me to the windowless room tightly packed with everything from hiking boots to winter coats and boxes of stuffed animals. I offer him the more comfortable office chair yet he opts for a high barstool so he sit at my eye level.

"Awright moe," I begin. "So shorty's your meal, your roof, your warm plus one?"

He mugs and postures like the brothers in lock-up . . . made more ridiculous because he's also struggling to corral those heavy lungs and calm himself. Won't look me, either. Getting a familiar itch—an unpleasant nostalgia—in my bones around this whiteboy.

"She's special, okay," he finally says after some long efforts at composure. "I mean . . . a friend . . . a friend before anything . . . she got me to come to D.C . . . .yeah, Ohio girl but moved to Austin. Her mom's from Texas."

"So . . . you *aren't* in a relationship, engaged?"

"I was engaged to a girl back home. But that was extra. Nothing." He grins. "Aw, but man ya know I'm hittin' dat perfect ass of Aidy's right. See, she's all artsy, techy . . . like Austin. Good thing she's woke, huh? Takes in strays."

"You a stray?"

"Yeah. As long as they're *pedigree*. Like a fuckin' Belgian Malinois, not a *mutt*."

"I see. The 'woke' and Biden stuff—what's up with that?"

"You're really coming into this cold, aren't you, dude?"

"I skimmed this file coming down here," I say in the monotone Daddy said disturbs motherfuckers. "Was cised to get your angle. You did canvassing for some group called the 'Gatekeepers' in college and worked for their media department afterward?"

"Princeton faggots kicked them off campus. Allowed Black extremists, feminists and Israel-hating Palestinians to run wild. Like the ANTIFA types and ghetto activists who plaster my face on the light poles."

Little turd. "I Googled the Gatekeepers on my phone. They're pretty much brownshirts. Stormtroopers . . . with a *pedigree*."

"Well . . . there're harmful Jews and then there's Israel kicking ass. Two separate things, okay? Look, are we gonna talk about my case?" There was a bit more bass in that comment. He's either claustrophobic or . . . un-huh, I'm on point getting that itch.

Fiending?

"You got fired by Senator Vitter . . . Brom Vitter of Texas who says there should be a new Civil War if Trump loses or goes to jail? I recall last year he sponsored a bill to strip D.C.

of home rule because of COVID mask and vaccine mandates, then called us 'savages and children' in a hearing, and during the Republican Convention I think it was 'Amos and Andy Taxicab Company.' Sounds like your kind of boss."

His head dips. "He's a squid. An asshole. See him supporting me on Fox? Tucker Carlson tweeting for my release on X? Nope."

Whoa. I'm supposed to talk only about the night of, get details on the crime scene. My nose and gut are telling me that's dead-end bullshit.

"Mr. Scholtz . . . I'm not saying you're a monster," *Yet.* "But something bad happened. You did something bad."

"White guy blasts on two black thugs . . . I mean, *youngsters*, tryna jack him up. Self-defense versus 'rampant urban crime.'"

"Simple as that, huh?"

"Only it's not."

"*Not* can mean reasonable doubt." Listen to my ass, sounding like I paid attention to the PI training vids on YouTube."

"Mr. Cornish . . . this is all tabloid. My side may have forsaken me, but these people here, *fuck* . . . I'm the gentrifier, the colonizer, the devil, the drooling . . . white privileged . . . leering Republican wolf. They're young oppressed babies. Genocide, remember?"

Devil's advocate horns sprout. "Then again . . . there're a lot of cats out here killing, robbing, plugging . . ." I point to his ankle tracker. "Many of them while they wear one of those. And no one's marching in the streets."

His pinkish face goes full vermillion as he sputters, "Mr. Cornish . . . um . . . I've never been in trouble a day in my life, never done anything violent. I mean . . . I wasn't exactly popular with the lib and lez crowd that's taken over the Ivies, right? Even my eating club . . . my senior year the freakin' president of the club was a *Pakistani girl*. Got into a . . . row with her. They almost expelled me."

"Best to check out the common ground than take false comfort in the fringes."

Those scary little blue eyes finally widen as his brows jump. "Well check *you* out, Dr. W-E-B Du Bois! When you came to the door, I thought were some big black 'Sling Blade' kinda dude. Guess not, huh?"

"I was . . . a scholar-athlete. I attended Howard University."

"An 'H-B-C-U.' What do mean 'attended?'"

He's smarmy, like a junior Bracht. Or a bullshit artist like Chief Figgis. Still, that Ivy League tee shirt's starting to stick to him as if the room's a sauna.

"I, too had a . . . mishap in college, Mr. Scholtz."

"Wait . . . some non-college homeboy ask you to help him rob a 'wreka-stow' for rap tapes?"

The punk's giggling . . . until the snot starts streaming into his mouth. He apologizes as he wipes with his precious Princeton ends.

"No," I say. "Drug-related. Speaking of drugs. How you feelin' Mr. Scholtz?"

"I'm fine."

Yeah, he's a stone fiend. The medical bills . . . something's up. He'll wilt in a minute. So back to the shooting.

"It's two-forty a.m. that eyewitnesses say a white man of your approximate description . . ."

"Approximate."

". . . wearing a Cincinnati Reds baseball cap was running down 18th Street, which was blocked-off for nighttime foot traffic . . . pushed through some people coming out of

Madame's Organ at last call . . . where your friends . . . all working for Republicans on the Hill, conservatives, whatever . . . were waiting, gave statements to MPD Homicide dicks that you were supposed to meet them to listen to a band . . . and you never showed. MPD put a lot of stock in this . . ."

"Why? Proves they're Keystone Kops, like my Grammie to say."

"Apparently, you'd been missing—as in not hanging, avoiding contact, shunning them—for months—and this was supposed to be your big 'return' to the crew. They were worried. So was Senator Vitter, per his police interview."

"That's why I have a public defender." He's grinning again.

"This figure in the Reds cap, fitting your description, fired on Diggs and Sellers, who were unarmed but for a hunting knife Sellers was carrying . . . blade down. I mean, except in the movies who stabs someone from overhead like that? In the street it's a slash and jab thing."

"He had a big knife, Mr. Cornish. Period."

"Some witnesses say Sellers and Diggs 'rushed' at you . . . but one claim they only shouted at you, and only ran-up on you when you didn't reply, then you turned around, fired. Which was it?"

"Have you seen pics of them? Like I said, they weren't 'boys' or the cute urchins in First Grade portraits. Sellers was a fucking adult NFL linebacker-size, Diamante Diggs was—"

"Short, slight, like you, Mr. Scholtz. Or hard and scary as—"

"*You?*"

"Your unlicensed pistol, with your prints, was found in the gutter . . . they ran the prints and got a match on the Senate employee database . . ."

"Heller . . . Heller versus District of Columbia, Mr. Cornish. Mr. Justice Scalia said the Second Amendment is sacrosanct . . ."

He's pluckin' me. "So if Diamante and Arthur were fetuses, they'd be sacrosanct." He dips his head again, bobs on the stool. "Five rounds of spent casings, nine-millie . . . about fifteen feet from Diggs' and Seller's bodies. That's some crazy shooting, man. In a crowd, and yet you don't hit anyone but them."

"Hey bro, I-I don't remember."

"Fuck's wrong with you? I ain't your 'bro'." My voice's still low, deep, slow. Maybe that messes with him.

"Listen . . . I'm not feeling well. Aidy's got to . . . go to Walgreens for me, okay?"

I channel Lil' Angie. "We aren't quite done. See, moe—a ROR now doesn't mean you aren't looking at hard time with the homies and the *vatos,* at a private prison hundreds of miles away from loved ones. Yeah, a place you rightwinger folk love to fund, own stock in, feel me? *If* or when you do get out, you'll a lot be older than me."

Now that smarm and asshole vibe's pretty much drained from his face. I finger through the report and I peep something I didn't catch in the ride over. Something Helen Yi didn't hip me to. So whatever gray and ache that left him was quickly immobilizing me, freezing my voice."

"So that's it, Mr. Cornish? Don't tell me you're going over to Northeast next, huh? Or to interview cops? Neither sounds terribly safe for you."

I digest the words on the page, then look at his fidgety, snorting form. "Um . . . maybe. "Cell tower ping. Ninety minutes *earlier,* your phone's way deep in the cut. Ward Seven, Deanwood. Northeast. *Close to where your victims lived . . .*"

He smiles. "My victims? I told the police I had two phones. One for work, which my friends used, one for personal stuff cause I still did freelance work for the Gatekeepers and fair and legit American media to counter lefty stuff. Maybe . . . maybe that's how they found me. They stole my phone."

Very troubling case, indeed. "But it says here . . . you never reported it missing or stolen?" Mater Maria. I pull my phone. I call Yi. That molasses slow voicemail greeting coats my ears and give it curt, "Dickie Cornish. I decided to meet Dean Scholtz, establish a rapport. We need to talk. Immediately, ma'am. *Please . . .*"

"*Hmmm . . .* Mom and Dad arguing?"

No sense bullshitting a bullshitter. "So the night of . . . your friends were bothering you on the phone you have now, onaccount they were bugging because you never showed up for their Adams Morgan liquor-soused frolic. And yet . . . it says here . . . the Homicide dicks wanted to amend the charges to first degree murder in light of the cell phone stuff?"

"Yet they didn't," he'd replied. "Ask yourself why."

Suddenly, like any true fiend hit with a wave of withdrawal, he starts drawing like a gallon of snot back in his nose, spits it into a little trash can in the corner. This stuff'd been collecting with the sweat, and I swear to God you don't need to have a degree in drug treatment to suss what had going on inside him so I finally I prod, "What are you come down from?"

"You starting to get a hint, Sherlock . . ."

Motherfucker . . .

I recite from memory what I did indeed read. " 'Victim Diggs lived in a rental house at Fifty-four Seventeen Gault Place, Northeast . . . in proximity to known narcotics distribution points . . . Arthur Sellers had one three month assignment to Youth Detention at Mt. Olivet for assaulting a teacher . . . father died in drug-related homicide, unsolved . . . '" I lean toward him, I mean lean strong so he can't squirm away. "Did you know them? Were they covering for a dealer you owed? Is that why all your little friends ain't here throwing you a kegger—because you're a fiend? Hanging with the dark people, huh?"

And he just sits there like the slinky weasel, the slippery otter, repeating the bullshit about his phone being stolen.

"I've been a fiend," I tell him. "You've been out there to Northeast." He turns away as if that'll dissuade me and I grab his skinny ass arm.

"Don't . . . don't you touch me. How *dare* you touch me!"

"Quit this strofin' and tell me something real, because this case just went south, man, yet someone on high's soft pedaling your ass as surely as your wingnut friends have cut you loose. How much are those dealers into you for?"

"If I'm a druggy why hasn't Pretrial pitched a fit drug testing me, huh? You don't know shit!"

I hear footsteps outside the door and then Aidy.

"Everything okay in there? Dean . . . you need your . . . medicine?"

"It's okay . . . okay, Aidy. Go walk Woody . . . seriously." He finally . . . finally locks eyes with me. Now teary, swollen eyes. "Mr. Cornish and I . . . are making headway . . ."

I school him, knowing full well this can't be the only answer. "They're lazy civil servants, using a lab that's the lowest bidder. Trust me."

"Okay. So you tell me what's my poison?"

"That part of Ward Seven . . . includes a piece of Deanwood, that's where Tina the Monster lives. Know her? I've seen whiteboys, hell hardcore Twelve uniformed officers, dicks, undercover—all party hard with her, cause she pumps you up then lets you down. Cocaine, a lil'meth and a lil' Benzodiazepine. That's Tina. That's what's got you in withdrawal."

"That makes me a murderer?"

"Even a dopefiends got a right to protect themselves when the plugger's done the algebra that you're no longer a reliable bank. But now I'm fittin' to have come to Jesus moment with Attorney Yi, most riki-tik as my dad used to say."

He slides off the stool . . . leaving a damp patch of sweat on it, I swear. As he opens the door to the room he whispers, "You think getting high was why I *may* have been in that neighborhood, eh?"

"Getting high's the *only* reason, man. It's the monster. That's what makes this all . . . *troubling.*"

"There're *worse* monsters out there, Mr. Cornish. You have no idea."

CHAPTER FOUR
Monstering

See, I'm keeping my voice low, my act all respectful but it's damn hard with her tripping in my ear. Blindsided. This . . . wraith . . . is seriously using words like blindsided? But I don't want to loose my money . . .

"Attorney Yi, this cell tower ping stuff . . . someone on MPD Homicide wanted to charge Scholtz with first degree murder . . ."

She's still slow, deliberate, hushed despite claiming to be pissed off. "*Mr. Cornish, your job was to introduce yourself, then leave. Inspect the crime scene, develop a schedule where you can re-interview witnesses . . .*"

"But the phone . . . I have a theory . . ."

There's dead air and then, "*I beg your pardon, sir? I am the attorney, you are the investigator, he is my client . . .*"

"Thought he was *our* client . . ."

"*You know what I mean. You don't develop theories, Mr. Cornish, I do.*"

"He knew those boys. He's a user. Getting high on Tina . . ."

"*Tina?*"

". . . . and is now sick on withdrawal. Pluggers use peewees to collect debts or scare users. Did you know that? I need to get over to Deanwood to find out what Twelve found out." More dead air and now I'm thinking I'm about to be fired.

Should have cashed this check first. "Very soon, he's going to fail a piss test. Then what?"

I discern a heavy sigh and then, *"That's not in your wheelhouse, sir. Do as you're told."*

So it's like that. I'm an ox, blunt tool. "Ma'am . . . maybe . . . maybe we aren't a good fit, because . . . you see . . . I'm . . . m-my wheelhouse . . . is I go into the cut, I do my thing."

"I am . . . under a lot of pressure, sir. You are compounding it." And she's gone.

Stay in my damn lane. Sit the fuck down, shut the fuck up.

Fine. Accordingly, I waste no time calling a car to beeline me out of these pleasant cobblestones streets and canopies of turning oak leaves to the grit and bustle of 9th and H, Northeast.

City Credit Union. Spot's among the few that help we denizens of public assistance with old school paper checks.

Got some green in my pocket. So please, fire me. Please, remind me that I'm still just one step above a bum, no matter how I scrub up or get decent clothes from Goodwill or get my choppers worked on or sores salved or how many pills I take or group hand-holding sessions up at the VA I traipse through. Just like Angela Bivens reminded me.

Outside I see a couple of jakes and toy cops on the opposite side of 9th running a roll of yellow police tape and between some No Parking signs. I ask this white girl what's up and she's almost in hysterics about an "active shooter" situation until a brother toting a little dog in his windbreaker schools us. Nah—some fool was just trying to house a couple of sets from the Nike store.

In that instant I clock the jakes roll out of the store, shoving a wriggling, handcuffed brother onto the pavement. Dude's got on the standard uni—dingy yellowed beater, skinny black jeans dipping below his ass crack. They stand him up and rip the COVID mask off his grill and nylon sheisty balaclava off his dome. All I see is a head full of busted locs and a stringy goatee. One jake is showing the dude's hardware and it's scary: a chopper . . . Hungarian-made AK-47. Get 'em cheap over in Virginia.

"*Yo* . . . *fam'ly!*" the dude hollers right at me, wild-eyed. The jakes are sneering my way, too, as if I'm some sort of aider and abetter. They swing open the door to a blue & white and are about to shove this nigga in and he will be gone from this world. But as they are shoving him in he's all smiley and calling to me, "Ain't no monsta, cuz. I jus' don't give a fuck . . ." Then they slam the door. No ROR for him, I bet.

Latinos and blackfolk disperse but the white people linger to give clap and cheer. Twelve hasn't heard acclaim in a long time. I mean, H Street's still got the yuppie bustle with the new apartments and Japanese-Jamaican-Italian-streetfood fusion shit, but it isn't the Shangri-La they hoped for. Lot of bars and retail closed during COVID, and that void, vacant buildings and such resurrected my old cohorts: squatters like my neighbors and wannabe stick-up artists like my man being driven away in cuffs proclaiming to the world he's no monster. The world answers in silence, with merely the timid strides and averted eyes of the Deans and Aidys as they exit Whole Foods down the block.

Of course, woe betide any sumbitch who tries to run up on me with $500 in my pocket.

With such flowery thoughts and that wonderful tableaux lodged in my brain I lumber up H, yeah, looking like a better-dressed Lurch, to Po Boy Jim's. Hadn't filled my belly since that bullshit early morning ice cream orgy so let's put some of Yi's money to work on something caloric and satisfying, shall we? Again, that's a fresh concept for me, relearned or maybe even learned: stress eating, or eating for pleasure rather than survival.

Edging past some hipsters and a couple of tourists I zero in on my poison; Verna once got me this jont when I got my new choppers. Steak, bacon, shrimp, a sliced D.C. halfsmoke and provolone. Okay shredded lettuce and tomato, raw onion and pickles for balance. Yes please. Maybe it'll render an instant coronary and overwhelm any stent the VA or Medicaid'd authorize. Sorry Lil' Angie, can't hunt him no more.

My phone's text tone sounds. It's Yi.

Meet me at the Moultrie Courthouse tomorrow. Will send location & time.

No riposte or reproach. Guess that's strike two. Guess I'm fucked. Oh well.

As I shove the phone back in my suit jacket the huge flat TV hanging above the cashier blurbs something about the case. Shit, from the murmurs I can tell the crowd's evenly divided between team Dean and team Diamante and Arthur, though the passion edge seems goes to Scholtz. I can see why MPD doesn't give a shit whether he gets charged with first degree murder or depraved indifference—they love someone doing a Charles Bronson on these b-boys. Closes cases easy and it's population control.

News switches to autumn's odd mixture of weekend NFL and baseball line-ups, then there's a toss to the hard politics talk. Poll numbers, presidential race. Confirms my jaundiced view of too many people, yet the girl behind the counter says, in a surprisingly mature, adept tone, "How could he be president—again? A criminal, a racist, a traitor, a liar about his businesses?"

"Abe Lincoln was a bartender and a pretty good MMA fighter before there was MMA," I joke.

"For real, the people lining up behind him—they look ghouls . . . have you seen that Senator, Vitter?" Wish she'd shut up with the *Meet the Press* shit and get my self-destructive order. "Glad Kamala's pushed that senile old guy outta the way."

"He tried to reduce y'all's student loans." For an instant I feel compelled to tell her the Vice President of the United States sat next to me in some gut class when I was a freshman and she was a senior.

"I hear he was racist, too, a long time ago? And what about Gaza?"

Lord have mercy. And mercifully my hot sandwich arrives. I retreat to a corner and I'm two bites into the heart attack when I hear another voice, as if talking to me.

Bivens.

I turn, with a shudder. This little chickenhawk, yes makes my big ass shudder.

Expected her blank stare whether she's in a business suit and severe bob . . . or it's almost thirty years ago and she's simpering in her pin curls and AKA sweatshirt. No, I swear she's looking right at me.

She going on and on about Trump and his legal cases and the Justice Department . . . and some patrons applaud, some hiss. The hissers look like hayseed tourists.

"All y'all shut up! I can't hear!"

They shut up.

"*This isn't a last futile gasp of a failed Administration, how can you say that? For us it's our duty.*" But . . . those almond eyes lock on mine from the screen like some sci-fi movie magic. "*Yet are those who owe the law a favor, and if they're wise enough, they will elicit evidence of such heinous lawbreaking that even the most cynical or the most brainwashed must pause, retreat. We can't look Satan himself in the eye and send him back into pit until we look ourselves in the eye. I think you what I mean."*

The news anchor babbles "*That was Deputy Attorney General Angela Bivens speaking today from Great Hall of the Robert F. Kennedy Department of Justice Building . . .*" and I clock the pundits muse not about substance, but instead why she chose to stand under the nude male brushed bronze statue of Law, rather than beneath the bare breasted and unblindfolded female image of Justice . . . or the irony of Robert F. Kennedy, Jr. shilling for Agent Orange. Blah, blah, blah.

I just feel small. I can't even finish my gooey sandwich onaccount, well . . . that statue of Law, he's got this banal look as he wields the a bundle of thunderbolts and laurel leaves in his fist . . . Justice, she looks like she's screaming. I saw fists raining down on me all my life . . . even in the place of law and justice. On *her* order. Parading a fake witch a phony sorceress in front of me who stole my life.

I try to do good, cooperate with the grand jury. *Nah.* I try to get a real gig and do real work even on behalf of these scum, Dean Scholtz. *Nah.*

Strike three.

I leave my tray on the table, return to the counter and the chick's maybe clairvoyant.

"You didn't get your drink with your po' boy, sir. Fountain drinks or ice tea, lemonade . . ."

"What else?" Amazing how easy that rolled off my tongue after rehab, counseling, scrubbing my soul?

"On tap . . . or cans and bottles?"

"Pabst Blue Ribbon. Tall boy . . . make it two."

Sixteen ounces a piece. Daddy, you'd say it was only hops and water, basically liquid toast. Won't hurt me. See, I'm *"uniquely situated."*

No, I'm a monster.

I finish my sandwich, chug. I empty the can and pop the second. I belch, in relief. Other diners stare. I laugh at them.

And I'm probably not going to remember catching an Uber home, because two cans of beer already got more buzzed than a whole forty of Mickey's and a puff of K2 would've done just five years ago.

Back in the crib, I stumble around, belch, do nothing to reassess . . . certainly not look in the mirror.

All I know is there's a cat in my apartment that I must've let in when I tumbled through the door . . . yeah, the thing that was scratching, mewling the previous night. Just a gray-brown blur in my addled state, yet I sense it watching me intently as I rush into the head to reverse the flow of po boy and Pabst . . .

. . . and this thing's still sitting there on the broken bathroom tile as I flush, crumple away to the wall. Weep. It rubs itself on my trouser leg. Amazing how need can disguise itself as empathy, love. It's just a hungry animal, neglected by a bunch of folks crammed into an empty jont . . . themselves conned into thinking this place would love them when it said it hated the government that oppressed them back home.

"No wonder there're so many monsters out there," I wheeze to the kitty. "And so many grifters, killers in charge. Because we set ourselves up to be lied to. We love being lied to. Even Linda Figgis . . . 'rescuing' kids? Nope, selling them off to the suburbs. Or me, lying to Stripe . . . telling him I'd train him, protect him. Ha! Look at me, cat. Look at me . . ."

It gives an emphatic meow. Like whatever, nigga. Feed me. Or, I don't care, I love you anyway? Does it matter?

I stand and look in the mirror. It leaps onto the toilet tank and stares.

"Yeah. I know . . ." I wash up, rinse my mouth. "I give a fuck," I whisper to it. "I'll show you my 'wheelhouse' Mizz Yi. Gratis. You'll thank me before this blows up in your face . . ."

In my dresser is Croc's lil' gift to me for getting my P.I. license—a "Mini" .380 Glock LCF. I fetch it and the holster, tuck the latter into my waist and slide it to the small of my back. The cat's still staring as I check the clip, pop it back.

"Pretty stupid . . . I'm still buzzed," I tell the cat as I holster the .380. "Go in the kitchen and I'll get you some tuna. Then you wait here for me to return, and we'll face the consequences together, because . . . I have a theory."

It's not even seeing me to the door, just eating.

I'm down Georgia under a setting sun and rippling purplish clouds and motherfuckers are literally ducking out of my way.

By time I reach the intersection that was my old haunt—corner of Florida and 7th—I clock Peach, seated on a vinyl folding beach chair right on the pavement among the local folk marking time, holding up walls. Got a smoldering bone in one hand, a plastic cup in the other and it's never just Fresca in there . . . always a little Tanqueray for flavor. She's got on her dinnerplate-sized shades so I don't know where she's focused; dry boney toes peek from Teva sandals. Her gray head bops to the D.C. swing . . . vintage Chuck Brown on a loop, *It Don't Mean a Thing* . . .

. . . "'if ain't got the Go-Go swing,'" I mouth.

And as it's dusk the store's picking up; the garish "Tobacconist" sign's all lit up like a circus now, with little tobacco being sold therein.

"When's your full weed license gonna come through?" I say, surprising her.

She chuckles as she composes herself but hits me back with, "You the nigga with the inside scoop, Dickie. Maybe I oughta ride your back. I hear you movin' up in the world."

The myth travels fast. If she only knew. I squat to peck her cheek but she turns away, full mockingly cold shade.

"Where you off to, lookin' all monster?" she teases. "And smellin' like a dang brewery."

"Nothin' like that. I'm *grinning and gung ho*. Speaking of monsters, kill—I hear you got a few sniffin' round here. Maybe that's holding your license up."

She's got some pamphlet or something on her lap; Spanish lessons? "What's that for—your new business partners? Sorry, investors. Partners can't be foreigners."

"They say I should go on vacation in Mexico not the D.R."

"Speak Spanish in the D.R. too, honey. What, you going to Cancun?"

"Ha! Place you never heard of Mr. College Boy. Manzanillo. On the Pacific Ocean. Bluer than blue water."

"Hmmm . . . you taking Kenny?"

Still can't see her eyes but I know I worked a nerve, as she retorts, "If you jonin' my my man, you tell yo' girls like that fat white bitch Katie to stop runnin' her mouth . . ."

"Invectives. Now-now."

"And as for my bid-ness investors funding my American dream, creatin' black millionaires, black employment, why folk think jus' because someone from Mexico they be gangstas? Thas' racist . . . an' how I gonna compete wiff these hi-falutin' niggas and white corporations runnin' THC dispensaries wiff their lobbyists and law firms, huh? They the monster, not *moi*, Dickie . . ."

"Just check things, Peach. Mexicans don't play unless you got something keeping them in the game."

"You'd know, huh? Esmeralda the Witch done turnt you out how any times?"

Ouch. "Peace, Peach. I gotta go see where I fit in on the food chain."

She calls to me as I break down 7th toward the Metro station escalators.

"You still near the bottom, baby. Don't do nothin' to remind y'self . . . and them . . . of that tonight, ya hear?"

Well, during the ride to Deanwood Station . . . and not a soul fucks with me. Leave the big, scary man alone, children. That's what my eyes flash when a bit of alcohol-induced badness fuels a look.

Once we go above ground the sky's moonless, dark but for blobs or pinpoints of light of different hues, and lines of red brake lights on Minnesota Avenue, and I'm no longer spinning, grinning . . . or menacing. Just sore in the head. Melty, in the eyes. Still armed, though. I'm a professional, an expert, eh?

Nope. I've trashed sobriety for pride. I'm a monster who gives a fuck. Praying I don't give life to Peach's words tonight, though.

But hey. You don't see me getting back on that train, do you? Nah son. That's not me.

CHAPTER FIVE
Skinfolk and Kinfolk

I GO INTO THE CUT, DO MY THING . . .

Ha! Well, here's the cut. Northeast . . . Ward Seven . . . Deanwood. See, each quadrant of the city is like a room in a home, each with its own flava and bouquet. As I hoof it across the broken bottles of Rock Creek soda and McDonald's wrappers, the taste's all bus fumes and motor oil, fried shrimp basting in mambo sauce . . . and suddenly I clock some OG burning the last detritus of summer with the first fallen leaves of September in his tiny front yard, despite the rules against burning shit in your tiny front yard. Anacostia—Southeast, D.C.—where many fools know me, smells like *rules . . . what are rules?* Yet over here it smells like *fuck the rules . . .*

I get to Sheriff Road and olfactory canon takes the form of some weed scented from the steps of a white frame house on the opposite side of the street. Two fellas in gray hoodies puffing away, and from the bouquet, it's not the 1980s Tysons Corner Mall Spencer Gifts bud the government-vetted dispensaries peddle, nor is the skunk stuff sold by any of hundreds of shadow headshops that sprung up, owed by Lorton graduates aided by the usual bleeding hearts who call them entrepreneurs.

No, this the Za tainted with the medicinal odor of Bivens' China . . . *sorry* . . . Mexican White. I cross at a lull in traffic.

"Cuz, this the way down to Gault Place, no eyes on you?" I ask.

Upon a hurried puff and cough one dude looks me up and down—disheveled yet still in a suit and tie—and says, "Dunno. You pay toll?"

"Don't pay toll, even when I was campin.'"

The other huffs nervously. He's been sizing me up and even glassy eyed I'm too big a creature for their frail, zooted asses to bag. "Wha' you get clean an' a preacher now? Social worker come ta save us?"

"Stamp moe . . . no hot tipping . . ." And this is where I should have turned my ass around and gone home, but the sight of them—damn. "Y'all fellas need some food?"

They both nod, showing rotted gums. But see, using again means I'm off my game and off my game means I miss the mass of shadows descending on us, cast by the streetlamps and headlights.

Four dudes yank the fellas off the porch, shove them toward a bus stop. One tells them to get on the Number 57 going into Capitol Hill and to never come back.

And now the group turns on me . . .

"Kill, big man," this dude with a belly hanging over his jeans calls to me. He got a bone dangling from his big lip smoked down to filter.

"Yeah, homie," says another, still in his DPW work togs and reflector vest, "you think you can post up here? We don't know you, brah . . ."

Now in my beer-addled state I'm getting the vibe of this spot. It's what Daddy said the East-to-West Berlin checkpoint was like when he was posted there after Vietnam.

Indeed, from down the sidewalk comes the sound of what I think are bike tires; the headlight beams on Sheriff soon reveal its anything but . . . and I'm thinking that the beer buzz got me hallucinating. A second later and I wish I was. It's a barrel-chested brother in a gray Dunbar High sweatshirt cut off at the shoulders to reveal the dark, oak-limb arms powering a wheelchair . . . and it's sort of rickety chair, certainly not Croc's Rolls Royce gear . . .

Uh-oh . . .

"Looky here," dude calls as he rolls further into the light. "S'up *Dickie . . .*" The emphasis is like a trumpet.

"S'up Mattel."

"You scared, Dickie? You sweatin', swayin' a bit. I mean, it's been 'least thirty years. We all just harmless graydicks now."

Yeah. "I'm cool. Small world huh. What's this jont you got here?"

"Neighborhood Watch. Stamp." He scans me as his non-plussed cohorts look on, mute.

He was chief of some bad Simple City Boys back in the day. Now—what . . . a cub scout den leader? I watch the bus scoop the two brothers up; still no crime not have proper fare so away they go.

"You importing fiends to the hipsters the way these crackers're sending these migrants up here from Texas?"

"Fuck 'em. These whitefolk wanna hug n' kiss'em these bums, they can do it face to face. Don't want my ride fucked with . . . especially now I got custom steering and controls. My daughter don't want her Amazon messed with, don't want niggas stabbin' my grannie. Cleaned out a tent city down Ft. Mahan just last week all up wid them homeless Tranq zombies."

See, this motherfucker always got my hair up as a teenager and even now that it's gray. "All due respect, Mattel, don't be fucking with peeps . . . just because they're in tents doesn't mean they're tricking the horse aspirin, you feel me, cuz?"

His boys tense up and he rolls a bit closer. "All due respect ta you, Dickie, but kill . . . I know you ain't living on Kalorama in some mansion, but it been awhile since you a camper, an' now you lookin' all clean an' shit, but it's a new jont out here now wid the Apache, 'specially here in the Seven. We got Youngs, sometime ten years old . . . linin' folk, causin' chaos, parents ain't nowhere. An' we got the *undead*. City ain't doin' shit about either. I testified to the City Council an' said this what happens when the po-po is the Klan one minute then a bunch of pussies the next. This white woman had the nerve to ask me if I was a Republican and I said no ma'am, I was a juvenile delinquent and a gangbanger and I'm sayin' you ain't shit!"

"Nice speech."

First dude who gave me the icy eye and words growls, "Mattel, you want us to bag this big nigga, Neighborhood Watch style?"

Mattel's got this sour ass look on his face I tell even in the night's dark but suddenly he's busting out in chuckles.

"*Hell no* . . . just fuckin' widchew, Dickie." He swings around to his minions, I bet all ex-bangers, now looking like a bunch of black Ralph Cramdens and Nortons now that they got mortgages on these little pillbox homes. "See, Dickie and his boy Croc was in the fancy faggot Catholic School, come down to ole Dunbar when I lived wid my auntie . . . play us in football, get their feelins hurt." He pauses, sighs. "Heard Croc in a chair, too. That's *karma*, nigga."

"Croc's got the sugar, bad. But he can *walk*." Mattel's quickly not liking the shade. Too bad. "You only played *one* game against us junior year and I recall catching a flare-out with ten seconds left and we won. That was Friday. Saturday night you got glizzy-tagged and, well . . ." I motion to the chair. "I'm still sorry about that, Randolph."

"Randolph?" a cohort says.

"That's part of my guv-name. At Dunbar they call me 'Mattel' when I was cursed to this here chair."

"*Hot Wheels*," I clarify.

"You and Croc fucked wid me!" Mattel sneers.

"We fucked with you by coming into that jont and takin' cash from y'all's juvenile delinquent asses in dice in the stairwells after them game . . ." Then Croc went to get head from whatever sad bopper cheerleader who was on deck . . . I'd count the money and pretend to be strapped. All while wearing our school uniforms, eschewing the team bus home. If Mattel handled his cash better or was more proficient with the bones, maybe he'd be on his feet.

"Why you really here, Dickie?"

Won't lie but won't spill the real jont, either.

"The whiteboy who shot two Youngs over in Adams Morgan. I'm involved with . . . finding some info. The victims . . . they're *your* peoples, over there at Nannie Helen Burroughs Avenue . . ."

The Deanwood Neighborhood Watch commences a collective belly laugh.

"What's so damn funny? One boy's dead, one boy's in a coma and the community from here down to East Capitol's about to boil."

Mattel's deadpan, though. "What boil? You see any boil?"

I shrug. "On the news, moe."

"Bullshit. It ain't nobody *legit* in the Seven doing that shit on no news. Man whatever you see is the usual suspects. Jackleg preachers on the city dole, mama Afrikka-bambalatta activists . . ."

I hope they're clocking my face this time. "I-I don't understand . . ."

"Them boys who was shot had it comin', moe,"

Getting dizzy and isn't the Pabst. Noise from a cop car and ambulance screaming by makes it worse so brace myself on a tree trunk. "What . . . are you saying?"

"Saying you best better g'won home and stop whatever stroafin' you doin here tonight. But if you got some itch, Dickie, be my guest. The answer's right across the street. But if you do go, you in 'Alice in Wonderland.' Up is down, down is up, all twisted and freaky and you ain't that rabbit with a free pass so you *will* be turnt, cuz."

Twisted and freaky: my theory's still good but now turned around. And the PD's looking more and more like either a fool or a co-conspirator. Yet with whom? No one wants to deal with this case who's intimate with it. Not Yi or the victims . . . or a community . . . or maybe even Twelve. Just some activists, the usual.

"I'll take my chances down there," is all I can muster.

And I must've sounded like an intrepid clown because as he backs his chair into the shadows, Mattel chuckles, "Watch out for the Red Queen, Alice . . ."

Motherfucker just waves and the rest of them part this checkpoint like I'm pushing a baby pram on fire . . . all giving me this dead man walking vibe.

Anyway, soon I'm not hearing a damn thing but crickets and cool breeze tickling the leaves . . . and ahead comes the roar and screech of traffic on Nannie Helen Burroughs Avenue; two blocks or so that-away is Gault Place.

In the streetlamp pallor I clock a wide veldt of tall weeds . . . some sort of no-man's land between the two hoods. The ragged vegetation obscures discarded electric scooters of various bright coral, lime, orange—each indicating a different rental service.

Could probably avoid this conspicuous invasion by entering the field but the ground's likely boobytrapped with busted bottles, whole car transmissions, rusted tool parts and Lord-knows. Back in the day I'd wade through the sea of grass, trolling the ground for goodies, unconcerned over the smell or getting tetanus from whatever's sharp there. But that's back in the day.

I check the Mini's clip just in case, not that the .380'd be any menace to anyone running around with a chopper fed by drum magazine like it's the good ole Marion Barry days. My only advantage: everything bad you can do to someone's been done to me by man, by God and myself . . .

. . . and yet I'm thinking I should turn my less than sober ass around head home.

Too late. An old queen, hobbling around as if both hips are locked comes out of the shadows towards me, calling for what's got to be a pet, from her tone. She's wearing gray sweatpants, fluffy bedroom slippers . . . incongruous vintage San Diego Chargers windbreaker wrapping her shoulders like a cape but hey, I'm not going to mess with her on that random shit because at least it's not Cowboys gear. Her hair's white and fleecy as a lamb's. She halts, gasps.

"Ma'am . . . sorry if I scared you. I'm looking for where Diamante lived, and Arthur . . . police arrested a man who shot them awhile back . . ."

"There go Tequila right there," she shares, totally inapt with what I'm saying. I turn and see a blueish gray Yorkie yapping and pissing where a hedgerow meets the sidewalk. "Fetch 'im fo' me. He ain't gonna do nuthin'."

I hold my breath, get as sweet and small as someone who looks like me can do. The little monster barks, snarls. "This ain't gonna work . . ."

Yet suddenly it leaps into my arms, and just as fast I relay it to the old lady.

"You not a Jehovah's Witness or up to any shenanigans cause Tequila knows good souls," she whispers, and I catch a whiff of Spanish. More proper than her English for sure.

"*Dónde aprendió español, señora?*"

"Ha! *Mi esposo era de Manzanillo y teníamos una casa en la playa. Era un hombre guapo*! Lawd he was fine. *Podía bailar . . . él murió.* Shit . . . *odiaba la ciudad.*"

"Sorry to hear that."

"You look like you ain't got no problem sneakin' round the city, like you jhi-campin' like them niggas drinkin', takin' that new zombie drugs in Fort Dupont Park?"

I nod in the darkness. Be honest—hey, she might be good for some leads. "Was in shelters on and off. Started at Mitch Snyder's, ended at St. Jude's, for men, attached to So Families May Eat—SFME complex. Father Phil Ruffino . . . he and the Order there took good care of us. Or tried."

"Lawd my kin was there! Petey P. hung wid ole boy they call Black Santa Claus?"

I'm flush and it ain't the lingering Pabst high.

"Lord . . . I knew Petey P. . . . and ole Black Santa, he was Jamaican . . . he was my nigga."

"Petey P. dead of the COVID. That rascal Black Santa Claus still 'round?"

Funny that. "Dead too." And I've long forgiven him.

"You caught me wiffout my teefs in," and the old gal grins a gummy grin. "But since you *kin* . . . I tell you don't go round Diamante's spot. Or his sister's. Don't do you good to snoop. Jesus say not all my skinfolk is kinfolk."

"You mean *Danelle Diggs* is a problem?"

I can see her eyes narrow now that mine are used to the darkness. "Why you really here, boy?"

"She pluggin'?"

She laughs like she's puckering for a kiss, showing pink gums again. "Diamonte's a lil' snitch, but I don't know 'bout nobody bein' a drug dealer."

"He's dead, ma'am."

"Oh yeah. And . . . the other boy. Now that was a damn shame. Art'ur Sellers. He mama trash. But he a good boy. Bad he got mixed up wiff Diamante, bad he broffer an' sista was born ta dopefiend trash."

"I was a fiend once, ma'am."

"Yet the Lawd save you. The folk who yo' skinfolk still destin'd ta use, be used. They up and re-up. Only thing good is maybe that money do useful things later on eh?"

Never heard it put that way.

"Well, dope money's got aways to go before it's clean money, ma'am. Anyway, look . . . I thought folks around here were angry a white boy shot Arthur, killed Diamante. I mean, it was on the news, there were protests."

"That so."

"Uh-huh."

"'*Le oye la calle* . . . ' What the street hears. That's what my husband used to say. Ya hear anything?"

"Nope."

'Then ya got yo' answer bout protests. Ha!" She gives me another look up and down. "You sure ain't a Jehovah's Witness? You ever been ta Mexico? Beaches down from Colima be the best, baby. Colima, nobody fucks with Colima!"

I'm not going to get anything more than riddles out of this ole abuela here, but coupled with Mattel's tale it confirms that

Yi is trash, and here I am, doing my thing covering for her malpractice. Almost feel sorry for Dean Scholtz.

"Speaking of kin—I know you aren't a fan of Arthur Sellers' mama but I can't seem to find her address even though I hear she lives here . . . but I don't want to bother her if she's with her son at the hospital. Can you help me?"

The old lady cackles as she cradles the Yorkie and says, "You best better leave, baby, and don't come back." She disappears like a witch with her furry familiar into a gloom cut only by dimly lit windows.

What is it with the "kinfolk and skinfolk"—some Ward Seven parable? It was Zora Neale Hurston's after all. And I'm laughing, nervously, because now the fog of years is clearing— adrenaline'll do that—and it was me who helped a freshman find a book in the stacks for her English Composition essay. Zora's *Dust Tracks in the Road*. That's where the quote's from.

"You're a good egg, Number Eighty-Eight," Angela Bivens said when I placed it in her little hand, years ago. That memory's returned through the fog of the street, booze, Kush. "Definitely kinfolk!"

Well, crickets' chirps and distant car horns and the like are never going to be loud enough to cover the patter of dunks and New Balance 990s on pavement . . . running up on me as the Youngs congeal out of the darkness. One, then three then five then maybe eight . . . ten? All skinfolk.

I hear, "Y'all old muvfukkahs ready ta die?"

CHAPTER SIX

The Street Never Fails

ONCE FORMED THEY MOVE AS IF those schools of sardines you see in ocean documentaries . . . a single creature. Rangy or stout, short or tall, slim black jeans or balloony gray sweatpants. Leggings with creased panty lines. Some kids are laden with the night's booty—in bags between their head and shoulders like those old racist Tarzan movie safari bearers—with what looks like various items of pilfered clothing, handbags, shoes, big jugs of Tide detergent. And the street never fails to break your heart: I clock two tykes who never bothered to change out of their middle school uniforms: khaki shorts or dresses, green or blue polos with the schools' logo.

No faces, as their heads are shrouded in the usual urban Taliban gear of sheistys and black COVID masks. Baby whiskers poking through some of those masks plus a bit of bass coming through in murmurs show the male leadership, yet the balance of the noise is the high-pitch clamor of children.

They don't target me immediately, and then I see why I was addressed as plural: there are two figures cowering on the asphalt. Diseased, hopeless.

"Lookit dat nigga hands . . . he fingers, yo!" One child taunts. "You the Mummy nigga? Zombie undead!"

"I bite you an' make you a zombie!" this old man yells in some last act of defiance. I see his fingers, yeah. Crushed and tar-black, as if dipped in acid, as if decayed fruit . . . nails about to slough. I've seen rot before, smelled it. But nothing like this. Got to be the Tranq.

A teen leaps in, unburdened by smash-n-grab spoils. He curses at the old man's companion—a smaller figure crumpled on the pavement in a long dirty cotton dress and jeans jacket—then lefts a foot to stomp at the figure. The old man deflects the blow with his hand. He screams. A decomposed finger's hanging by threads of tissue . . .

. . . and so I come out into the light. The smaller kids gasp.

A large boy, locks poking from the forehead seem of his bala-clava, brandishes a long screw driver. Oh, not for stabbing. "You goin' git lined, comin' at me like dat, uncle! So where yo' whip at, uncle? It *my* whip now, so you pay wif it fo' actin' a fool!"

Another holds up one of those big ass mobile phones, screen glowing in the night's dark. The sound's shrill, words imperceptible—but I can make out images of bodies plucking clothing off hangers, shelves. Designer store names Verna'd know are evident in the background. Then it looks like someone car's being boosted.

"On code, you goin' be out, Old," this kid shouts. "Less you wid Gestapo. She don't want no smelly fiends in her hood. Take they shit an' go like a Happy Meal is the rule."

Is that what this toy motherfucker said . . . *Gestapo*? "Who?"

"Then you *ain't* wid Gestapo," he sneers.

A girl, tiny with pink hairclips popping out of her head gear empties nail polish covered in Walgreens stickers, into a another bag, all gleeful. "Watch, this nigga goin' piss hisself an' cry and say somffin faggot like 'I don't want no trouble.'"

Mater Maria, COVID bent them all. My deadpan stare and the monotone pushes the smaller kids away, though. "Kill, y'all best jump. Now."

The old man takes this distraction to be a geriatric Flash, injured finger and all.

The other one, the woman writhing on the street, mutters, "They ain't goin' hurt me . . . that jus' Bill, my friend . . ."

"Man fuck this ole nigga!" a teen female screeches.

One of the huskier boys reaches for his waist at that prompt. "See me?" he shouts.

I pull the LCF from my holster, crouch, . . .

PANG! PANG! PANG! I behold the ricochets terrifying these kids more than if I'd put a dot on someone's forehead.

They scatter. Crying, cursing, screeching, hollering.

I drop to my stomach because one or more of them will likely return fire. Whether now or the bad ole days in the '80s when Croc and I ran the streets in our proper Catholic school gear, teens aren't known for having the sand to stand off and aim. Hell, the outlaws and sheriffs didn't even do that in the Old West.

Sure enough . . .

POP! POP! and then one more POP!

And then it's quiet. And should be cursing myself for using, for sliding on children. Sure, breaking sobriety's got my street sense stymied, but I'm not out here to hug. The older ones will steel them; they'll regroup. And I doubt that old lady and "Tequila" will be my refuge as I watch the lights of each row-house and duplex dim or blink off all around me.

I hear, "N-No . . . ova there. It's safe, thas where Bill an' I was goin'."

It's the woman in the dingy cotton dress and jacket. She's beckoning to me.

Across the street, with a chute of light slicing obliquely, is a Ford van . . . same Econoline panel "truck" as we bums rode to empty-out evicted folk. The thing's the same color as the rust around the wheel wells; the rear door's two glass panels are taped up with some sort of black paper from the inside, as if a ramshackle vampire had taken up residence therein. The windshield's occluded by what looks like bedsheet with little curlicue designs.

"I swear, it's safe. Help me up."

If she's as much a fiend as Bill, I know to lift her gingerly, like an antique doll.

And then I hear, muffled, by the Detroit steel, "That you, mommie?"

"Goin' open the door!"

Kill, each wheel is up on a cinder block with nary a tire in sight. The door squeaks open, hell I'm in. A small arm pulls it shut.

"You from Chile 'n Fam'ly Services, come ta hinder me?" the lady I rescued chides me. "If so you stupid cause them boys'll kill ya, leave ya in the trees."

There's a little LED light illuminating a face with dull blue glow. A small face, yeah—plump, framed by braids. Then a bigger face materializes . . . a boy's. He's the one who opened the door.

Finally, I see the adult as she unwinds a muddy scarf that had wrapped her jowly face. Eyes are bright, wide, and earnest for someone fiending in zombie shit. Yet there's an incongruous blonde wig askew on this head, almost comically. Forces me to point to it but the wearer, who's indeed female from all outward signs, ignores my gesture . . .

"My kids, they goin' Ridgeway Elementary an' get Title Three meals," she whispers, I wash 'em when we go to the motel and this summer we get air condit'in and pool there. It get cold las' night so I start this mug and put on heater. We ain't filthy so no doody or pee in here . . ."

Yet thanks when the stink hits me. No not from piss or whatever. From her right forearm. It's split, as if dissected in a lab yet with edges as black and sugary as this dude Bill's rotted fingers. And as she moves her own fingers, I swear I see white tendons twitch and flex, exposed open air . . ."

"Baby git mommie a wet cloth and some ointment for my sores . . ." she whispers to the boy.

I'm about to speak but now I hear those feet coming back. She shushes the children and me. The little girl points, mutely, at my face.

There's mumbling . . . I hear the hum of those rental scooters . . . and sure enough they take off as I peep a siren in the distance. More like EMS—I can tell—but hey if they can't, I'm good.

"They trash," the woman whispers to me. "They mamas is trash, they daddy's is prison trash. I di'n't raise no trash." When I look around the van, she clocks my tracking eyes. "My husband kidney's messed up and bills messed us up. Finance company took all but his van. Then my oldest, he gone . . ."

"Lemme take you to a hospital."

"*No!*" she shrieks. Damn loud enough to catch the ear of any lingering Young.

"I'll take your kids to a safe place, no Child and Family Services, stamp . . ."

"I said no!"

"Look . . . okay . . . sorry I put your little ones in danger. I'm Dickie Cornish. I'm a . . . um . . . I work with the . . . *Courts.* I was here . . . and I shoulda been more careful."

"You not Twelve?"

"No ma'am." I'm watching the kids pull two of those Lunchable things from a Coleman camp cooler behind the van's driver's seat. "Those are good eats," I tell them. "Trust me I know."

"I like cheese," the little girl whispers to me. Then, "Are you a giant?"

That's when I notice the packs of syringes, on the floor near the food cooler . . .

"If you not Twelve then you a rough nigga huh?" the mother hisses. "Wif yo' iron shooting in the air. Wha', Gestapo think jus' cause I ain't paid up I sill a zombie like Bill? Bill goin' get his money from his nephew and then them kids chase us. For fun. For sport. Older boys they chase zombie woman for the *you-know* . . ."

"What'd mean, ma'am? This spot's where fiends get Tina."

I'm no getting a chance to elaborate because she's leering at me real hard, as if her arm's already amputated, a painless memory. "Who you be—*really?*"

"I told you . . . I would lawyers in the Superior Court," I lie, "I'm looking for someone who knows Arthur Sellers, or Diamante Diggs. They got shot about a month ago . . ."

I'm watching her face almost melt in the shadows, her kids suddenly cling close, minding that rotted arm of course. Her mouth forms words but nothing's coming out.

"*Go,*" I hear, barely audible.

I nod. "Sure." I'm about to crack the side door but then she grabs my arm with he good arm. Good because the needle sores are only bee sting-sized, for now.

"Why? Why you want Arthur?"

"Trnya peep what's going on. If cops are right . . ."

Guess I made an impression on at least one of them. The boy moves close to me, brushes away his mother's grasp, mutters, "My brother he asleep an'll never wake up till he see Jesus."

"*Shush now!*" the woman yells, almost rocking the van.

The boy's reeling into a dark corner and the girl crawls to him. I watch the mother weep and pantomime an apology but the kids don't budge.

"You are . . . Artemesia Sellers?" *Mater Maria* . . .

Breathless, she spits out words. "Yeah. You don't think I love my son? I love all my babies. You tell that to Twelve, the social workers . . . so big nigga I ain't afraid of you an' I ain't goin' be shamed. That not my boy wiff tubes and wires stickin' all out him. His soul a butterfly with the Lord now."

Learned a long time ago, when I saw boys Arthur's age turning tricks in the same men's rooms they had to turn into a bed for the night—never cry for them. You'd run out of tears, even the ones banked for your own suffering.

"Police say a whiteboy shot him in the head because he was robbing him way over in Adams Morgan. Did the whiteboy owe money . . . for Tina? Did Arthur and Diamante follow him across town to collect?"

"Don' be stupid." Her face is suddenly dry, fierce. "Why Diamante need money fo'? His sister be growin' money like a farm for e'ry one us fiends, janky foreign thieves . . . like fo' housin' that pandemic money."

"How so?"

"Unemployment checks, drug sto' money, money for sto's what got closed, Medicaid. Rent help. Danielle figure she help folk get it. Just not the right folks. Steal you name too . . . use that. I say so even though it bad. White man taking *billions*, put it in his pocket and ain't feed a soul, ain't fly medicine an' vaxx to no one!"

"No . . . I mean, how so you knew about this, and Danielle—the sister—don't come by and shut you up. You could tell the cops, the Feds . . ."

Artemesia chuckles and reflexively so do the kids in that dank stink van. "Diamante the one wiff the big mouff. Beside . . . I ain't afraid of her. What she goin' do to me . . ." She bears her festering arm, ". . . what she already done do?"

I nod, but something beneath her words have hooked me. I give her a business card. One of my old ones, the first ones I ever had done at Staples. As I push the rest back in my jacket's inside pocket I tap my phone. The little girl's washing her Lunchable down with a Rock Creek orange soda.

"The best," I tell her. Then I tell them all I'm just making a call to let my people know I'm good. I'm really recording neat trick Stripe taught me—as I fake the call, ask their names, have Arthur's mother repeat as much as she's willing. "So again it's Thursday, September twenny-fifth, ten-forty p.m. . . . with Artemisia Sellers and I'm going to speak to Danielle Diggs. So Miz Artemesia, what you mean Diamante's got a big mouth?"

She shrugs. "Ain't mine to say."

"Arthur, was he mad . . . mad at Danielle for slinging the dope that got you hooked. Hooked on *Tranq.* It's the Apache, right?"

"I look hooked to you? Bill, he fucked up. I get off that shit. But they say sin don't heal . . ."

Amen.

"Finally . . . any police, anyone from the U.S. Attorney's office discuss any of this stuff with you, other than to tell you Arthur's been shot?"

"Nah. Nah sir."

Time to take my ass out of here. Fuck yeah, re-assess everything Yi dumped on me, but I need to clear one more thing.

"So now I know about Danielle. Maybe can you tell me, real live, if some whiteboys may have been coming here, hangin' with her?" I don't say it. I won't say it. Just want to hear her reaction . . . .

"Ain't seen no whiteboy."

"Miz Artemesia, thanks. I'm gonna check to see if it's safe to—"

She cuts me off. "Spanish boy, pump weights like Arthur. He not scrawny girlie boys like what hang wiff Danielle's bitches. But *my Arthur* . . . he was hard as stone so none these fools messed wiff him! He only sin was defendin' that Diamante. Boffem—brother an' sister—monsters!"

"I can help . . . help you visit Arthur again in the hospital."

"I tole you. That thing ain't Arthur. But Diamante, he trash. He dead. In Hell."

I tap the phone off. "You need anything you call me at that number." Yes, fomenting an ever-bigger conflict of interest. But I'm just using my *uniquely situated* talent . . .

In a few minutes I'm out into the weeds and garbage toward the lights of Nannie Helen Burroughs, sussin' out a route to the Metro because no Uber or cab's coming here. I'm actually believing this crap about doing good, teaching Yi a lesson on my "wheelhouse," until another wave of nausea—longtime coming—combined with the ebbing adrenaline, finally ends the night's delusion and empties the last of the Pabst and everything else into a dark empty lot.

Yeah, the street never fails to break your heart. Yet it will always tell you the truth. Tonight, I did stupid, questionable things, goddammit. Tonight, I was reminded that people charged with upholding the law, adducing fact, still lie to my face.

"Verna," I'm now speaking into my phone. "P-Please . . . I need to see you. Your boy's in over his head. *Again*."

CHAPTER SEVEN
Sentimental Vanity

KATIE'S SIDE-EYES ARE A BLUR, HER chides are hollow.

"Sh-Shut up . . ." escapes from my lips and goes straight up to Katie's pink, pudgy disapproving face. It's better than saying, *Hey I drank for the first time in years and was running fade on some children . . .*

"Whutchewsay, hon'?" she squeaks. "I know you didn't tell me to 'shut up!' See, Keesh, this shit is indick-tive of what I've been saying. Something's wrong with him . . ."

I'm on my rack, shirtless, shoeless and sockless but still wearing my suit trousers . . . cold rag on my forehead. Praying the serpent that's my Daddy doesn't rise in my throat, coil in my brain. Pills and sessions and rehab might not put me back on track. Maybe a nuclear bomb will, I dunno. Still, shame and regret's got me tight-lipped about Yi likely firing me and I'm still not sharing a damn thing about Bivens in the federal courthouse.

Now, Katie's just finished sanitizing the head with Clorox wipes . . . and maybe from the stench of the night's leavings, to wit: po boy and beer, she's guessed I'm off the wagon. Maybe. Even so my crib never measures up, and she keeps supply of wipes in her faux leather purse anyway—a sort of PSTD from being on the street when her accoutrements included a shopping cart filled with empty plastic bags.

Now she's standing over me. Giving me the what-for.

"No cap, Dick . . . them boys could've put you on a milk carton last night. I hear some kids robbed two grown-ass men right up there on New Hampshire Avenue, middle of the day, flashin' pistols or some shit, jumped into a whip and then ran over some lady jogger."

LaKeisha's waddling to my desk, opening my laptop. "Migraines, eh?" she grunts. She ain't buying what I'm selling, either. She starts tapping away on my keyboard . . . .

"Migraines, suddenly the excuse," Katie huffs. "This *ain't* like you, hon. More like foolishness Stripe would've pulled. Gone over Nannie Helen Burroughs like 'John Wick,' no backup, no word."

Shows how far off she is. John Wick?

"Dammit Katie leave Stripe's name outya mouth, okay?"

"Nah-ah, not 'okay.' Them Deanwood sumbitches don't play and they ain't never heard of you. They ain't afraid of you like them savages in Anacostia got."

LaKeisha reminds me, "If you'd use this Nexis I stole and hooked up here when I fixed your jenkty modem—you're welcome, by the way—you'd have known all about your client . . ." Former client, I suppose, ". . . and maybe had better background on those Ward Seven folks. Example, Jon Snow: Danielle Diggs, Diamante's sister, owns five houses, all Section Eight."

"So what?" I snap. "Look at my crib—it ain't the Mandarin Oriental and y'all know why the city's paying for it."

"May I continue, m'lord? Fifteen citations from HUD in the last ten years for tenants who were trickin', pluggers, other felonies, hot bunking with double capacity . . . putting other landlords out of business by helping their tenants keep COVID back rent collection tied up, Lord—couple years now? And look at this here. Helping shops and property owners in her hood get fraudulent COVID loans?"

I'm groaning into my pillow now and the cold rag flops off. "Perhaps you dip out to the donut place on Rhode Island and get me a toasted coconut and a twenny-four ounce joe?"

LaKeisha sighs and instructs, "This is important. The Dickie I know would have—"

I feel the serpent bite my stomach as I cut her off, mean. "'The Dickie you know?' Fuck is that—me sleeping on a steam grate over at the Smithsonian? Look, your databases and shit didn't reveal damn thing about my client's alleged victim, Diamante Diggs, having a sister slinging some no-medical-card weed and very likely Tina. I had to find that out the old-fashioned way." Like Yi, lying to me.

Katie shudders, stands off in the kitchen. She was always more fragile despite the bravado. LaKeisha, who called down artillery in Afghanistan and seen her kids taken away three times, is her usual matter of fact self as she tells me, as mono-toned as me, "Your client is no 'Lannister' nor a knight, nor a squire. Father's a salesman, mama works at Walmart super-vising security video. Salt of the earth pilgrims who, well, only want to 'Make America Great Again,' m'lord."

Katie finally plops at the foot of my rack, almost squishing my calves and feet. "Well?" she prods.

"*Well*, what?" Jesus, Mary and Joseph these chicks're split-ting my skull.

Her skeptical gaze's aimed right at my pinkish eyes. "How could you miss that info? I mean, that big-ass brain of yours, that thing don't forget nothing. But ever since you walked outta that *courthouse* . . ."

"You're trippin'!"

LaKeisha toggles up her own TikTok and Twitter because I do not partake of either. "Here's more on your client. What the 'Gatekeepers' are all about *before* you jumped at the money," she counsels. "I was in the Army with the skinheads in the early two-thousands . . . who were the daddies of the ones today. Redneck females, too, as mamas."

"You pester them with computer shit too?"

"No. Took the back off metal hairbrushes cause back then they wouldn't let us wear plaits and braids and stuff. After lights out we'd teach them what *woke* truly meant . . ."

Yep, now—as Katie's eyeing me, frowning—we're clocking social media footage taken by Scholtz's phone and a fancy little attached mic. I see these preppie brownshirts with their tiki torches from a couple of years ago. Then it's mask and COVID time and he's got clips of protesters who say they could give a shit about George Floyd—they just want to see whitepeoples' shit burn, and in the comments it says the Gatekeepers paid rando teens and street people to say that. More clips: his old employer Brom Vitter's causing a ruckus on the Senate floor by declaring Trump 2020 election winner and survivor of a wacko's bullet by divine intervention . . .

. . . and here's ole President Orange Hair giving the billionaires winks and tax breaks, the bumpkins marching orders to terrorize folks. Scholtz's getting it all on video. Strangely, though, I don't discern the affirmations, pants of delight, lips wet with each swipe of his tongue—all the noises of the *true believer* chronicling a miracle.

Rather, silence, as if a mere task . . . or he'd otherwise does not want to be there.

I force Katie to lift her hips off my legs so I can swing own around and lift myself from the rack to get a better look. Katie eyes my hands. My fingers are trembling . . .

"What?"

"Seen that before, is all, hon'"

"*Pssssh* . . . seen what, huh? Keesh—speed up your show 'n tell."

LaKeisha eyes Katie and I know they know I fucked up. Still, Keesh continues with the Dean Scholtz vids.

"Okay . . . this is from affirmative action stuff in front of the Supreme Court on First Street. He's the one with the tee shirt 'Choice=Murder' 'Pro-Choice= Lazy Feminist.'"

And still—silence and detachment as he records his cohorts facing his phone lens to beef on his behalf how lucky he was to get into Princeton when there were too many spaces allocated to "*weaklings who can't handle the workload so they commit suicide.*" He pans over to some kids, maybe Chinese, Korean, Japanese extraction, a few South Asian—all of them pulling for *his* side, frankly, yet he dishes on them. "*Fucking zipperheads and curry eaters . . . they should be on their knees, me-so-horny thankful for what we just did for them. Well, when they're distracted celebrating the Year of the COVID Lab Rat or worshipping cows so we'll neutralize them, easy.*"

I mean, the words are harsh but it's like he's reading from a stage play script like we'd do in Catholic school and the nuns literally wrote "emote here" or "shout this part" in the margins.

A brown-skinned dude appears, with a Texas Lone Star tee shirt and Trump regalia, eyes obscured by mirrored state trooper shades. Odd look for kid with a soul patch of facial hair, shorn head and what looks like an Aztec pyramid tatt on his forearm. He's cajoling Scholtz to come harass a clutch of Black Lives Matter protesters climbing out of a van, yet Scholtz waves him off.

"*Lemme see those eyes, Wetback!*" I hear Scholtz tease. This time, I see and hear genuine emotion, jocularity. No script.

And when the fellow pulls off the mirror shades the lens is filled with eyes that make my peepers look snow white and pristine. So this Latin pal was fiending too? But this doesn't look like a Tina gaze. Last I saw it in person . . . it was on Coats' face. But Apache? Nah . . . no way the White is among these kids. No way . . .

"Dean's just a voyeur. A poser. He's not down with this shit." Katie demurs. "Yeah pull this titty and it plays *Ave Maria*! Dick, I got a nephew in the Gatekeepers out in Manassas. No 'voyeurs.' They chased anybody who wore a mask in public during the pandemic including nurses, teachers . . . they tossed smoke bombs . . . wanted to be 'deputized' to bring their long guns down K and 16th Street to go after Black Lives Matter. My brother-in-law brought my nephew to the Capitol on January Sixth to hurt people . . . all them assfucks need to be under the jail before it's too late—and it's coming up on being too late!"

"Not saying he played you that first you met, Ser Richard," LaKeisha adds, "but sociopaths like this are glad to have confidantes. Affirms their charm, power."

Lord, if they only heard Mattel and his Wonderland talk . . . seen Arthur Sellers' mama and siblings in that van, they'd've run my ass out of that apartment straight up to the VA headshrinkers. "Back, off. Please."

"You shouldn't have taken this gig," Katie hammers.

Perhaps it's time to be a good Catholic and confess, bear the truth. Yet I just freeze up, yell for the cat, who I haven't even named. "One loyal thing in this room," I grumble.

I see LaKeisha's shoulders go stiff, her eyes shut behind those soda bottle glasses. She's starting to coil up like a pillbug. Quietly.

Katie's not a pillbug. "Remember that one winter, night it rained, then ice, then cold as fuck in hours and you got a bed at St. Jude's but you didn't go . . . and you *scavenged* all those pieces from the Dumpster behind Staples, and made glue from rubber bands to mend the tarps you found . . . and you stayed with us, when you had a warm bed, three hots."

LaKeisha finishes . . . mumbling, whispering, "And the tuna cans you and Princess stole . . . when we finished eating you shoved cardboard you found the Dumpster . . . in the vegetable oil in the cans . . . made little firepots . . . we boiled hot tea. We all would've died that night . . ." The next words are clear, crystalline. "Where's *that* Dickie Cornish, huh? When we left the courthouse, you shared something *bad* with Croc but not us. Us . . . who've been with you since *forever*."

Yeah, I'm hearing but not truly listening. Can't . . . see, that serpent's twisting its way up from my gut, bringing the bile with it, the blood.

It's in my mouth now. I mean . . . *you're* in my mouth, Daddy . . . Oh Mother Mary . . . I'm so sorry, ladies.

"Fuck is it with you bitches, huh? *Huh?*" That shuts them down. Oh they are quiet now. "Do this, Dickie, do that . . . save us Dickie, take care of us Dickie, and what'd you bitches give a nigga in return, *huh?* Like you got room ta question my black ass when you both still living in a fucking halfway house? I shot at children last night . . . after I used. Yeah . . . I drank. Happy now?"

Hear the sniffles, the moans? They be weak tea, Junior. Like your mother, like your sister.

"Y-You sumbitch!" Katie cries.

"And nothing happened in the courthouse that's *any* y'alls motherfucking business!"

"He used," LaKeisha whispers, as if to herself. She's mumbling, shaking, taking herself away to that place of dragons and seaside castle keeps.

But Katie, through her squirting eyes and wet snorts hits me once more. "Gonna ask you one last time. What happened when you left us in the courthouse?

Guess must spill, huh? Dr. Gupta, and the rest of the Mumbai Medics up there at the VA's rehab and psych spot wouldn't appreciate my candor.

"Esmeralda Rubio. She was there. She's alive. She's a witness in this shit about Bracht that never went away. They . . . they brought her back once this shit about Figgis, the Antonelli came out . . . they paraded her in front of me. Hurt me."

"Oh *God*, hon," Katie whispers. "Fuck didn't you say? Coulda helped, coulda gotten you to a group, to the docs . . ."

I'm nodding, crying like a little boy like when Gunnery Sargeant Daddy'd give me the what-for and I'd be so stone-faced and then Mom'd find me ask what happened and why I was bruised-up and he'd call her a redbone bitch and bruise her up, too but she'd still hug me . . .

. . . and so both women allow me to hook them with my arms . . . my whole giant mutant wingspan . . . .and I bring them to the gray curls insulating my chest so they can hear my heart. They clutch me tight until Katie giggles into my flesh and I hear a muffled, "Boy you need a bath. *Got my bleach wipes* . . ."

"King of North . . . *and Lord of B.O.*," LaKeisha snorts.

All's not absolved nor forgotten. We just know one another. We know we're human.

I add more tearful laughs, until the apartment door opens. Whichever woman who'd come and didn't trip the new lock, it doesn't matter, as here they are, close to my bed, me shirtless and swallowing them in my body.

Verna's mute and gaping.

We must look like what we are—all sloppy, dingy and dappled, former shelter dwellers—farting around on a weekday morning when regular folk are out being real, doing real.

She, on the other hand, looks like she'd come from a 1960s movie's office party: sharp-toed leopard print high heels, matching gloves, beige knee length skirt, tight embroidered waistcoat, thin scarlet purse, small knit beret topping her head. Her hair, now natural and upswept, is the only contemporary feature. Her lips are as red as that purse and they finally form words, "You all, above all, should know to keep a door locked. Anyone could walk in and cause drama . . ."

"Hey," I mutter. "Been calling you."

"Been with my lawyer when I haven't been with my banker and my dad to liquidate stuff . . . so I can be with my lawyer." The vinegar in that statement should rub me raw, given how it ain't my fault she needs a lawyer.

"We're sorry," Katie pouts, child-like.

"There was nothing from HR on whether we could come back to funded jobs," LaKeisha adds with more adult officiality. "I'm due to see my kids, Verna."

"I understand," Verna huffs, again as if that's on LaKeisha, not her getting hooked up with Chief Figgis and her bent Amazon cops nobly pilfering kids from poor bamma mothers, place them with bourgie families, with wealthy childless whites. "I've spoken to the Board. You two may continue at SFME. The children's residential wing'll stay open. She tugs off those print gloves. "But I've been terminated, effective yesterday. I built that place from when I was a grad student, a single social worker . . . and they are boxing my stuff, mailing it to me. Not even telling the kids, the moms. I brought in Amazon, the Nats, Commanders, Wizards, Caps as matching sponsors to our Medicaid, D.C., TANF grants. And they are terminating me."

I can manage nothing but, "There's coffee . . . I'm getting up . . . gotta wash, evidently."

My bed provides the only furniture for her. She sits next to Katie as I rise, smiles that dimply smile, albeit with a nervous reserve. See, it wasn't just Figgis she endorsed. By doing so, she entered the cop civil war between Figgis and Antonelli— the one I firebombed, like in the childhood books I'd read in the library. Jules Verne: *Captain Nemo, Robur The Conqueror*. Why choose a side—when you can wipe out both? Though . . . my heart was a bit with Figgis, yeah I'll cop to that. At least she wasn't killing people or impregnating helpless women in shelters.

At least LaKeisha takes the hint. "Jon Snow . . . you have free Nexis another month, and access to basic Fedlaw database. I wrote the new password over there."

"Public Defender hasn't even cleared all my paperwork."

"Paperwork? I am *Valeryian*." She motions Katie and says, "Let's go to get a proper breakfast. Ethiopians up Georgia's got some nice eggs sprinkled with sumac. Used to get kicked outta there all the time . . ."

Katie gives Verna a hurried smile and almost weird curtsey as she brushes by. LaKeisha halts, however. Still avoiding eye-contact when speaking, she declares, "Please be kind to him. You treated him better when he was big and hairy and smelly than when he is clean and I could tell you wanted him to kiss you—"

"*Keesh!*" I intercede.

"It's okay, Dickie . . ." Verna answers, solemnly.

"He saved your life!" LaKeisha snares.

"He saved us," Katie adds. "But he's going to kick *us* out. Chew on that hubris, Dick. Good-bye."

CHAPTER EIGHT
Always a Price

BEFORE SHE CLOSES THE DOOR BEHIND her Katie geeks on the cat that still wants to make my acquaintance. "Don't get close to Dick Cornish, lil' puss sweetie baby. He'll get bored and hurt you . . ."

Verna waits for the footsteps down the stairs to abate then observes, "They are fierce, and they fiercely love you. And they are pains in the ass." When I shrug, saunter into the head to soap up and rinse my head and face, my pits, I hear her add, "And . . . they're right. I'm so sorry. Dickie . . ."

"I don't give it a thought, Vee," I lie. "You got sucked in by Linda, bamboozled by Antonelli's spy Roffe. I'd never let Roffe hurt you." Yeah, by putting two ACP rounds into his chest when he came at me with Big's knife.

I take down my trousers, sweaty draws, wash and rinse below. I pull on the draws I slept in last night, grab my frayed, red plaid rob off the door and wrap myself.

"I wanted you to be the first to know. They've granted limited immunity next time. Here I thought I was going to federal prison and see some of the same women I failed to help."

I dry my head and ears with my towel as I face her. "Funny because Linda Figgis's been in the Outer Banks with her wife and their kids for the last month. Sweetheart deal, so why they need you?"

"She's hasn't gone to trial, Dickie." I don't give her permission to remove her waistcoat, that weird little hat but she does anyway.

"She won't serve a day." I tug a clean tee shirt over my head. Settle into my office chair. Pretend to check my email as she speaks.

"Why were you at the Federal Courthouse the other day? My stuff's pretty much closed to the public."

"Because Esmeralda Rubio's back," I say, nonchalant, almost aloof. Not to get a rise out of her. Just to keep myself grounded. I've got two cans of Pabst and discharged .380 to atone for.

"Damn. She's . . . *still alive?*"

I nod.

"Dickie, oh my God . . ."

"You got too much on your plate. You don't need to the deets. But the bitch's back. She's federal property."

I settle beside her. She clutching my pillow now, scanning me. She's the horror show that is my body before so I'm not modest: scars, misshapen bones of my knees, Godzilla-like processes running the length of my spine, tortured horror feet, nutsack of an octogenarian, hanging to mid-thigh, dick that hasn't worked so well, if ever. Just once for her, last year. shows that are my feet before so I'm not modest. Lord have mercy it's good to seen her again!

"Vee . . . I never told you how that dude Mr. Sugars . . . the white man . . ."

"A killer and I'm glad his gone. You were very brave . . ."

"Listen, he cleaned me up from Bracht with . . . stuff that's still experimental, so you can imagine what the folks up at the VA said when they first got my bloodwork back. I mean, I didn't have an honorable discharge so they didn't have to take me. Closest molecules are *acamprosate* for the booze, *buprenorphine* for everything else but the Kush. And if I didn't get a come-back bump from Mr. Sugars directly it would force the opposite reaction and then I'd need naloxone within a few hours or I was history. Ticker's not the best and my kidneys and liver're standing on a banana peel. Just started meds for that. Nothing has hurt me in years on the street. No bullets, blades . . . Hi-Five, COVID. But now . . ." When she takes my big Herman Munster paw in her little hand I admit, "I'm glad . . . *glad* I got Esmeralda—and some goosestepping yuppie client—to take my mind off it all."

"Long before I got your message last night," she reveals, "I'd emailed LaKeisha. I was feeling mean, feeling sorry. She said you'd gotten a contract with the public defender right outta left field. I'm sorry it's that shooting in Adams-Morgan, amarite?"

"Uh-huh." Time to open the sluice all the way. "I had some beers . . ."

"Aw Dickie, no."

"Made me sick. Not before I was out with the three-eighty doin' gumshoe shit."

"I'm not gonna preach," she whispers, squeezing my hand. "Who am I to preach?"

"I never, ever said you were tainted, that I was better than you. Your fall's recent. I've been down a long, long time . . ."

I won't lie—she's right where I dreamed she'd be, starting intently at my troubled mug . . . here on my rack . . . in my wreck of an apartment. That she's damaged, too, yeah her wall's crumbling. Okay, maybe I told her to building it . . . as I wrapped my mind around she and Linda Figgis. That a bourgie like would muse about kidnapping kids from the dirty, the cold and placing in the clean, the warmth . . . all toys and dancing and Spider Man movies—that's no crime. That you'd actually cover-up someone doing it? Nope . . .

. . . yet we are kissing, nonetheless . . . she's parting my robe with her hands, and I let those hands roam all over me as devour her throat, her earlobes. Hope the door's locked this time. Hope after the night screams, the pain, the meds I can keep it up and inside her . . . and I came and she giggled how all gentle and oozy I was when she saw the fully laden jimmy because I hadn't before made love so many years and I guess she expected a firehose.

This morning, I give her a firehose.

She'd already finished herself astride me, and I'd turn her on her back . . . and I pulled out because there's no jimmy . . . and I been tested so many times for the Hi-Five and other badness inside me, yet she doesn't gasp or berate me when the stuff goes everywhere.

I roll off her and into the damp sheets. Not a lot of avoiding the mess in a single bunk. "I-I gotta get right, get it together."

"Shush. Two to tango, Big Man. Otherwise I wouldn't have even set foot in here."

"What are we gonna do?"

"First, Im'a clean off this mess you made," she says with a snicker, thumbing away the my essence of me lingering between her small breasts. "Then . . ." with a big sigh she just pauses. Looks at me. Strokes the deepening lines in my face. "Let's be king and queen of our own world a little while. No one else allowed. Deal?"

"So decreed."

"Hungry?" Verna posits. "Proper grub, not your ramen and cold cuts, man . . ."

"Got money in my pocket."

We take turns washing up, I throw on some baggy khakis, an oversized plaid flannel shirt; Stripe always said I looked like a big black Mexican when I dressed like that, shirt buttoned to the neck. If the khakis were slim and I wore some Tims and a red silk print shirt, then I'd be a proper *Salvadoreno*, he'd joke.

Good to see the Mini-Cooper again. Indian Summer sun's made it warm enough for the top to be down. I'm relieved Simon's not there on the sidewalk, comatose or jacking off. Never want to say these folk embarrass me because I was them. Still, I want nothing that adulterates this vibe. Maybe our last, decent vibe . . .

She guns us down to 14th, in the thick of shops and bistros that were once the porn shops brothels my father frequented when on liberty, while Mom had to remain chaste on pain of losing a tooth, eh Daddy? We sit outdoors at this spot called Chicken & Whiskey, not too far from where Melvin usually posts up to panhandle and throw shade. We have the outdoor COVID shed seating all to ourselves. Dean Scholtz and Esme and pills occupy zero space in my dome now.

"Just chicken for you, no whiskey," Verna jokes.

I'm mouthing "Thanks, Lawd," yet absorbing a familiar scent through my nostrils, displacing the roasted goodness of the Peruvian yardbird.

At noon on the dot, on a Friday yet, decent warm weather—the sidewalk's not exactly sparse with people. I can fix on Verna's smile but so long, see? Something's always pulling my gaze—it's instinct, a survival thing. Like Jaime Bracht said: scavengers gotta look out for predators and prey.

And I clock a swaying Trader Joe grocery bag . . . attached to an arm as delicate and small as Verna's.

A face freezes me in my chair. *Nooooo* . . . a doppelgänger? Hair more playful, a jog top and yoga pants replacing a stiff skirt. White Birkenstocks and painted toenails.

Okay. It's no twin . . .

"Hullo, Mr. Cornish . . . *Dickie?* What a coincidence!"

Angela Bivens is oddly coquettish, swishing in place like a little kid. I mean, like she's high or this is Dr. Jekyl.

"*Mater misericordia* . . ." I mumble. Bad habit from Catholic school.

She hears, knows she's gotten to me. "And a *Supercalifragilistic-expialidocious* to you, hey!" She comes right up to the curb. Nods to Verna. "Hello."

"H-Hello . . . uh . . . I'm . . . Oh my God, you're with . . . the government . . ." Verna's sure enough gasping from an invisible pinch. The little person making eyes at equally little self is the boss of the U.S. Attorney presiding over the federal grand jury putting the tit of every cop and social worker in the District in the ringer. "Verna . . . Verna Leggett." She flashes me a frantic glance. "Dickie, I had no idea you know—"

"Angela Bivens." Bivens gives a grin, takes her hand, shakes but doesn't release for a few agonizing seconds "I love your hair, queen, and the outfit . . ."

Queen? Yeah, even her voice's pitch, the cadence of her speech, all fucking off-character. Like she's tripping. I try to compose myself, hit back. "You don't follow protocol do you, just coming up on *certain people* like this."

"Beg your pardon?"

"Howard alums. We aren't supposed to run-up on one another so close to Homecoming."

"Ahhh . . . haven't heard that one. I guess I'll see you on the Yard if the crowd hasn't gotten too young. My sorors always do something but I've been an invited speaker at so many bouls and hotel rubber chicken conclaves and caucus black formals it all becomes a blur. Years ago when I was with the FBI . . . pregnant, no friends . . . I was too shy to come to the Yard . . ."

Verna taps my arm. "Dickie . . . I-I have to go to the ladies room." She shoots out of her chair and rushes into the restaurant proper.

"Dunno what's got her thong in a bind . . . she's not going to serve any time. But yes, bad form, maybe even spirit if not letter of the rules breach me swooping in like this."

"You . . . you *jhi*-clocking me, scaring my friend?"

"No . . . I just happened to be at Room and Board over here, understated urban chic furniture for my new apartment, and I decide to get some other shopping done. I have days off, too! Can even shake my security detail. So—I thought you lived up on Georgia, per my intel?"

"You come for your favor?"

"Matter of fact, yes."

My sphincter's tightening, prepping . . . *stay away, Verna.*

"The favor is—do you recommend this spot Lupo Verde up at the next corner? Some friends of Joe and Jill—"

"*That* Joe and Jill?"

"Yes. They are coming in from Delaware—one is a federal judge—and are looking for some decent Italian. As I alluded, I just sold my spot in Capitol Hill for this high rise in Navy Yard but that's a bit too trendy for older Delaware guests and there're no Nats homegames this week . . ."

Lord. "I wouldn't know about Navy Yard. Closest I come was St. Jude's Men's Shelter, attached to Verna's SFME. At least you won't have to suffer too many poor people running around there, huh?"

Her eyes narrow and her expression and voice flatten to the frosty menace that buffeted me in the courthouse. "You really need keep up on current events, Dickie. First, Navy Yard is now part of Ward Eight. '*Souff-east.*' Second, you must have it confused with The Wharf, where a lot of my subpoena targets live in penthouses or superyachts paid for from addresses in Eastern Europe, Panama, Channel Islands, the Middle East and such."

Verna sheepishly returns. Mumbles, "H-Hey . . . what'd I miss?"

Bivens ignores her and keeps playing.

"So refresh my memory, Dickie—you're private detective, right? How's that working out? Very dangerous, I hear."

Verna's staring at her water glass as I say, "I dunno. What've you heard, Ms. Bivens?"

She laughs and bounces to a startled Verna. "What do *you* think, Ms. Leggett—I mean, he's very gentle giant, laconic sort of a man. But I suspect when things pop off, he's very . . . un-gentle?"

Verna's looking me up and down like she wants to leave. Yet this little woman running a game on us has got us penned-up with just a vibe. Just a vibe . . . *shit.*

"I handle myself," I grunt.

"They never see you coming."

Got to get her heart before both Verna and I have heart attacks.

"Ms. Bivens, um . . . our food is actually coming, real talk . . . I'd ask you to join us but . . ."

"*Protocols*, yes. But I find this fascinating as I'm just a pencil pusher, C-suite flatfoot. What kind of gumshoe are you—John Shaft or Sam Spade . . . triggering name notwithstanding?"

Perhaps Verna's trying to rescue me when she says, "Neither he's just . . . a working man . . ."

"More like Sam Spade," I crack, just to keep her bizarre vibe at bay.

"Or . . . since you're a strong silent type—John Klute. Ever see the movie?"

Is she baiting us or just off her fucking rocker today.

"Nancy Drew."

"Dickie, *stop*," Verna whispers.

Bivens' little round face hardens; the dimples seem to ripple like gills.

"Shaft got all the hoes," she quips. "Sam Spade . . . and Klute . . . they fell for that *wrong* woman."

To my shock, Verna finds a little sand and fires back, "I'm a social worker, not a *femme fatale* or a *Manhattan call girl*. Just his buddy."

"Ah, a movie fan, too! Amen, queen—he's one of the *good* ones, I hear." She sighs—again like this act's sucking something from her.

She extends her hand to Verna. I have to nudge Verna her with my knee to get her to shake it so she'll get the hell out of here before my head explodes.

"Miss Leggett, protocols aside," Bivens begins as she grips Verna's hand. "If you're honest and cooperate, I'm sure you'll have nothing to worry about regarding your grand jury issues. We live in troubling times that require a look in the mirror."

Verna gasps and is looking at me more than Bivens. Our tiny tormenter lets go, offers me her hand next and I put that little thing in my big mitt and squeeze to show I'm not afraid.

"I'll see you at Homecoming if I haven't jinxed it," she says, all those fakeass smiles used up, I guess.

"Maybe. I've got a lot of work to do, not a lot of time to do it. Like you, huh?"

"You are . . . uniquely situated . . . to do what you do best, I hear."

Off she saunters. Still in character. One of many, I suppose.

And then it smacks me like one a knight's steel gauntlet in one of LaKeisha's tales . . .

"Mother Mary . . ." I can't catch a breath.

I could be dying right there, defibrillator be damned, because Verna's not listening or looking, just muttering into the ether . . .

"Dickie, maybe this was all a mistake. Getting together . . . *always a price.*"

I'm frozen in my chair and she's up, bolts down the sidewalk in the opposite direction as Bivens.

I know better than to take off after either of them.

CHAPTER NINE
Come to Jesus

"Imani put your uncle the phone!"

I'm coming up the escalator at Judiciary Square Station, surrounded by tourists and court workers. Head's on swivel while I talk, as this where fools like to jack phones when you're distracted, though from the looks the tourists at least are tossing me I guess they got me pegged as already stolen this one.

"You know damn well this is Dickie, come on now—find Croc and tell him cut his loafin'."

"*Who this?*" I finally hear Croc clown.

"You owe me a call."

"*Is this about the E. Barrett Prettyman Federal Courthouse? You gonna finally come clean about what really went on in there while we were sweatin' it out with these grand juries?*"

"Esmeralda . . . I saw her. She's back. She brought her back . . ."

"*Who brought her back?*"

"Angela Bivens. Little chick I went to Howard with. Pay attention, man. She ain't so little anymore. Justice Department. Big time . . ."

Quick step across the square and now I'm on 4th Street.

"*Tole you the Feds lie, bait n' switch. Thas how they fucked Mama n' Pop. So what's the haps, what's thing, moe. Y'all sound stressed as a mug.*"

"Might be loosin' my mind, moe. Listen . . . got this new PI gig with the PD's office.

"Whiteboy shoots two b-boys from Northeast. Turns out he's on the Tina and I figure they're soldiering for a plugger but . . . but something's even wrong there. I get this gig *right* after I see Esme. Right after this chick, on high at Justice Department, shanghai's my ass, has Federal Marshals jack me up in a damn closet. She's tryna put a case on Trump's people . . . and listen, she said something out on the street the other day . . ."

"Stamp . . . where you at, man? Out on the street . . . lemme have Melvin pick you up, bring you here . . ."

"Don't interrupt me, brah! She said something word-for-word what the PD who hired me said right to my face, Croc. Word-for-word. You know I ain't crazy."

I'm in sight of the Moultrie Courthouse. That's where Yi said come on by. Sure enough to fire me, face-to-face.

"Dead ass Croc . . . I'm . . . I'm slipping. Both these women are squeezing me. Hell, I even had to deal with Mattel. Yeah, *Mattel.*"

"That nigga's still on this planet?"

"Got his own fief over in Ward Seven . . . and then this Bivens straight up jack-in-the-boxed me right on the street, when I was having lunch with Verna and—"

"Kill, Romeo. Verna Leggett? Who betrayed you with Chief Linda Figgis—herself now likely in retirement rather than serving damn time?"

I slink past MPD headquarters in the Daly Building, then head over to Indiana Avenue and halt in front of the concrete, granite and glass pillbox that is Moultrie. It bookends the officialdom anchored on the other end by the federal courthouse where I was violated . . .

"You think I'm trippin', geekin', don't you, Croc?"

There's dead air and then I hear him repeat every curse and epithet he's ever leveled at me for questioning his lifetime of friendship. But that's not what I did.

"Look fam'ly, I dunno what fuckery you got goin' on wid the PD's office, who this woman Helen Yi is, okay? It all might be coincidence cause you all these high powered females especially lawyers all use the same damn lingo, stamp.But . . . this Bivens woman . . . are you insinuatin' she be catchin' feelins for you? Or, better still, caught feelins when she was eighteen and decided to show that love by having you lined in a broom closet like she be Queen Nzinga?"

I'm looking up at the white granite courthouse steps. "I-I dunno, gee."

"Well, she's on TV now with Lester Holt, NBC." I hear his snorts, diabetic grunts, then, *"Whatever she wants from you, I'd do, cause even Lester's like 'dayum, gurl.' This bopper says she gonna lock Trump up and all his niggas, moe—even Supreme Court Justices and this Senator from Texas who also on, talking shit."*

Something ricochets off the inside of my dome. "You said . . . Texas? Pale nasty-looking motherfucker named Vitter?"

"I look like Wolf Blitzer to you? Real live . . . Brom Vitter. Why?"

"Cause the whiteboy I was fittin' to help used to work for him. Now the PD's gonna fire me. More coincidence?"

Only one balm and shield for this drama, trouble, and we recite in unison what the nuns and priests beat into us as boys: *"Det tibi Deus veniam et pacem, et ego te absolvo a peccatis tuis . . . in nomine Patris et Filii et Spiritus Sancti."*

"Amen," I finish. "By the way, license paper on the Mini— the LCF—it's good right?"

"Whoa, where you goin' strapped?"

"Best you not know."

"Long bammas don't do a secondary track on the social security number from the barcode," Croc says with a chuckle, *"or it's gonna come up Gladys Thorndyke from Harrisonburg, Virginia. You the need, I provide. I got your back, Dickie . . ."*

Too bad he's on his niece's sofa watching Netflix, because I must enter the Moultrie Courthouse, alone for the first time through the front door and not a van from the CDF or after the friars at St. Jude's had dried me out. I'm awed, awkward. Scared.

And here come the rent-a-cops and U.S. Marshals ahead of the metal detectors.

Look, this place is no more a gilded and granite and marble temple to justice or even law and order than the Feds' at Prettyman. Got this minimalist *Clockwork Orange* crypt vibe whereas the Fed is like old bus station with polished floors. Get you in an out, chains and manacles optional.

The Marshals at Moultrie seem a little less buggy than my pals Equal Protection and Due Process, though. Guess the more mundane ghetto gunman, petty thieves, divorcing couples and scofflaws are more chill than the political Ringling Brothers Barnum and Bailey jont going down at Prettyman. With smiles they ask for my ID and I tell them I'm on the Public Defender's investigator panel. I pull out all that temporary mish-mash and then, oh . . . I'm carrying, right under my oversized billowy shirt. Here's my fakeass permit . . .

. . . and as easy-peezy-skeezy as Croc scarfing my Mom's sweet potato pie they scan the permit and it all goes into a cubby. I'm getting a big head as I step to the elevator.

I find Yi where she said she'd be, in the biggest empty courtroom on the third floor, I mean rows of benches and lots of polished oak paneling, beaded gray carpet. She was sitting on counsel's desk, leg swinging and totally chill—as she said, she was a different person in the courtroom. At ease, adept.

To her right, gesticulating as she was deaf, is this white man close to my height, short cropped dark hair, gray suit, striped red necktie. He's wearing a mask so he's a good little boy when it comes to the viruses out there still causing coughs and chaos. Meaning he's got a stick up his ass, and that notion's now being confirmed as Yi introduces me.

"Jake, this is our investigator on *U.S. v. Scholtz*, Richard Cornish . . ."

Kill, not former investigator? Insubordinate, incompetent, hulking brutish investigator?

Dude gives me tight handshake. I mean like he's been to the gym.

"Jake Markowitz, Assistant U.S. Attorney."

I see a bit of a gray-flecked goatee peeking from the mask. "Pleased to . . . meet you. I don't bite, even though I'm on the other team," he guffaws. "Helen and I were just conferring on other matters and we're about to talk about Dean Scholtz. Do you have a minute?"

"That's not why I'm here . . . is it?"

"The situation with the ROR and ankle bracelet has gotten out of control," he begins. "And the optics are killing the jury pool if this goes to trial. I need a reverse *Batson* issue or a mistrial as much as a hole in my head, Helen."

"Pardon . . . *Batson*?"

Helen Yi explains to me that it has to do with striking people from a jury based on race.

"Well, what if Scholtz knew them?" Uh-huh. Stir the pot . . . Yi loses it. "Come . . . come with me! Please!"

She leaves all her shit in the courtroom and a nonplussed

Markowitz standing alone. He's shouting after us, something like, "I'm not a nudnik, Helen! We need to talk!"

Boney and tiny as she is, she manages to herd me into a corridor near the restrooms and some vending machines.

"How . . . how *dare* you!" she hisses.

"Nothing you told me and half of the shit in the files makes any sense. Artemesia Sellers, Apache fiend . . . Danielle Diggs . . . not just pluggin' Tina and Za weed but got her own hustler's empire over there in Deanwood . . . and very likely's pluggin' the Tranq that Arthur Seller's mama's bitin' on."

"Apache? Tranq?"

"Fentanyl . . ."

She sucks her teeth, groans. "Walk with me. Back to the room. Jake's gone." And then, "Help me with this cart of exhibits . . ."

Mater Maria. When I leave the courtroom and enter the hall echoing with murmurs and shoe leather I'm pulling her shit like I'm toting her damn groceries.

"Like I said, I was over in Ward Seven," I recount.

Her usual timidity returns. "Why? Why . . . so soon? All you had to do was wait. Wait on my instructions, Mr. Cornish . . ."

She sounds like she's had worse day than me.

"So I'm not fired?"

"I-I need you, Mr. Cornish. What . . . what else did you find out?"

Whoa . . .

"Sellers' mother lives in a damn van on cinderblocks, in fear of Child and Family Services and not thinking about Arthur beyond memories. She's afraid of Diamante Diggs' sister and that's a wise thing. That woman's dirty and I'm betting the prosecutor there knows it. I figure you need to sit down with Dean for a come to Jesus talk."

She halts and gives some lame waves to folks s near the elevator bank. "Mr. Cornish . . . Dickie . . . perhaps . . . perhaps we—"

"Need a come to Jesus talk, too?" I finish. "Yeah. This shooting wasn't random foolishness on the street. Arthur and Diamante were after Dean for something else. Could even have been a hit, not a collection or an attempt to scare him, gone wrong."

Inside the elevator we both wait a couple of floors until no other human soul enters to speak.

"Attorney Yi, do you know Angela Bivens, Markowitz's penultimate boss at DOJ?"

"N-No. Why?"

"Spooky . . . nothing." Might just be my brain re-wiring from a fall from the wagon.

As the door opens on the ground floor she tells me, "I'm increasing your panel stipend to an additional thousand dollars."

"Real live?"

She nods. "Meet me on Indiana Avenue. We'll both talk to Dean. It's better . . . that we both talk to Dean."

Spooky, alright. "I have to pick up my gun first."

"Oh my God. This is no time for jokes."

"Am I smiling, Attorney Yi? I'm not going near that kid without it."

Her ride's a suburban hoopdy: a busted and dog hair-filled old-ass Volvo station wagon but she's got priority parking right there on Indiana Avenue. We make it over to Capitol Hill in about fifteen minutes, which is just the amount of time Scholtz takes to call her back and confirm he's home, even though he can go nowhere else but home or maybe a thousand feet down to Eastern Market for deli meat, some shea butter soap . . . or Mylanta.

He answers the door as I spy the girlfriend or whatever she is across the street with the Malinois on a taut leash. The sky's already milky and there's a spritz of moisture in the air; she's only in a tee shirt and yoga pants and is looking sad, grim so maybe there's something she needs to get off her chest, too.

"Your friend's out here," I tell Scholtz as he beckons us inside. "Might rain."

"I got nauseous so sent her away." he answers, curt and utterly uncaring that his lawyer's clocking the man without his mask. "She'll stay out as long as I say."

The glib bullshit returns when he has us sitting on that leather sofa, opposite himself on the hassock. Ok, Katie. I'm an insect now. All instinct, no intellect. Let's see what pops off.

"Attorney Yi and I have some . . . concerns . . . about your defense."

"*Whoa*. The dream team assembles, with *concerns*. Did you know D.C. still doesn't have it's crime lab re-accredited? That's why now inconclusive gunfire residue results. They wasted hours getting my sample to the FBI lab." He leers at Yi. "Here's to you, Lucy Liu . . ."

"Dean," Yi says, sighing, "We stipulated that you were firing in self-defense because that's what you told the police. That issue's a nonstarter for us."

"My bad, huh."

"Kill, you wanna go to prison to dry out?" I press. "Cause that's where you're headed. *Diesel therapy*, man—the District don't operate a prison anymore. It sends inmates into the hinterland on big buses, belching fumes . . ."

"I want a gummy without a piss-test. Been able to finesse the piss tests, but . . ."

Yi tries to honcho things. "Listen, Dean . . . Mr. Cornish here claims to have uncovered some . . . discrepancies in the background info . . ." She crosses a glare with me, ". . . rather than reconstruct what happened the night of the shooting, *as he was instructed.* Be that as it may . . . were you buying drugs, non-regulated marijuana or any contraband from the two victims or anyone associated with them?"

Damn. Someone's interested in the truth suddenly.

He gives me the stink-eye then grunts. "No."

"Good."

"I never had to 'buy' anything . . ." he quickly follows-up, and Yi's papery skin is pulsing again as she struggles to keep a professional chill as her case ferments. "Diamante and the Sellers kid were in the wrong place, wrong time, and suffered. But it wasn't my fault."

"Stop the wellin'!" I yell and it startles Yi.

"Speak *white*, dude!"

Daddy always said a barking dog ain't shit. A dog in low growl means your ass. I'm at a low, low growl. "You little fuckin' Ivy League weasel, no more riddles . . ."

He criss-crosses sheepish looks with Yi on the couch, spills. I still think he's holding back . . .

"I'm a pogue in the army of the Christ, not a combat soldier. A pretend patriot . . . I wasn't at Charlottesville or the Capitol, I wasn't in the front rank in Lansing when ordinary people raged against the masks, then the vax . . . or when fools and cucks and pushy bitches and whole families of idiots pushing baby carriages and 'pussy hats' joined the BLM scum and Antifa on the streets. Nah, I was in the rear, taking phone video or interviewing young conservatives for Twitter feeds and Fox News guests . . ."

"Because you were *scared*," Yi says. "Like you were that night in Adams Morgan."

Nah, I've seen this before. In a hundred doses, pills, tokes, sticks, sucks on a Green Grenade or pint.

"Unh-unh, Attorney Yi," I correct. "He was scared, yeah. But not how you think. You were scared this whole rightwing jont wasn't your thing, huh? That you were trapped."

Scholtz nods, slowly. "Trapped. Yeah . . ." he mutters.

"That why Senator Vitter was beefing on you? Heart not in it? Maybe he thought after January Sixth you might flip, snitch him, others out?"

Yi clasps her boney fingers across mouth, talks through them. "That's not relevant or material, Dickie."

"Don't you think it's important?"

"Not within the law and fact controlling this case. I'm the attorney, not you."

Of course.

"So tell me truthfully, Dean," Yi charges on, "Inside this room, just you and us—did you know Diamante Diggs and Arthur Sellers, and were they attempting to rob you or otherwise cause you harm?"

No pause at all from Scholtz. "Yes, I knew them. Diamante more so."

Her grimace looks painful.

"But I knew they were coming."

The grimace drops to no expression at all. "My God," Yi whispers.

"Who snitched them out?" I press. "Same person who said you'll be the hitter, huh?"

"Diamante was a big baby. Arthur was like his bodyguard, tried to harden him up so he wouldn't take shit."

"That's not what I asked."

"Wouldn't take abuse from who?" Yi adds and I swear she sounds like she's crying but, like her skin, her eyes are dry. "What are you saying?"

"Wouldn't take shit from his *half-sister*. Older. Like a mom. *Happy now?*"

I got him. "Danielle?" Oh, now his chest's pushing out short breaths. "Lives on Gault Place Northeast, where your phone pinged? Was a C.O. at the women's block at the CDF."

He turns to Yi. "Guess we're all inside the circle of trust, *Helen . . .*"

Yi gets as close to a sneer as her desiccated face can manage and shoots back, "This Diggs woman, sister of the victim, set up her own brother?"

He's not even looking at her. "I told you when you *first* set foot in here, *you fucking ogre.* You were hearing . . . you weren't listening." Guilty. "Was I using, yep. Was I getting it from Danielle, yep. Is there more to this, yep. But the truth would fry your brains. Especially you, Helen. Lawyer question: can someone engaged in illegal conduct claim self-defense if the person they . . . kill . . . wasn't victim of that conduct? Bad . . . *bad* people get the benefit of law, right?"

I'm watching him rise off the hassock, step to the window and part the curtains, study the rain-slick street, blowing leaves, all a dead, dull green that will turn fire orange, then dead brown as they paste themselves to the city's filthy pavement.

"Come to Jesus time, man . . ." I implore.

"My boy Ben. Ben Ortiz. He came over from the House side to work for that assfuck Vitter, doing the dude's podcast but mostly because of his family. Border Patrol Mexicans who frickin' hate Biden, came to U.S. the 'right' way. Great optics."

"That's the only reason?"

The tears give way to the most sardonic smile I've ever seen, surpassing that of my old handler and tormenter: Bracht's goon Burton Sugars. "Maybe, Mr. Cornish. Since we're coming to Jesus. In any event, he's a *good* Mexican, okay?"

"Got Aztec ink on him?"

"*Yeah* . . . how'd you know?"

"My mind focuses on little, dumb stuff. He use?"

Scholtz nods as Yi's shaking her head.

I have to ask her . . . "We don't have some Constitutional thing about disclosing this to that Markowitz asshole, do we?"

"N-No . . ." she mutters. "But . . . what's stopping him from finding out?"

I'm snickering. Dead ass, I never snicker. But they are staring at me as if waiting. "You tell me, Attorney Yi. Somebody's got to tell me. Because nothing's stopping him, or blocking reporters or TV folk from digging . . ." The bass comes to my voice. "*I'm the only one digging.* They don't want to know, that's the answer." I gesture to Scholtz, who's now turning away from the window. "Ain't that right, *whiteboy*?"

Scholtz's weasel face blossomed red. Again, Scholtz yanked off those damn Charles Dickens-looking specs. "You people got no clue what power is all about. It's all getting high, fucking, being loud, flexing for you. You too, Helen or whatever your parents named you. You all are just termites. Jews without the finesse and the Old Testament vouching for you."

"Don't test me, Dean," and yeah I'm not raising my voice. Still I don't like the physical vibe . . . got this chill in my nuts so I instruct him to stay away from the window, and sit down.

Thankfully, he complies, and he's back on the hassock, adjusting his glasses. I do not turn on the table lamp in that living room, I don't know why. "Okay . . . Ben Ortiz . . . where is he?"

The kid swallows hard, mutters, "He OD'd. He was DOA at Medstar. We told his parents he'd hit a tree root on an off-road bike thing in Rock Creek Park. Fell, hit his head on a rock wall."

He's right. Jont's crazy. "How the Hell'd you get over with that?"

"People's perceptions beat toxicology protocols and reality. So does a rock to the skull."

I'm still all monotone, all stare. Not going to lose it. "Did you hit him . . . or did you stage it?"

"*Fuck you, Cornish!*" he yelps.

"He wasn't chasing Tina, like you. Because only weak tea ODs on Tina."

Breathing hard and that steady vermillion hue again, my client reads the floor and whispers, "No. Tranq . . . Apache. *You know what that is?*" I definitely can't feel my nuts now because he's the second person to ask me that, and I'm seeing the chickenhawk in my mind's eye. "H-He wasn't shooting it. He was . . . mixing it with the blow."

"Was . . . was he getting it from Danielle?" I stutter, trying to keep Bivens out of my words.

"No, he was getting MILF pussy from Danielle."

"Let's take a break . . . please," Yi protests.

He rolls on. "She's freaky, likes younger guys. Hairless, sort of. Thinks light-skinned black guys, white guys are 'delicacy like Chesapeake Bay oysters,' she says. I guess . . . Ben's new dish . . ."

"Twinks?" I say. And I'm just throwing it out, no coy move. Oh, but he's boiled. "*That's a fucking faggot word!*"

I nod. "Yeah. You and . . . Ben? You're no twinks, eh?"

Those blue eyes in that otter-like head shrink to slits. "Wasn't just sex. She really liked him. Liked me too." The slits part just enough to give me what I wanted to know without him saying a word, yet he affirms, "Liked us . . . more than her own flesh and blood."

And I hear Yi groaning.

Girl, coming to Jesus ain't supposed to just sting a little.

"How'd y'all even remotely get involved with this chick?"

"Because Ben broke the rule."

"Falling in love? *Pssstit* . . . don't clown."

I'm expecting him to say something truly frat boy and nausea-inducing, like she was a security guard or concierge in their condo, or Metro'd into Ward 1 to be their Trader Joe's grocery bagger.

Oh no. That'd be merciful . . .

"He broke the rule about not to get high on your own supply."

"*Fuck you say?*"

"He supplied her, not the other way around. *Tranq* . . . fentanyl and horsey meds, Cornish . . ."

See, inside my dome's what Daddy called the jigsaw puzzle due to my supposed mental infirmities and the pieces are clicking hard. That's why Sholtz is broke, alone? That's why Artemesia and Danielle aren't on TV crying for their kins' spilt blood, demanding Scholtz's? I'm on overload so I don't even hear the doorbell gongs that first time.

Aidy and the dog are still out there, and at least one of them presumably got a key.

"You order a pizza or DoorDash?" Yi asks.

He shakes his head. "Maybe Aidy did?"

I cut off his path, to the door, check the peephole.

It's Aidy, her top soaked through to her bra, that brick hair wet and stringy. She's wedged herself between the wide-open screen door and this one.

"M-Mr. Cornish . . . I can't find my key. Someone in a car . . . they bothered us . . . and Woody's run off . . . he . . . he won't go far but I'm so scared. Please open the door!"

"Then how'd you unlock the screen door?"

CHAPTER TEN
Jesus Replies

I SEE YI CRANING HER NECK toward the front door just as the sound slaps my eardrums. A noise, generated from the window where Scholtz lolls. But no . . . two noises?

PLINK!

PAMPF!

The throw pillow about an inch from Yi's lap . . . explodes in a bloom of foam and yarn.

PLINK! A wall poster across from the window's gored with a round.

"Dean *drop!*" I yell. "Everyone *down!*"

I'm on my ass as the door splinters off its hinges, and I make out a "*Go or die, bitch!*" barked as Aidy's shoved towards me . . . a human foil for two huge cats in black wave caps, black COVID masks, work overalls that janitors or car mechanics wear.

Got the .380 out before she lands on me, and I take the full impact and terrified thrashing . . .

POP! POP! POP! One of these motherfuckers is firing in the hallway, wildly. My brain says that's got to be a different round . . . the sound? It's not muffled . . .

POP! POP! I get off two, and though they connect with a mirror and dry wall rather than flesh and bone from the sound of them, they do elicit a "*God-dam!*" from one big motherfucker and a hollered order from the other to turn tail.

Scholtz takes what strength he's got in that scrawny form and peels a hysterical Aidy from me; I note a spray of blood on the rug and it's not from me.

"Oh my God Dean," Aidy cries and points. He crumples to the floor, realizing his knee's taken a hit.

No time to help him. I jump to my feet then flatten myself against the wall I've ventilated . . . in the early wet gloom the streetlamps have yet to buzz on but I spy the bastards legging down North Carolina Avenue, cutting to Sixth like NFL half-backs. And they're shouting toward invisible cohorts. Yeah . . . who'd likely been pumping the bullets through the window with a suppressor or silencer.

What's next is all D.C.—violence in plain sight. Brakes screech, traffic congeals, mouths gasp and scream, pedestrians either scramble like squirrels or freeze like foals. And here I am bounding into it, my pulse gonging my throat.

But see, whoever these motherfuckers are, this is my *jont*. Me and my boy Esteban . . . Little Stevie . . . and use to come over to Eastern Market to scavenge the Dumpsters for shit to build nests like we were gorillas or orangutans. I take the short cut into Seward Square, cursing *my* old gams and feet and lungs and heart. But I catch them.

I crackback one like its high school, with Croc as pulling guard on the sweep. That'll hurt in the morning. The other does a Carl Lewis over both of us and a hedge row, and as we struggle on the clammy, peaty ground he stops, dead, and I'm seeing his piece drawn.

My dude gets in a decent kick to my face. Know this—it isn't the first time that's ever happened. I shake off the stars, catch his other leg and twist it at the knee.

It's then I hear familiar barking, snarling. Got to be Woody, somewhere in the shadows and then I dude grappling with me hollers, "Shoot that mug, nigga!"

Over the hedge . . . there's Woody the Belgian Malinois, mounted on a park bench . . . foam spitting from his fangs, body coiled to jump at this brother who's already pulled off his wave cap, exposing a bald brown pate reflecting the traffic light hues.

Now, it might be that the adrenaline's fucking with my head but I swear the dude answers, "I-I can't!"

Dog lover?

To make it more surreal, around us is now a circus of pedestrians either scurrying in terror—or whipping out their phones for the latest Instagram polemic on D.C. lawlessness.

No choice. I let this bastard go, pull the Mini from the holster.

And then my brain goes blank as to what the PI videos say when it's gangsta time. Something about pointing your finger when you got a little-ass gun like mine. Didn't do it with those kids when I was buzzed on Pabst. Hell if I'm going to be a slave to style here.

Let it fly . . .

. . . and ACP round hits this asshole in the upper right shoulder, spins him . . . and now Woody owes me one.

The dog's stunned, confused, however . . . and I suppose this dude's been tagged before because he gathers his wits and is already tearing right by the animal, screaming for help . . .

. . . in Spanish?

"Fuck . . . *coño* . . . *Ayuda me!*"

Okay again that might be fear playing tricks on me. The other hitter's turned on the jets and is rushing headlong for the Eastern Market Metro escalators on Pennsylvania so there better be some damn video later . . .

No time to dwell on that shit because here comes the roar of a hemi or bad-ass V-6 . . . that's when I savvy that the dude I shot is stumbling toward what looks like a bull-headed and boxy Ford pickup . . . white or silver . . . like an F-150. It's screeching to a halt at 5th Street.

The driver cuts off the headlights but interior's and lit and I can see a thin dude, camouflage baseball cap . . . he's white. And so's the guy in the flatbed. An ogre of a man, flannel shirt open to what looks like a bare chest. He's exhorting this wounded asshole who's black as coal but whimpers in Spanish to jump aboard. Looks like white things on his wrist . . . wristbands to cut sweat like at a gym . . . but I can't make out a face as he bounces in and out of the light . . . *oh shit* . . .

. . . there's a muzzle flash from the flatbed and some rapid pops and I realize the big man's firing at me with a long gun . . . a chopper? AR-15? Somebody had a suppressor aimed at Aidy's crib but they aren't interested in stealth now. Anti-racist anarchists avenging Diamante and Arthur, my ass!

I send two his way just as whoever this poor stupid spook they got stooging for them does a Batman leap right into that flatbed. One pings the side panel. A .380 ACP's not going to penetrate an F-150, but one sure as hell tags the brother again. Sorry man, I was aiming at the ofay ogre firing at me. I hear him hit the truck's bed with a dull thunk so I've done everything to him except give him cancer.

Before bare-chested man can fully scream his dismay, the driver's gunning that pickup the fuck out onto Pennsylvania, sending that big man down as well, legs flailing almost comically.

I'm on my feet, chest heaving.

Hear a low growl, at my six o'clock.

Yep, Woody still doesn't know me from Adam and now he squared up on my ass.

"Woody *down* . . . good boy Woody . . . good *buuuuooooy* . . ."

Using his name keeps him ripping out my epiglottis.

That's when I hear Aidy. Fuck she doing out here?

She calls to the dog . . . stamp, the damn thing whines like a child and stands-down, retreats right by me after giving me this weird *it was almost your ass, too* look. I shout over my shoulder, still leveling the .380, "Get back in the house with Dean!"

"*I want my dog!*" she yells back as she hugs the jumping, prancing wolf-eared pooch.

I'm hearing sirens now. Seems like hours passed but it was really no more than five minutes. One of the mobile phone brigade members pops up from behind a park trash can, asks if I'm okay, if I'm a cop.

"I'm a private detective."

Accordingly, Jesus has replied. He's not pleased, either. Oh yeah, the sky opens up and it's Jesus is sending down a chilly rain as if our asses haven't already gotten the message, washing away whatever evidence was laid down . . . .

. . . and here's Helen Yi, soaked to the bone and lingering at the open hatches to the DCFD EMS unit. I've still got my chin aimed at the blinding light above the secured gurney, holding an ice pack to my nose.

"It's not broken," the paramedic assures me with a smile. Cute little thing with kinky, ruddy hair, green eyes, freckles. Yeah, like my mom. "But there's so much scar tissue and cartilage up there you should still get an X-ray."

"Mr. Cornish . . ." Yi calls, pulling me from my infatuation.

"Keep it elevated," the paramedic cautions.

"If . . . if you want to take the money and back off this contract I'll understand. But now . . . Jake Markowitz just called to find out what happened. I-I think I can push back, say it's his aggressive public statements, the activists, local pols that caused lunatics to stalk my client, threaten his life and the lives of others . . ."

The paramedic wisely excuses herself to the front of the ambulance.

"*That's* the scenario that scares you the most?"

"He'll twist it to support the Show-Cause Order—that Dean . . . Mr. Scholtz . . . belongs in the jail for his own protection."

"It was a hit."

Yi digs in ."I can't rush to that determination."

"*It was a fucking hit*! Tell that dude Markowitz you want twenny-four-seven eyes on your client . . . *our* client."

"Sir," the paramedic calls from the front seat. "I'll fashion a little bandage to catch any bloody discharge but then we'll have to roll."

Last time I was in a "bus" I was getting an IV for the DTs and snort of what was newfangled Narcan. Now a cutie's calling me *sir*.

"No problem baby I'll wrap this in a second." Then I look to the Public Defender. "*You* have to quarterback this, Attorney Yi, not me. The cops are easy. But in a minute it's gonna federal marshals. Prolly FBI, too."

"Helen . . . call me Helen. Just tell them . . . what happened. No editorializing."

"*You* were there . . . are you crazy?"

"I'm not joking, Dickie, please. You're covered by my attorney-client privilege . . . a prisoner on home detention has just been attacked, so just feed them the minimum until we can regroup."

I lower my head. My nose throbs, my neck cracks. "I'll say it seemed to me it was someone wanting an eye-for-an-eye. Reacted to protect my client's life. His . . . girlfriend . . . had been assaulted and used to gain entry . . ."

"Um . . . that works. Please be calm."

"Don't I look calm to you?"

The slow, timid cadence retreats. Her courtroom persona returns and flushes her face. "Do *not make* any moves until this is sorted out. Once they're finished with you—and it will be short time, owing to privilege—go home, wait to hear from me. It might be as late as tomorrow morning."

"Advance the next five hundred dollars."

"Do not talk to the press—your engagement isn't under seal, so they might contact you, given that you've been newsworthy in the past."

"Advance the next five hundred dollars. Please."

Now I know what a big fat rockfish feels like there off Hain's Points, hook ripping into my gills. People say nothing scares me. No. Nothing *rattles* me. I'm *scared* all the time. Big difference.

Uh-huh, my interrogation with the Marshals lasts a grand total of ten minutes before they let me go—sore face, ribs, ankles, knees and all. Quite a different jont than my time with those bammas Equal Protection and Due Process.

Their and the FBI's conclusion: radical cadre of Black Lives Matter folks from the hood and yet no one's been to Deanwood to question anyone over a beef since my beer-addled ass was there. No one's spoken to the Sellers or Diggs families . . . such as they are. Even better. Those white guys in the truck? They were ANTIFA. Lefty anarchists . . . in a Ford pickup. Ha! Makes total sense.

Last thing communication I get from Yi is at midnight, with the cat on my chest, purring, staring. She says this Markowitz clown's asked for a continuance on all of his motions, yet won't drop the charges on Dean Scholtz.

And Dean? Oh he's now in an "undisclosed" hospital with a GSW.

Funny, this is the first time in a while I have slept though the night. No screaming . . . not even a piss to relieve the pressure from my ever-expanding prostate. Don't need the Valium Melvin's late in delivering. Don't need to call the VA, weeping for an appointment. All it took was getting shot at, being lied to, used, wrestling two big niggas . . . facing off with a Malinois.

Kitty's mewling wakes me and the morning's a dull butternut pallor . . . damp, ugly, chilly. No more Indian Summer. I'm fiending for grub and nothing's in the cupboard or my noisy, rusted fridge. I wash and brush-up—careful not to disturb my nose bandage.

"I'll bring you back something, cat."

Mickey Dees on Georgia's thick with jabber: construction workers joking in Spanish, Howard U. students complaining about financial aid, truant high schoolers boasting about Lord-knows because I can't follow the lingo. I get my order and ease into a sticky booth, crumbs

tumbling in my wake. The truants melt off when two figures in these Dick Tracy or Untouchables trench coats
through push through the doors. I recognize the female
and she zeroes right in on me.

"Miss Monica Abalos," I welcome. "I'm glad I brushed my
choppers, put in some hair grease."

She's laughing, and her cherubic eyes compliment the
brightness. Stripe was right—she's a Filipina, not Ecuadoran
or Peruvian as the old-boy white homicide dicks presented.

"*Sargeant* Abalos," she corrects. "And this Detective Bob
Gentry. May we sit?"

The whiteboy's edging in next to me anyway; Monica slides
over to face me.

"Sargeant huh?"

"Promotions are faster when the old fellas ahead of you are
either retiring or being indicted, thanks to you, Dickie."

Now I can't tell if she's messing with me or playing the role
for her partner, as the tone's not complimentary. She's a solid
cop, and fair, and saved my ass from that Uncle Tom, Detective
Woodman, and his master, Deputy Chief Antonelli. Heard
Woodman ate his Glock rather than face prison. Makes me
smile . . .

. . . so I tear off a morsel of sausage biscuit dipped in
ketchup for her. She declines.

"Nose bleed, a shiner. You got off okay. The assailants,
though, left pints of blood all over Capitol Hill. Too bad the
rain got to it."

"Story of my life. And?"

"And. Sorry, Dickie. The Marshals and FBI are closing
the matter. 'Reverse hate crime' they say. Local assholes,
lefties tryna make their bones by satisfying the

community's *hard-on* for your client. Client's whereabouts are classified. In other words we know where he is, too and it's not very secure."

Jesus Mary and Joseph. "You aren't buying it."

"No, Mr. Cornish," this dude Gentry adds. He must be a rookie dick because he's being polite to me. "We had to beg for the ballistics report on the rounds from the residence. They don't match anything the database."

No shit, Columbo.

Abalos nods and tells me, "There is a lot of tension in DOJ these days. Reminds me of the shit in MPD when Linda and Antonelli were at loggerheads . . . but it's more . . . dunno . . . crazy. Said they be in touch. Your statement was truncated to say the least."

I like Monica. But now I have a job, a purpose. "I got no comment. My thoughts and work product are privileged . . ."

She squints my way. "Everything about this case is off. Like no one's holding their breath as to the outcome, just as to *ancillary* drama like this. Nobody in Homicide did the deep dive on your client, or the vicks. 'No altarboys,' per the statements but turns out Arthur Sellers actually did assist the pastor at some storefront church on East Capitol. There's intel of phony protests over in Ward Seven, and that at least one of these kids was not well liked."

"A troubling case," I say, repeating Helen Yi's observation, aging well.

Monica moves closer. "Crazier stuff coming—if my DEA sources get clearance from this Bivens woman up at the top of DOJ, because the U.S. Attorney sure isn't saying shit."

Now's the first time I'm hearing Lil' Angie's name used in my case. I try to stay stone-faced.

"I'm going to ask you, for the home team, not the Feds—anything you want to tell me? Even a hunch. It stays at this grubby table, I swear on son . . ."

I search her face. Round like Biven's, except true earnest, not scary earnest. "If I come upon . . . questionable stuff . . . I'll let know. Just nothing that can hurt my client."

"You be *careful*, Dickie," she huffs. She motions with her head for Gentry to drop a business card. Like I'd really call his tight ass and I'm sure he's all puffed out at feeling included, but it's street kabuki, a signal. I know where to find her.

They leave and the Mickey Dees denizens can go back to their usual endeavors as if the spot's a ghetto Rick's in Casablanca and the Germans have just booked. I send a call to Yi and yep, another prompt for a voicemail. *Goddammit.* There was a time when inertia was everlasting. I could sleep on a steam grate in snowstorm for hours, like a polar bear. Now, I'm jittery, ready to kick down the stall like a stallion only without all the horniness and it ain't from the Mickey Dee's joe.

I stroll back to the crib. The block's strangely quiet . . . the store's not open till noon, and there's a paper sign saying "Do not loiter or form a line." No cluckers or Simon . . . and no students across the street rushing to Howard's campus for morning classes. Just a jake . . . yeah in an MPD blue and white, parked across Georgia. First, I think it's Abalos sending me a message but why surveil me? He doesn't even clock me yet pops his blue runners, let's them shine a bit, them kills them. Starts reading what looks like a magazine. *Shit . . . he's scaring folk off the pavement?* Nothing here to raid.

Even the building's hushed, like it's taken a deep breath. I get in my spot, hit my laptop and there's what I've been holding my breath for: an email on the PD webmail Yi had me upload . . . okay . . . LaKeisha uploaded.

Has anyone from the press contacted you? Do nothing until I have a conference with Judge Barnes and AUSA Markowitz. Your second payment's been authorized. H.D.Yi, Esquire

Indeed, good prompt to get over to the D.C. Housing Authority account with my green and give them my rent co-payment. My preppie magnate landlords won't be pleased that I'm still paid up on this two hundred square-foot shithole.

So I hit the head and produce nothing . . . at least I yank off that nose bandage as I sit there, constipated in thought as well. *Do nothing?* I text Verna and get no reply . . .

. . . an hour goes by and am on my rack, watching the cat nibble a morsel of harsh browns. Useless. Stupid. I miss Stripe.

Suddenly there's pounding and weird popping noises, muffled by my door, downstairs. Shouts . . . then few shrieks. I swing off my mattress, reach for the .380 I've had under my pillow since the Marshals and FBI allowed me to depart Seward Square without handcuffs.

Footsteps on the lower landing . . . until there's a meek almost imperceptible knock on the door. That's when I hear the mewls of that cat . . . and sniffle and whine of a what has to be a child, and *"Por favor . . ."*

I check the peephole. Lots of screeching and cursing in English and Spanish downstairs, yet nothing till I see the hair on top of a small head. I shove the .380 in my dresser, open the door and it's a little boy, holding that cat . . .

"Habla pe . . . causa." No clue what that means—it's not Stripe's Salvadoran Spanish, but the kids quickly beaming a big smile despite the tears gobbing-up his eyes. Then in English, "Here . . . p-please . . . they take us."

The squatters. "Immigration?"

I hear down the stairs a coarse, "Everybody has ten minutes to pack this trash and get in the van, asylum application or not!" Then, "A police officer is here to observe!"

A woman screams, "Ernesto!" and "*Dios . . . Dése prisa . . .*" Then more bawling . . .

"*Ese es tu nombre?*" I ask him. He forces a smile again, nods. More coincidences. That was Stripe's name: Ernesto. "*Me quedaré con el gato y le buscaré un buen hogar . . .* I promise." I bring the squirming tabby to him.

"*Buenazo!*" he gushes, and he barely gets a kiss from the whiskers when some fat clown in with a 1950s crew cut, blue polo shirt with some stupid logo but it isn't Fed. Well he comes up the stairs, grabs the kid, shoves him off the landing into a woman's arms.

"You don't touch him," I warn, pushing the now hissing cat back into my crib.

"We know all about you, fella," he sneers, "so don't get in the way or you'll be next. This is a trespass eviction, we're private security for the development company."

Not going to tell him Stripe and I did the same thing for about two dollars an hour plus a donut and stale coffee. "Doin' God's work, huh, motherfucker?"

"*You people* should be thanking me, getting rid of these cockroaches who take the minimum wage jobs . . . Biden's letting 'em all in here, *your* mayor and these other libs welcoming them with open arms."

I joke inwardly that this must be an uncle of Scholtz's. Outwardly, my face is hard and my tone Frankenstein low and slow.

"They were bused up here illegally by pieces of shit that look like you, I hear. Left on account you turned their countries over to gangsters, generals on the take—all so you could have cheap bananas on your banana splits at Friendly's . . ."

"Let me enlighten you, asshole," this cracker snarls. "This ain't about communists or bananas. Criminal by the name of *El Pescedor* . . . big money gangster, trafficker, out of Colima, Mexico, makes money off every one of these here folks. So slow your roll, big fella."

"Wait . . . what?"

"*The cartels.* Watch real news on Fox, not lib crap. They're here. Been here. Right in our capital! Now mind your business or you'll be in cuffs!"

The shouting and screams end and I'm alone in this three-story brick slum box, with a cat on my belly meowing and it sounds like, "What now?"

Yet that shit's all dissolving in my dome, replaced by the cackling of an old lady on the fringes of Deanwood, and the yapping lap dog.

"*Colima,*" I whisper. Mexicans? Bringing in the White . . . the fentanyl. Didn't Bivens say that? Threatening the migrants, using them as mules? The answer's not here on my rack in this dingy ass apartment . . .

. . . and I'm feeling something I haven't felt in a long time since I got out of St. Jude's, out of the VA.

A purpose.

Okay, this poor cat's stuck with me, now that her humans were just scooped up like garbage. Lots of garbage here actually stays in uncollected heaps, rots, permeates the ground and air. So fuck these people who kick folks around like garbage. Fuck these people who chose to live as garbage, too, huh? Never that simple.

And so we lay still until the cat's silent but for an occasional yawn and purr. We lay there so long that the gray, wooly sky and clammy air outside my sole window gives way to a bloody red vista before sundown, and then I whisper to the tabby, "Time to into the cut. Do my thing."

The tabby sounds off, likely hungry but I'll take it as an exhortation any day. I reward it with a dish of water, more tuna.

This time, I'll try not to look like a ragamuffin or a Jehovah's Witness. It's the panda dunks Stripe got me, in case these old dogs got to run from trouble, black jeans I got from Target as a shopper not a shoplifter . . . dark gray canvas jacket with a leather collar I found behind one of the whitefolks' toney urban outdoors shops off 14th after a smash n' grab. I returned . . . it along with one of the midgets who stole it. The manager let me have it as a reward. It's good for hiding the .380's holster in the small of back, when running's not an option.

"I'll call Katie to come take care of you," I tell the cat, who's doing yoga stretches on my floor. I shred aged sheets of the *Post's* Metro section in the bathroom and leave the light on in there. "Use that for your convenience, if you please, not my bed. Hopefully I'll see it again."

Let's find you, *Gestapo*. I got a theory . . .

CHAPTER ELEVEN

Dying to Tell

I LEAVE THE CURB FULL OF squatter flotsam, all picked over by Simon and the cluckers.

They don't even say a thing; they can tell by my look got business, and I find my first order of business with Peach, right where I left her, on the corner.

"Nigga when you come off the Metro the other night all sweaty and buggy," she shades, "you say you was gettin' paid work to find out about the two boys shot over on Eighteenth an' Columbia. Now I hear you workin' for the *white mother-fucker* what killed them?"

Uh-oh. "I ain't on the cops' side."

"What do it matter? Still wrong side. I know you ain't here to buy gummies so lemme make it easy f'you. Gestapo, she ain't goin' let you jus' walk into Deanwood and knock on her door even if you was on the right side. She a queen, Dickie."

"Stamp—who?"

"Gestapo. *Danielle Diggs.* When she a C.O. at D.C. Jail . . . Women's Detention Unit. Thas' what the bitches be callin' her."

Shit. No wonder nobody from the families, from that hood, came up to protest . . . grieve. Cops, the U.S. Attorney—they must've known Diamante's sister was dirty. And if LaKeisha could've found shit, than any reporter worth their ink could've dug and down without getting shot and come up with the name "Gestapo."

So why didn't Helen Yi?

"Gestapo retired?"

She nods. "Back in the day, she was frontin' Oxy for some rich rednecks from Roanoke . . . you know them jailbirds always got they menstrual cramps and broke teefs and she filled the need, then on the come-back they fiendin', in and out of the jail. City fires her but she a union steward and them bitches around her circled the wagons, took 'em five years to get rid of her and she take her posse wiff her. By then, the big crews was fallin' apart from prison or death, right . . . the only bad niggas leff over there is some dudes up Sheriff Road, an' couple a middle aged gangstas from the old Simple City crew. The rest are youngsters. Run amok. Not to soldier for product. Nah they dead ya jus' to get 'likes' on that TikTok bu'shit. After COVID killin' off big mama, auntie an' uncle . . . no school, no money comin' in, years of Trump's folk—made 'em all crazy. So Gestapo, she make a dollar oughta a dime on COVID like whitefolk, rich bankers."

"There's more, Peach. Gotta be. Something that scares folks away worse than her little real estate scams. Tina?"

"Yeah, well, why I tell you?"

"Say less then."

"Awhite, Big Man. How about I say this. You swear to do for me, I do for you. I don't wanna see no whiteboy beat a rap for killin' no kids, but . . ."

"He might not. He might be guilty. Or this might blow up and suck in a lot more motherfuckers, but I'm gonna get at the truth, dammit."

She gets this coy grin on her face and says, "Truth. Tha's what I want ta hear. Onaccount you good. Onaccount you do what you promise so you gonna promise to help my Melvin." She pulls me close, away from the corner banter. "My man, Kenny . . . these bitches be sayin' he raping chickenheads in the tents under K Street bridge before the City pushed them out. Some a these bitches gone to the cops . . . some a these snitchy curs be friends of *yo'* bitches!"

"Kill. Watch it, Peach. Those ladies're my friends."

"Awhite . . . my bad . . . *stop.*" Christ there're tears tracking under the shades. She's jumpy to the touch. "Dickie, stamp . . . my Kenny, he a man's man, like you. He don't need to *take* no pussy. Ain't no reason anyhow onaccount he my man now, I cleant him up. Ain't no monster. So you promise . . . promise you *fix* Kenny. Talk to yo' new lawyer friends. An' I give you what you need wiff Gestapo. A transaction, not no snitch."

I kiss her cheek and this time she lets me linger. I smell the tobacco and cheap perfume. "Okay," I whisper. "I say she was plugging Tina to back up real estate, COVID scams. But then, my gut's telling me she's going on full blown Mexican White, maybe mixing with the horse pills to make the Tranq . . . the Apache. Sound familiar?"

"Lawd, Dickie . . ."

"Maybe uses her landlady gig to sling it through some traps . . ."

"You done your homework."

"Say less."

"Well boy . . . Mexican White . . . that Tranq . . . it dangerous, nigga, if you don't keep an eye on the product an' more fenny gets in. But you wrong about one thing. See, she don't got traps. Use her cash ta buy up spots she call 'clubhouses' wiff legit stuff inside like braiding spots, storefront churches."

"Stamp?" Now, the real deal. "You hear anything about a broke white college boy, a Spanish boy, maybe she's buying from them?"

I don't care how she takes the question . . . and she isn't taking it well.

"You standin' way out on the thin branch, boy. I got cover, I got peeps who throws me a rope if I get out too far. Call right up in my sto' right on a *satellite phone*, an' they solve my problems. Get me my license in two days, no more head shop. No more politicians telling me I'm too close to a damn liquour sto'! Who you got? That fat nigga Croc? If he parents was the dinosaurs then he same fat furry thing from my grand baby 'Ice Age' movies gone extinct, too. So you cover for you?"

I hold my hand to my own chest. Grin. "Gotta get to her, Peach."

"Jus' tole you it ain't happenin'. And nigga, it's Friday night. She at one a her 'clubhouses,' doin' her thang."

"I'll help Kenny. I told you. Now gimme more. A kite."

She gives me a wistful sigh and whispers, "Back in the day wiff Black Santa Claus and y'all . . . they was ugly times . . . but we had good one's, too, di'n't we, Tree Top?"

I nod.

"Well, when we partying, back in the jail they also called her 'Lotto' and 'Gym Girl' onaccount she addicted to them scratch-offs and lotta fruit for lifting weights. Only grabbed that shit from corner stores, never Giant or big grocery stores like that."

Corner stores? Not just any. Says Ethiopians, Arabs sold spoiled fruit. Old school Koreans, who inherited stores directly from the Jews and Greeks, are the only purveyors of fruit Gestapo trusts.

"Find a sto'—you only goin' get one shot. Should lead you to which clubhouse she an' her girls—*an' they boys*—be at."

"Fetish, huh—fresh young boys?"

Peach laughs. Takes everyone by surprise especially when she removes her shades, looks me right in my eyes.

"Don't you get kilt befo' you fix my Kenny, hear?"

The PD's Uber voucher's used-up in the trek from 7th and Florida, Northwest, all the way south of Mattel's fiefdom in Deanwood to the cut along Nannie Helen Burroughs.

The driver—a Somali from his face and name on the app—wasn't pleased about the destination, bitching the whole trip. If he had a ramjet powering the car back to ferry Kennedy Center patrons to curtain time, you'd have seen his vapor trail and I don't blame him, as two girls barely out of middle school like the Youngs I scattered the other night snuffed a driver near the Navy Yard just a couple months prior.

Me, I'm in my mix. And now I'm surveying these brothers who turned plastic soda pallets fronting a corner store into ersatz lounge chairs. The streetlamps are buzzing on, and up on the boulevard thick-thighed women with hair extensions and puffy bedroom slippers tow their whining tots and tongue-lash their lagging tweens . . . graydicks in baggy trousers and ragged baseball caps shuffle and mumble to themselves . . . dreadlocked fellas hawk customers outside identical weed shops like hood carny barkers.

"Gestapo?" I ask them.

My audience arranged on the pallets stare, mute yet they aren't so drunk or zooted not know what I want. "Inside . . . wiff Candy," one finally mutters.

That was easy. "Candy . . . she work in there?"

"Candy ain't no woman. Thas a Chiney man."

Another fellow on a higher set of pallets erected as thrown retorts, "Korean, fool!" Then he turns to me. "Big Man, whatchew want Gestapo fo'? You know some whiteboy kilt her lil' brother so she be inside herself."

"I heard about her brother. I bet that whiteboy's been round here, too, showing his ass."

The group members exchange nervous, hardly furtive glances, until the first dude who deigned to speak to me rephrases his first response. "She keep these youngs, old Sheriff Road and Simple City niggas from fuckin' wiff us. You ain't here to fuck wiff her, are you?"

"No." I give them each five bucks. That's one three-piece tenders with mambo sauce each, right down the street.

Indoors, the Burroughs QuickMart is as retro D.C. as you can get. Dim, expired shit on the dusty wooden shelves. Cigarettes, cheap-ass cigars. Hood Bitcoin—aka Tide, Advil and Pampers—all locked up behind the Plexi-glass. Grumpy looking young Asian dude in a terribly incongruous black tee shirt bearing Bob Marley's grandson Skip's likeness and some Rasta parable is stocking the Rock Creek soda, and I watch him sneak a gummie and it ain't no Sour Patch Kid.

A gray-haired lady, face furrowed with age and I swear no more than four and half feet tall appears out of nowhere and yells *"Kang-Dae, Kang-Dae!"* then motions at me—the dark *kaiju*—with her head.

Young dude looks me up and down, then shrugs at her as if to say I might kick his ass. She snaps at him in Korean and says, "Damn . . . okay," then to me says, "Can I help, you, bruv?"

"Picking up some soda, Lunchable . . . basic shit. Pepto, too. Bad gut. Y'all sell ice, too?"

"My grandmother thought you were, uh, someone else. Sorry. Um, that stuffs in the cold cabinet, aisle two. Stomach stuff's in aisle four along the wall. Ice machine's broken, bruv."

"What's your deal, *Can-dy*? Don't sound like you dig place . . ."

Trying to push him yeah but I don't get the reaction I expect. He whispers sideways, "Dude . . . first, no diss . . . I'm not Kang-Dae no more I go by Cole, cool? Second, look . . . I'm helping my dad and grandmother with the jont, but this mug shoulda been my gap year after COVID . . . was supposed to be in Tanzania, Africa, studying agronomics."

"Real talk?"

"Real talk, moe."

Moe?

"Hate this spot, OG. I mean look at this neighborhood. But this shop . . . an' my auntie's wig and hair spot . . . damn, it's putting me through Harvard, dude. *Harvard.* And put my sister through Stanford. Then she wins the Asian slot machine out there in Silicon Valley by hooking up with this white dude who's an angel investor. Know what that is?"

"No."

"Well, she's fucking rich. With her mixed kid, looking down on everyone. Can't get with that, moe. A banana."

"Yellow on the outside, white inside?"

"Yeah!" he chortles. Then his stiffens and he tells me, "Pack up each night, pick up auntie, head to Virginia burbs, repeat the next day morning, crack of damn. It's bullshit."

The gummy must be kicking in. He's *perfect.*

The grandmother's posted up behind the Plexi-glass and is staring. Some of these folks got choppers or AR-15s under the counter. Shotguns are so Nineties.

"So you good Cole?"

"Nah, we good here. Ain't been robbed once since I been home. Up on Sheriff Road, Benning, Minnesota Avenue it's twice a day it seems." He draws close. "And um, Dad's got a redneck AR-15 up there."

See?

"Stamp, I'm looking for Danielle. No shit-starting. Just want to peep-out where she's at. We starting up some biz, this is what they call due diligence."

"Huh?" He's scatching the soul patch. "No shit? I mean . . ."

"If I wasn't chill, I'd have put a nine milly on you and made you show me where she hangs, then waxed you. I was Twelve, I would have put a nine milly on you and shoved you in a sur-veillance van . . . so this is really about how she's handling Diamante . . ."

"Oh snap, yeah! They killed him, bruv. I mean, he was a trip, but they killed him . . ."

"A trip?"

"Ye-eeeah something strange about him and I don't mean to trigger by saying he's neurologically challenged or got iden-tity work to do. Just you know . . . annoying, like a gnat. And she's . . . *phew.*"

"Uh-huh. Well look great talk, man. Gonna grab my gro-ceries and dip if you can't—"

He cuts me off. "Hold up." The grandmother shouts some-thing. "You're in luck. She wants a delivery down the way . . . some of her old correction officers union friends, plus they have a hair braiding thing biz, real estate . . . wanna come? We safer than Wells Fargo down there."

"This delivery order just happened to arrive when I walked in?"

"No man! Waitin' on new pick six to spit: September Scratch-off. Plus some tangerines, Fuji apples." He leans close again, whispers, "Dad gets his fruit from Costco."

"I'll never tell."

"Um, sure you ain't a cop? I mean I never seen one like you even when then dude on the news now for killing himself was running ops all over the place, shootin' brothers."

"Antonelli."

"Right! Fuck that porky pig. Um . . . lemme get the stuff from Dad, can I meet you outside, I'll say you ain't soldiering. We open till midnight, man."

Lay on McDuff.

This "clubhouse" is an old gas station off 49th Street, Northeast, flanked by the big boxy ramshackle apartment buildings endemic to this boulevard, and backed by a wooded creek. Nope, not a trap—jont's painted like the tons of day-care centers and charter schools all over the town. I mean laughing black and brown kids, historical figures. I note the latter's all female, from Sojourner Truth to my seminar class-mate the Vice President . . . to Queen Nzinga of Ndongo and Matamba of Angola.

"Pretty sick, huh?" my Harvard guide asks. "I'm so gutted I had to look this queen up on Wikipedia, and here I am a scholar, yo. My Dad says this is all nonsense, doesn't need to be taught, doesn't need to be on the SAT. I told him let's all learn how Korea bent over and took it from Japan for centuries, then the Czars, then the Japanese again and then communists."

"She fought the Portuguese. Tried to fuck up the slave trade."

"Wait here, they get a little suspicious."

"Of men? This a dyke spot?"

"I know you're an OG but that's a real bad word. Second, no. It's like . . . the opposite. Check it."

Indeed a young dude—lanky, tall as me—rolls out in baggy boxers and a tee . . . the streetlamp and traffic back-light his dick and nuts swinging lose . . . and I think I'm hallucinating. He's barefoot despite the bottle caps, broken glass, and such glinting on the lot's surface.

From inside I hear a woman's voice, "Put yo' damn slippers on!"

"So he's the clucker?"

"It all twisted sexually, OG. Wild shit, boy . . ."

"Well Cole . . . I'm gonna my stuff with me and see about an audience with them tomorrow."

He wants to do some chest pound but I back him off. He's running like Jeremy Lin on a fast break against my poor Wizards back down the block, looking over his should every now and then to make sure I'm not lingering.

I take up across the street in a incongruous stand of bushes, elms . . . and discarded tires. It's away from the streetlamps, and the headlights can't penetrate brush. I sip soda, grub on my Lunchable . . . no better or worse than I've supped on a ward or cellblock. The Pepto's a decent dessert.

And all this time, I see some big women, dressed to the nines, wigs and jewelry, head in that spot with brown paper bags . . . BYOB. And BYOD—slender tall boys, most light-skinned and indeed one straw-haired hillbilly looking kid, tethered to them.

Finally, I here comes my kite. Short Indian-looking dude with a long pony tail, weird handle-bar mustache poking from each side of a blue COVID mask is emerging from a Rav-4 lit an Uber sign. Got some liters of soda and two big brown bags. Grease stains at the bottom of both bags are evident even at this distance. Yeah, that's theirs. I leap from my blind.

"Don't panic, bro'." I tell the driver as I run up on him. "Gimme the food, Here's the tip." I only have a twenty but that, a view of the Mini's holster and my size gets him in the vehicle fast and he's gone.

I figure the mask means he comes right up to the door rather than drops whatever this shit is putting my snack of processed "meat" and crackers to shame.

Sure enough, they don't send the boy toys for the precious grub after I press the buzzer. This lady's got herself a wig with one long blonde horsetail and eyelashes out of a Disney cartoon . . . pneumatic tits under a silver lamé type top, jeans skirt tight around her pooch, thick thighs, matching silver slide sandals, claws painted silver too, like those toes.

"Well hul-lo, Big Man," she coos. "You new?"

"Started drivin' last week. Just put it . . . wherever?"

"Put it in wherever you want, baby. Lookityew in your cowboy coat . . ."

She's framed by this wild red glow, like red light on the bridge of a diving nuclear sub. Spilling out is this Eighties R & B, I mean KC & Jojo *All My Life* stuff . . . the odor, even without what's in the bags, is an amalgam of fry oil, garlic, onions . . . ass . . . and that army surplus Estee Lauder they sell in Marshalls.

"Bring it down then have a nice night, less you want ta knock off early and chill? You yo' own boss . . ."

I make sure my six is covered by a cinderblock wall. My eyes quickly acclimate to the red glow; I another heavy woman in a wrap dress and heels that look like weapons sipping a drink at a vintage Mrs. Pac Man arcade console. She seems more concerned with her bare-chested plaything than my the game or intrusion—as she's flicking his nipple with her fingernail, nuzzling his neck. Whatever's in his high school gym shorts moving is scaring me so move to a makeshift bar tended by similarly half-naked young cats.

"Set it there," Silver commands. "So, you goin' stay?"

"I just might. But if I do, mind if I keep my draws on for now, maybe get a scotch?"

She's cackling like a Bugs Bunny witch and then I see some attention thrown from a couple of women surrounding a felt-top card table covered in dice and stacks of chips. Laughing in between hungry looks at my old broke-down self. I see arms rooting under the table . . . guess they are fingering each other or whatever twink's cuddled up on them.

All but one. Her big eyes have targeted mine and there's no blinking. Dark coffee skin, head adorned in a short pixie cut yet accented by meticulous finger waves and pin curls. Top layer died blue, and it looks violet in that red pallor. She's got a figure eight shape: heavy breasts barely held by a leather tanktop, leather leggings on tree-trunk thighs.

"Silver," she calls over the music and merriment. "Does this big nigga look like 'Vivek' to you? I'm clockin' my Eats and he don't quite seem like a Vivek."

"No bullshit." I call, intriguing plan gone awry.

The loud talk drops to murmurs in an instant.

"No bullshit, then," she acknowledges. "And I ask for none in return, else you leavin' in the trunk of my car, suffocated on your dick, and we drive to Chickenbone Beach, toss your big ass in the Chesapeake Bay attached to some kettlebells."

"Sounds detailed."

She points at me with this painted saber like fingernail. "Practice makes perfect." She looks me up and down, sighs. "I heard of you? You runnin' ops here, nigga?"

"I wanna talk about Dean . . . and Diamante." Yep, in that order.

The murmurs go to a hush and someone kills the music.

"Dean. Who that?"

"And Benny, the Mexican kid from Texas?"

She's cool as a fan. Just a hard swallow. "He dead, right?"

"Funny, you haven't mentioned Diamante yet. I have. Grieving over?"

"Funny, you ain't tole *me* yo' name."

"Someone hit Dean."

Another hard swallow despite the controlled visage. "Yeah. Well . . . my boy okay?"

"GSW to the knee. Maybe he come limpin' back to your arms."

Guess that popped the balloon. Her face contorts, the makeup and eyeliner crack. "Peep this, *Herman Munster.* If you real, than talk. If not, you be lucky to walk. I meet you outside."

I back up, and I'm fingering nothing but the Mini now. When I hit the night air I draw my phone and do a quick pic of the "clubhouse" and her emerging from it like some ghettofab sphinx or gorgon out of her lair. I leave on the recorder app.

"Okay. Who you pluggin' for? Dean's fiendin' for Tina, going through withdrawal . . . but it ain't Tina *you're* slangin' It's Tranq, right? Apache?" All this time she's trying real hard to frost-up. "Who's the source? Benny was reppin'—am I right? Just wanna know for who."

Weird. Now she's giving me a smirk.

And that's when I feel the jab of something much bigger than an LCF in my right kidney.

"Don't move, OG."

"*Kang-dae*," Danielle applauds. "Take him to the yellow house, put him in the basement . . . there're handcuffs and chair down there."

"Handcuffs?" is all I can manage.

"But mind the washer. My tenants be doin' laundry prolly."

"It's *Cole*, yo. It's not like I holla *Gestapo* at you."

She gives him a carnivorous side-eye and chills real quick, escorts me across the dark parking lot. If she wanted dead I'd be in a hoopdy's trunk headed for the shore ten seconds ago.

So he's shoving me through weeds and garbage toward a yellow ranch style house; looks like it's already festooned with Halloween shit though summer's barely over. I check him.

"Kill, if the white boys want you to join one of them Hasty Pudding clubs up at Harvard, you gonna put this on the application?"

"Man fuck you, okay. She buzzed us on the two-way and we got her back. This is *our* hood, too . . . I mean yeah in a fucked up way, but it is. You're an *outsider*."

"Protection?"

"Kill, moe, we little meek buck-teefed gooks look like we need protection? Cash, gee. Hooked us up sweet with COVID loans, no payback, COVID ghosts on the unemployment payroll an' shit . . . District government only checked in to make sure we was prettying up this block at *our* expense, just so it don't look so ghetto . . ."

In the dark we approach a side door that looks like it's fashioned from sheetrock. It opens and out comes yet another pretty boy, this one a white kid who looks like he models for the same stores the pee-wees smash-n-grab, appears in it and ushers us in.

Cole mumbles to the twink and then presses, "How you know about Hasty Pudding, OG? No offense."

"None taken. I'm educated, gee. Plus . . . rando things get into my dome, they don't leave. My father used to think I was autistic and then when my mom and docs said I wasn't he'd just smack me and say act normal."

"Staaaaaammmmp. Sounds like my single parent dad—cray since mom left. Yells at me to 'work harder.'"

"Glad you can at least bond over crime."

"*Shut-up!*"

The twink's in the lead, down a cramped, dim stairwell like the ones in Croc's fucking catacomb of a house. Same smell of mold and corn chips. I can probably bounce these two and rabbit, even with one armed, but my knees and back are killing me. And, well, curiosity's killing me too and hopefully not literally.

We head through another door, the Korean kid strips me of my Marlboro man jacket and my piece, the jumble of paper that's my ID. The other kid pushes me onto a chair. Handcuffs clink my wrists together behind a sadly solid back. Now I'm next to a washing machine and I catch my reflection in the door glass. *Not how you thought this go down, eh Junior?*

No Daddy. But I'm in. You know how I do.

I look down at my feet. Normal ancient basement linoleum. I look up. There's oxidized brown blood—another material with which I'm intimate—all brown, sprayed and splotched on the ceiling tile. I hear you Daddy . . .

You better pray someone's dying to tell, or else you be dying before I hear it.

And here she comes down the steps, leading a waddling, double-chinned entourage. Vapor of drug store Estee Lauder in their wake; panting from the exertion expel the undertone of fried food, liquor. As they struggle in the cramped, starkly lit space I see Silver's toting a jimmy stick. Puts the model I fashioned from a Chuck & Billy's Balabushka cue to shame. Too bad it's under my rack, at home. Spikes from tiny beheaded nails just above the handle are artful. That'll leave a mark . . .

"Didn't come here to fuck with you, Danielle."

"You impress me most . . . muvfukkahs be pissin' theyselves now."

"Just want the truth is all."

"Truth? Truth be that word 'Gestapo.' When them jailbird bitches used the word, I claimed it. Like that dope and dick-suckin' so-called 'mother' Artemisia. I claim that shit to keep'em in line. Fear, not love. All to takes is one to stop lovin' you and you got a problem. Don't believe me? Ask God about Lucifer . . ." She surveys her meaty coven. "*Right?*" They all signify and testify and co-sign, loudly.

Silver hands Danielle the stick. I don't grit my teeth because that always puts my tongue at risk when the hurt arrives.

Instead, she pushes the handle up under my sore nose.

"Benny . . . an' my lil' Dean . . . they wasn't cut out for none them stupid games the big shot white boys play here. Drugs or pussy. Like we all animals to serve them. Never ends . . ."

I sound crazy with the thing all in my snoot. "Dante Antonelli . . . his undercovers were frontin' for all kinds of savage shit . . . turning out poor women in shelters . . . helped bring him down . . . it's all up in the TV news . . ."

She pulls the stick away. "You done all that? Yeti-lookin' nigga . . . I don't give a f-*uuuuuck*."

"Figure not. Pluggers be pluggin' not caring about their own . . . just as cattle to be milked, turned into hamburgers."

The peanut gallery's making faces at my insolence.

"Kill, you bes' stop that lunchin'" Danielle snarls.

Real live I don't have a choice. Push her and maybe she slips. Says something I can use. Or stay chill and die.

"And those Youngs . . . out here jacking cars, robbing. Doing a great job of clockin' them, huh so I guess the way is to turn them out on the Apache too, make young zombies. Isn't that what the whitefolks packing the China down in Mexico for Benny, Dean in their lil' REI or hiking bags want for us?"

She pounces on me like a lady tarantula on a grasshopper. I can smell the Henny and mambo sauce, her mouth's so close to my face as she fucking shrieks.

"I oughta tattoo my trademark on yo' eyelids, Big Man, yo' ass talk to me like that! Benny and then Dean was runnin' from their them crazy rich Trump-ass fools who paid them to fuck with people. They come running to my titties, literally, after the deals we done. You understand? But Benny, he weak, he say he wanna stop. He say he getting high on he own Tranq. He say he can't rehab."

"And Dean? You got that boy thinking you love him."

"Who say I di'n't? Him back? But he weak too . . . he runnin'. You an' me, Big Man, we prolly cop a lil Tina like the whitefolk do a Friday martini. My sweet boy was scared of that fentanyl but hell he couldn't even handle that Tina onaccount he couldn't handle what he was asked to do. Be a businessman, underneath all this politics cover. *Bet*."

"Doesn't explain setting up Diamante and Arthur . . ."

The scream that hits my ears almost cuts my eardrum, as I'm on the wing of a plane. Then, in the dim basement light I see her arms raise. I feel the whoosh of motion . . .

. . . and when the jimmy stick slams onto my upper thighs the pain doesn't kick at first, even as the tiny spikes tear through my jeans, bite into my flesh.

The ladies look down at me, agape. They expect wails of pain. A low moan is all I give them. Danielle lifts my lowered chin from my heaving chest with her adorned fingernail.

"Now explain ta me why you out here, fuckin' shit up."

"Serving . . . my client . . ."

"*I say fuckin' shit up!*" she screams, and this time she brings the cue down so hard it breaks in half. Luckily . . . on the chair's arm, not mine. "All sposed ta be self-defense! They spose ta come at Dean, he give them the nine-millimeter beat-down, they die. Simple. Thas the law. Self-defense, Twelve shouldna even charged his white ass! Don't nobody care if two black boys die, even if some cracka wastes 'em cause they doin' dirt, right? Spose ta be *simple* . . . "

"Baby . . ." I wheeze. "It's never simple. You're walking proof of that."

CHAPTER TWELVE
Family is Hard, Money's Easy

"ALL YOU GET OUTTA HERE!" DANIELLE shouts to her minions.

It's Silver who comes to my aid with a cryptic, "If you kill his ass in here, you goin' have ta tell *her*. She goin' be *pissed* . . . she goin tell them Mexicans *an'* the whitefolk!"

"Bitch who makes the money?"

"You do."

"Repeat?"

"You do."

"An' what do them burrito eaters an' them white muvfuk-kahs in they penny-loafers an' pickle-ball shit care about?"

"Money."

"Now *step!*"

With little more resistance she and rest the women trundle up the stairs. See, now I'm glad I took my bladder pill. Now I'm scared. In front of she's just given me the whole damn world, a theory given a skeleton, muscles, viscera. Which means unless Batman with some shit in my utility belt my ass is grass.

Yet now that we're alone, I get a sob story, not a jimmy stick in my ear or a bullet in my head . . . and her eyes are wet, her nostrils sputtering with snot as it tumbles from her ample lips.

"That lil' pussy Diamante was touched in the head, from birth, like he daddy, like he uncle . . . he daddy a big dullard taco-eatin' fool. The boy was pushed on me by my dear, dear sweet auntie when I lost m'own baby. Make me raise him as if he my brother, when I had a life, a job, a man who didn't want no crazy lil' boy. That lil' nigga used to say to my sweet Benny Ortiz he was my 'enforcer' . . . like this some video game or gangsta shit on Netflix. I mean he hated Benny . . ." Her mania ebbs, as much as it seems, there in a traphouse basement with me bound to a fucking chair. "And when Benny fucked up . . . .and Benny had to go . . . Diamante, he thought he had *me*—his 'mama'—back, till Dean . . . my Dean came along."

"But . . . you had a fetish to feed."

"That was some good dick, my Dean . . . lil' sweet college boy ass."

"And Arthur? He was gonna make something of himself. A good kid."

"So I be a monster? His mama was a dopefiend in that van long before the Tranq. Shit when she was one of my jailbirds she was always cryin' for the Oxy for her damn aches and pains. Now, Arthur, shit, *I warned him*—Diamante ain't none his business. But I guess he want to show his nutcase mama he could stand up to me when she couldn't. Always watchin' Diamante's back when the boy cry an' whine 'stead of makin'im stand up for himself . . ."

The sweat's pouring off my face now so I'm squinting up at her. "Y-You still can't tell me why you set them up . . . for Dean to smoke 'em. Two boys . . ."

Should've known better than to play mind games with an ex-C.O. She starts rubbing on my crotch, whispering. Oh but that stick's not far from my face . . .

"You know what Dean'd be doin' when I be suckin' his dick?"

"No but . . . you're gonna tell me, I got a feeling."

"He'd be on his phone, on that Twitter, wid he Trump folk, wid one hand, fingerin' me wid th'other—I ain't wellin'."

"Say less . . ." I think I got one chair leg and the back loose . . .

"I'd tell him 'Ya know Diamante got some hole dug over by my vanity table' an' sometime he watch me an' Benny an' maybe he watch now. An' I say that how Diamante found out Benny using, cause he see Benny get high in my bedroom an' I say to my new boy Dean if you ever get high in my bedroom I'm goin' kill ya . . ."

She digs her claws into my sack but good, and I don't make a sound, at least outwardly. Inward, yeah, the serpent in my belly can hear the scream, *right Daddy?*

"See, when then cops who our backs was out there, no cap. But then they all started going to jail."

"Imagine that."

"And Diamante say to himself, I can get rid a this whiteboy too by snitchin'. He was tellin' me Chucho Benny was a liability onaccount Benny was getting' high. Or maybe he already snitch out Benny, huh? DEA. Imagine DEA takin' calls from a retard chile wantin' to be an informant! Well, this time he got the balls ta do it."

"Made you nervous?"

"Made me mad, like you made me mad. Diamante, I beat his ass and he say he ain't goin' ta prison, juvie or not. One my girls heard him fuckin' around on his cellphone with Arthur, about how they goin' set shit right . . . Candy's daddy tell me he seent them buyin' irons from some other Youngs. You figure out the rest, Mr. Private Detective, in the short time you got left. Family's hard. Money's easy. But money always got a *cost* . . ."

The moisture and shine belies her otherwise hardscrabble, cruel face. She grabs the broken pieces of jimmy stick and swishes up the stairs.

The second she's gone I slide into the light reflecting off that nasty washing machine door. I'm using the heel of my left shoe to pull on the one on my right. Nice soft leather, peels right back because I watch the YouTube lessons, bitch. Out comes my little shim, steel. I shake my left shoe now. Ferro rod from Target. I'm smiling because back in the day I'd light fires with cast-off Bic lighters not this frontier shit but that's not why I got it.

No more voices or footsteps upstairs. Lessons say nobody but movie spies can dislocate both shoulders and swing the cuffs to the front of your body when you're seated. Nah, when you're a big motherfucker like me, aged yeah, but still big, and you've already got some of the chair parts loose, you do this: jump!

I twist and land on the back rim between the washing machine and this old defunct oil furnace like the videos say. Chair's pile of sticks; I'm wriggling free of the debris then laying backward to finger the shim and stick.

Never done this before. Never practiced. Yet thank Mother Mary for my afflictions, Daddy. The ferro stick sparks up the steel shim—I can hear it and smell it. Nice and hot and energic and yeah it hurts, but my callous-padded fingers have felt worse. The hot shim pops the lock and I'm on feet, ready to find Candy or Cole or what-the-fuck, knock him out, get my .380 and shit back . . .

. . . until I hear a BANG! like something hard and frightening bashing into a wall or door . . .

"*Freeze! Drop it! Comply!*" Above me the floor beam quiver and dust flies.

Silver come tumbling down the stairs, her sandals in each hand. She lands right at my feet, and looks up at me in a weird plea for help.

Big spook rippling with body armor's tearing down the steps right on her and suddenly I'm blinded by his cop torch.

"Down on the floor with her! Hear me nigga? Hands behind your head!"

Sort of ironic. And when I get sight back I clock his shoes on her wrists, and he's frisking her chemise for a little .25.

She's moaning something. "W-Why y'all devils . . . gotta shoot her?"

And as the bells in my ear ease up on the pealing I hear po-po radios calling for EMS and a van for their quarry . . .

. . . and after a drink of water I'm collected enough to answer the questions from this white female jake who's squatting by me on the curb. The spot's lit with ghetto suns like it was midday.

"You the private dick?" she asks.

I nod and massage my wrists, roll my achy shoulders and then the utter horrible oddity of the question registers. "Fuck's all this, officer?"

"We been after her for a long time. The dicks got a tip you were coming down here to shake some shit loose. Guess it got ugly, huh?"

"Danielle Diggs . . . her brother Diamante was one of the teenagers Dean Scholtz shot recently. dude's facing a murder rap . . . I work for—"

"I'll let the dicks fill you in," she interrupts.

The street fronting the house looks like a dirty-laundry-and-carryout container bomb detonated and buried everything in stinking refuse and bloody linens. I may be dazed, but I'm certain this is Monica Abalos in a tac vest coming toward me.

"Danielle Diggs might be joining her only family very soon," she says, coldly. "Come with us."

... and so I'm in an unmarked's back seat with an icepack around my neck, and gauze under the tears in my jeans. Monica's next to me. We're in a daisy chain convoy of sorts following blue and whites—running lights and sirens full blaze and blast—and an ambulance. Behind us are cars from the neighborhood; near as I can gather, the fate of someone nicknamed "Gestapo," has produced more heart wrenching and teeth gnashing as the supposedly unjustified shooting of her brother by a white man.

We scatter the traffic and cross over Kenilworth Avenue into areas more familiar to me.

"I put a tail on you, on a hunch," Monica shares.

"I shake tails," I mutter.

A jake turns around from the front passenger side and hangs over the seat. A pretty thing, slender nape and oval head like a queen of the Nile's, hair drawn back in a bun. "I'm Officer Jessica Goins."

"She looks like a Howard sorority girl."

"I was, at least last year."

"Dickie, you're as much a gentleman as you are paranoid. You might've looked at Jessica but you wouldn't have made her as an undercover. When you got to the Burroughs QuickMart, it was pretty clear what you were up to."

This doesn't add up. "Just following me? That's it? And then you blasted on her?"

"She was screaming at my officers," Abalos tells me. "Something about her aunt and white people betraying her?"

"No clue."

"You telling the whole story."

"I am *jhi*-straight. But did you have to kill her? I wanted to talk to her when she wasn't pyscho and I know the Feds are going to trip when they find out a potential cog is this wheel is dead . . ."

"Maybe she was high, drunk, it doesn't matter wehn she draws a vintage Colt auto on us . . . look at me, Dickie—I didn't authorize kill shots! Neutralize only. But . . . *coño* . . . my officers are not for target practice and frankly anyone plugging Zombie Tranq deserves to die in my book!"

I gesture at the ambulance headed straight for Medstar. "They'll all be together," I muse. "Arthur, in a coma, her . . . and Dean . . ."

"As far as I am concerned this Scholtz case is not cleared and I'm going to bat in the Daly Building to say just that and don't care what this prosecutor Markowitz says. You are coming with me."

"Those chicks jacked me up. Look at me. I'm not going anywhere with you until I'm checked out at the ER. It's my right."

Monica groans and says, "Jessica go with him. Then you run him back to the Daly Building."

"Good. I don't like that preppie white boy who bugged me at breakfast. Real talk though, why wait till now? You had her on PPE fraud, Tina, pills, protection rackets . . . ."

She offers me some peppermints I gobble a few and she pretty much corroborates every Gestapo ranted. "It's as if Linda Figgis and Dante Antonelli were still running their fiefs in the Department. Only Feds got our back. I can't prove this, but there's some kid, from Texas . . . who may have been pushing your girl into the China White. We'd made contact with a potential C.I. DEA was developing. We had to back off."

"Ben or Benjamin Ortiz? That's the name? Or was it Diamante. You can tell me now, because his sister sure as hell did."

Even in the darkness of the car I see the Filipina's Pacific eyes get as wide as dinner plates. One of the narcs in the front seat whispers, "Maybe you should tell him . . ."

"Our . . . our potential C.I . . . was this kid Arthur Sellers. He said his knowledge was personal and was coming from someone close to Danielle, and there was a Mexican guy who was the source of the fentanyl and xylazine cooked into Tranq . . . ."

Jesus, Mary and Joseph . . . "Danielle had it right, yet wrong. So *Arthur* was the snitch . . . with Diamante Diggs just feeding him info by beefin' on the sister."

"*Hay naku*," Monica quips in that Tagalog stuff. "And the beef? Money . . . side deal with the pills, COVID fraud—what?"

"No. *Neglect*."

Neither my voice or my facial expression give a ticket to the furious permutations all *clickty-clackity* inside my dome. She's literally frowning until we both clock my phone in my hand. A jake returned it from Kang-dae's fingers along with my ID, wallet, and, grudgingly, the .380 and phony license.

Seems Attorney Yi's been blown up my voicemail. Her wellin' ass can wait.

"Your turn, Monica," I say sleepily and ignoring the trembling phone.

"Much of this activity was back during your Summer of Love, big guy. Last we heard, this kid Ortiz breaks his neck biking in Rock Creek . . . we then see he worked for a *senator* . . . and then our C.I. and Diamante supposedly try to jack a white guy in Adams Morgan . . . and then he's brain dead. The shooter's arrested and we're told to stand down, allow that to run its course, likely a manslaughter plea."

"My client worked for the same senator at one point. Brom Vitter."

Monica shakes her head. "Walk away from this, Dickie."

"Say less." And I decide to answer the call this time.

"We've been fired, Dickie. Dean fired us today from the hospital."

I'm eyeing Monica so I'm not hiding my shock too well. "I-I'm on my way to the hospital. What do I do?" That's a serious, no bullshit question.

"I doubt his new attorneys will need you . . . or want you, for that matter, given what you've 'agitated.' Quinton & Breedlove. White collar crime, D.C. white shoe. Repped many of the January Sixth defendants, been devil's advocate, literally, since Watergate, Iran-Contra . . . even second chairs with Casino Jack Abramoff and Marion Barry. Rumor is perhaps one or two sitting Supreme Court Justices and of course the former president's legal team have consulted with them."

"He has no money."

"Someone does. Dickie . . . I fear a threshold was crossed with this raid tonight, and I owe some . . . disclosures . . . but I'm too wrung out to do it now. Try to forgive me. For what it's worth, a friend at the Marshal's Service says he's admitted to the hospital under the name 'Mr. Blue.' "

"And?"

And she's gone. And they're all staring at me in the backseat.

"Money's easy, family's hard . . ." I repeat. *Mater Maria*, got to think fast. As the caravan of lights roars onto North Capitol Street I groan, "I-I'm feeling dizzy."

"Those wounds on your thigh're ugly but they'll heal fast," one of the dicks observes.

"Yeah, get your antibiotics and tetanus shot, get patched up and *then* I see you at HQ," Monica adds.

"No . . . it's . . . my head, my chest . . . like I need a gallon of Mylanta, *fast . . .*"

It works too well.

Who knows—I'm a wreck for my age so maybe there's something indeed wrong with the ticker and such. So real live, I'm half-naked and hooked up to some monitors. At least I'm alone behind a blue curtain and the nurse told me to sleep. I clock that chick, the cutie, Goins talking to another black jake and hey—they both book, leaving no Medstar guards I can see.

The bonus is who's cuffed to a railing, one curtain over. "Hey Kang-dae . . . I mean *Cole.* It's me."

"Fuck you, man."

"Heard they busted a rib while pinching you. You're a *for real* nigga now."

"I said . . ." I hear a grunt and groan, ". . . fuck you! My peeps'll get my bond . . . they'll empty the *hui* for my ass . . . I'm a first son!"

"That's not how bond works anymore here. Plus you assaulted a cop in a drug raid."

"Whatchew want?"

I tell him to chill. I gingerly slide my ends back on, my shoes. I make a command decision to yank my drip. I've done it before in the bad days. I disconnect the other leads and there's low tone; they'll investigate soon but I'm not here as state property so I'm betting no one will trip . . .

"Kill, I know a little about the system," I whisper as I part the neighboring curtain from the wall. "You can call me, I'll help you the best I can, keep you on ROR . . ."

"You can do that?"

"I'm an OG, stamp."

"I can't snitch. But . . . my community, they'll protect me. My uncle's a lawyer in Bailey's Crossroads."

"Yeah. That's Virginia. This is the District, homes, so spill."

I wish I wasn't such a wooly mammoth, ancient and dumb—should've had pics on file from LaKeisha . . . right onto my phone. I take his pic, thumb the record app. Ask him about a Mexican dude running around with Gestapo.

"Was his name Ben or Benny Ortiz?"

He nods. "They called him Chucho Benny or Benny. The 'chucho' part was his rap, like this dude was a whiteboy wannabee so he had to invent some street shit. Always came around in a shitty whip so he b-boys would leave it alone, but had cash. None the ladies would say what he was all about but when I'd hang after deliveries, they say Danielle'd be smashin' with him, and he's got all these connections, right down to the border . . ."

"Kill . . . hold up. *Mexican* border . . . for . . . ?"

"You the OG!" He winces a little on the exam table. "Fennie . . . the white. Mix it up here or down there, depending. Make that Apache or Zombie Tranq with it. These junkies in Northeast be sprinkling like on cupcakes by the time Benny was through."

"Then you did or did not see him? Twelve never touched him?"

"Slow down, shit, moe. No, Twelve never fucked with Danielle as long as his ass was there, then he was gone, she started fucking someone else . . ."

I swipe my now busted screen till Dean's face appears. "Him?"

"I can't tell. Some whiteboy. Could be him. Dunno. Ain't fuckin' with you, gee."

"Did he . . . look like the whiteboys at Harvard?"

He sighs. "Yeah, maybe so. Didn't talk but had that look when he'd come by the store, maybe couple times for rolling papers."

"That's specific."

"Hey, he was white. And not Twelve unless he's undercover."

"Name?"

He shrugs. "Never came up."

"One more thing. Diamante—he wasn't happy with his sister's bedmates, was he?"

"Nah. He'd come to the store after school and like, act like a baby 'Nino Brown,' but when this shit started really comin' in, the Tranq, he became a little pussy. I mean, I guess I would, too. You start to see the people, all fucked up, the tents would pop up down the block and they'd be all dazed, toothless, crazy looking. As long as this street was okay, man, fine by my dad and the other merchants. Gestapo kept the zombies away. But they were there. More an' more, an' it made Diamante crazy."

"Go on . . ."

"He and that big kid, Artie, they'd come by, buy Pop Tarts and shit, and Artie'd say how old you got to be for them to move you from juvie at Mt. Olivet to adult prison or Fed prison if you were around family members plugging Apache, making zombies. Like I know? I'm at Harvard!" Kang-dae raises up, obviously in agony. "Um . . . just in case Danielle pulls through, she gotta know I was a good scout, a good soldier, okay? Keep my cover, keep my family safe."

"Oh, you be back up in Cambridge soon, my man."

He smiles just as I'm turning to part the curtain and says, "You my nigga, man!"

I say nothing. *This* motherfucker . . .

I'm off the ward and smiling at anyone in scrubs. Quite the turn from back in the, when I'd abscond—no eye contact, nuts swinging under my gown, shunt still sticking in my arm, laying a blood trail.

I go up a floor for shits and giggles and luck out because there's an info counter, not just a busy nursing station. There's a big grim brother in security garb, looks like Equal Protection's twin, backing this little Indian chick. I make sure he sees my nod, all my now useless PD stuff and roll the dice.

"The Marshal's Service has *my client* under 'Mr. Blue.'" Info passes slow in here. I one absconded from the dry-out ward in a gown and draws, and it took an hour before they sounded the alarm.

The Indian girl nods. "He's out of critical care, sir . . . but there's a notation on the record . . . he was to be transferred for physical therapy on his knee wound. Now there's a hold as of last night."

Jesus. "Well again I'm the investigator and I just need to wrap things up, ten minutes."

"There's the added problem that it's very late."

"I'm not a visitor."

She and the guard exchange glances. "Ok it's up to the Marshal on duty. Take the elevator then follow these directions." She scribbles out something on a pad.

Good thing I'm wandering hospital corridors, huh, because I have to vomit as there's so much in my dome now. Clickity-clackity, clickity-clack. And as I pass a small waiting room wall

TV I clock incongruous news on Israel and the Orioles, and then Senator Brom Vitter, mouthing something about his boy Donald Trump.

"Vengeance will follow vindication," the Texan rails.

"Sounds like the kinda asshole who'd gladly help someone murder a fungible family member," I say to myself as I spot the room . . . and empty chair outside its door that should have had a guard or Marshal's ass parked therein. "Because money's easy."

CHAPTER THIRTEEN
Requiem Mass

I LINGER THE LENGTH OF THE average piss and still no marshal; I overhear a young woman say "Mr. Blue's midnight meds don't seem to be working but let him watch TV, note it on the chart."

This confirms my guess that everyone's guard is down, and Quentin & Breedlove's name is definitely deep the government rabbit hole. At least until I'm finished.

My "client" is sprawled on his bed, knee wrapped like a mummy's and elevated, Cinci Bengals tee shirt, pair of clam-shell style headphones wrapped on his skull and eyes darting between Fox News and the phone he's fingering. No wonder he doesn't note my big lumbering ass enter.

Upon creeping closer I realize the multitasking is even more multi than I figured. He's watching the news with close captioning, listening to music on the phones while texting.

Something catches his attention on the screen. Black Lives Matter marches from prior years, during the pandemic . . . warehouses on fire, protesters presumably transmogrified into snarly beasts.

"See, you've gotta take back the messaging and put this on *them*! Especially that smiling clown from Minnesota!" he hollers at the narrating pundit, who's switched to chaos in the

Congress, internecine Republican warfare between Trump's folks and who Dean calls the 'cucks.' Now we're the one who are the thugs, lusting only to rule, not govern." He pauses, I guess admiring his prose. "Yeah, I'll use that . . ."

"Hello, Dean."

He turns, fumbles the phone like too many Commanders running backs handle the pigskin.

"*Fuck*! It's you . . ."

"If you think security's coming, there *ain't* any, at least from the Marshals." I run up on the bed, knock his phone to the floor. Luckly a rug muffles the racket.

"I'll scream, Mr. Cornish . . . I swear!"

"Then Gestapo might even hear you. And if you're *real* loud, you'll wake up Arthur Sellers."

"*Wha-what*? Danielle's—

"In surgery. Couple of bullet holes, compliments of that one piece of MPD that Dante Antonelli didn't run like the Waffen SS . . . that Linda Figgis didn't rule like Queen of the Amazons. It was doing its job."

"*Danielle!*" he snorts, instantly overwhelmed by tears, phlegm.

"Danielle. Your and Ben's ghetto MILF, huh . . . nigga *rolla*, mommy sex thing?"

"*F-Fuck you!*"

I shut the door. Take out my phone. Tap the voice recording, find my pic of Kang-dae.

"Recognize this Korean dude?"

"Huh?" He's trying to compose himself. "W- Wait . . . is that the dweeb at the corner store down on Nannie Helen Burroughs?"

"He's a Harvard dweeb. Can't a Princeton dweeb tell?"

"*Shit.* Okay . . . look Mr. Cornish—that guy's a nobody, an asshole."

Sounds like my admonition to Bivens about Esmeralda.

"He ID'd Ben. Your Ben. He knows you took Ben's place in Danielle's bed. Your *boss's* bed."

His face hardens and yet as I remind him no one can hear, he shouts nonetheless, "*Boss,* asshole? Do you even know how this shit works? She's just a retailer, okay? I'm a sales rep, so was 'Chucho Benny,' and we work for a marketer . . ."

"The supplier . . . the *bichote* . . . big shot."

"Whatever. You forgot the product advisor. This is capitalism."

"Glad we're being honest. Guess it took you getting shot, me getting shot at, and us getting fired. So as long as we're being honest, who hired the goons to come take you out— your 'boss?' Or this mystery person—the 'product advisor?' That an Ivy League term for shot-caller? I mean, just like Benny, you started getting high. Maybe not on the Apache because you didn't want to die or mess up your pretty face with fentanyl sores, but all that other shit Danielle and them crusty bitches and your fellow boy-toys were dealing was tasty, huh?"

"Get outta my room, Mr. Cornish. My new lawyer, Mr. Graydon, will be in touch."

"How'd you get back on the inside, Dean? Who's paying the bills? The *bichote* just gonna let you live, fly your family here from Cincinnati?"

"Yeah, matter of fact."

"Matter of fact, if I can find your *anonymous* ass in this big place, people who took potshots at you down Eastern Market way shouldn't have any problem. Matter of fact, I'm sure they are getting your location from Mr. Graydon right now. The heat's not off you, man. *Matter of fact* . . . you're going from a D.C. hipster who fended off two little black muggers to a drug dealing, drug using whiteboy who shot the street dealer's brother . . . and a potential C.I.—yeah, Arthur on a ventilator in this building. So man-up with me. Who you working for, running the product coming out of Texas, across the border you say Grandaddy Biden's made porous, same one Ben's family wears a uniform and federal badge defending? Who's the shot-caller, the *guarantor*? Your friend Senator Vitter know?"

"You're . . . a bastard."

"I'm betting the shot-caller's a Mexican. The cartel . . . in *Colima*. Someone working with them?"

He's swaying like a scared little kid though his knee's locked in that hanging brace. "They . . . they were still coming to kill me. Arthur and Diamante. Still self-defense."

"I've seen too much on the street to believe that. Your girl with the charming nickname . . . in this hospital morgue . . . already gave me what I needed to know. You're an amateur assassin." This wasn't a set up.

"You'd be surprised what people will do . . ."

"No, I'm not. The street is a very simple ecosystem. Every creature out there's doin' dirt."

"And you?"

"You see a cape on me, Dean?"

He turns away and shuts his beady blues as if I'm a *for-real* spook that will disappear if he wishes hard enough. I give him two seconds, but he speaks first.

"Arthur was a dumbass noble kid. Diamante was a numb-skull. They were coming to scare me, maybe beat me up? I'd run squealing home and stay in my whiteboy lane. So . . . yeah.

I'm a killer. I'm a murderer, of children, Mr. Cornish. I'm going to Hell. Danielle, Benny, they'll all be there, too. For what? So those . . . *fuckers* . . . can get revenge—on a city?"

Last time my pupils got that wide, I was smoking the Kush, watching Peach trading smooches with Black Santa right down on the Mall, Capitol lit up, G-Dub needle lit up, like it was our backyard. "Go on . . ."

The door swings open with a couple of people in scrubs, and two beefy security guards entering. Yeah, the guards in the hospital carry.

They pounce and yank me the Hell right out of there and some suit passes me. Mousey looking K street jerk, with perfect hair, like Bracht's old barrister.

Before the door closes, I hear, "Thanks for saving my life once. Wish you hadn't. But I'm gonna save yours . . ."

I'm on the elevator and it opens in the lobby with Monica Abalos and a lot of cops waiting for me. My thigh sutures have busted.

"You fucked up," Abalos sneers. "Put him in the Suburban this time, cuffed."

"Is he under arrest?" a jake asks.

"*Do it!*" the little Filipina hollers.

"You should be up there guarding Dean Scholtz," I match in volume. I can't follow up—I'm coughing . . . on my knees.

Abalos comes right up under me. "Fed problem, until Chief Patterson tells me otherwise."

"He killed your C.I. Admitted it to me." Don't know what my face features now as look down on her whole five feet of height—forlorn? Defiant? Nope. Bone weary, done. "Then I'm *dead*, too. You . . . all of you . . . are just the *Introit.* A sad song."

"Get in the Suburban. You've obstructed and disturbed the peace."

"I was . . . debriefing my client."

"He's no longer your client."

"*Dies irae . . . dies illa . . .*" I smile and tell her, "If you remember your Confirmation when you were a little girl, that's how the Requiem Mass began as the *Introit* was sung."

"We'll discuss this at the Daly Building." She pauses when an ABC affiliate news van pulls up outside the lobby windows. "Can't we catch a damn break?" She orders the jakes to herd me out one set of doors as another news truck rolls up and the first crew scurries into the lobby, garish camera lights blazing.

The night air's cool and it for an instant it soothes my sore *everything*—body, head, thighs, soul—as he head toward the dark blue cop Chevy.

Suddenly, a couple of jake shoulder radios buzz. That Goins chick asks for clarification from security and the medical staff then tells them to get off that frequency.

I hear someone shrieking . . . I see a dude maybe a hospital staffer looking skyward, mumbling "*God-damn*," as if UFO's have invaded the black sky.

It's shards of plate glass from Medstar's huge picture windows—glistening like icicles as they fall, shatter into dust and diamonds on the pavement . . .

Then there're shouts, another shriek, "*Oh my God, look!*"

Silence, weird silence, follows the shriek . . .

. . . then a hideous THOOMP! Square onto the roof of the MPD Suburban.

I feel moisture on my cheek and it's too heavy for a raindrop. Abalos thumps it off and it's red, with a speck of flesh . . .

"*Sarge!*" a white jake calls, unhinged. "Holy shit . . . you aren't gonna believe this!"

Under the harsh lights of the main hospital drive, splayed out from the crushed SUV roof, I clock a bloody bare leg . . . wrapped, braced and casted at the knee.

CHAPTER FOURTEEN
Probable Cause

THIS FELLOW CAPTAIN "BUSTER" PATTERSON HATED me from the first time saw me . . . back in those misty, gauzy days . . . and Chief of Police Linda Figgis showed up in my two-room shithole with the entire fucking MPD command staff. Like Abalos, he should thank me for clearing the organizational chart above him, enabling his cream-like rise to the top.

Yeah, *cream*. Fat, sludgy maybe—a redbone, green-eyed version of my ole Black Santa. His dumpling ass is parked in Figgis's chair and it just looks wrong.

"You speak when you're spoken, too, Hobo Jim!" he shouts at me. *Hobo Jim?* He's the motherfucker in what I'd swear are 1960s sitcom striped pajamas under a 1970s blue Adidas track suit.

"How do you all know it was suicide?" I repeat from previous protests, this time monotoned. "Not that he was pushed by an intruder?"

He aims the stink eye then calls on Abalos, "No sign of a struggle in the room after the medical team and his law firm's rep left? Security had controlled access after they expelled this fool here?"

She eyes me nervously. "Yes sir . . . uh . . . it was medical staff with one guard in the hall. Deceased Scholtz was agitated, refused sedation or requests to get back in his bed despite clear knee pain from a GSW. Nursing staff and physician left the room to obtain assistance in calming the deceased. Maybe a minute. The guard heard a crash . . . it appears the deceased broke a window with a chair . . ."

"Detective Abalos may I speak?"

Abalos sighs. "Dickie . . . Mr. Cornish . . . the only evidence of a physical struggle in that room was you fighting the guards."

"Hobo Jim, I'd stand mute if I was you."

"You ain't me, *Acting* Chief."

He sucks at his teeth, scans the other uniforms and plain-clothes jamming the office. "Anyone been in touch with the Marshals as to their absence? This boy shoulda been in a secure facility like the jail infirmary not ROR."

"Your Homicide dicks cleared the case," I push. "With alacrity, sir. Shot two b-boys plain as day like some vigilante hero and yet I'm the case two weeks and what do I find?"

"Don't you mock me, Cornish! Shit, all this drug rehab at the VA nonsense and I'm supposed to treat you like you in law enforcement?"

"This is counterproductive, man."

"Ain't playing whitchew, Hobo Jim. I'm gonna find out *all* the artifices you've been trading on all this time, fella—from that sumbitch Jaime Bracht and his Latin hooligan friends, to what you and my predecessor cooked up to roast Dante Antonelli."

A voice from the back calls out, "Meeting at eleven later this morning, Chief . . . confirmed. U.S. Attorney, Public Defender, Marshals . . . and there's some guy from a law firm in on it, too."

Monica comes to the rescue. "Uh, sir, in light of that, maybe it's time we get our story straight, and I indeed my intention was to bring Mr. Cornish here, straightaways given his intel on the matter of Danielle Diggs, aka 'Gestapo.'"

The old man nods. "G'head and tell him."

"Wait, you gonna treat me like I'm *not* a piece of trash?"

"Cornish I ain't too bright and not the tough sumbitch I think I am. I advanced through the ranks and survived by playing angles, and you, sonny, your shit's 'bout as Euclidean as they come. I got feral teenagers run amok, fentanyl, random folks getting shot in the streets. I got a City Council that says my officers are doing Klan lynchings, I got a U.S. Congress that says I'm not lynching enough. So I guess it's time kill this department's left-hand-not-knowing-what-the-right's-doing crap once and for all. Sargeant—it's your show."

"Dickie, you were—correct. We weren't there for Danielle on our own intel or tailing you. The raid on Danielle Diggs was based on a tip from the DEA, with supplemental information from Main Justice, circumventing, obviously, the U.S. Attorney for the District of Columbia."

I let that sink in. Main Justice. "Ah shit . . ." I'm feeling all warm from nuts up to my forehead. Then fire, like, my skin, roasting, just for a second. "Bivens . . ."

"Angela Bivens communes with a low-life like you?" Patterson grumbles. "I don't need you runnin' a game, too."

"N-no . . . no game."

Patterson still thinks I'm talking shit. He's smirking like I'm still a homeless rube . . .

"We had probable cause to hit that particular 'clubhouse,'" Monica begins, "otherwise the warrant would have been *prima facie* no good." She pauses to draw a deep breath then says,

"The tip included intel that we should tail you, Dickie, for location of possible fentanyl and fentanyl precursor materials, xylazine etc. And other contraband within the proximity of the subject, Diggs. So yes the intel was based on long-standing information from . . ."

"Arthur . . ." Yet the only person to whom I was relaying info was a highly skeptical Helen Yi . . .

Monica sighs and says, "We have no idea why the Deputy Attorney General of the United States would augmenting intel from a sixteen year old snitch in Ward Seven, effectively cutting her own U.S. Attorneys out of the chain."

"Unless she couldn't . . . trust them," I whisper.

"Or she's clownin' us all," the Acting Chief chortles.

That too.

"Okay Cornish," Patterson says, "it's your turn to answer our questions. Your client confidentiality ended the millisecond that fella Scholtz's head hit *terra firma*."

"No, it caved in one of your Suburbans," I mutter, with my dome playing all these versions of Bivens, all monochrome and frenetic like those Lumiere Brothers kinetoscopes in centuries past. No sound. Then I look the gruff fart in his sleepy eyes and speak. "You have a potential C.I. shot publicly by a suspect about to go on trial for the C.I.'s murder . . . the suspect then jumps . . . r is pushed from his hospital room window because he's scared, feels useless now. And he's in the hospital because someone tried to kill *him* . . ."

"Go on," Patterson grunts. "I want everything in the bucket . . ."

"Diamante Diggs is mad at his sister, Danielle. He tells his big dumb friend Arthur and Arthur prolly Googles at school how to call Uncle Sam out of the blue, not very subtle, so

Gestapo finds out; meanwhile the two boys go to jack Dean Scholtz up, and Arthur's got his own reasons because his mom's a zombie, dying of Tranq sores. Danielle drops a dime and turns the tables on her own brother, making it a hit. City's in a crime wave, these two are just b-boy thugs who got smoked by a righteous young patriot and the Second Amendment. And why Dean? Because previously, Dean and his boy, another baby wingnut named Ben Ortiz, were tasked with setting up Danielle in the bad biz, Chief. Mexican White, was called China White. Processed into the shit you all are seeing along with this street mayhem. Both Dean and Ben were her lovers and business partners, but . . ." Hey, he wanted everything in the bucket . . .

"But what? You gonna blame us for arresting Dean for shooting them while we're in the middle of teen crime wave?"

"Just realizing something. The boys'd already fed the DEA and y'all a taste . . . but maybe there was more? Not just about Danielle dealing Tranq, could be who the *bichote* was—I mean the supplier behind Dean and Ben . . . or maybe somebody even closer to the operation?"

"Huh?" says the Chief. "Care to share?"

First chilling thing Bivens said to me. A business model: A guarantor, shot-caller. Typically watching over the whole process. "Maybe the info that was forthcoming was about who was guaranteeing the shipments, mixing the xylazine and White into Tranq. Dean had the opportunity to wax the boys because the boys were acting like boys—impetuous. Your Homicide dicks never bothered to go to Deanwood investigate any of this shit . . . they just up and arrested Dean . . . closed the case, spoonfed it to the prosecutor. With great . . . *alacrity*, Chief."

Yeah, I'm getting a little woozy so Monica's nudging me. "Are you alright?"

"No."

"Chief," Monica says to Patterson, "I'll need to take this man to sub-two for some first aid. His bandages on his thigh and stuff from the ER . . . need re-dressing."

"Be back here to help with a briefing statement then we can get our usual two hours of sleep before this meeting at eleven."

"Chief . . ." I ask. "Figure I'm not invited to this meeting, right?"

"Are you smoking the K2 again, Cornish?"

Monica intercedes. "*Chief* . . . in light of what he just summarized . . . and the DOJ connection . . . we need clarification on the supplemental info they supplied for the probable cause affidavit to have Cornish shadowed."

"Chief . . . whether you believe or not, Angela Bivens as much as told me who the supplier is . . . a syndicate of 'em. Dean and this Ortiz fella, they worked this syndicate, the *bichote*. Angela Bivens *also* told me no one had a clue who the street dealers were and that was a lie. You and the DEA had info it might be Danielle Diggs. Real live, with Danielle, the plugger, gone, and a mess with the supply, someone's going to start pointing fingers and running fade. Watch for bodies to start turning up. Typically, that's the shot-caller's job."

"You been watchin' too many Discovery Channel shows. Abalos, take this big biscuit eater downstairs before he bleeds all over my carpet."

"Chief!"

"Dickie, let's go," Monica insists.

She takes my arm. I shake her hand off. Can feel the wetness in my eyes no matter how tough I posture.

"I'm a professional, not a piece of shit! I bleed yeah . . . I bleed because for two years I was watching you cops act like your own street gang, and I was the one protecting folk! But I couldn't protect my best friends on the street from that merc Burton Sugars . . . couldn't protect my . . . my Ernesto . . . Stripe. He was like my son, y'hearme? Your jakes been making sport of me out on those streets for years and then what, your Dante Antonelli . . . Deputy Chief of motherfucking Police, Special Opps . . . tortured my Stripe him, killed him. I'm no piece of shit!"

"I said get him outta here!"

It's a comic sight. Little Monica yanking giant-ass me from the room. As we hit the doorway I hear the chuckles and sighs from the cop braintrust, and then Patterson's voice.

"I'll handle this, Hobo Jim. Cause Lawd help us if we got to leave it back to you. Again."

"That went well," Monica snarls at me on the elevator.

"What . . . what did he mean about leaving it back to me?"

The doors open on the basement level. "I told you in McDonalds. If it wasn't for you, he wouldn't be Chief, I wouldn't be doing this. You're a bane and a hero . . . *Hobo Jim.*"

The nurse's station in the Daly Building's staffed by folk who look like they need a vacation, like some MASH unit after a battle. Not too much blood, though, but if anyone needs a tape-up, a spritz of lidocaine spray, some antibiotics and quick sutures—and pills, oh *lots* of pills—this is the place so they don't have to fuck with the civilians in the ER.

I'm getting a combo of all that stuff for my thighs, by throbbing head, as Monica finally lays down the law. "I'm sending Detective Gentry home with you. He'll post-up outside for awhile. You're right, you're the *ultimo hombre*, last one standing so let's keep you standing."

She's not even averting her eyes as I step back into my jeans. I tell her I'd rather have that Goins girl as bodyguard. She's looks like tough cutie-pie. "Bet she'd teach me some respect . . ."

Monica grins then we share a laugh. Haven't laughed, for real, in days.

"Real live, you might want to put someone on that Korean kid, from the corner store, if the judge holds him over. Anyone claim Dean yet? Parents?"

She radios for that Ken doll white guy Gentry then says, "So far a female, age 25, Aidy Voss? Come across her?"

"Most definitely. He was her spot those 'unidentified persons' shot up when Dean was on 'geographically restricted ROR' with the ankle bracelet. Figured it all scared her all the back to Austin . . ."

"I thought it was Cincinnati. That's how we found her because the marshals have all the details and intel."

Odd. "What do you mean?"

"Her father owns that house, not her. Investment property, I guess. But he lives in Cinci and she uses that address for college alumni mailings, IRS. I mean, there was some other address listed . . ." she monkeys with her phone, finds some digital notes. "Susan S. Voss . . . *oops*, yep . . . *Austin, Texas*. Must be her mom? Anyway, she's gotten in touch with Scholtz's folks."

"Still don't understand that relationship . . . Dean and his parents, this chick. They basically disowned him, but Hell, my girl LaKeisha says they were pretty much white trash so how you get disowned by white trash—he's the Princeton Man, got a new life . . . like this Ortiz fella."

I was the scholar-athlete. I was fixing to escape, too. Then came Esme . . .

"By the way," Monica says, "the Chief—he does respect you. In his own . . . way. Laid some crazy metaphor on us. You might not like it."

Girding my loins . . .

"He says he's got a spot on the Eastern Shore, bad cesspool. Shit's all hard and forms a seal and then there's gas forming under that. See, I told you it was bad. Well, he says someone's got to come 'bust up the crap, even if it's brown soup.'"

"That's me, huh? I've been called worse. "

"Keeps the whole place from exploding."

"So he's on my side?"

"Look, you never asked how much Apache we confiscated from Danielle's spot, fully cooked with the xylazine? A kilogram. Some plastic containers of NPP that add up to a liter or so. Actual White? None."

"Someone's been holding the main supply. Now I bet they are hoarding for a re-up."

She nods. "That's what used to happen for the meth, the rock. Even the K2."

"Detective Abalos, where you been all my life?"

She grins impishly. "Sadly, Gentry's waiting in the garage to take you home. I have paperwork . . ."

First thing I notice back at the crib is the red stop-work order's gone off the jont. With the migrant squatters gone and the garden variety ghetto phone store doubtless on a shit lease, I guess the junior robber barons can begin "rehabbing" the jont and get the City to move me.

The cluckers bumrush Gentry the Ken doll. I hear Patsy offering her *curriculum vitae*: blowjobs she gave jakes in parking lot down on 9th and N.

Gentry tells her to fuck-off; I'm too tired to teach him manners. He escorts me upstairs to tuck me in, says he'll be in a car parked on Georgia till after lunch; another plainsclothes will swing by tonight. I'm happy to have the .380 returned to me and you best believe I'll have that Glock Mini bump under my pillow. The second he leaves I shove the desk chair under the doorknob then dive into my rack . . .

. . . and so I got damn clue how long I've been out—the sun's still out but it's lower in out the window so it had to be at least three hours with me dreaming about Stripe coming here Jacob Marley style, telling me he's got a college diploma, he's married, he's got some high money gig and a baby.

It'd be nice.

My phone's rattling and I'm so mooshed I'm pulling the Mini from under my pillow and answering the spout. Could blown a hole right to my brain but, hey given the last couple of day would I have missed a beat? I check the nightstand and I can't believe what I'm seeing on the screen.

It's Verna.

"Can't talk long but . . . just got the word. Grand Jury disbanded."

"Huh . . . what?"

"My case. Aiding and abetting Linda Figgis. The government dropped the case." Suddenly we're laughing in unison. *"No probable cause to say I should be indicted."*

"I'm . . . so happy for you. I mean, you cooperated and they were only hanging some bullshit over your head anyway."

"Uh-huh . . ."

"What's your lawyer say?"

"She's . . . flabbergasted . . . never seen anything like this. It's as if—"
The flush of blood through my temples feels like it will burst head open. "Kill . . . oh Verna . . . I am sorry."

"I-I'm scared, Dickie. What the fuck does this bitch want from me?"

"Listen, stay home get things together for work. I'll . . . try . . . to . . . get to the bottom of this."

Tears are palpable over the radio frequency wave silence, then I hear, *"You wanna know what makes this worse, Dickie? It's because yeah, she wants you to 'get to the bottom of this.' Don't you understand? I'm a voodoo doll. She pushes pins in me to get you to jump . . . spending time with her, not me."*

"Vee, this murder case . . . it's crashing down, crashing in. I fear . . . fear Bivens might be the common ground here, too, but I don't know what the play is, I'm boxed in. I don't know what she wants."

I hear a sigh then, *"Don't be stupid, man."* And she's gone.

There's knock on my door and in the romance movies it'd be her. I pocket the .380 anyway because this is D.C.

"Who is it?"

"Open the door, Dickie, damn . . ."

Familiar yet not. I part it a crack. Must be over tired like a baby because I think I see Mattel and two dudes out on the landing. Mattel . . . how'd they get his chair . . . up three narrow flight of rickety-ass stairs?

"The fuck you get in here? Got a whiteboy cop babysitting me . . ."

Mattel rolls in like Ironside or a James Bond villain flanked by the dads. "You mean the whiteboy who was grubbin' Chipotle in his unmarked, then out on his lights and chased a couple Youngs in Civic what ain't got no plates zooming up Georgia? Five-O too short-dicked to watch yo' big ass, Mr. Touchdown." He looks around. "Man it ain't a shelter but I figured you'd be doing better than this shit."

"You saw the news . . . about the whiteboy who shot the kids from your hood. Case closed. And the Apache plugger, case closed." I squint at the chair. "How you get up here?"

"My boys lifted me."

"That's loyalty."

"That's the Deanwood Neighborhood Watch, nigga. And we ain't here to laud you. Hell back in the day I'd've sprayed your door wid my chopper for what you did to my jont, man!"

"You saw the news . . ."

"You missed one thing, man. Shit the news kept small onaccount it wasn't some Young shooting up a store, or a zombie bashin' in another one's skull fo' they benefits card in a fucking tent city, or shovin' a housewife in front of a Metro to take her purse for ten dollars. Some fat mug in a wave cap waxed two dudes used to deal for the Tranq for Gestapo right out front of a Exxon Station off Southern. Jumped in a black Nissan, driven by another motherfucker ain't nobdiy seent before. Hour later, two of Gestapo's lil' gigolo's bought it."

Jesus Mary and Joseph.

"Just like I told the Chief. But I was selling wolf tickets, bluffin' for time . . . but . . . kill . . . you blaming *me* for this?"

Mattel nods.

"Get a grip, moe."

"You ask your boy Croc. This stuff is old, old school from '80s, '90s, man. Clean up, for the re-up."

"You mean . . . shot-callers?"

"You the college boy. What's the college words—they don't cotton to a 'power vacuum.' There's product out there wid nobody to move it. Money ain't comin' in. Zombies to be fed. My folks here say if shit really gets bad we goin' see mo' Mexicans come here, like that shit in *Scarface* . . . grapplin' hooks and choppers with banana clip magazines. Trust."

Yeah, I'm back on my rack, head in my hands. No way Bivens noodled this part out. Unless her girl . . . my girl . . . Esme suddenly became an expert on . . .

"Cartels," I think aloud.

"All this game is a new game, not like old days, but if shot-callers be out here cuttin' ties, that's who they be checking the product for. Like I say, some *Scarface* bullshit. And you stirred that shit up in my backyard, my nigga."

Suddenly there's a news update streaking across my awakened laptop screen. Looks like Bivens has struck again. Like a thunderbolt . . .

> . . . D.C. GRAND JURY RETURNS PROBABLE CAUSE DETERMINATION THAT INSURRECTION, CONSPIRACY LAWS WERE BROKEN BY TEXAS SENATOR AND CLOSE TRUMP ALLY BROM VITTER. TEXAS GOVERNOR VOWS STATE WILL SERVE AS "SAFE HARBOR" AGAINST FEDERAL PROSECUTION OF VITTER, AND HONOR THE SUPREME COURT'S TROUBLING IMMUNITY DECISION PROTECTING THE FORMER PRESIDENT DESPITE RUMORS OF DRUG TRAFFICKING BY DONORS OF BOTH MEN. IN A STUNNING REVERSAL OF FREE SPEECH POLICY, CERTAIN SOCIAL MEDIA OUTLETS SAY THEY WILL REMOVE ANY POST LINKING EITHER THE FORMER PRESIDENT OR SENATOR VITTER TO TRAFFICKING . . .

"That don't concern us here at all, Dickie. Thas Mr. Charlie versus Mr. Charlie shit."

Maybe not.

"You still haven't told me what you want, Mattel. Coming all the damn way across town, middle of the day."

"Croc. Got a biz proposition for his fat ass."

Bullshit. "This a shakedown because you know better than to bring your middle-aged posse over her to bag me."

"Look . . . I ain't the feeble mug sellout y'all think. Been keepin' an' eye on your big ass since you stumblin' through my hood, Dickie. Yeah, bad shit come like the plague behind it. Somebody—wonder who it be?—blast on some junior gangstas down near Gestapo's territory . . . then Gestapo gets lined by Twelve after I hear you come back, fucking wid some Koreans?"

"Get to the point," I'm zipping up my Goodwill shop canvas jacket. They're snickering at my ends but they're the one's dressed in FedEx togs and janitor overalls. "So you still the man."

"Oh, stamp. You know your jont in Capitol Hill . . . Seward Park near the Metro Station, while back? Wild west shit. In my new role as grant recipient and 'certified violence interrupter' I gots a po-po monitor in addition to monitorin' yo' ass. You had a run-in with some swole niggas in wavecaps. One took some ACPs from your mouse gun, another be speakin' Spanish?"

Now he's not wasting my time. "Yeah . . ."

"Ole school assassins. Paid for but maybe not. One of my guys say they made two muvfukkahs like that. Muscled-up niggas, peas in a pod, throwin' down lots of paper all through Ward Seven. First indication of their nouveau -riche-ness was at a cabaret, down Benning Road, 'round Fourth of July, maybe? They was armed to the teeth, sellin' wolf tickets on any other crew . . . which was crazy overkill if all they doin' was featurin' titties an' ass. I mean Putin versus Ukraine hardware. I ain't stay alive this long widout cataloguing weird shit, I know you know whut I'm sayin'. They local niggas but weird not just wid the guns and money but onaccount they speak Spanish ta each other yet it ain't Puerto Rican, Dominican . . . like any other dark niggas what speak Spanish . . ."

"Interesting. Like Mexican, maybe?"

"Uh-huh. So whether they the niggas what fucked wid you or not, I can't have well-armed niggas in my backyard especially wid a zombie plague as well, wiff-out bein' a well-armed nigga too, catch my drift?"

I do. "You got Croc's kind of cash?"

"Now it's your turn to get a grip, Mr. Touchdown. Your boy needs to just sell me what he got, and the ammo, and we deal wid a reasonable price."

"It's the 'funny' paper that costs. Only suburban moms and Trump lovers at gunshows who get the easy permits. Second Amendment never applied to us."

"Stamp—Second Amendment was *onaccounta us*, bruh. See, I can be book-smart like you! But I ain't got *all* these bleeding heart pale people and sistas wid P-H-Ds an' African soundin' names fooled: still can't get licenses for some of the weapons we *do* got." He hands me a slip of high school, three hole notebook paper filled with scribbles, figures. "Call that our purchase order tell him we a five-oh-one-C-three nonprofit organization so he can write it off. Ha!"

And with that they literally dismount this motherfucker and piggyback him down the stairs . . .

. . . and no real food up in here so I head out on the street, down to Harvard and Sherman to my new go-to now that the CVS on 7th Street's been erased. Was convenient for all my meds from Dr. Gupta, but then VA switched to "mail order" so I got to put the word out the folk at Chuck and Billies, and the Spirit Lounge so it filters down to the cluckers and random package thieves: don't fuck with my deliveries. Okay yeah things have slid but Katie's only half right. Wasn't the armed robberies that closed the store, mind you—I fucked up my share of knuckleheads in that jont—but rather, the *siafu* army ant-like shoplifting. Could've given less than a damn when it was Tide and Advil they were housing and the city was literally letting them sell the shit on the card tables at the corner, but when my tinned meats started disappearing I knew it was the endtimes.

See, I'm sussing all this out as I amble down Harvard Street toward a blinding, setting sun. Shades are pretentious; I'm using my left hand as visor and it's tough to clock anyone coming toward me. If they're ghosting me I'd be pretty obvious turning my big ass around to look every five seconds. Since Mattel took off and there's no sight of my MPD babysitter.

The Pleasant Plains MiniMart down on Sherman doesn't have the ambience of disdain Kang-dae's jont effused. Just an Ethiopian brother at register, no Plexiglass. He knows my brand of bologna to fry, white bread that's not sprouting mold, apples with few bruises, cheap yellow mustard. That's good eating, I don't care what anyone says. It'll calm me better than the food my occasional windfalls allow me to get some-times, in places that used to shoo me away with the end of a broom or snow shovel. I guess I could take what's left of Bracht's money and get the fuck out of the Nation's Capital, but how far could I get when I have a peculiar little valentine who runs the FBI, DEA, Marshals?

When I come out with my vittles and coffee, the sun's casting distorted shadows up the block, now making it impos-sible to scan for trouble. Yet trouble seems to find me, easier. I mean, I got a good catalogue, to use Mattel's terminology, of the local colonizers, from the young couples pushing $900 prams to the hipsters who either barely tolerate me or their hounds who bark on sight.

Yet the two Caucasian fellas lingering at a light pole . . . never seen them on this block before.

I stop and pretend to take a call but tap the phone camera; one of these dudes looks like a Japanese manga character— thin build, squinty eyes, oval face with a pointy chin . . . stiff blond hair covering half of it. Blue pullover . . . camouflage patterned chinos, dusty cowboy boots. The other's hulkier and in Jordans, a pair of black sweats, black hoodie. Hood's up and drawn; no way it's that chilly out here with sun still out.

The proof of the pudding is when I do a right-face into the narrow walk connecting Harvard Street with Girard. I'm a big old man, so like a big old boat I can't turn on a dime like I used to when I was Number 88, but the cut's abrupt enough to—per my camera screen—peel those two off the pole. I'm moving fast but not frantic so they won't think they've been made. This would be a route home anyway, taken by someone who skulked in alleys not so long ago.

When I turn up Girard, back toward Georgia, here comes Manga out the alley first, then Muscles in the sweats.

Aw . . . shit. It's all swimming back into my dome now. I check .380 in my waistband.

The sumbitches from the Ford, the F-150, there in Seward Park. Minus their darker skinned minions whom Mattel's now claimed to have made. Hell, if they're pros, real gunsels working for a *bichote*, they likely were on Mattel's ass as well. We're all amateurs when compared to Mr. Charlie's level of thuggery. Nah, Burton Sugars, Bracht, even Chief Linda Figgis and her erstwhile rival Deputy Chief Antonelli never taught me that. I learned that loosing my scholarship, enlisting, suffering fools in the Air Force who dropped fire on people who's third cousin might have been a terrorist, watching rich landlords bounce single moms' from apartments then me and Stripe'd come along and scavenge their shit we'd pile on the curb in the rain not an hour before . . .

. . . and so I dawdle to draw them out and the sun's going to dip out very soon and there'll be ample shadows to give me chance to find a blind, but what fucking sense does that make? Like I said, am I up to ambushing them? Too many old folks and kiddies and hipsters still lingering around anyway.

Yet I'm catching a notion. A tactic, from my "Hobo Jim" days . . .

. . . so I'm doubling toward Harvard Street . . . lead them way down to Euclid. They're going to have earn this. Give me enough time to get home and fort-up.

Not a soul on this particular piece of the block looks like them; all the whitefolk are at the gym or out sampling artisanal mustards. No bourgies or buppies or Howard students, either, to save them. A minefield and a sliver of pure hood that rivals Gestapo's little patch of paradise, and on what's probably going to be the last warm late afternoon until Spring, so the folk will all be on stoops and porches as if it's midsummer at midnight . . . chilling and milling . . . toking, drinking while obnoxious pee wees skitter and scream.

The minefield? Fall's sumptuous, tall ginkos lining the block . . . leaves already a brilliant yellow despite this global warming shit . . . and fruit all over the damn sidewalk like orange snotballs . . . smelling like a combination of semen and vomit . . .

Folk wave, nod at me. The duo tailing me, already bogged down by the stinky slop soiling their no doubt prize boots and kicks, are now getting some hood love. Thrown shade or having shit thrown at them. Hopefully no one will try to bag them but these two will likely duck and cover rather than draw a glizzy on folk in broad daylight. Indeed, I crouch under the stoop of an abandoned rowhouse and watch as Manga and Muscles retreat.

Welcome to D.C. Probable cause that you fucked up. And the probability that I might get shot at again, real soon.

CHAPTER FIFTEEN

Ain't Your Ride or Die

SECURE AT THE CRIB BUT BY no means safe, I scoop up the mail, jump inside, double lock the door.

The mail's some junk, some shit from the VA . . . and a square peach colored envelope, no return address. The cat's flat on its back, dead asleep as I come through the door, doesn't even get up to stretch. It's breathing and looks like it's dreaming and I envy the little motherfucker. I grab my skillet, light the stovetop burner for my fried bologna feast. You got to cut the round pieces so they'll tent-up properly. With three slices sizzling the cat wakes and I finally check this nicer stationery.

Postmark's D.C.; it's a parchment and tissue paper greeting card and I immediately go to the signature. Aidy B. Voss.

Mr. Cornish, thank you. You saved my life, Woody's . . . and put your own on the line to protect Dean. It was not a fool's errand. He could have been saved. He chose not to be.

Funny, how'd she get my address? Probably Helen Yi.

I make the toast in the grease, fetch a plate. Guess Aidy's like me. Everyone else is dead. Me with no faith in Dean, her with blind faith in Dean. I jump on my phone, text LaKeisha. Be nice to find this girl and talk. Nothing else nice out there . . . two gunsels ghosting me and I'm waiting on Twelve . . . or Bivens . . . to swoop in and tell me what I should do.

Mom would say go to Mass and pray.

I implore the cat to chant with me. "*Sancta Maria, Mater Dei, ora pro nobis peccatoribus, nunc, et in hora mortis nostrae . . .*"

Amen. And it's got my dome clickity-clacking . . .

I punch up the girls' room phone.

"*Lord of Night's Watch . . . you just texted me so why the call?*"

"Yeah . . . um . . . in addition to finding this girl . . . can you find me reports, articles on when the China White combined with the xylazine really started messin' up town? Already know the White's arrived."

"*Yep. You died for awhile from that hot dose.*"

I let that slide. "By the way . . . stay away from here. I've had some weird company lately and Twelve's nowhere in sight."

Takes a couple of tries before I get through to that Goins chick, the sorority-looking young MPD dick. She apologies. Yeah, short staffed. But there's something popping off she says, Feds ae all abuzz about this Vitter thing, threats on witnesses and it's got nothing to do with me.

I let the cat lick the mayo and crumbs from my now empty plate. And then there's someone at the door, again. "This better be Abalos and more cops!"

She says nothing and hangs up on me. Yeah, thank you MPD . . .

I move to the side of the door as the knock repeats. The Mini's out, I pull the slide, trip the safety.

It's a deep syrupy female voice next. Bivens, playing cute? Not even she's this nutty. "Open the door. It's okay."

Something's not right. "V-Verna?"

I trip the deadbolt, the knob lock . . .

"Come in." Those are the only words I get out when the scent hits me.

Coqui Coqui.

It's a couple of seconds to adjust, compose myself, think it out . . . I mean, in the lunacy that's followed the fucking nano-second she floated back into my life on Bivens' AnnTaylor coattails, I've almost consigned her back to universe of abstractions. But here Esmerald stands . . . no red dress, no make-up really . . . jeans, sandals, plain white tee shirt, simple short jacket . . . stygian hair with that swirl of gray pulled into a knot and ponytail . . .

The obvious question isn't how, it's why. And don't say you still love me after decades of thieving, squatting, lying . . . pushing me from sherm sticks to blow to rock and finally skin popping. You don't get redemption for that by saving a couple of mestiza teens from being slaves to old fat men . . .

"Because I could," is the answer that fucks with me. "We're alive. People who are alive, Ricardo, should not play dead to each other. We are not *los monstros* . . ."

"And you're Uncle Sam's property . . . they just let you up and slide out the door?"

"I came with a guard. Outside."

Those two gunsels, Manga and Muscles I left in the ghetto gauntlet and sticky ginko? They out there, still?

"May I . . . come *in*, Ricardo?"

So I motion with my head. I stumble to the kitchen sink, douse myself with cold water. When I turn I watch the cat leap into Esme's arms and she squeaks a bit, delighted and surprised, it sounds.

I'm not delighted. "*La bruja*, with her familiar?"

"Don't be cruel, Dickie." I never liked it when she'd shift to my nickname; always sounded like "Dee-KEY" with her accent.

I motion her in, scan the landing and stairs, shut the door.

"I thought you were a dog person. *Me dijiste que los gatos te asustaban . . . no se podía confiar en ellos, eh?*"

"*No, son las mujeres en las que no se puede confiar.* Cats are good company because they give you space. Dogs are all up in your shit twenny-four-seven."

She doesn't even ask to sit, she just grabs my desk chair, plants herself as she strokes the now purring cat. She gives the furrball a smooch and looks me over. "Look at us, with our gray hair and our eyes, all ringed. You have a tummy now."

"You have a big ass."

"I always did, and the thighs. And the *tetas.*" She grins, hoping I will but I'm trying not to even look at her, head-on, as if a real ghost. "That's why the boys couldn't stay away. In Mexico . . . or here . . . at Howard. But see in Mexico it was a curse to look like me. Used, thrown away, or kept in a cage? At college, with *los negros Americanos* . . . well . . . I could set the terms, as long as the sistas didn't kick my big ass, eh?"

I lean on my meager, unstable kitchen counter. "I recall."

The cat bounds off her lap, curls up on my braided rug in the middle of this embarrassing hovel, this sty. "Listen. They don't let me out often and I must admit something to you. I didn't want to come here. *No.* I was frightened of so many things between us . . . I couldn't."

"Kill . . . *Angela Bivens* sent you?"

She nods. "More like, allowed me to leave."

"She's been clocking me this whole time."

She nods again.

"She know there's about to be a war over in Ward Seven, not to mention a couple hundred sick fiends looking to get well and yet no Tranq?"

"We're prisoners *mi amor* . . ."

"Don't call me that."

"Remember how I read the *Washington Post* always to help me with my English, understand things? I read much this week about a case she says you were working on . . . yes, she knew of it. She wants to help you, and you, to help her."

My phone's buzzing from a call. As I reach for it on the night table I mutter, "Why can't she just leave me alone."

"Because she knows you will not leave *her* alone."

"You're tripping now."

"Because you love the truth so much. No rest for you till you find it. That's the difference between you when I first met you, when we first made love, in the dorm, and smoked our first sherm stick . . . and I had you, Ricardo."

"Stop!"

I answer the call without looking. It's Verna. *Of fucking course*, Mother Mary, why not? "Vee . . . I can't right now."

"*Dickie . . . listen! I'm about to—*"

I click off. "I'm a husk, Esme. And old, pained husk . . . in over my head."

"*No.*" She moves next to me on the counter. Takes my hand. Lord our hands look so different now, the even her scarlet polish has dimmed. "You are the man *now* you were always supposed to *be*. I envy you that, *mi amor. Lo juro con mi vida . . .*

She lays her head on my shoulder and fuck if there's another knock on my busy door.

Through it I hear, "Dickie I tried to call but you were duckin'." Yep. The universe is in full fuck mode tonight. "Dickie? Come on let me in!"

Esme touches my arm as I get up. "The woman from the shelter, SFME?" she whispers with a tearful smile. "The one who was always trying to clean you up? *Brava chica . . .*"

When I open my dor Verna looks up at me and smiles . . . looks past me and the smile disintegrates. The cat runs into head, sensing what's coming . . .

"Oh my . . . my . . . *God*," Verna stammers, as if coming out of coma and the first thing that happens is she's punched in the face., "That's . . . *her*?"

"Sit . . . please."

"Fuck's she doing here?"

"I came to—"

"I-I didn't ask you. I asked *him*."

"It's Bivens, Vee, all her at DOJ . . ."

"*All*?"

"Don't trip. Please, Vee."

I know her look, her body language. Hell, and Esme's. One's getting as jittery as a mongoose, the other's coiling like a snake. Only this time they have a common enemy. Or meal. A pigeon. Me.

"Dickie, called my lawyer's office thinking, like shared with you, that dissolving the grand jury meant I was in the clear, or at least I'd have immunity. Then I find out the government did *not* grant me immunity. They just dropped the fucking charges . . ."

"I don't understand why you beefin' on me for that? That's *good news*."

"No. It's not."

Esme's shaking her head . . .

"Yeah, this bitch knows the score," Verna sneers, crossing her arms, cocking her head.

"Please don't call me that," Esme says. "We're both in a trap."

My big brain in my oversized head finally breaks through the sentimental bullshit and hips me to back reality.

"DOJ . . . can reel you back anytime? Shit . . . that's worse than immunity . . . at least there you can testify and you're done, clean slate."

She's nodding tearfully, retreats into the head, slams the door.

Esme recites the obvious. "She was probably very happy until she heard the details, read the fine print. Like I was. I missed my home here, despite the pain and the horrible things. I missed . . . you. I'm not a smoking-gun. I'm only a walking-talking evidence authenticator, adding nothing new. Bivens could have kept me in Mexico, guarded, taken my statements. But she wanted me here, to push *you*."

"Dammit." I'm trying my best to ignore her, or at least compartmentalize her bullshit because it's all bullshit whenever she talks, rationalizes, asks for understanding. I knock on the door to the head. "Vee?"

I hear, "They said I was a little fish not worth the effort, nor were the Child and Family Services people they were going to indict on. *Poof!* Moved on to shinier toys. Did you give 'em the shinier toys . . . you, with this murder trial now *over* because a racist jumped out of a hospital window?"

"It's not over, truly," Esme adds, talking into the door. "I'm the reason all of this started, years ago, when Jaime hired Ricardo to find me, the girl . . . the baby. I was weak. I was Ricardo's—what do you call it, 'ride or die,' but I was afraid and could do neither for him . . ."

Before I can swim in the thoughts Esme just imparted, Verna bursts from the head, leaving a flushing toilet and numerous tissues wetted.

"Again—bitch did I ask you? *Huh?* Huzzy who destroyed this man's adult life . . ."

"I did that, Vee, not her." I can't believe I just defended *la bruja* . . .

"*Nah . . . .nah,*" Verna hisses, now pacing the room and both the cat and Esme watch, intently. "I believed in you. She bugged out when you needed her, almost dead but for some defib shocks. I allowed you put my life in danger because I know you'd protect me. She runs for cover. She comes back *why*—because her life or freedom's on the line? I came back because all I have is you. *I ain't your ride or die.* I just want some peace and normal shit with you and I know that just isn't going to happen . . ."

She moves for the door but I block her. Time to end this. "Don't. No. We are going down to Main Justice if I have to storm the place and get her attention. Or this new crib of hers at the Navy Yard, I don't care." I look at Esme. "Your escort knows how to get in touch, right? Their supervisory agent, up the line?"

She plops back onto my rack. "Yes."

"Oh no, you get up, you just may have to take us, then."

"Are you mad, Ricardo?"

"In both meanings."

"You're straight-up bullshitting," Verna huffs. "I'm going home.

"Unh-unh. You're coming too. You got lucky coming her safe."

We hit the street and it's dark and would be somewhat calmer but for the streams of sharp white headlights and dim red brake lights on Georgia, the honking horns, the loud-talk of the usual customers and loiterers in the neon glow of the phone store.

I sense something's not right two seconds after we hit the street. The banter's flipping into bewilderment . . . and here comes my clucker Wilhelmina, skittering fast, boney arms flailing. In a flash of headlights I see her prominent cheekbones wet with tears.

"What we goin' do—'bout that man back there?" She's squeezing me like I'm her daddy and the looks Verna and Esme are throwing now are priceless.

"Willy what's up, huh?" She smells like stink fixed with hair spray.

Suddenly, Esme cranes her neck toward a parked car, shakes her head and moves away, first in a slow walk, but then in a frenetic trot . . .

"That man . . . in the car, Dickie . . . he chokin' an' I seent blood. I ain't goin call Twelve..I ain't no part of this shit. Fuuuuck . . ."

I hear Esme scream. Heard it before so many times.

Yet only Verna and I are running toward the trouble, along with random whitefolk and a Howard student from the campus across the street. Everyone else is moving away, *fast*.

It's a tan Chrysler . . . D.C. plates . . . recall from my YouTube vids, how-to on being a PI these things are usually the unmarked Fed car of choice.

And in the driver's seat, slumped onto to the armrest, a young white man in a gray suit is wide-eyed and gurgling, wheezing . . . grabbing at his throat to plug the geysers of blood spraying the windshield . . .

. . . so there's common gasp before the hollering. A yuppie's already on 911 . . . I'm shouting my lungs out "MPD! *Monica!*" like I'm a crazy person, waiting for the promised babysitter to materialize.

I yank open the unlocked door and the Bison kid, then another judging from his sweats and windbreaker, pull this dude out and Esme's pointing, whimpering, "A-Agent Butler . . ."

Verna tells them to tear off his suit jacket blazer, his feet elevated and use the jacket to put pressure on the wound.

I'm grabbing at an agitated, pacing Esme. Never saw that coming. And then . . .

"The fuck?" *Is that real?* A hole in the passenger side window. Size of finger . . . spiderweb cracking radiating from it.

I'm pulling Esme closer, just to calm her. "Ricardo! *Alguien nos va a matar!*"

Finally I catch a that Goins chick charging up the block. She's carrying radio and stops at us, breathless and probably wondering who these other three women are, one wraithlike in stained.

I point to the Chrysler, the frantic efforts to save this poor guy. "He's a Fed. Someone just shot him. Call all your backup!"

"He's almost bled out!" Verna calls from the pavement.

"Hold up," Goins says, grimacing.

PAMF!

The Chrysler's sideview mirror just above Verna's head explodes.

Sound-suppressed shot. Can't be anything else . . . just like at that chick Aidy's jont . . . and coming from the dark, just like that night.

"*POP! POP!* POP!

Those aren't suppressed and Lord knows where the rounds landed. Or maybe that's the point, as a tumult of gasps and hollers hits my ears; the sidewalk either clears or everyone's diving for the pavement. Goins draws her Glock puts both me and Esme beneath her so I know this chick's not a poseur. But where to return fire in the bedlam? The stampede of terrified folk even surges onto Georgia Avenue. Cars are screeching to a halt on Georgia, one's rear-ended with a frightful crunch and I'm smelling gasoline.

Goins is calling for backup and I'm already hearing a siren from the first 911 calls. I grab the cop's arm. "Get us outta here!"

"What, no way. I have units coming in and an ambulance!"

"That Fed was guarding her!" I point at Esme. "He was executed. You're guarding *me*. Nuff said!"

She cries out some weird noise then calls Abalos on her radio and on-rushing units dodging traffic. I literally have to hook Verna away from Fed and drag her.

Esme's already in a sprint, shouting, "Where is the car? How do we get away?"

Goins points to a Buick across Fairmount. We duck and tail Esme to the car, Goins unlocks the doors as I swear another suppressed round whizzes by my head. We tumble in.

"We're going . . . to the Daly Building . . ." Goins pants as she starts the Buick in one providential twist of the ignition.

"No, Kennedy Building, Main Justice!" I yell. "You radio the Chief, the Marshals, the FBI I don't care . . ."

She hits the siren and activates the small running lights and we blast down Fairmont to Sherman, close to where I first clocked those two gunsels. Guess I can call them gunsels now because I'll bet a *hell yes* over a *damned if I know* the round that took out Esme's driver came from the same sound-suppressed iron that aerated Aidy Voss's jont . . .

I look to Verna and Esme, hunkered down in the back seat. "Looks like you both are ride or die now. I'm sorry."

CHAPTER SIXTEEN

No Favor

THE CHATTER AMONG GOINS' RADIO, UNITS on the scene a by my crib and the MPD command staff is pissing me off: the gunfire is listed as just more of the same knucklehead bullshit, random street violence. The Fed took a stray round.

"You believe that?" I growl at Goins as she guns the Buick across Rhode Island, almost taking out some dumbass nighttime cyclists. "Now are you taking us to the Justice Department or not?"

"Not," this chick huffs. "HQ is the best place to be until the Feds and the Chief get on the same page."

"Ain't a page to get on, Officer. Fed's been shot . . . whomever did it pumped in rounds to flush us out. It's textbook."

"The Hell you know about 'textbook,' Cornish? You learn this on the street because you've taken fire? Or at some academy? Nah, I heard it was YouTube! Now get outta my face!"

"You're a real sharp lookin' sister, Officer. Be a shame if I were punch your damn face in if you get either of these ladies shot." I look back at Esme; she's shaking her head. Verna's spattered with that agent's blood. "This woman back here's a Federal witness. She just called her handlers and they are likely chewing Patterson a new one so let's just get to Kennedy and—"

My phone is rattling in my pocket. It's LaKeisha.

"We're okay, did you hear?"

"*Yes . . . good . . . safe?*"

I toss Goins a look. "More or less. Look, Verna's with us."

"*Us? I don't—*"

"Keesh no time to explain. Esmeralda Rubio is with me and Verna in an MPD unmarked. Headed to the Daly Building but I'm tryna get this jake to take us to Main Justice. The Marshals, FBI, should be all over this . . . anything else?"

"*Oh . . . alright . . . yes. A lot. M'lord the Tranq . . . Apache . . . it started as a trickle, a novelty, around Twenty-nineteen, right when I went to rehab the first time. All those rumors about it being dry through the pandemic—it's true, as if by design. Only exception is the little bit of powdered blow the Mayflower people still use . . . and prescription pills. Appears Deputy Chief Antonelli in his Special Opps Division knew about this and the 'displacement' starting around Twenty-twenty but never briefed the Mayor until new personnel took over at Justice as the Trump Whitewalkers went back north of the Wall.*"

"Where'd you get this?"

"*Washington Post, MPD's own reports . . . white papers with USDOJ after Trump's out and the January Sixth mess. Right in D.C. Public Library database, ain't a thing.*"

"Keesh I got to go."

"*Wait . . . forgot . . . I tried to get word to that Aidy Voss woman, regarding Dean Scholtz . . . there's something strange and—*"

I'm hearing Patterson himself on her speaker now. "Keesh—text me. Bye." I turn to Goins as I see she's cutting straight through the light once we reach Indiana Avenue, rather than left to access the main Pig Poke. Nor are we busting a right to get to the RFK Building.

"What?"

"You were right. I'm to take you to new location, turn you over to U.S. Marshals."

"Main Justice—RFK Building?"

Guess not. We're heading across the Mall, Capitol to the left, Washington Monument to the right . . . straight toward the restaurants and toney shops of the Wharf but that can't be right. I get my answer when Goins jerks the wheel left, as if avoiding a tail, and hits the entrance ramp on the 695 Freeway.

The only secure Fed jont this way is across the Frederick Douglass Bridge into Anacostia to Homeland Security's HQ— but has this gotten so far out of hand, so big as to put us in that James Bond shit?

No, we exit right here. South Capitol Street. Where we started, at least Verna and I. St. Jude's . . . the men's shelter, connected by that glass corridor to SFME, with its brand spanking new children's dorm—Verna's legacy.

"Dickie . . . what's this all about?" Verna calls from the back.

Esme gasps. "No . . . no . . ."

"*Tu sabe?*" I ask her.

"You . . . you will see . . ." she whispers, almost as if she'd rather be a sitting duck out on the boulevard.

We're smack in the Navy Yard's Oz-like gentrification ground zero. I eye some high rises east of the baseball stadium. And I now I feel like I'm sinking into the seat as two cars with blue running lights intercept us. Goins cuts hers and the siren, lowers her window as the suits approach.

"Good luck Cornish," Goins says with a sigh, looking cute again. "My orders are to take Ms. Leggett home. I'll leave a unit in front of her place."

"No . . . Vee, please . . . stay with me."

"*No* . . . this sounds good. I want to take a shower. For days," Verna says. "Good-bye, Dickie."

Stamp, I wondering if I'll see her again.

Outside the window in the blue flashing lights one of the suits overhears, barks, "You two then, out of the car . . . get in the back."

"Vee, please." I mutter. I swallow and get a little more sand into my nutsack. "I'm not going if Ms. Leggett's getting kicked out. Go tell your boss that. She lives down here now, right? That's why . . ." I gesture, ". . . all of this mess?"

"Go," Verna whispers. "Dickie, I'll be okay."

Esme's already out of the car. I nod, I get out. She's not even looking back as Goins peels out. About a hundred people are indeed looking at the spectacle from the street corners on M, so the Feds shove me in the back of their boxy ride and away we go . . .

. . . five minutes and a quarter mile if that . . .

. . . into a warren of smoked glass and terraced condo buildings, with weird sounding pizza and sundry shops in the lobby. You'd never have known this was the pre-industrial heart of the District at one time. That's why the British burned it all first after drubbing "a well-regulated militia," leaving the Capitol and White House as an aperitif.

Esme's trying to hold my hand. I glower her fingers away.

The suits park in a garage off Tingey Street, named for a commandant of the Navy Yard, and shove us into an elevator that opens in the lobby of avant-garde art and a waterfall. They glower anyone trying to get on away, and we are soon on the 7th Floor, stopped in front of door decorated with a huge wreath of fall leaves, nuts, pinecones and rosemary sprigs. All real, living until they were shellacked and glued.

A beefy sister wearing short tan blazer and black answers the door the door and ushers us in. I see her badge and those of the suits in the cars now in more detail. She's a marshal— an Amazonian version of those biscuit-headed niggas Equal Protection and Due Process. The suits are FBI. All except one depart; he posts himself in the hallway.

The place is filled with cardboard boxes of various sizes, some open with packing paper or bubble wrap spilling out, some still sealed. Beyond them are floor-to-ceiling windows . . . through the clutter I can see the twinkle of the Douglass Bridge and it's reflection on the Anacostia's wavelets.

The only thing unobscured is a huge bare wall off the foyer, and there're paintings stacked below, still wrapped and padded. Yet someone's already mounted a few displays. Framed front pages from the *Washington Post*: twin psychopath serial killers die, a whole crack rock crew and its network taken down along with a self-styled South African Zulu witch doctor. Massive Medicare fraud uncovered. Oxycontin docs, drugmakers bankrupted. I get closer. No pics of her. Just her name . . . under the bigshots' by a paragraph or two.

Yet when I move further into the enclave, two of my senses instantly overload.

Smell: bacon cooking. Burning, even.

Sight: a cloud-puffy long beige couch to my left. On it, a laptop and a few papers scattered on the cushions . . .

. . . and the Public Defender, Helen Yi.

It's like my tongue's been cut out, shoved down my trachea and I'm about to pass out . . .

. . . and the wraith stands, smooths out her skirt and all she can manage after all her bullshit is, "I-I apologize . . . and I'll explain."

I hear, "I'll apologize, too . . . for the smell. Can never get it right—something as simple as bacon."

Whipping to my right . . . over Esme's and the Marshal's shoulder . . . there's a long galley kitchen and wisp of smoke hanging over a shiny stovetop. Angela Bivens saunters closer, carrying a sandwich on a plate.

She's yet another incarnation: flip-flops, Georgetown gym shorts, a gray sweatshirt with faded letters spelling out "FBI Academy Quantico, Virginia."

"BLT. I get peckish at night because I never seem to have a proper dinner." She looks me up and down, sighs. "Too bad sandwiches only taste good if someone else makes them. Marshal Greene, you hungry? There's a dill pickle on here, too."

"No ma'am," the Amazon snaps-to and replies.

"Dickie?"

I'm stung. Poisoned. "Wha-What?"

"*Dickie?* Hungry?"

"Fuck . . . fuck no. W-Why is Attorney Yi here?"

"Let's all sit down," Bivens says as if this is a cook-out spat between cousins. She calls out a male name. "Michael!" A young Asian dude, looking like he could be Yi's son, I swear, navigates the towers of cardboard boxes and other crap and dutifully presents himself. "Take Ms. Rubio to the bedroom where Special Agent Saloniki has set up his gear, make her comfortable.

"I want to stay," Esme insists. "I am not happy. I saw a man shot!"

"That man was a seventeen-year vet of the Marshal's service named Charles Blount. He left behind a wife and four . . . *four* . . . children. Now please go with Michael."

"Dickie . . . *por favor*!"

"You heard her."

Dude pulls her away and I hear mumbling, curses in Spanish. Not cursing. *Curses.*

And thusly cursed, I point at Yi. "*Why* is she here?"

"Dickie," Yi begins. "I owe you . . ."

"Helen . . . stop," Bivens calls, grabbing a glass of water from her sink. "It's a debriefing."

"Bullshit!"

"Alright then," she brings her sandwich and water over to another chair, moves a box out as a makeshift table. "Sorry for the security but since new indictments came down, especially on Vitter, rightwing radio and social media have been publishing my personal information, enabling the MAGA cult to phone-in bogus police and fire emergencies at my mother's house, at my old address."

"Bully for them."

"Aw Dickie you don't mean that." She looks to Yi. "Helen he's a big man but a gentle giant."

"You been marionetting this from jump, haven't you?"

"*This?*" She takes a bit of her sandwich as if we're all friends about to watch a movie in that huge living room.

"Dean Scholtz . . . Diamante Diggs, Arthur Sellars," I begin. "Three nobodies, who died . . . all conveniently to serve your scheme to fuck Bracht's pals, cronies of the old president to save the current one."

"You a nobody?"

"Yes."

"Well you're *not*. Neither is Helen. Helen here was a Three-L and mother hen for our section when I was a first year evening student at Georgetown. She took care of me when I was utterly lost and surrounded by the kind of type-A personality sociopaths I thought I was supposed to be jailing at the FBI." She wolfs the rest of her snack. "Never cured me of stress-eating, however, right Helen?"

I can hear my pulse thumping in my ears . . . her glazing and gassing has got me just two seconds from . . . *what*? Jumping through a window like Dean Sholtz? Punching them all and running from gun-toting Feds?

"Stamp . . . I jumped right onto y'all's spiderweb as if it was kid's trampoline, didn't I? You needed me on this all along."

"Uniquely situated," Bivens says with a sigh. "I believe you verbalized it perfectly for Helen when you jumped the gun a bit, stirred things up too early: you go into the cut, do you thing. I needed someone to stir things up."

"What, did you give my predecessor a heart attack so I could get the job?"

Yi, almost in a whisper, replies, "No . . . he was corrupt, sick anyway. We had a legitimate opening . . ."

"Right. What if I were to walk out of here now and straight to CNN or the *Post*. Better still Fox News? Imagine what your staff, the people disbarring you would say, *Helen* . . . and you'd have it easier than your girlfriend, Mighty Mouse."

I hear the Marshal, pacing. She probably heard me. I go no issue with grappling to get out of her and I will certainly leave Esme's ass here no matter what she "testifies" about me.

And yet is just sitting there, all calm, as Yi sheepishly searches the papers scattered around her. "First, *Mighty Mouse*?" Biven squawks. "Second, she's not a girlfriend, she's a mentor and friend. Third, I think you know that going to the mass media is neither your style nor your forté. Being a tool. A blunt instrument, is . . ."

I shut my eyes. I've heard this before, like a reel that never re-loops. Dipped in shit.

"Then tell me, *both* of you," I groan, as if I'm running my tongue along a razor. "What was plan B if I hadn't taken the bait or wasn't geeking for work . . . hadn't left that sob story message on Yi's answering machine?"

Bivens sets down her plate, walks right in front of me now. I'm a tree to cut down. A por troll in chains and helpless.

"Here's the story, then. When I read the files on Jaime Bracht's death I saw a familiar name. When I allowed Police Chief Figgis to spend two weeks with her wife and children on the Outer Banks before reporting to Federal prison I asked her about that same name. She said it belonged to a homeless ex-addict . . . whom she *also* hired and who's testimony was putting her away albeit for thirty-six months rather than the twenty years she deserved . . . and I asked her, if you were me, besieged by Republican traitors on the Hill, armed nutcases out in the hinterland believing anything on Twitter, troubled by infiltrators and incompetents—would you trust, even hire this man again, despite his betrayal?"

I swallow hard. "She said yes, didn't she."

With a nod Bivens adds, "And when the *Federales* on the plane at Dulles turned Esmeralda Rubio over the FBI, the first thing she said in English wasn't 'I want a lawyer.' It was a *name.* I would have had you out there, working for me . . . .*me* . . . one way or another."

I'm sinking slowly onto a small, rusty metal folding chair, inapt with the style and expense of the other furniture, a temporary convenience. "You're no better than Bracht, or Linda

Figgis . . ." a voice says in my dome and somehow escapes from my mouth.

"Dickie," Yi begins.

"Helen, you don't need to—"

"Angie . . . he's *owed*. Dickie, the only January Sixth defendant that my office represented was a joint effort with my federal counterpart. That person was a friend of Dean Scholtz. Dean was merely videoing the charge on the building and attack on the police but didn't go inside and it appeared neither did our client. Until sentencing on a plea deal . . . the client went berserk, attacked the marshals, my staffer, the federal PD . . . even his own friends among the spectators in the Gatekeepers . . . Dean included . . . allowed to attend and were on TV and conservative talk radio the previous day proclaiming his innocence. Before he was tased, tackled . . . he screamed at the judge something like, 'What they can't take, they'll taint, rot from the inside, and you all are too stupid, animals, *p-word* fools to see it coming.' His first night in the jail—"

"Central Detention Facility," Bivens corrects.

"Thank you, Madame Deputy Attorney General. First night in the CDF . . . he's supposed to be in COVID isolation. Rather, he's put in with a known plugger . . . who's being held pending trial for transporting Mexican White. By the second night, he's shanked by this inmate. This inmate eventually dies of COVID-inspired pneumonia six months later, before his trial, reneging on a deal he's made. His deterioration sped up when under the watch of a C.O. transferred to the hospital pending numerous misconduct charges that couldn't be dismissed outright . . . she was union shop steward entitled to temporary transfer . . ."

"*Gestapo* . . ."

"Fentanyl . . . xylazine . . . was arriving like a plague, displacing . . ."

". . . the rock, the smack . . . the boat, the Tina every-thing . . ." I muse, recalling LaKeisha's research.

Bivens adds sternly after sitting, "Coinciding with waves of migrants who're seeking asylum from gangs and such, from Peru to Mexico. Coinciding with the renegade Chinese pharmas transferring more lab capacity to sites in Mexico, as Esmeralda has witnessed, among other things. Coinciding with utter chaos at the border that we are laboring to control and certain allies of the ex-President who I am putting on trial have exploited . . ."

"And Danielle was getting her first taste of the new product, because Tina, COVID fraud, slumlord shit was boring her, huh?"

Yi and Biven nod almost in unison.

Bivens says, "Thanks and quite by accident to you uncovering what you did on Dante Antonelli, DEA realized why it was running into the same walls and denial with the fentanyl that AFT repeatedly faces with right-wing law enforcement, legislators and gun show operators—when the end users are not people of color. Linda Figgis was more concerned with the murder rate, keeping a truce with Antonelli, PR with Congress and maintaining the funding with the mayor and your circus of a city council."

"Dean . . . this kid Ben Ortiz . . . how'd they get mixed up with Tranq?

Yi adds, "Dean . . . and Ben . . . I suppose they were true believers. From what we pieced together from our old Capitol Insurrection client and sadly, Dean's own words . . . Ortiz genuinely felt he was doing his patriotic duty—*revenge*. Flood this evil Capital of Deep State World Government Mixed Race Toilet with zombie makers—this Capital that holds January Sixth patriots and Christians hostage. I can't say there aren't millions of sick people out there who agree."

"Then he was sicker than Dean."

"You ever been to the border?" Bivens says. "He comes from a family of Mexican-American Border Control agents who have no issue with jumping on a big horse and riding down mothers and their children who look just like them one day and supervise trafficking of fennie precursors like NPP the next."

She stretches, kneads her temples like she's recounting some old ABC After School Story.

"People have *died*." I turn to Yi. "So you were going to supervise me digging up shit to sabotage that poor bastard Dean's defense till he turned, became your big witness?"

"No . . . *no*," Yi fumbles.

"MPD Homicide in on this too?"

"*No*," Yi again says with a gasp. "They're in their own world, obsessed with closure rates."

"*Helen shut up and let me handle this*!" Bivens commands. "If need be, *scare* Scholtz into cooperating, when he was looking at real time. Markowitz didn't know. He's a lazy arrogant lifetime civil servant who thought he had a headline-grabbing slam dunk. Who was I to disabuse him of that."

"Until you swoop in for the *deus ex machina*, right?"

"Listen to me, Dickie, you're a bull in a china shop . . . yet you fancy yourself a surgeon."

"The new Chief of Police called me a shit stirrer."

"He was paying you a compliment. But you *are* a neophyte . . . sometimes that works in your favor. Sometimes it doesn't."

I anticipate the next question. "Speaking of favors . . ."

She throws me a weird smile. "Ah, well. *This* isn't the favor. I'm offering you a gumshoe *job*, cutting you loose from Helen, here, basically."

So I am no longer the jock then, homeless dopefiend hobo, goon . . . stupid animal?

"Go fuck yourself."

That's my answer.

Both her and Yi's jaws go slack and the marshal's headed over here to give me some black girl magic up'side my head. I stand but this Amazon's not impressed.

"Back down, Mr. Cornish," Marshall Greene admonishes.

"Dickie," Bivens offers, "the election's now barely a month away. Don't you want to save your streets . . . save a nation . . . ?"

"Nah, nah . . . street won't change no matter who's in charge. You send two motherfuckers to beat me, make me more pliant—and you're better than people like Vitter? You bigshots, you profiling on Martha's Vineyard. When I was on the street I was just a filthy animal to y'all. These kids out here robbing—throwing away their lives—just ignorant little urchins, monkeys to y'all . . ."

"Dickie *no*—you are being—"

No privilege to speak, not this time. "*Listen, goddamit*! But whenever you need to put something on Mr. Charlie and show him you got the juice, suddenly y'all're loving us with equity, telling us we're kings and queens. Well, I wake up every morning and I smell the equity. Know what'll make us just as crazy as Mr. Charlie beating on us night and day? More equity. We need honesty. A foot in the ass when we fuck-up and a ladder to get over the walls. We don't need more equity from you even though you got us trained like parakeets to say it . . ."

So she's quiet now . . . doesn't even look at Helen Yi. She moves to the huge picture windows with the panorama of the illuminated Douglass Bridge and the Nats ballpark glowing like a giant holiday punch bowl for the final game of a dying season.

"You aren't that naïve," I hear her whisper.

The Amazon counsels her to stay clear of any line of sight but the mighty little chickenhawk just stays there, bravely, or maybe utterly absorbed or self-absorbed. Rather, I watch as her breath fogs the pane. Not so . . .

"You ever ask the street 'why you?'"

"I don't understand."

"Why'd you survive the indignities, even death?" she murmurs into the glass, "when most human beings last only one cold winter, one scorching summer. But you lasted . . . *decades*."

"I dunno."

"I ask 'why me?' When I faced terrors worse that bullets. Alone, usually. No cavalry to the rescue." She turns, faces me. For the first time I see . . . fear. "Listen, I was wrong, so wrong . . . for manipulating, orchestrating. It's not me . . . I wasn't always like this . . . schemes within schemes, power. I was mentored by people who only knew those things. I don't even know who I am . . . depending on what pill I take to go to sleep, and what pill I take to smile at people in the morning. I am *so* sorry I hurt you. I'm one of the most powerful people in this country, Dickie . . . yet I am that callow little black girl in the library . . . worshipping . . . *a bronze god* . . . who ignored all those skeezers swooning at his feet yet would always smile at *me* . . . when even my vain sorority sisters took me because they needed my GPA . . . then ignored me, teased me. *That* little black girl's asking for your help, just this once. *No favor.*"

I nod. What else am I to do? Walk out?

"You got your cross, I got mine. Let's not compare nails, okay. I just want to know what you want, within reason, so I can get out of here, make sure my friends Katie and LaKeisha are alright . . ."

"Thank you," she mouths. "I tried to do right by Ms. Leggett. I hope you and she will, well . . . ."

"Ms. Leggett's already done with me.

"I'm . . . so sorry."

"You did *me* a favor. I'm no good to anyone. Never have been."

She neither smiles nor sighs.

"Would a two thousand dollar contract do it? Three? Probably nothing compared to what you have hidden away of Bracht's . . . while you eat catfood and freeze or boil in that your hovel on Georgia Avenue. That I'll never understand . . ."

Bivens motions to the Amazon to approach, and together they disappear down the hall, leaving me alone with Helen Yi. Finally. She doesn't get off the hook either.

From the concrete-topped long kitchen island I say to her, "Attorney Yi. There is still the vegetable that's Arthur Sellers . . . his Tranq zombie mama, a brother and sister living in a van. *They need help.* And—I can't find Aidy Voss."

"Um . . . I don't know about any of—"

"Your girl Angie here basically said the game's up so stop playing me. You and that Markowitz fella need to get this woman and her kids off the street, her into a hospital and rehab and them into a shelter and I don't mean like the old Munie. I mean Verna Leggett's SFME."

"I'll see what's possible . . . even it's not really my issue anymore."

She won't even look at me as I press, with more bass in my voice, "Of course it is."

"I-I'll try. And what about Aidy Voss?"

"She took Dean's personal stuff for his parents I hear? I want to send the parents my condolences but I'm confused . . . does she live in Ohio or in Texas?"

"The house deed was in her father' name it turns out. The Marshals will get any message you want to Ms. Voss."

We both turn as we hear footsteps on the hardwood. And I smell the Coqui Coqui.

"Fuck's this?"

Esme's toting a small suitcase and slinging a cross body clutch.

"MPD has the street your street on lock," Biven says, "so no one would suspect she'd go back there. Just one night, she'll be safe."

"Or she's bait?"

"Don't be melodramatic or silly. Give Marshal Greene your phone . . . she'll fix it up with an app that will allow you better communication with our group. And us to track you incautiously when you call."

"Like Burton Sugars did when Bracht pulled me out of the St. Jude's shelter?"

"One night for Uncle Sam, for *me*."

"Until you call in your favor."

"And you'd be wise to say yes." She winks.

I hand over my phone and get a lecture from Marshal Greene on signs and counter-signs. She's getting an attitude with me—the phone's a hood brick job LaKeisha helped re-up after—and Bivens has to hip her to what she calls my "photographic memory" or what Daddy called yet another affliction.

"Mr. Cornish . . . this here," she hands over a padded envelope with something that literally looks like a fat button inside, "is the jewel so don't mess it up. There are instructions so study them carefully, read them through at least once first . . ."

"What is it a grenade?"

"Don't clown me, Mr. Cornish. It's got a range of about five to seven miles and a two-hour battery once activated. It will transmit, as long as it's relatively dry and not too far underground, to our data center in Greenbelt and create an audio file. A last resort."

"I get cyanide, too?"

That re-engages Bivens' gasface.

"Marshal Greene," I say to the Amazon, "you know Marshals Adonis Taylor and Frank Siddiqi at the E. Barrett Prettyman Courthouse?"

"Yes, Mr. Cornish . . . Madame Deputy Attorney General's staff already briefed me on your interaction."

"*Interaction*? Please do *me* a favor. Give them this message word for word: I don't blame you. Despite that—mind what I told your asses about a one-sided beating."

Now, I am owned by the Feds. Now, I am haunted by the truth. Can't say I'm better off. But at least I'm alive, for now.

CHAPTER SEVENTEEN

Family Ties

We eschew the fire escape and slip into my building through an old coal boiler basement entrance. I can hear the rats rustling in the dank darkness as we feel our way through cobwebs. Even down there I'm wondering where we are going to sleep. I guess I'll be on the floor.

The Marshals and FBI assholes bunking at Bivens' taxpayer-funded palace in Navy Yard basically handed Esme a big Macy's store bag containing a pillow and some linens! Ain't that a bitch. Guess the national debt won't worsen; the floor will be fine for me, then. I've slept on worse.

Indeed, Esme's said nothing since we got dumped back on Georgia Avenue. Good, as I've not said a word to her, nor am I interested in what she has to say.

I pause at the landing, about to insert the key. I hear the floor squeaking beyond the door and unless the cat's grown to the size of a puma someone's in there. Only two others share a key but given the last couple of hours' lunacy gesture to Esme to stay quiet. No way anyone laying in wait inside the apartment wouldn't have heard us trudging up the stairs but I move to the left of the door, give a rapid knock.

"Dickie! Don't play!"

I exhale whole lungful then say, "Katie nobody said anything when you came up, no cops, no one greazey-looking?"

"Nah-unh." I hear the locks disengage. She peeks out her
ruddy round head, brick and gray hair tucked under a baseball cap. "Feedin' the cat is all. Keesh been blowin' up Verizon
lookin' for you." Quickly she realizes I'm not alone.
"Oh . . . dayum."

"She's staying here at least overnight.

"She the rolla who turnt you out so long ago huh?"

My girl doesn't mince words.

"*Muy mala!*"

"Esme go inside for God sakes."

"*Coño* . . . don't order me around . . ." She pushes past us
both with her stuff anyway.

I shut the door and give Katie a look. Yeah, I don't like
defending Esme but I don't need shit now. My head's already
pounding.

The cat runs to me, meows and mewls then runs back to
Katie's slippered fat feet.

"I'll be goin' now anyhow. It's fed and you best better get in
touch with Keesh." She's leans into Esme, who's already parked
herself on my rack, the only other proper spot for a lady to sit if
you don't count my desk chair and the john. "Kill . . . Miss
Thang, actin' more like a white woman than me . . . I wasn't
throwin no shade. Like the Bible says, everything's connected
under Heaven. If you hadn't turnt his big ass out . . . we wouldn't
have been with him on the street . . . and ain't none of us woulda
survived, regardless of all the evil your Morticia Addams lookin'
self brought back with you. So *thank* you . . . and *fuck* you."

Katie grabs a denim jacket, keeps on those damn slippers. I
catch her arm before she moves toward the door.

"I'll walk you to the bus stop."

"You got business. I be okay." She eyes Esme. "Watch her."

"Yeah."

"By the way . . . Keesh say that Aidy girl . . . she work for the President, alright, but her Daddy, shit, go on Keesh's Facebook, if you wanna see . . . Aidy's daddy worked for your girl here's brother Bracht . . ."

"Half-brother, *puta*!" Esme shouts.

"Esme! Chill!" I take Katie aside. "Fuck you saying, Katie?"

"Uh-huh," Katie sneers over her shoulder at my guest. "Conrad Voss? He was partner at Jaime Bracht's equity . . . finance . . . whatever-shit jont . . . in Virginia . . ."

"The Argyle Group."

"Yeah, before it all went to Hell, thanks to you, Big Black Man! But check your email."

I nod, give her a hug. The cat protests her leaving it alone with us . . . strangers.

The clickity-clack's up and started again but I mumble something to Esme like, "There's nothing in the fridge but bad milk I guess . . . some juice . . . I got crackers . . ."

"We've lived off less, Ricardo. I'm not hungry. I need to wash up. I'm sure the bathroom is nothing worse that I've seen . . ."

She rolls into the head and I don't even give it thought that she's the only person beside Stripe who's devious enough to find my larder, my stash, my past—all holed up in the tiles behind the john. I don't care. I replace her on the mattress, resting my chin on my fist. I'm staring at my dresser and what's in the top drawer: the "Mini," loaded with a full clip. Now, on the dresser top: Mom's rosary. On the walls . . . my smudged mirror, my framed pics of Stripe, Black Santa . . . Mr. Fred,

Miz Eva . . . and suddenly I'm thinking about the Mini again and those gunsels and how a .380 isn't quite going to cut the muster.

Luckily Melvin's been by and I got some Valium in here somewhere. I spot the vial by the kitchen sink, pop it, swallow and hang my mouth under the faucet to chase it.

As it eases down I dig my phone from my pocket and see the three messages from LaKeisha but I ring Croc instead.

"*I told you to use my niece, fam'ly.*"

"It's way beyond that shit now. By the way, I saw Mattel. Says s'up. He's neighborhood watch . . . on city payroll as a violence mediator."

"*Another hustle. Whatchew need, then, moe. I got shotguns . . . in case your girl don't put Trump in the cellblock and he's back on the block. I plan on being an expat in the Caribbean. Wanna come? Same old-ass Israeli dude up in Silver Spring who does the gun paper does flawless passports. No logjam from gubmint shutdowns. Brown yet not too midnight black motherfucker like you might like Belize or Guyana. I'm checkin' Nassau . . . more good trouble with the tourists.*"

"Might need something bigger than the LCF. Nine milli-meter? No shotguns. That's your and Melvin's thing."

"*Back in the day it was comic books and jimmies. Now all your ass wants from me is irons and my damn rides. Kill . . . you should come to my crib and check out my toy though. Mossberg. Best shotgun in the world, baby. Not one of them booyahs Melvin rocks in his damn jacket to house a 7-Eleven if I wasn't payin' him! Peace.*"

It's then I notice one of the LaKeisha's texts . . . "*By accident on Facebook,*" and there's a screenshot. The caption: "*Florida vacation, Christmas back when Santa was real, and he brought Mommy back her brother my Uncle ♥.*" Aidy's account.

I slide to my desk and get on my laptop as Esme comes out of the head. Just a tee shirt, gym shorts, flip flops. Hair, half split over both shoulders—one section reaching down to that ass . . . one that would rival any woman half her age, the other covering breasts that have lost only a small bit of lift from the dirigible pneumatic aggressiveness of her youth.

Maybe it's the Valium . . . tough to shake off the vision. She's lingering behind me, clocking the screen.

"This girl, who works at the shelter under the Leggett woman . . . she lets you use her Facebook?"

"She does a lot for me. We all trust one another. When you left me, when I O.D.'d . . . they were my family . . ."

Wisely, she shuts the fuck up.

I find Aidy Voss's profile. Only a few pics are public but there's the family shot, from when Aidy was in middle school, if that. But it's her. And . . . it's weird. Dude with the BDUs . . . sandy camouflage pattern not standard for any branch of the military I've ever seen, he's got on aviator frames, balding, maybe in his forties . . . but with a brown Grizzly Adams beard and is kissing a woman who's clearly Aidy's mother while holding little Aidy's hand.

Dude is familiar. In a prurient, itchy way . . .

"Ricardo . . . *que es?*"

"*No sé . . . pero este hombre . . . mírelo con atención.* Strange . . ."

The last text from LaKeisha says, *These people are bad. These people of Casterly Rock. The uniform I recognize it: DoD standard for all contractors in Afghanistan, m'lord. But which? Blackwater? MPRI?*

"He's private . . . security," I say, as if she's in the room with us.

But it's just Esme and me. Like old times. Her hand's on my shoulder, her hair's draped over the shoulder, cascading down to my chest—that macabre ribbon of silver accenting the black. Yes, her cheek's now touching mine and I swear I want to tell her to move but I don't. You'd think I'd know when this bitch was salting me with those titties on my back. But . . .

"*Oye.* Can you show me . . . the boy. I know all about what you did. Bracht's old lawyer, the family. Bivens told me. She knows everything."

"Why am lunching? Of course she knows. "Aleksander Nimchuk . . . he handled it. I paid him with Bracht's money."

She nods. "She doesn't know the baby's new name. Or his new parents. *Mi corazon* . . . my dear Piedade's baby boy. Maximiliano. She'd be smiling from Heaven."

Still, she protects that little bitch. I'm too tired to fight but I draw the line anyway. "I don't think Purgatory's quite done with her yet, Esme."

Remarkably, she relents. "Or any of us. Do you have pictures?"

I let her rest her chin on my shoulder now. "Even better."

With LaKeisha's Facebook account I find Donna Marino and Kevin Merrick. Two pretty ordinary whitefolks. She was an old Obama campaign worker who got a cushy job at the Labor Department when grandpa Biden was elected. He just left the Navy and joined a software design firm. Can't access their pics but LaKeisha taught me how to switch over to Instagram, which is private, but then to Donna's TikTok listed in her profile, which is not . . .

"Oh my God . . ." I hear very close to my ear—with a little gasp, a little giggle. A big boy named Jagger, celebrating his fourth birthday and a full three years with Donna and Kevin, shows how brave he is by jumping into a foaming turquoise wave with his daddy at a resort on Puerto Rico.

But then her mood darkens. "He looks like his real father did at that age. He's has bad blood in him."

"He's around good people. They'll raise him to be good."

"*El Patron,* he would bring me around Jaime, he'd say 'Play with your tiny sister, she is your blood.' He would say, 'She is from one of the pig-bitches you fucked.' He was only eleven, maybe twelve, when he said that . . . so blood is blood."

I push away from the desk. Bracht hired me to hunt her down and when I found her, all I wanted to do was hold her, kiss her, when I had every right and reason to choke her out. Now, she rises like a ghost yet again, and the compulsion to grab her by her neck . . . is slowly, God . . . stupidly . . . ebbing.

"You ruined my life, left me . . . twice . . . to die, and then to wander, alone . . ."

"You were not alone. You had that woman. That *Verna . . .* who always wanted to save and fix you *Dee-key . . .* and she did. Where is she now, eh? I took you as you were, when you were a baby . . . a fucking boy . . . in the body of big, muscled monster with your nose in books when you weren't playing boys games . . . when you were a fiend and drunk and your dick didn't work . . . and now . . . an old man. I never tried to fix you." She's standing over me now, chest heaving, face florid. "And you know what, *cabrón?* You never wanted me to change either, eh? You came for that baby, for Maximiliano . . . *and me . . .* that night you killed Jaime."

I'm flushing all warm on neck, my ears, like an instant fever. I don't feel the serpent in my gut. Just it's laughter, in my ears. *Go an' get that pussy what kills you, Junior!*

No idea how she just lands astride my lap. Like it was planned, like it was a pre-cut puzzle piece.

No, I'm thinking about Verna. I'm not thinking, period.

She yanks off that tee shirt and I see those tits again . . . yeah sagging, a few blue veins . . . but still the ones dudes drooled over even when we were dirty and squatting when I got out of the Air Force . . . because we dudes are foul. And she shimmies out of those draws, genuinely sticky because you can't fake that. She seems shy about her how those ample hips, that ass has grown. Lord, even the white fellas, used die over both whenever she'd dance. Not a thing wrong with what the years have done to them since.

She doesn't seem to mind what the years have done to me. She smiles at how the crane needs a little more steam to crank-up and I take no offense because she does so as she caresses me, whispers wet encouragement in my ear.

And when we're all hugged up . . . and I'm inside her . . . she weeps.

I try not to weep myself . . .

. . . and so I have no clue what time it is, just that it's dark . . . no traffic or sirens on Georgia, no damn dogs barking or rats flipping garbage lids in the alley.

"This is the first time we've done this . . ." I begin during this a lull in the sweating and gasping, "when you didn't get all crazy with the Mayan-witch-*hechizo* . . ."

"That was just to piss off the Castellan white people in the family. And scare the *babosos* and all those mean girls at Howard saying they were going to fuck me up for stealing you away. Ha!" Suddenly she sits up, knees to her chest points out in the shadows. "*Mira*. I don't have to be *la bruja!*"

I clock a pair of green eyes peering back at us.

"Katie should've taken that cat. They can't have mammal pets at their group house but they can at their job, ironically."

"She works for that Verna?"

"Uh-huh."

"Verna who helped the Chief of Police take babies and children from their mothers on the welfare to give to rich white lesbians."

"*No*, not exactly," I grunt as I twist onto my side. My sweat's made me cold, so I gather up the sheet and blanket around me. She's glistening yet seems fine, silhouetted against the alley light diffused through my grimy blinds. "Verna looked the other way. Lot of the woman . . . shit, teenage girls . . . were in the SFME shelter. Some of them were in and out . . . reached thirty years old with five kids by five different dudes and the oldest often was making them grandmothers by thirty-five, easy. Verna got frustrated."

"No excuse."

I don't want to argue. I yawn and ask her to come under the covers.

"Run out of steam, *viejo*?" she teases.

"Sometimes . . . Stripe'd call me that."

"The boy . . . I thought he bedeviled you? He was a thief and the Malva Salvatrucha boys wanted to kill him because he was an annoyance."

"Turned his life around. Worked with me. Racist cops murdered him. Too many people around me got killed, and then the pandemic came and more died in the hospital or on the streets. None of the people who really had it coming, though."

"Just Jaime?"

"He's the only one I'm glad is dead beside a few cops and Burton Sugars."

She relents, folds her voluptuous flesh into my poor dry skin under the sheet. "I know many powerful people in

Mexico," she whispers, "who love Jaime, *still* . . . and they know people in Texas. Bivens wants more names. Connect to people in the Congress. Donors, businesspeople . . . and they all know about the fentanyl. If they make money from it, give the money to the Trump folks, she says she wins."

"She was never going to use you to hang a murder rap over my head, was she?"

Even in the dark I see her shake her head.

"But she is reckless, *mi amor.*"

"Don't call me that."

"Sorry. Look at us. What do I call you?"

"My name."

She sighs and continues, "Bivens . . . always seems to be plotting but she isn't. She fights with the little man her *jefe* . . . Garland . . . all the time, in front of Biden they say. She says there are men in her Justice Department . . . who think like Jaime did, who love Trump in secret. Certainly, the FBI, but also Marshals, Border Patrol, even DEA, Customs. I hear her say she cannot guarantee my safety. I think she just wanted me out of her sight tonight because I reminded her of how out control it's become. I feel more scared," she takes my hand, "then when I was on the run with Piedade and the baby. At least Jaime was not going to kill me."

I think about those two redneck looking gunsels then check my phone. There's a message from that Amazon, Marshal Greene, in the elementary code she didn't think my street-addled brain could handle at-a-glance. Bivens wants me to deliver Esme to the RFK Building at ten a.m. then stand-by. They'll send a black Ford Explorer, Maryland tags, running lights clearly visible on the dash. Pick-up on Georgia and Euclid at 9:30.

"Let's go to sleep."

And we do . . . okay, at least she does.

The Valium keeps me from staring at the ceiling all night but I'm already awake once the first taste of orange light tinges the curtains and the birds out there chirping. There's a cryptic text from LaKeisha. She doesn't sleep either.

How late did you keep Katie at Winterfell?

Check that later. For now, I get back on Facebook and enlarge that old pic on Aidy's page . . . the dude in the BDUs . . . the contractor. On another window search for the dad, Conrad Voss. So I'm sitting there, naked in the chair as Esme snores, musing how any ten-year-old kid could find shit on Conrad Voss better than me.

Turns out he's easy. He's from Ohio, moved to Texas, then Northern Virginia for his stint with Bracht's fund, then Ohio and back to Texas. His wife, not so much. So let's roll the dice and hope they land on anything connected to Conrad in any way.

Elizabeth Voss? Elizabeth S. Voss? "Betty" S. Voss, of Austin, Texas?

"*Dee-key*, what are you doing?" Esme groans from under the blanket. "What time is it? *Hay café?*"

Then, on the screen, in Google . . .

"What the—"

I stand and the chair almost flips. I haven't taken my piss pills in a day so I swear a drop or two spills on the floor . . .

Betty Sugars, of Austin, Texas. And her brother, Burton, announcing his retirement from the U.S. Marine Corps.

I click back over to that Facebook pic, on Aidy's page.

I don't realize for a few seconds that Esme's right beside me, wrapped in a sheet, and she's gasping through her fingers, mumbling in Spanish and then, "It is *him* . . . but who the fuck is she again?"

"The . . . ginger," I mutter.

I'm not the one who pranced into the spiderweb. It was Dean.

"You . . . you must tell Bivens . . . *now,* Ricardo. This girl . . . she must . . . must know you then, and me."

Ice cold . . . to sit there with me *and* set him up. Probably hired those two in the wave caps as expendables, decoys? Great actress; leaving the dog out there was a nice touch. The gunsels . . . they must be with hers.

"We don't have time to tell Bivens and wait. Get dressed."

My phone rattles and LaKeisha.

"Yeah . . . Keesh, you would not believe what I found based on your lead from Facebook!"

All I hear is sobbing. This from a woman who neither laughs nor cries. "*The House Manager woke me . . .*"

"What?" And I feel like I'm sinking in the dirty floor.

"*Bed check. Katie never came back. That's why I texted you. What's happening?*"

"Baby . . . shush . . . call in sick at SFME and stay put. Tell Verna to do the same. I'll explain later, okay? Tell the House Manager to call Dickie Cornish if there's a beef . . ."

I cut off the call just as another's coming in. I don't recognize the number and when I've seen this shit before, it's been from a burner, not spam. I tuck up my nuts . . . literally this time as I'm nude . . . and answer in a slow bass, in my monotone.

"If this is who I think it is, don't touch a hair on Katie's head. Speak."

"*You're in no such position to break bad, nigger.*"

That's a voice I've heard before. Yep. "You're made. Seward Park? That damn F-150 pick-up. You hurt Katie, I'll kill all of you, except the dog. I like the dog."

"We got family all over the place. Including eyes on you now. Stand down and let's talk as if you're a civilized white person. Nothing's stopping our return, election or not. But we aren't savages. Taking the fat bitch was to get your attention. Speaking of dogs, you wanna be a street dog all your life, or a rich man, not worrying about what these apes and insects from shithole countries are doing next, able to take care of the ones you care about?"

"I'm listening . . ."

"Welcome to the family then. Here are your instructions."

CHAPTER EIGHTEEN
The Low, Low Down

"*YOU WERE TOLD NOT TO CALL this line directly,*" Marshal Greene barks at me, clearly groggy.

"Wake Deputy Attorney General Bivens up."

"*I'm not at liberty to do that.*"

"She's not with Helen Yi. So who is she with—Merrick Garland? I want her now."

"*You need to stop. Now, she's been called to a seven a.m. emergency meeting at the White House, yes with Attorney General Garland and others so what's this about?*"

"My friend Kathleen Molly McCarthy has been snatched. I think by fentanyl traffickers, making the Apache Tranq out there. Same motherfuckers she thinks dabble in Republican politics, right? I don't know what they want. Can't be a swap. Esme's too important to Bivens and they never mentioned her."

"*Go on.*"

"No *you* go on. You get Bivens. I need a shitload of Fee-bees down here on my jont, ones you all trust, to get Esme out. You getting this?"

Dead air. I put her on speaker, as I'm pulling my one decent piece of black fleece over my head. Indian Summer's long retreated and the air's frosty this morning . . . radiator's commenced the season's first spit and clang in celebration. In another couple days it'll be summery again. That's D.C. Unpredictably predictable.

Like me.

Well, finally . . . *"Dickie, what the Hell?"* Bivens intones. *"Do you have any idea what you've interrupted?"*

I have indeed moved up in the world. "They've kidnapped my friend."

"Who?"

"My friend Katie."

"The homeless woman?"

"My *friend*. Katie. Your targets, or people who can lead you to the assholes in charge did it."

"How do you know?"

"You loafin' that much to ask me *that?* Look, they snatched her, and you better fucking get the FBI on Aidy Voss. Her uncle was Burton Sugars, the merc who was Bracht's cleaner, his muscle."

"My God . . ."

Something lil' brainiac didn't figure on, huh? "Aidy set up Dean Scholtz in business, like seduced him away from Vitter when he turned out to be a pretty lame MAGA soldier. Then he, in turn helped Danielle Diggs set up Diamante Diggs and Arthur Sellers. Now you have to find out who orchestrated this whole mess."

"My Lord. Rubio . . . is she safe?"

"Yeah."

"Still cooperative . . . after a night with you?"

"I didn't ask."

"Come in from the cold with Rubio, then we discuss Katie and next moves. But this meeting today has a direct bearing on all of this . . . including you."

"No. I left my friend Ernesto . . . Stripe . . . out in the cold and crooked cops wasted him. I got leverage. I won't let it happen again, this time to Katie."

She's anything but stupid. *"Dickie! You do not play chicken with my witness! Dickie?"*

"What did she say?" Esme presses as I swipe off.

"Hold tight. Stick close to me. We have to move."

This time I finally get Croc, who passes me mercifully to Melvin the Henchman with no lip. "You got anything for me?"

I guess this is why there was no lip. He's got extra clips for the .380 but nothing heavier. Just a patronizing quip about how the ACPs will do some damage. Yeah. If I'm right up on a motherfucker. I prefer not to go toe-to-toe with gunsels who are toting all kinds of hardware, and all got is an expensive mouse gun.

"Bring some duct tape," I tell him.

Indeed, Esme's eyeing me suspiciously as I fetch the LCF from my dresser, pull the slide and shove the holster into the small of my back.

"The FBI, the Marshals will protect us. You don't need that."

"I do. Come on. I'm making one last call, then we're out that back door."

"It's nasty."

"Uh-huh. And no one sees us."

I hit that last number. "Okay, where to?"

"You coming alone?"

"I'll have a driver. He's harmless."

"And you said something about collateral. They're pretty interested in that."

I eye Esme. *"Good. Give us an hour."*

I bring up this wonky app the Amazon put on my equally wonky phone last night. Hope it works . . .

. . . and so we're in Melvin's ride, rumbling across the Potomac with the Lincoln Memorial at our backs, I-66 sign ahead. The car's a bit too ancient for Croc's tastes—a dusty, musty 1980 beige Pontiac Catalina with a stained white faux-leather landau rear roof panel. But like everyone associated with Croc, their hoopdies had one common feature: V-8 engines that never seemed to get legit inspection stickers. And the clowns out ticketing on the street never seemed to get it that they were being conned. I suppose when folk were out getting jacked or shot . . . and plenty of money was coming in from speeding cameras . . . whether a sticker's phony or not isn't a priority. Good for me, though—past and present. Out to Bracht's jont in Pennsylvania, or where Linda Figgis had parked that girl in Harrisburg. A hoopdy with a V-8 engine's better than a helicopter!

By the time we negotiate the knots of Northern Virginia concrete ribbons leading to the Dulles Toll Road, Melvin's suddenly grumbling about not having an EZ Pass. Got to exit, head to Reston by regular streets . . .

Esme's not happy. "He's a fool. He's not a federal agent."

"No shit."

"Then who is he . . . he looks familiar."

"Senorita. I be Melvin Jackson. I work for—"

"He works for *me*. You're safe. We're all gonna be fine. Just stay cool."

I'm relieved all we have to do is stick to Loudoun County, Virginia. Figured these crackers'd have me headed out to a jont inside the Luray Caverns or some bumfuck bullshit like that. Still, it's unnerving to know that such neo-Confederate, neo-Nazis are *suburbanites*—likely on their way home from some pee wee soccer match or a couple holes of golf rather than cow-tipping and cross-burning.

We exit near the airport, follow some signs into an industrial park bounded by rows of squat, identical townhouses. Melvin's in his own head, and rather than repeating our battle plan he's musing why anyone would move way out here just to live in a townhouse or apartment.

"Some whitefolk will bend over backwards to get away from niggas an' Go Go music, eh?"

"Melvin shut the fuck up. There . . . the second warehouse. Get frosty."

Esme's now squirrelly and I don't blame her. I'm making this shit up as a go along and I'm a little shaky, too.

"*Coño Ricardo . . . qué demonios es esto,* huh?"

"Calm down."

"*Fock* you."

"The man say calm down, senorita," Melvin adds. He's chewing on hard on a coffee stirrer, I guess that's how he unwinds.

"*Fock* you, too . . ."

The place his huge . . . a white building maybe only two stories tall yet covering an area—eyeballing it—that could eat half a dozen of the fields I played on in college. There's an open bay, and the instructions said enter there.

"Melvin, text Croc. Tell him where we are, then go in."

"In there? Inside?"

Esme co-signs on the reticence. "What . . . is this?"

"Probably a bonded warehouse. Airfreight and such comes in from Dulles, they store it out here . . ." We enter and the space is well lit and indeed cavernous; just mounds of crates, other containers in isolated piles, seems like miles apart.

"They come in and load and unload. I'm sure this spot fills then empties daily."

"This they jont, moe," Melvin muses. "We a million miles from the street now." He pulls open his windbreaker to show me the taped-up grip of a sawed-off shotgun. A booyah . . .

"I asked for duct tape."

"Oh snap, I saved the roll . . . look in the glove compartment."

I do. I pull out the roll, then turn to the back seat and an incredulous Esme. "You aren't gonna like this part . . ."

That's when Melvin mutters, "Sheeeee-it" and I hear a car horn. Headlights flash . . . and the bay door behind us closes.

Ahead maybe twenty yards is that pick-up . . . the damn Ford. And another car. An idling Benz SUV, black, Texas plates. I'm siced. Everyone's at the party.

"Get out and distract them!"

Melvin's not a smart brother so he does what he's told. He hops out, hands up while lunge across the seat at a woman I hate and a woman I just blended not a few hours past . . . shoved my fist under her chin and in my best monster tone snarl, "Play along!" I slap a piece of tape over her mouth, red lipstick and all, and I twirl layer upon layer of it around her wrist as she writhes and kicks at me till the roll's almost spent.

Now, did I mention Melvin's not a smart brother? The booyah's clearly swinging from a strap affixed to his belt and that's making my old pals the gunsels nervous. To the point that I hear another horn and look up and even at that distance I clock Mr. AR-15, alright . . . no suppressor this time. Muscles! So where's Manga?

"Nigger . . . is that a sawed-off shotgun or your dick? Either way it's about to get shot off if you don't tuck it away! Now where's Cornish?"

"Here he go right here!"

I get out of the Catalina with Esme in tow and Christ I'm not sure whether she's in drama class or not when it comes to the muffled shouts and squirming . . . I now have an oozing cut on my cheek to prove it from one of her nails. Some verisimilitude, I guess? The pain in no way's reassuring nor are all those videos from pro PIs on setting up stings and shit. So easy when you stage them with your middle-age wife and fat nephews. Pretend you're pointing . . . extend the index finger . . . pull the trigger with your middle finger. Easy-peazey.

"Kathleen . . ." I call, monotoned, in character.

Manga in the house! The elf-looking gunsel pops out of the Ford and moves around to the truck bed. He and a third dude then wrestle with what looks thickly and sloppy rolled black carpet or large blanket . . . with plump pinkish feet flailing and flopping from one end. Feet missing a couple of toes. Fucking savages had her back there, exposed?

Funny, the third guy's white . . . but kind of dark, a bit short. As in darker than Esme and I swear just bit more Aztec in him but not enough to trigger the diehard racists in the leadership of who I think is responsible for all this bullshit on their side of the border.

Indeed, Manga shouts to his compadre, before I can warn the motherfucker to ease up on Katie. "She ain't dead yet, Pee-dro, careful!"

"*Cállate . . . cabron . . .*"

"Is that the collateral?" the musclebound gunsel with the long gun calls.

"Yeah!" I shout.

"Someone wants to talk to you about that. If they're happy, you all leave with this fat loud bitch, some money your pocket . . . maybe even a new job." He looks to Melvin. "Put the shotgun on the deck, Kanye. Cornish, you and cooze advance . . ."

"No!" I holler. "He's my insurance, you can keep yours. Besides, at this range, what's your worry?" I got this redneck thinking I'm an Army Ranger I guess but it's common sense. Melvin's booyah won't do shit unless it's close but I'll send some lead down-range aways, to disrupt . . .

Melvin snickers, fingers the damn thing anyway. "Stamp. Do yo' thang, moe."

I pull Esme forward. "Play it *cool.*" I whisper at her. "No one dies here, okay?"

The look she gives me, well . . . scares me more than the mare's nest I'm walking into.

"Oh my Gawd Dick they crazy!" Katie cries as they free her from the rug. The Latinish dude keeps a pistol to her head, however.

I watch the rear window of the Benz SUV lower. Yeah, I am far, far from the street but suddenly I feel a tingling in my throat, around my shoulders. Something brutal and primordially bad, you know . . . like I'm meeting Satan himself. This this the trash, the dogshit, that rolls downhill, that pollutes the street; it never spontaneously generates in the gutters, on the curb. Like the OGs used to say, no poppies grew along the shores of the Anacostia, no coca plants sprouted among the boxwoods on New York Avenue Northeast.

"Is this him, sweetie?" a silver-haired, well-tanned white man says.

"Yes, Dad," Aidy Voss hisses. She's glowering right at me. Very well-dressed, in a flowered dress, blazer, her red hair upswept . . . as if this dude had scooped her up at work for a pleasant father-daughter bagel and coffee and a chat.

Another male voice—disembodied yet and sounding pretty much executive whiteboy and nervous says, "Conrad, he's on the phone . . . the burner. And he's pissed. This is a lot of exposure. I mean he's—"

"Graydon gimme the damn phone!"

Graydon? Supposedly Dean's new attorney, right? The arrogance. They think they are so untouchable they don't even bother to come up with cover. Or . . . they're going to kill us all in a second. Time to find out.

I make sure I keep Esme very close to me, one arm across her chest and my head on swivel.

"You ape-looking *retard*!" Aidy screams, much to her daddy's chagrin while he's on the line with a big shot. "You fucking killed my uncle!"

"Aidy *shut-up*!" Conrad counters, holding the phone away. "Mr. Cornish here also killed this woman's brother. My friend. Didn't you?"

I nod.

"Just business, nothing personal."

"It was personal."

Conrad groans and says into the phone, "I can reason with Cornish."

"Put the phone done, Mr. Voss. Hands where I can see them, Mr. Graydon. Reduced to chauffeur now that Dean Scholtz took himself out?"

"I-I don't carry a gun," says a voice. "I do what I'm told."

Now I'm hearing some yelling from that burner. Conrad Voss's more concerned with that than me, and he spits into the phone, "I don't care! How dare you insult my daughter . . .

you know how long it took to get her into these idiots' good graces: college, grad school, the DNC? You tell those Spicks it was *their* idea to front the product here with these . . . kids, and that idiot Dean and muscleheaded fool Benny Ortiz!"

"Focus, Mr. Voss."

"You don't talk to my Dad, nigger!" Aidy adds.

"This like a *Love n' Hip Hop* episode," Melvin clowns.

Undeterred, Conrad shouts, "Revenge is bad for business. Wrecking this city merely to impress a bunch of hillbilly halfwits who go to jail on our behalf . . . embarrass local mongrels and corrupt lickspittles and a senile clown and a mulatto whore in the White House who embarrass themselves daily . . . and *you* have the fucking *gall* to lecture *me* about risk? You go back tell them we'll be concluding here soon—in a stronger position than ever!"

Finally, I watch him toss the phone back up to the driver; simultaneously the Latin in the F-150 leers at Esme and whispers, "*Puta.*"

Yeah, he's cartel . . .

Conrad Voss turns to me. "Apologies . . . *truly.* Not a good multitasker like Aidy's generation."

"Uh-huh. Someone mentioned jobs?"

"Yes. This game is a bigger P-I-the-A than anything in Mar-a-Lago I swear. But pretty good ROI, though . . . and those stupid Chinks turned over the fentanyl works for a pittance. Alas . . . Mr. Cornish, I'm just a bean counter though my opinion does count—I saved your life when my little girl wanted our South of the Border pals like Mr. Ybarra over here to bid out a contract on you."

"He's a homeless junkie nigger, Daddy. And that crazy old bitch wouldn't back me, either. She could have ended this a week ago!"

"*Aidy*! One more word, for Godsake . . ."

"Crazy old bitch?"

He calms then smiles. "No one you need to know—yet. Especially since you come bearing gifts. Ms. Rubio can connect too many dots. Too many people close to our true leader, our true president, our true destiny. You have spot in the hierarchy. Even in street dealing."

"Wow. Who were talking to on the phone?"

"Why?"

"The head white man makes the decision as to employing me, and it isn't you."

"It is me . . . sir. Listen . . . I know you don't like the police. I don't blame you. Here's what's going to happen . . ."

"Daddy don't tell him shit," the pretty ginger hisses. "Just kill his ass, take this bitch and let's get to the airport."

"As I was saying . . . we're re-upping. The more MPD is pre-occupied with street crime, the more so-called Apache or Zombie we can move into the region. When order is restored—"

"When Kamala, all the other 'mongrels' are gone?"

"Legally, by voting acclaim, not armed violence. The *vermin*—as the term has been used the true president—will be exterminated or banished, then we'll figure out another way to make money off the new droves of surviving Tranq addicts. We'll need seasoned security here and in the out there in the future. You want a fresh start. I mean . . . that's all Jaime Bracht was truly offering you when he set you after this cunt here, right?"

Esme moans under the tape, and it looks like her tongue's just about to work it free when I say, "Actually he wanted his baby from an underage *metiza* he was trafficking from Guatemala because she looked whiter and so did the baby . . . if we're being honest. So let's be honest. I want a thirty large retainer and that will cover my undivided loyalty. Give me a thousand in cash today plus five for Melvin and his gas. The rest by transfer."

"You have a bank account?"

"I have a savings account the City's Adult Services set up for me when they found me an apartment with help from the Veterans Administration. Fixed my teeth and feet, too. Your tax dollars at work. Send the transfers by Zelle, in under three-thousand-dollar increments."

"Done. My colleagues will take this person here."

He gestures to Esme, who starts to squirm again and swear. I can't savvy if she's playing along or on her own tip. Guess I'll find out.

"When shit started getting personal with Danielle Diggs, why didn't y'all just wax her, Benny, Dean. One to the head, pick someone else?"

"She had existing infrastructure. And we ourselves have joint venturers to mollify."

"Stamp." I look in at the ginger. "Aidy . . . I really liked your dog."

She fumes, fidgets.

"My brother-in-law was a philistine, but Bracht found him useful." Voss explains. "Bracht had a lot of truly awful people he put trust in, eh sweetie?" He cranes his neck. "Mike! You and Ybarra grab this woman, let the fat, mouthy one go. You're lucky I've been to the ATM, so to speak, Mr. Cornish . . . got some cash here."

I feel my phone buzz in my pocket. "*Lo sciento*, Esmeralda." I pivot around her check out the beefy dude with the AR-15. "You know what else you are, Mr. Voss? Basically, an amateur, sadly like me. But I'm what you people call streetwise . . ."

Before he can grimace and form a word I shove Esme to the ground, pull the Mini from the small of my back . . . extend my index finger and point . . . send four rounds into the gym-rat's direction. I think two hit because I hear an ugly "*Fuuuuck!*" as I turn to fire on the others at the truck, praying Katie's ducking, as the street's taught her to do.

Melvin charges, sending lead balls our way and by the grace of God that shit's not hitting me or Esme but peppers both the pick-up's and the Benz's grills, pop the windshields on both. The Mexican's head disappears in a meaty shower.

Echoes in the warehouse amplify the noise, adding to the horror and disorientation.

The Benz's driver, Graydon—I guess he's wounded because I hear a scream that isn't Aidy's . . . he hits the accelerator and the Benz shoots forward . . .

. . . just as the bay door we came in caves, splinters.

Sirens now echo with the popping rounds. Unmarked vehicles swarm inside.

I holler to Kate to stay in the truck bed as I roll Esme under me. Manga ries to lift her up as a shield but immediately sees me aiming the Mini right at his pecker; Feds have already dragged his pal away.

"Let her go!" I shout.

He's flushed turnip red, suddenly bathed in sweat as if someone hit him with a bucket of water. What's with these fools? Why won't they stop, give up?

"I don't wanna die like this Dick!" Katie whimpers.

Esme's tape's long off her mouth. "Get me out of here!"

Some Feds in body armor try to decide the issue. "Freeze, drop your weapon!"

Before we can make a move, however, screeching brakes and revving engines turn our heads, irresistibly. Even the motherfucker holding Katie, and Katie herself, are mesmerized by this macabre dance unfolding behind us in this artificial cavern: Voss's banged up Benz playing bumper cars with two Fed unmarked sedans and a Virginia State police unit. It can't escape, yet they can't box it in.

Katie snaps out of the trance and finally uses the distraction shove the gunsel away and leap from the truck bed . . . just as the rolling circus flies toward all of us. I don't know if the dude driving has passed out or he's gone kamikaze, but the Benz grazes the Ford, bounces the gunsel into the air and onto his ass, flips . . .

Jesus, Mary and Joseph . . .

The thing careens into some metal air freight containers.

It explodes.

I see Conrad Voss try to protect his daughter from the flames. Then I don't see anything but liquidy gray smoke until the sprinklers cut on but its still too dark and poisonous to stay in there . . .

. . . and outside in the parking lot, door to the Catalina swung wide, I hear Melvin on his phone to Croc.

"Yeah, all them niggas is fried whiting at the Shrimp Boat cept two muvfuckahs who prolly ain't gonna snitch. That's the low, low down . . ."

Some asshole in an FBI windbreaker follows Marshal Greene in her own garb and they are charging straight at me as I feed Katie another granola bar from an EMT who's fetching Katie something to wear on her bare, almost toe-less dogs.

"The Deputy Attorney General wanted arrests!" The FBI dude hollers.

Marshal Greene, heavy lips aquiver, isn't pleased either. "Now it's a shitshow!" She points to the fire being extinguished by a number of big and loud red pumper and ladder trucks. "It's all over the local and national news . . ." she grabs my arm, I yank it away yet she drives herself closer regardless. "The Attorney General of Virginia and the head of the Republican Caucus of the legislature are former principals of the Argyle Group . . . partners with Voss . . . and Bracht . . . and these State Troopers and VBI agents are their minions, *brutha*. You've given these whitefolks an excuse and Ms. Bivens is very upset."

"Champ, *sista*. Are you sure she's not cross with you for being a bit tardy to the party?"

"Esmeralda Rubio is on her way back to D.C. and refuses to testify now. She says she'd rather go to a federal prison. There is a chopper waiting at Andrews right now to take her to Lewisburg, Pennsylvania to cool her heels and get her to think about that decision. That's on your head, too, like this bloodbath . . ."

The words gut me. I mean I don't let her see it but I'm about as tall as my knees now and I want to vomit.

"Dick," Katie says, "I be fine. They taking me all the way home, then over to work to see Keesh. I'm good, really. I'll call you."

"You don't want a lawyer?"

"Why?"

"Don't say nothing, okay?"

Melvin shows up. "Let's book, cuz. Twelve don't want us bammas here."

"And who is this?" Greene's pointing at Melvin.

"I be Melvin Jackson, Ma'am."

"Cornish, yes, maybe you should go before reporters or these Virginia Bureau of Investigation people see you. Seriously."

Yeah. The low, low, down . . .

CHAPTER NINETEEN
Maxine Nightengale

THE SUN'S SINKING ALL BURNT ORANGE across on the tree-tops, way past where Pennsylvania Avenue shoots across the river . . . way past Seward Park, and I think of Aidy Voss's fiery red hair . . . in real flames. Yeah, there it is, making the cloud tops a garish purple . . . way past the CVS where Hakim "Little" Alexander "lost" K'ymira Thomas years ago, and I think of the girl's fakeass mother, there at the VA, hiding in plain sight right in front of my face in the waiting room with all the mumbling, sick men. I think of her husband, blowing his brains out in a flophouse after making me promise to find his little girl.

I'm thinking of a lot of stuff. Bullshit. All bullshit. I've done nothing since I've been clean but feed a bullshit machine . . . like how I imagined all those boiler room sweaty mother-fuckers on the *Titanic* when I read *A Night to Remember* when I was a kid, or the shovellers buried in the mountains of ash in *The Great Gatsby*. Saw all that in my dome before I saw any movie. Imagined I was them, not a brave sailor rescuing kids, or Jay or Nick.

So I draw up the collar on my jacket because it's gotten cold and the Halloween shit's dangling in the October breeze. And I wander . . .

. . . and I find the bar. Yeah, Daddy. Uh-huh, Katie. *A bar.*

Daddy, it's one of your favorites, Mr. Henry's. Venerable, ole school as fuck. Whenever you craved the company of your people, Cutty Sark scotch and ebony boppers in tight skirts and sweet blues music, right around the corner from a shit-load of the cracker Leathernecks you called your real family.

The place is a shadow of itself, I suppose. A little dingier, a little stickier, darker. Still cozy, huh? Not how he described it when Mom would demand to know why he was off-post and and he'd smack the shit out of her, and say he'd bought Freida Payne or Roberta Flack a Chardonnay, like they'd give his liver-lipped monster ass the time of day even in his dress blues.

The bartender says the show upstairs doesn't start for another two hours, asks me what I want.

I want some cheap-ass Mickey's or Wild Irish Rose. I want some rot-gut vodka. I want to be left alone and maybe score the Apache because if you can't beat 'em, join 'em, as on the screen beside a pre-season Capitals hockey game a fiery commentator on a lesser, more strident cousin of Fox News is screeching how the "confla-gration" out near Dulles was "Waco, redux," and a supposed Mexican national among the dead, a cartel torpedo sent to aid in some illicit enterprise implicating poor Conrad Voss or his lovely daughter, is all fake news, Deep State propaganda . . . and the pundit's quick to say Aidy was an analyst in the Executive Office of the President . . . shows pics featuring her prominently with Grandpa Joe . . . and then Grandpa Joe's son Hunter, as if either had a damn thing to do with Aidy. Brilliant. Bullshit wins.

"Can I get . . . a Coke. No ice."

"Coke? That's it? You sure, big man?"

"You got fries? Small order of fries. Put . . . um . . . a little gravy on 'em. A little cheese."

"Sure thing, man. Want me to change the channel? Some Repub Hill staffers were in here, ya know the types. Real siced there's gonna some big comeback . . . as if, right, man?"

"Right. Just . . . Coke and fries, cool?" No other conversation. Please.

He's shaking his head, grinning. Like this is the last stop before I really start asking for the below the shelf vodka, or saunter over to the brothers huddled by the Potomac Avenue Metro score some shit adulterated with Danielle's product. Lose all my nice government-installed crowns and bridgework. Danielle's product? Nah, the product of whoever was on the other end of Conrad Voss's burner, aptly named as it was crisped in the car fire, and yet its being rugby-scrummed by the Attorney General of the Commonwealth of Virginia and some dickheads on the Hill to keep Bivens and the FBI from getting at till after the election. It's all up to some federal judge now . . . appointed by well . . . you-know-who.

My stuff comes and I'm not hungry, not even thirsty. I can hear you chortling, playing a fool, Daddy . . . singing along, stomping your feet . . . fucking with the bouncer.

The serpent uncoils in my gut, bumrushes my heart . . .

. . . I smash the plate of fries, knock the glass of cola across the bar and the bartender's fingering something lethal under the POS station while a scrawny waitress with dyed blonde hair's on the phone to 911.

Imagine her shock when, like djinns, Monica Abalos and that chick Goins walk in right as the bartender's barking at me to back the fuck off and I'm wiping grease and gravy off my hands and sleeves.

"How'd you find me?" I ask.

"We followed you," Monica says. "You walked all the way from Seventh and Rhode Island down here."

"I used to walk a lot. When I had no place to go. Ironic, isn't it."

"I have orders to find you. Not from the Feds. Chief Patterson. Couple of Danielle Diggs Last-Knowns . . . they've been found with GSWs to the head. Two in the women's detention center awaiting pretrial have been strangled . . ."

"I heard."

"How?"

"That Croc person?" Goins chimes in. She whispers to Abalos, "Crazy-looking old fella who fakes needing a wheelchair. Drug dealer back in the early two-thousands . . ."

"I know lots of fellas in wheelchairs, baby. Y'all're dealing a bit of a 'realignment' over in Northeast . . ."

"We found NPP residue in containers, pill presses in places other than Gault Place. Someone's burning bridges, moving the product." Abalos explains.

"Even Diggs' boy toys are getting unalived," Goins adds. "Found them buried in shallow graves in PG County and Dahlgen, Virginia."

"That's a spread."

"Yes, it is. Because we found pieces of the same young men I both PG County *and* Dahlgren." She swallows hard after she says it.

"Meanwhile, if that isn't enough to drown us, we got even more teenagers pistol whipping yuppie moms pushing strollers, or Apache zombies tossing feces on joggers, breaking into home, even dognapping.

"Ladies . . . not my monkey no more, not my circus. That was made very clear to me by the Feds."

"Come get in the car. Please, Dickie."

Well, she said please. And I guess I'm the second Richard E. Cornish unwelcome anymore at Mr. Henry's . . .

We step outside and the air's a little colder, the sky darker. With the streetlights buzzing on, illuminating the dirty sidewalk I got lots of white people this time staring. Quite the site seeing my big ass in a long coat getting in the back as if it's my limo, and two small, very exotic looking young women in leather jackets—gold shields glinting from their belts— jumping into the front. Pimpish in fact.

Goins busts a couple of tight turns and very soon I'm clocking familiar sights. For a second I'm even dreading a return to Biven's lair at Navy Yard proper but there's the steeple—at St. Jude's. The 1950s smoked glass of SFME.

Back to where I started from, like that old disco-y song my sister liked, by Maxine Nightengale. So why am I terrified at being back . . . "home?"

The lady cops dump me at the chapel.

Father Phil Ruffino and the Brazilian novice nuns and Sister Maria-Karl are distant memories. Couple of civilians are sweeping up but it's nice that the jont's open "after hours" and the smell of candlewax and philters of incense are filling the nave . . . I give my forehead a dab of oil and holy water and oil and genuflect and roll to the pew, bow, slide in, kneel, pray . . . all mindless and mechanical. I don't care. Haven't done it in months.

Feel a hand on my shoulder. I turn to see an old white man. Very wrinked, very bent and brittle, wearing a hooded robe.

"Wanna hear a Pollock joke?" he says in a raspy voice. "How do you make an old Pollock happy?"

"I dunno," I whisper, trying not to tear up.

"You answer his prayers," Brother Karl-Maria says with a grin. "Look at you."

I rise. We hug.

"So Peter Gunn, Private Eye, what's shaking lately?"

"Nothing much."

"Oh, we both know that's not true. Quite an entourage showed up here, waiting for you. Not since your friend Antonelli and his goons disrupted the *santus sanctorum* had I seen so much brass. Sort of yearn for the days when we'd have to hose you off downstairs, kill the crispy critters in your clothes, eh?"

"Simpler times."

"Let's walk."

"Is . . . Verna here?"

"You'll see . . ."

I'm more jumpy here than in that warehouse out by the airport. Yeah, the undercroft of St. Jude's still carries that homecoming smell of Lestoil and Clorox to fight the B.O. and vomit on the men saved any given night. But something's different about this new, remodeled SFME. As the guards buzz us over, I don't catch the timbre of a damn thing. Not even loaded diapers. Sterile. A tad corporate.

Soon I pass where steel doors used to guard the larder called "Fort Knox," repository of all things Pampers, Tide . . . painkillers and gripe water . . . cartons of Sprite and tubes of hydrocortisone and bottles of Benadryl. Now it's a mini-data center and it hums with a small wall AC unit to cool the computers, all tended by LaKeisha. The new cubicle farm off the corridor ahead is where I hear Katie cackling and LaKeisha's heavy fingers on a keyboard, both working overtime to process the single moms, the kids needing beds, the families needing to eat—all as Federal money's in peril and grant money from rich wallets might stall. All depends on the election. Bivens is right.

And here's Verna's new suite. Brother Karl-Maria, like Dicken's Ghost of Christmas Yet to Come, points a tremorous boney finger right to the door.

"Why here?"

"How else are they going to get your attention, boss," the cleric says, "then for you to be at the beginning, when you cleaned up and stood there and said somebody hired you to be a friggin' detective. ' . . . *in saecula saeculorum . . .*'"

"Amen," I whisper sheepishly. I knock on the door, as I have so many times before, filthy or clean-shaven.

There's Verna, neither smiling nor scowling, rocking in her bosswoman highbacked high-tech mesh chair behind a desk piled with both archaic manilla folders and two flat computer monitors.

She looks good. She smells good.

Arms folded, fat ass about to slide off Verna's credenza is Patterson. He chuckles, shakes his head upon laying eyes on me.

It's not until I enter the office fully that I see who's been seated behind the door, legs crossed, high heels scraping the carpet. She's still wrapped in a bright green peacoat over her skirt and blouse despite the stuffy heat in that place.

"I always wanted to see this place," Bivens muses. "Did you know that Ms. Leggett and I are sorors? I'm older, yeeees, but . . ."

"It's fascinating." Chief Patterson teases, gruffly.

"Yeah." I'm standing there dumb as a mug until Verna points to another chair. I don't sit.

The Chief fills me in. "Last night in Deanwood there was a triple homicide after two shootings the previous night. Immediately afterward, a vehicle answering to the description and plate number of the suspects' . . . carjacked earlier of course . . . was spotted heading west on Benning Road, then later right over here on South Capitol Street. It stopped on Ms. Leggett's doorstep long enough to drop off two children with a note pinned to one's sweatshirt 'Please take care of them, they are orphans now. Signed Richard E. Cornish, Jr. Private Investigator . . .'"

Fuck me . . .

"They killed Artemesia Sellers?"

Verna answers. "The kids are traumatized but it's clear that's the case."

"We know someone's messing with you, son. There's an old-school drug war there over the Tranq now that supplier's been compromised."

Trying hard to look hard. At least two people in that room know how to read me. "I was told to stay away. Right, Madame Deputy AG?"

"That came from Merrick Garland, and the President, Dickie," Bivens says. "Yes, you moved up in the world."

"I've seen the polls. Your bosses don't seem to want their jobs. That Twilight Zone jont's not my fault: teenagers out protesting for terrorists, black folks out shilling for Trump. What, Esme hasn't rolled on anyone yet? Those gunsels taking the MAGA *omerta*? I hear GOP wants hearings on Voss's death, not his drug dealing. Your shit's *backfired*."

"Smartass," Patterson huffs.

"Your girlfriend . . ." Biven begins, and I watch Verna shift uncomfortably in her chair, "will crack and give it up soon now that she's among the sistas and don't mean back at HU. I mean on the cellblock with no Coqui, Estee Lauder and eating Chef Boyardee."

"She was squatting and using with me She's dealt with Bracht, cartels, MS-Thirteen, so don't hold your breath, she's tough."

"We aren't going to hold our breath for you. Neither is whomever dropped those kids off."

Bivens rises, approaches like she's cross-examining me. I swear Verna's trying not to eye-roll.

"The Mexican national who was with Voss's men was finally ID'd. Francisco Ybarra. He's muscle—a torpedo, as you say. No direct connection to NPP importation or final fentanyl or xylazine chemistry, trafficking and the like but he came up from Mexico in an odd way—freighter into Norfolk."

Patterson adds, "Colima Cartel. That stuff's their thing now. The switch to Tranq."

"On the west coast of Mexico. Up a ways from Acapulco."

"How'd you know that?" the Chief presses me.

"Elvis, *Fun in Acapulco* . . . the cliff divers?"

"This isn't funny, Cornish."

Verna oddly comes to my aid. "It's one way he remembers things, Chief."

"Well, if it don't come through Texas, then the White'll feed up into the States by way of—"

Clickity-clackity. "San Diego?" I say.

Biven's head swivels. But Verna fixes on me. She's seen my look before.

"Dickie, *what?*" Verna says.

"Vee . . . I need you to . . . get those kids . . . I need you to get them, let me talk to them."

"Oh no. They just finished with the counselors and the police."

"What are you on to?" Bivens says, the little chickenhawk affectation in full effect.

"Arthur Sellers . . . he's still on life support, right?"

"Far as I know. I'll have to ask Markowitz and Helen."

"Who's paying for that?"

"Prolly the taxpayers," the Chief grunts.

I loom over Bivens' small form. "Ybarra the torpedo . . . you said he got here on a freighter. Port would have been . . . Manzanillo, would it?"

She crisscrosses a look with the Chief, then with Verna, I've yet to see on her, in all of manifestations. Surprise . . .

"How did you . . . know? That was in a confidential Department Homeland Security Memo"

"Vee . . . *the kids?*"

She hits her intercom.

"Katie, the Sellers children MPD interviewed . . . are they still with the nurse or did Mr. Jimmy take them over to eat? Oh . . . and Dickie is here, by the way . . ."

I stoop to Bivens' eye level, meaning my knees are truly bent and creaking. "You told me, way back, about the third leg of this stool. I think that's how I can be . . . of use again."

The adults hang back from the cafeteria yet crowd a double doorway. Katie leads me into the room festooned with jack-o'- lantern and black cat cut-outs, orange crepe paper, ears of Indian corn. A bunch of kids eating in the late shift of emergency admissions are all cutting up or fussing. But they go quiet and look up, like I am whatever lumbering Halloween creature their generation fears or cheers. For me it was Herman Munster.

It's hard to recognize the two at a table in the far corner, away from the others. Cleaned up. In bright light. And they're the only two not staring. Rather, they are digging greedily into bowls of spaghetti with pale red sauce, couple of small meatballs.

I pull up the biggest chair available. The custodian, Mr. Jimmy, rolls up with me and takes an eavesdropping station nearby, as does Katie.

The boy freezes suddenly. He throws me some evil, pushes his bowl away. His little sister keeps eating. In between forkful she says to him, "See, I tole you he was a giant. Giant's ain't all bad."

"No. We don't like it when folk hurt lil' kids."

"He's a muvfukkin' liar."

"We don't like it when lil' kids talk like that, either."

"See?"

"You can't help us."

"Mama's gone . . ."

"Stop that shit! Snitch-bitch!"

"What I tell you about talking like that?" Just the bass in my voice straightens him out. "I don't want to know where your Mama is. I just want to know . . ." I throw the dice hard here. I give as high a pitched bark as a can. The murmurs of the other kids eating in there turns to a few snickers but it has he effect.

These kids aren't amused. They both give me these wide-eyed stares.

"Was Tequila barking, when your Mama went away?"

"Tequila mean," the little girl moans.

"What's her name?"

"Tequila a boy and you got the name," the brother replies.

"No, the lady who has Tequila. Did she make your Mama go away? Did she hurt your Mama?"

They crisscross, then study the bowls.

Guess you have me back, Madame Deputy. I stand. "Look at me." They do, straining their necks. "I am a *giant*. I used to live here. This is where I started. Now, I protect every child who stays here. You ask any adult who works here what the giant's done did to bad people here."

"Her name be Miz Flora."

"Your Mama scared of her?"

The boy says, "Mama, she high. But e'rybody scured a her but Arf'r. He ain't scured a nobody."

"Diamante's big sister, Danielle . . . Gestapo . . . she scared of Miz Flora?"

The boy shrinks but the little girl nods with alacrity.

Katie says, "Dick . . . you never asked their names. That's Michael. That's Tina."

"Apologies. Like she said my name is Richard."

"A giant . . ." Tina says, going back to her spaghetti, blocking out all the awfulness.

"This is where you started from?" Michael says.

I nod, and as I leave the room, and the din begins to rise, the sound of plastic utensils digging into food re-commences, Tina calls to me.

"Giant! Miz Flora, she mean to Diamante's sister but she don't gotta be."

I halt, turn and bend to her. "Why's that, sweetie?"

"Cause she her auntie, say Mama. Don't you auntie gotta be nice to you?"

Still crouched, I twist my head to the adults, the supposed experts and veterans, all aghast yet crammed together like helpless spectators.

Verna's probably breaking a dozen promises to herself when she comes over to me, gets really close.

"They want to know . . ." she whispers, "what's your angle."

"I've met this woman before. I could have stopped this. They're not gonna be able to do it. Not their way."

I haven't seen her smile at me in a brick. "Then go it your way. Just like in the beginning, where you started from . . ."

CHAPTER TWENTY

Barbershop

They call it the Visitor and Family Center now at the CDF, as the trend to make everything sound sweet. Like I was "unhoused," or the dozens of ex-cons I know are "returning citizens," as if any of them ever did anything indicative of a citizen.

So I sit there literally twiddling my thumbs on sticky table . . . there was a kid who spilled one of those pouch drink earlier. The tables just opened back up again after COVID. Before that you had to check out your loved one via video. The C.O. shrugs when I ask where the dude is so he has to shout again, "Park Kang-Dae!"

Finally, my Harvard Crimson friend shuffles out, hangdog.

"Don't you know your name, dickbrain?" the C.O. snarls.

"It's Cole . . . *Cole!*"

"If it was that easy, huh," the C.O. says with a sigh. "Table four."

Cole eyes me, groans. He's gotten a nice cellblock haircut—resembles a young Mako . . . one of my favorite Asian actors, *The Sand Pebbles*, 1968, with Steve McQueen. Daddy hated it because he hated swabbies and Chinese.

"Guess the family and neighbors over in Bailey's Crossroads couldn't convince the judge you were a good boy, give you an ankle bracelet," I muse.

"Hey, I offered to surrender my passport . . . fucking judge thought my grandmother was gonna fly me to Busan."

"Was she?"

He buries his head in his arms like a little boy on classroom detention. "Fuck yeah," I hear with a muffled chuckle. Then the smell hits me.

"You been avoiding the shower? Prolly a wise move . . ."

"Whatchew want, dude?"

"At least you've been snacking well, now that they moved you to a single."

His head pops up. "My folks wouldn't recharge my book. Was that . . . you?"

"Western Union 'Offender Connect.' And a phone call from the cops got you the single."

"Stamp, bro' thanks. But again, my lawyer says that raid on Danielle was unconstitutional and says I'm out at the next hearing in two days. As long as I didn't rape anyone, Harvard's cool; these days they can't afford to lose woke brilliant Asians like me, gramps, *so* . . ."

This motherfucker. "So . . . where is Flor?" His eyes widen. "Who are her people . . . besides her niece? Yeah. Danielle is her family."

"Aw . . . man, why you on me, dude?"

I lean in. "Because I was champ on myself, playing too clever. Thought I was the last man standing when in fact it's *you*."

He's quiet for a few seconds, searching the table. "Like I say, my lawyer is—"

"Stop wellin' on me with this shit, y'hearme! Uncle Sam is your only play. Flor's the guarantor, the shot-caller—Colima's eyes and ears—okay? They are cutting ties and loose ends to this Tranq operation, moe, and a wannabe like you isn't satisfied with bagging groceries . . . nah, you liked playing hard b-boy, like this is a PlayStation game until you get here and suddenly taking showers doesn't seem safe and it *ain't* because you wanna keep your booty hole pure."

"Come on dude . . ."

"If you get out they won't need to shiv you in the shower. They'll wait for your arrogant ass to go back to Cambridge and you'll be walking to a fancy coffee shop in Harvard Square with some rich WASPy chick with big titties who you've waiting all semester to blend . . . and two zooted cowboys they paid fiddy each will come up behind you both with rusty lead pipes. Notch-up another brutal street crime . . .

He can't even look at me now. "Cops hittin' the wall with the peeps?"

I nod. "You know the opps." I settle back in my chair. "It was her. Couple of nights before I met you, just up from Nanie Helen Burroughs . . . walking her nasty little dog . . ."

"You watch that *Game of Thrones* shit?"

"I know someone who's seen 'em all, and read the damn books. Why?"

"All them mugs with their white hair—they be Danielle. *The dragons*? They be Flor."

This kid's phony streetwise, but if he had a last name for her, he'd have spilled it. So I push the rest. He puts his head on swivel as he speaks. He's learning.

"My Dad said whenever Danielle's hardass women couldn't handle collections and shit she'd call Flor and Flor'd send her sons. That's why he paid on time. But then they stopped coming. Be after the zombies instead. Help the zombies jack folks, rob houses and shit to score. Guess they're Danielle's cousins."

"Describe them."

"They mixed Mexican and black but them Mandinka chromosomes of Flors' prevail . . . big gym-lookin' brothas. Bald but always wearing silk wave caps cause they got skin conditions on they heads from too much conk . . . Danielle'd clown 'em and say they wanted to look like their Daddy . . .

Bingo. Mental note—thank Mattel. Yet now I'm the one searching the table. "Tussled with them. Shot one of them."

"Oh shit. If you shot them you better have killed them, bro'."

"They got names?"

"Government? I got no clue. Just Oso and Lobo."

Heartening. Bear and wolf? Silly me thought this was going to be easy.

"So dude, O.G., um . . . Uncle Sam's gonna have my back, my family's real live, right?"

I nod, "That's the plan."

"Rather have you, man."

I smile. "That's not everything, Cole."

"Yeah . . . um . . . they own a barbershop."

Shit. Maybe this will be easy. "Address."

He gives me this look. "Not that kind."

I shut my eyes. "Shit."

"Last locale . . . maybe . . . okay . . . maybe was they was setting up a house . . . fun house an' the barbershop an' shaves bc a perk, like a hood day spa . . . for gees . . . while the ass an' titties be out"

"Kill . . . if it's a house . . . you think, as a smart Harvard man . . . the White, xylazine, shit like that might be stored there. Stuff they maybe took from Danielle before Twelve raided her?"

"Oso and Lupo ain't that smart but Mama is. Then again, Mama don't wanna be too wrapped up in their mess is my guess, Big Man."

"So where's the house—your guess?"

"The Angle . . . if you had po-po stake it alla Northeast from Deanwood over to MLK, man, they'll see the heat's comin', pack the shit up."

"*Angle?* Ward Seven ain't my jont."

He starts describing this ninety-degree angle where Southern Avenue and Eastern Avenue come together . . . literally the most eastern point of D.C. "East Capitol Street below, M.L.K. above. You don't catch 'em there, they be gone."

I better mollify him.

"See that C.O.? He and another one named Smothers are gonna watch you until your prelim. Because you're being as smart as you claim to be, the U.S. Attorney will drop the charges before your lawyer even gets a chance to speak. Then you go to Massachusetts and stay there. They told me your family will be safe, no charges, no moves against the store."

"Stamp, O.G."

"And stop talking like that . . ."

I don't feel like such a big man when they give me the claim check for the .380. Keep thinking about the Infirmary basement here. And Stripe.

Never again will I leave anything to chance. That's why today, I'm leaving things to Mattel and Croc.

On the subway I'm contemplating how close a shave I'm going to get at the barbershop. Can't directly involve MPD or the Feds because the kid's right, they'll blow the whole thing yet who's to say the old bat and her sons haven't booked—either for Mexico, or just up the parkway to Baltimore, to scout out new zombie fruited plains with the damage already done in the Capital, retracing the Limey's scorched earth in 1814?

Still, need a back-up. Hate myself but I need it.

I call her. Uh-huh. Her. Pray she won't shit and mess it up but I'm her only play now. She doesn't even ask why the street's got to handle this business.

Streetwise? Nah, street-*whys* . . .

. . . and by the time we pull into L'Enfant Plaza I'm texting Katie, LaKeisha . . . and they're reminding about the last time I was at one those moveable feasts called a *barbershop*.

Dig it: screwdriver buried in my thigh down to the handle, and asshole who did it still after me for housing his coat and radio. Good thing I brought my own anesthesia, so to speak. But they were a bit low on antibiotics, or antiseptics for that matter, as the owner had broken up with his bopper who worked at a Walgreens in PG County. They used Listerine while an overweight stripper did bottomless splits to TLC's *Creep* played on an underpowered boom box. Next thing, I'm in a regular folk ER a week later with blood poisoning. Checked myself out AMA, naturally. So yeah, the old medieval barber does indeed survive in the out of sight, out of mind spaces where GSWs and STDs and abscessed teeth and nose jobs for motherfuckers on the lamb are dealt with quickly, surreptitiously, by cash or barter. They cut heads, shave, too . . . minus the leeches, plus a floor show.

I get home and immediately head to the head, open up the panel behind the tank and dig into the larder.

Past the old photos, the papers . . . any memories . . . I bite lip and ignore them . . . straight to the cache. Bracht's money. I peel out enough bills to put together a gwaps that will speak a Gabriel's horn of decibels on the street.

No need to pack an extra clip of ACP into my trouser pocket though; if I can't do what I've schemed-out with the bullets allotted I'm a dead man anyway. Besides, the .380's got to fit in a special spot if I'm to survive the usual frisk.

Katie's been there, as I requested. Yet despite a filled water bowl and ample mounds of spongy meat the cat's mewling and meowing at me. Can only imagine the barrage of questions . . .

"Yeah, I called Croc," I tell it. "He's siced about kicking some ass. Not happy about who with, but no way we're doing this alone." It rolls on the rug still fussing at me. "Got some eyes on the jont right now." The tabby stretches, yawns, disappears under my rack. "Yeah, that's a good spot to hide if shit goes south. What happens then, you ask? Bivens commits *seppuku* before Trump Part Deux can put her in front of a redneck firing squad. I get neutered and put in a shelter before you do."

My phone rattles and pings and it's Abalos.

"Nothing really from Kang-Dae, Monica."

"He didn't give you any intel we can use?"

"Nope. Just two names: Oso and Lupo. No clue where they are. Or the woman."

"What are you doing now?"

"Staying in, making some calls. Something will shake loose and I'll find you, I promise."

"Don't bluff me, Dickie, or get in over your head. Again."

"I'll check in this evening."

"By the way, Esmeralda Rubio was moved to the prison hospital at Lewisburg."

A wave ripples across my body. It's not euphoria. "Mother Mary . . . *shit* . . . did they get to her? It was only to teach her a lesson . . ."

"No . . . apparently . . . she's hypertensive. Been hiding it well. But the last couple of weeks, well . . . she's ready to come back and testify if there's anything left to testify to, so stay frosty and stay in

contact! The Feds are letting us go primary on this. Looks like DOJ's got bigger worries now."

I click off. Step to my dresser, grab Mom's rosary. Looks like LaKeisha's came too, did what I asked and played nice with my uneasy benefactors. I grin at what kind interchange they must've had. I drape the beads around my neck as ersatz jewelry. *"Sancta Maria, Mater Maria . . . remitte sacrilegium meum. Protege me in praelio venire."* I pause after genuflecting then speak into the crucifix. "Did you catch all that? Testing . . ."

Before I hit the door the cat swipes my shins. Swear it called me called "Rain Man."

Melvin picks me up in the alley off Fairmount as soon as it gets dark. Croc's in the back and I smell fried whiting and hot sauce, hear lips smacking.

"Want some, fam'ly?"

"Nah, I prefer them not finding that in the autopsy."

"Want something other than your mouse gun?"

"Gotta stay hid, so no."

"Hid as in?"

"As in they'll frisk me, check my ankles. But toxic masculinity will stop them from checking anywhere else, moe."

"Kill . . . it ain't like we infiltrating the Kremlin, cuz . . ."

"You trust what the Korean kid say?" Melvin quizzes. "Them Koreans lie ta us like mugs."

"I trust him."

"And you trust these Deanwood niggas?" Croc adds.

"Be nice if we could stick together, too. They bought your shit, didn't they?"

"Stamp," Melvin cosigns.

"Ain't nobody ask you, employee!" Croc snaps back. "I mean, independent contractor without benefits. Just drive, nigga."

"Just be cool."

We whip around old RFK Stadium and zoom east on East Capitol Street as MPD units stream west to rectify the usual nocturnal shenanigans. Swerve left onto Minnesota Avenue, blend in as best this Catalina can, then onto Sheriff Road. Just as lighted sign heralding the border with Maryland comes into view along with directions for FedEx Field, I clock parking lot fronting an old diner, long boarded up. Couple of cars are await us, red parking blinkers flashing.

"Here they go right there, boss," Melvin cautions Croc.

We pull into the lot, slowly, windows down despite the wind. Not quite the hawk of winter. Maybe a hatchling, of Fall but that's not giving me the chills. Second thoughts, Rain Man?

Shadows emerge from open car doors, then reconstitute into bodies with faces. They linger by their vehicles until a lane's cleared. And through the lane rolls a dark-skinned figure in a wheelchair. Across his lap is an old-school chopper with an extended banana clip.

"Lookitchew, Mattel, Goddamn!" Croc calls from the window.

"That you, motherfucker? Dickie truly brought the B Team, huh?"

The dome light pops on in the rear of the Catalina and Croc showcases his weapon of choice. "Mossberg, nigga. This ain't a ghetto demonstration for the white gentrifiers in the bamma museum of natural history. This is internal business so why you brought yo' daddy's drug dealer rifle from the '80s like you Karma Chameleon who's addicted to love an' you beat it wid Billie Jean on MTV?"

Can't let this shade this spiral into jonin' on Croc's parents because I can see Mattel's jaw go taut. "The sitch, Mattel?"

"I tole you, Dickie, ain't none of them givin' up that old lady down there. And ain't none them zombie fiends saying shit about the shop . . . but couple y'all's homeless muvfukkahs posted up on the bus stop on 63rd and Clay finally came up through the park. Said some Youngs chased 'em off on account Oso be payin' cash outta there for jacked whips. Couldn't make Lupo, though. But they say Oso went into a duplex, right on the Angle. Saw a few dudes go in with him with some cases of beer...one came out with a clean-up."

"That's our jont."

"Dickie you sure you wanna do this?" Croc says. "You know these fools prolly made you even if that Aidy girl ain't say shit to them. And even if it does work—all the heat's goin' be on *you*, fam'ly. And I don't just mean Five-O or the Feds. I mean Colima."

"We'll find out. Got to grab one or both of them to get Mama. With luck she's not far. We don't get Mama, they will re-up and half this city's gonna look like *The Walking Dead* within a year, the other half's gonna be some *Mad Max* shit, dead ass."

I let Mattel quarterback the rest.

"Aw'hite . . . we head down Eastern," he says, "no caravan, just cool . . . we all gray dick mugs so Twelve ain't goin' fuck wid us as if we was Youngs. There be a America's Best Chicken An' Waffles two blocks before you hit the Angle and it turns into Southern, almos' there at MLK. They mind they own business, just doing Halloween carryout and shit. Thas' where y'all cut the headlights, we dismount." He pauses, looks at Croc, then down at own lap, chuckles and says, "where *y'all* dismount, we be the chariots."

One of this fellas, showing dad gear like loose jeans and fleece pullover, asks about the teenagers posted as lookouts.

"We ain't here to kill children. Ain't none us ninjas. Shut them up any you can, but remember, they ain't as hard or brave as they wanna look."

Melvin speaks up from behind the wheel. "An' them toy gangstas inside, we let them go? They goin' shoot back, too."

Mattel sucks his teeth and says, "If they hands up, then run, rabbit. If they in there bein' stupid," he pulls the bolt in his chopper, "then we do a public service. Regardless, soon as it's done git back ta America's Best, or break for the park. Any unpapered weapons, you shove in a storm drain." He's looking at me now. "So Mr. Touchdown, got anything to add?"

"Nah." I pull the gwap and peel out a couple of cees and hand it out the window to Mattel. "Fee for services."

"We the Neighborhood Watch, we ain't no mercs."

"Then use it for the neighborhood."

Mattel hands the cash to a minion still wearing his WMATA bus driver uniform, toting a revolver.

"Man, back in them Simple City days I'd be siced ta feed you this chopper and you'd give up that whole roll."

Croc grins, beats me to the punch. "But we grown-ass men now."

CHAPTER TWENTY-ONE
Cabaret

FOR ALL I KNOW, PATTERSON MAY have double-crossed my double-cross and could have MPD's ERT jackboots busting in the spot with a battering ram and flash-bangs any fucking second. But right now, I'm just making sure my nuts don't migrate up to my throat as I saunter past two Youngs with these cornrows and dyed top-knotted hair as if they're warriors and not two people who need to be doing algebra homework. I got at least two feet on each of them so they don't eyeball me too much.

Sad-looking, squat cinderblock and wood-frame duplex . . . that's what I'm staring at. A cookie-cutter barrack, like so many on the eastern edge of the city. The abandoned, darkened left side of the house . . . geographically in Northeast D.C. . . . .is probably where the White and xylazine, pill presses and anything else they had to shanghai from Danielle before cops found it is stored for later use.

The right side, in Southeast D.C., is the tight side. Shaking with an oldie. Faith Evans' *Love Like This*. Since it's R&B and Go Go and not that trap or mumble bullshit I'm thinking the cabaret has started.

There's a bizarre steampunk Jules Verne-looking peephole mounted in an otherwise frail builder-grade plywood door; the camera above me buzzes and beeps.

I'm not disguised or hiding my face, but I am wearing a pair of Croc's cheap shades . . . at night. I just knock, hold up the gwap.

Beware of Greeks bearing gifts. Doubt if these niggas read Homer. But they love investors.

The peephole opens as if it has a metal eyelid and I hear, "Five seconds ta say you ain't lunchin' or Twelve. Or you be unalived. Fo' . . . Free . . . Two . . ."

"Gestapo's dead, got my good faith kite here in my hand. Want a piece of her jont the Tranq . . . with the re-up. Plus I need a shave. Wanna see some titties."

It's only a few seconds but it's an hour to me. The door opens. I roll in and as soon as I do Faith's beat hits my ears, three sets of hanging breasts striated with stretch marks and punctuated by purplish areoli hit my eyes, along with accompanying shaved pubes and high heels . . . oh, and one gun barrel's pressed to my temple, another's aimed toward my dick . . .

"Kite, nigga?"

"Nah...not till I get my wet shave."

"Who vouch?"

"Croc Morrison. Ole school, in Southeast. But this is *my* money."

The guns retract. The frisks begin. They only find the burner Melvin handed me.

"Cover is a C-note. You get the phone when you leave."

I peel a bill out. The show continues. For $100 I get the smell of Old Spice, weed and ass.

Once I sit to wait my turn, however, I'm overwhelmed by the odor of chicken and fish frying. Indeed, I see grease spitting in the weird glows cast by the DJ's makeshift lightshow. I turn down a sopping paper plate offered by a brute wearing a shoulder holster that cradles one of those scary 40 calibers that can splatter your dome like a rotten tomato on sidewalk.

No real barber chairs—just folding card table chairs plus a few lucky customers get reclining nylon beach chairs. The barbers got LED spotlights on their heads like coal miners; one customer balances a gray Pitty on his lap and the dog's panting like it's got a fever. A dancer avoids its huge head for the slobber, not for the teeth, then hands me plastic cup of something strong and nasty. I pretend to drink and eye the room for anybody who's eyeing me for anything other than my height.

Working the last chair is a big fella, sweaty, adeptly swigging a beer bottle, taking a forkful of greens in his mouth, grabbing a pair of forceps to dig for something in a very still and stoic brother's back, then repeating the process.

"That be Big Mike," the nude dancer says. "He do wet razor shaves an' bullets. He got you next. Then they say you talk to Lupo. Wanna lap dance till then, Big Man?"

"Maybe upstairs . . . um?"

"TwoLip."

"Tulip, like the flower?"

"Nah nigga, look down."

"*Stamp.* So, upstairs?

"Nah," she leans close to my ear and I can tell she's been eating more fried shit than she's been slapping those cheeks. "That ole bitch up there countin' money like some Jew so ain't no *private* dances today and it a shame cause I done my menistration, right? But I hear she maybe goin' home soon so . . . be ready, Big Man." She pulls away, smiles a grill of gold and slivers of chicken and green pepper, and slinks down the row of hard, dangerous men. All of them, like me, wearing shades in the disco-ball darkness.

Sure enough Big Mike motions me over and I sit. He swallows his vinegary greens, covers me in a short smock and asks if I can remove my shades and I refuse. "You in luck for the wet shave—got hot water ready from the twenny-two I dug out that dumbass nigga's scapula and hadda close it wid glue cause he want a lap dance. You want essential oil in yo' hot towel, cuz?"

The yammer ceases when a new brute limps by, left arm dipped. Head covered in a familiar wave cap. Big Mike's the supplicant, almost forgetting I'm there but this dude's staring right at me as he strolls by, even turning when he hits the stairs.

"Stitched two holes in ole Oso, man. Small ones, must've been ACPs. Kill, his brother goin' talk atchew in a bit so lemme get to this."

He readies the steamed towel as the DJ queues up the Junkyard Band for a few beats of Go Go so the local talent can show off their footwork.

"Leave my eyes uncovered." I take off the shades.

I hear a woman-like scream a few chairs down and Big Mike laughs, assuring me that's typically when some fool's too stupid or poor to take bootleg antibiotics for a "love disease" and his fellow barber's got to take drastic measures with a scalpel and cauterizing tool. Yet even the tortured brother calms and bobs his head as the Go Go blends into the electronic pop and thumping intro to Strafe's *Set it Off*. Song never fails to get any blackfolk distracted, and indeed it even tugs me back to school, just for an instant . . . that time before Esme . . .

Sausage fingers massage the warm lather into my scruff just as Oso returns, eyeing me again. Big Mike sways to the song and sings the lyrics as Oso nods.

"Yo man. The buy-ins been accepted. My brother be down directly."

I note he's now toting a sopping paper plate but it's full of flautas and dripping with frijoles. "No fish?"

"Don't fuck wid this D.C. shit man," he explains. "Ya know it's Koreans and Vietnamese who make it and these Negroes just reheat or deep fry it like it's theirs." He pauses. "*Oye* . . . I know you, bro'?"

Can't shake my head because Big Mike's just taken the first swipes with the straight razor. And his he's still dancing, singing along, ". . . *on the left . . . I suggest . . .*"

Dickie Cornish isn't afraid of a damn thing, they say, probably because he's endured life as one of the damned. Ha! Tell that to my Preakness Stakes ticker about to bust my sternum. Tell that to the serpent, wriggling in my belly, whispering in my dome. Not know, Daddy . . . *slow down . . .*

. . . and now everyone starts moving in slow motion, almost to the music, to that fool Big Mike's razor swipes and dance steps . . . and the buck-naked dancers have set up an impromptu line dance, yeah, *slow*, like my heartbeat now . . . and Oso and another figure pass me, look me up and down . . . slow . . . converse with some captains . . . stroll back . . . slow . . .

Set . . . set . . . set . . . set it off . . .

. . . so they stop in front of me and I see the second dude's got on a wave cap as well, but this doo-rag's a brilliant sateen, picking up the glint and glitter of DJ's lightshow.

Big Mike almost genuflects to this man. This is sumbitch with whom I tussled in Seward Park.

"Didn't catch your name, moe, " Lupo says.

"Didn't give it. Just who vouched." Right about now, who

vouched is *hopefully* rolling up the sidewalk with Mattel, two old farts in wheelchairs, the last generation of innocuous, ubiquitous causalities of the War on Drugs . . . with the rest of the brothers creeping up on the back across the treeline, and next door without any teenagers sounding the alarm.

"Lupo, man. Means wolf. Not wolf tickets y'hearme."

"Uh-huh." He's squinting hard and it isn't because of the dim light.

"Things got fucked up, bad. But they gonna get better, specially if these *putas* put Trump back in, we can operate, we don't gotta run. So we wait and will call ya on who the next supplier gonna be . . ."

All the time the song's bridge is playing, and it's Oso tilting his head. I wasn't wrestling with his ass but damned if he's not making me. He taps his brother yet Lupo oddly waves him off, gestures to the cabaret talent.

"You see anything you want?"

"Say less," I clown with a face full of lather. "Her." I gesture to TwoLips.

"That bitch deformed," Big Mike opines. "Should call her FourLips!"

"All four do the job, *muy perfecto*," Lupo says with a laugh but Oso's really nudging him now.

She comes over. I look down at my crouch and she shrugs and kicks off those heels and hunkers down . . .

"This gonna be a first," Big Mike says. "Ain't no faggot so let me get these last hairs and get some Clubman on ya befo' the boppin' and sloppin' begins . . ."

She tugs at my trouser zipper to as Strafe returns to the chorus . . . the crescendo . . . I'm lifting my neck to take that last upward scrape of the blade . . .

"*Que?*" Lupo abruptly hollers. "Mike . . . cut that muv!"

Before Big Mike's synapse's can process the order and turn the blade to a ninety degree angle to slit me like a hog I'm shoving her face with my left hand while yanking the Mini out with my right . . . *twist your wrist, Junior . . . squeeze . . .*

. . . two rounds hit poor Big Mike as I'm swinging the gun forward now, lunging . . .

. . . I hit Lupo in the upper thigh and fall on he and his brother. We land with me aiming the pistol at Oso's face and Lupo howling and squirming like a wounded canine.

It's surreal . . . the screams and Strafe stop just for an instant, as if a deep breath's coming, then . . .

The door's being blown to bits and I hear Croc's lusty shouts . . .

"Mossberg, niggas! Mossberg!"

The only swinging dicks dumb enough not to already be on the floor are Oso and Lupo's minions who were about to rescue their bosses. Dude with .40 automatic opens up on Mattel's fellas but he's literally cut in half by the stream of lead spit by Mattel's chopper. Nothing else makes that awful sound but an AK-47. On a residential street.

Any dancer who didn't take a round comes screaming out of the front door into the night's chill and blowing leaves, with that Pit Bull close on their heels. Whether Mattel was going to St. Valentines Day Massacre the other gangsta customers as a public service and message to the Youngs, I left up to him. My focus is upstairs.

"On your feet, both of you, *muevete!*"

"You . . . *shot* me . . ."

"Now you and your brother are even. It'd be worse if I turned you over to them. They got relatives y'all turned into zombies."

"You killed Big Mike!" Oso cries.

The barber's bleeding out, razor twitching in his hand. I feel a soreness . . . a trickle of my own blood across my Adams Apple. I swallow and all the plumbing's still okay but I got to fight off the dizziness and I don't know if it's my ticker blasting at my ribs again or a I took a round.

"I-I still . . . am gonna see Heaven . . . before all of you. Now get up. Time to see mama."

I pull their irons from their holsters and shove them forward, both whining, limping and wincing and I'm responsible.

"Somebody back me up!" I yell, and a couple of Mattel's dads acknowledge yet I don't hear anyone coming up the stairs past the kitchen with me, Just Melvin shouting at Croc . . .

We're up one creaky, cheaply carpentered step at a time, and either of these two monsters could easily dig in or fall back on me but they know the house is crawling with an unknown enemy armed to the teeth and it isn't the cops, subject to the Constitution. Help is somewhere in Mexico. Maybe get me closer to their mom where they got more weapons stashed . . .

"*Mamá . . . Flor . . . tengo a tus hijos aquí. Estoy cansado de hacerles agujeros. Y lo siento por Danielle. Hay que hablar.*"

"Mama! Fuck this muvfukkah . . . kill him!"

"Lupo shut up!" I hear. Guess she's got her teeth. It's punctuated by some growls, a high-pitched bark.

"*Bah! Sabia que eras tu! Donde aprendiste español, chico?*"

"My girlfriend . . . in college. Taught me many . . . many things. And a friend . . . Ernesto. Police killed him. But that's past, now is now. *Mira*, Flor . . . you, your boys and Tequila can live or die—just do as I say, okay?"

The barking gets louder and she's cursing. Probably got an iron while trying to corral a squirming little dog. Probably torn between escape . . . and leaving a lot of product. I get my answer as to the priority. "Take those fools, give them to the po-po. What's up s worth more than alla us. They comin' for it from Manzanillo if we don't get it all re-upped, then they come for us. So why don't you an' I and whoever you got down there do it. And Tweedle Dee and Tweedle Dum and they hoes and strippers and that hot mess'll take the hit."

As we get to the landing her offspring mutter, "Mama?" in unison, and she berates them for fucking up like the amateurs—Conrad Voss and his pals.

I see her in a doorway. Jack dangling from her red wrinkled lips. Yeah, her teeth are in she's powdered and got on her best wig. I'm sure she was a fancy redbone back in the day, enough to sway whoever these two clowns' daddy was. Yet now she's holding a Glock in one leathery hand, that Yorkie in the other and she is shaking both.

"They know better than to snitch. They be taken care of, and we make the money."

"Confession time, I want it all. No cops, no Feds here. Just us. A street, thing Mama."

"Voss's peeps—an' them others like his partner, made it personal, politics." She spits in derision, and the Yorkie barks. "I saw you stay wiff what ya'll know. Gettin' a real man back in our White House. Let the expert slang the Tranq. Then . . ."

"They fuck up?"

Hard to have a casual conversation at mutual gunpoint, dead and wounded motherfuckers laying all around . . . trigger happy dads mopping up . . .

. . . and she's squinting. "Then you 'round, baby. Messing shit up."

"Me notwithstanding, Voss's people'll want back in, right?"

"They pussies, RINOs, too country club despite all they redneck bu-shit. Now Bracht . . . yeah . . . he was a real man, iron fist and but could go country club with the girlies, drink the men and slap them around. *El Jefe.*"

Whoa. I almost lower the .380. "You . . . you *knew* him?"

"I cry when I hear he was killed . . ."

"You know who killed him?"

I hear, "Mama, you ain't serious about a deal wid this big nigga are you?"

"Baby, you got big balls. I wasn't down wiff them nobody touchin' you when that damn white girl fount out you kilt her uncle, and I did my adds and takeways and come up wiff maybe you kilt Bracht, too. Her own daddy said no to her . . . then she had the nerve to come to me! Silly heifer."

I thought a bullet was coming yet now she's cackling like the witch she was out on the street that night and even the two sons are quiet, breathing very hard at something maybe they feared deep down . . .

"I think Mama's knows what biz and what's personal and y'all might have to call me uncle."

"*No! No!*" the squirming sons protest in unison.

"See, I don't care about freein' all the crackers from prison long as monkeys like these niggas who my boys entertain or these damn teenage hoodlums I gotta pay off will be in cages again . . . *maricones* and perverts'll be buried along wiff that mummy Biden and his silly black bitch, Lord have mercy! Don't matter 'cause we got people around Voss who gonna make sure the president *really* win this time, who know the game. No more stupid college boys. No more crazy perverts like my niece. You an' I be making paper, baby . . . and we be *safe* 'cause *this* time, the Justice Department'll be eliminatin' the competition. The politics is good long as it serve the money and the product. El Pescador told me that shit."

"So they say hate China but, do business with the Chinese to get the White . . . they do say hate the Mexicans, the border is fucked, but do business with Colima to bring it in, bootleg the xylazine. That's gonna make America great again?"

She shrugs. "I smarted myself up an' been to an Inaugural Ball. Have you? Nope. You was prolly beggin' for change at Obamas! I been ta the White House. Have you? Nope. I been ta Mar-a-Lago wiff my husband before he died. His dyin' wish . . . he loved the President's *estilo* so much!"

"Mama shut up an' help us!" Oso blubbers.

"Sit!" I order them. "I don't need a human shield. Arms behind your head POWS style."

Lupo complies. Oso can't do the arm raised thing because he's still recovering from the shoulder GSW I gave him.

Faint hints of sirens start coming through the blasted windows downstairs.

"You aim ta keep me here for Five-O? They too stupid. You sure you won't deal for real, share in this shit wiff ole Flor?"

"How'd you know Bracht?"

"Tell him boys. Tell him your mama was an American success story like Mr. Trump."

Lupo clears his throat and says, "She . . . she used to clean his office when he first opened over in Virginia. Cleaning lady to shot-caller, you pussy muv- . . ."

"Shut your mouff now boy. Yup . . . Alexandria office. The Argyle Group. I'd stop dustin' an' read his shit and take an' interest an' he'd never get mad. He was flattered okay? He taught me shit. But thas' not God talkin'. God talkin' is my late husband and Bracht knowin' some a the same folk down Mexico. Same badasses. Jorge Molina. Memorize that name. Jorge Molina. Manzanillo Pesce Tours. Fishing . . . *Pescedoro. Ha!* We'll do some good biz together."

Sights and triggers're still on one another but I'm getting tired of her doing all the talking. "I hope whoever's listening got all that," I say to the thin air, but mostly to Mom's rosary, worn as a prop.

"*Que?*"

"This *puta*'s wired Mama. *You fucked us, ole lady!*"

"You don't talk to Mama like that!"

Tweedle Dee and Tweedle Dum start going at it and I don't know if it's bullshit or real but she's squawking. I lower the Mini just a few inches and get my answer. Lupo's the smart one. As his brother wails on him he lunges for me.

"*Mátalo!*" he howls.

Yet all he manages to do is topple me, heels up. Still, the old lady advances, shrieking, cursing. If I can't get turned around . . . and aim, then I'm dead . . .

. . . because I can hear the music, the beat . . . watch the dancers, right? Cabaret . . . Lord, I love myself some cabaret! Garish and nasty and fun and I don't even feel any pain, right?

Don't even hear the shot.

Yet I swear I see Croc, on his swollen feet, climbing stairs. Mossberg smoking.

Ready to see me, Rain Man? I missed you...so did your mom, your sister.

CHAPTER TWENTY-TWO

In a Deep State

NO FLAMING WHEELS, SPINNING ME IN the clouds for a thousand years.

No rolling boulders up hills for ten thousand years.

None of that, unless Purgatory is the hum of a pulse oximeter, or the incessant yet reassuring beep of a heart monitor. Oh, and the pleasant repartee above me . . .

"This sumbitch may be an amateur but he's indestructible I'll give you that. This negro'd beat nuclear fallout . . ."

"I want the guard on him doubled Chief. I also have FBI agents checking the medical staff. I cannot have him hurt . . . I cannot have him leave *me* . . . I mean . . . my case . . . I cannot evaluate him as a witness until he can give me a statement . . ."

"Hold up. My officers found him surrounded by a dozen bodies . . . and half nekkid women running through the neighborhood screaming . . . felons who got outstanding warrants hiding in trash cans scared out their minds. My lab did a quickie on some of those shell casings—some weapons are licensed to phony addresses out in rural Virginia, so now I'm tellin' *you* what happened—I figure he infiltrated this traphouse or whatever, like what happened when we raided Danielle Diggs' spot . . . let in his friends who shot up the place. There-fuckin'-fore, he ain't under 'protection.' This big motherfucker is under arrest!"

"This is a federal city. You can't prosecute a bedbug without my U.S. Attorneys."

"We'll see about that. Your girl Kamala ain't got no October surprises left. It's November today . . ."

My eyes, crusty and pained, open to Patterson's meriney jowls flapping. "C-Could y'all keep it down . . . maybe get me some water?"

"Dickie? Oh my God . . . *look at you!* I mean . . . nice to see you on the mend."

Odd to hear the chickenhawk gushing . . . there she is, looking severe in her glasses, hair blown out no doubt for the whitefolk on a network news show. Smiling, though.

As for Patterson, well . . . "Trick or Treat, huh! I got some good news and bad news for you, Sonny Jim. Looks like Flor Jackson Mendez-Garcia blew a small hole in you before somebody blew a big hole in her. Good news is they plugged the hole. Bad news is the round you caught nicked your ureter. They patched the plumbing pretty well but every time you drink, you gonna have to piss standing on your head for about a week . . . *in your jail cell.*"

"Chief!" Bivens intercedes.

"We ain't done by a damn side, Hobo Jim. Now if y'all'll excuse me, I got to get to a ribbon-cutting with Her Honor the Mayor." I watch him top his bald pate with his cap. "She's back from her overseas junket . . . now that her girl Linda Figgis has finally reported to federal prison from her beach vacation." He pauses at the door, looks at me and smiles. "Dickie Cornish—Lawd have mercy . . ."

When he's gone Bivens opines, "He's a philistine but he's our philistine."

"Funny I didn't . . . get that feeling." Yeah, I'm cotton-headed, numb.

"That was quite the 'Hail Mary' with the transmitter, we're still reviewing the audio file."

"I am a Papist after all. And a tight end. Where am I?"

"GWU Hospital, Foggy Bottom. Same security wing they bring wounded terrorists or unsuccessful presidential assassins."

"Jesus, Mary and Joseph. What's the damage? I don't mean on me."

"I suppose you heard some if you were awake. City officials are hot to pin the entire O.K. Corral on you unless you talk. You knew the MAGA machine on social media, the extremists in Congress even main street out there already circled the wagons around Voss. Deep state conspiracy, the fake moon landings, right? The audio with Flor . . . it's great so far but, again, the cult abides to blindness, power. It got some play on Fox News . . . a miracle . . . yet even a mountain of circumstantial evidence, inferences connected—is still circumstantial, still inference to too many people."

"You pretty much . . . weren't subtle, *Lil Angie* . . ."

"Yes. I didn't want to nail everyone at Mar-a-lago and donors and toadies with insurrection, election fraud. I want them on drug trafficking and RICO."

"Uh-huh."

"You're still woozy, in some pain?"

"Uh-huh."

She laughs. "And I'm remarkably calm, given things."

"Uh-huh."

"What is it you all . . . when you get clean . . . what do say when you go into rehab, therapy?"

"Grace, wisdom . . . because there's shit you can't control."

"Yes. Streetwise perhaps like you?"

"Look at me, you call this wise? It just had to be."

"Cops say Flor Jackson Mendez-Garcia was about to deliver the *coup de grace* on you but someone killed her. Imagine that."

Don't have to.

"Olivier Mendez-Garcia, Junior, aka Lupo is here in the ICU . . . conscious yet refuses to roll on anyone. Roland Mendez-Garcia, aka Oso has two recent bullet wounds, healing. Piecing together what we and MPD know or should have known, yes— they were the button men sent to clean up Dean Scholtz, make it look like they were going after Aidy Voss, too. You and Helen were going to be collateral damage. Those other two worked for Voss. Oso . . . he wants to flip on his mother and brother but wants 'Kanye money and a new face' otherwise the Colima people will come get him. Again, perfect inferences don't seem to be enough to prevent a coup by criminals. Then again . . . it's not a coup if the average clown votes for it, right?"

"So we come . . . back to me," I wheeze. "You want to know if I want Kanye money and a new face too?"

"I've run out of time. Have you run out of Hail Mary's?"

A nurse and an Indian resident, given his name plate and apparent youth, arrive and will likely usher her out despite her title.

"Ms. Rubio is giving testimony now at an undisclosed location. She recorded a message for you. There's an iPad on the side table—you can view it. Some raspberry mini-popsicles in the insulated cup to keep you hydrated, too."

I lick my lips. Cracked but sweet. "Thanks," I whisper.

A little mirror on that moveable side table shows something odd after I clock her face, however. Her lip gloss is a little smeared at the corners—with the same red stain tinting my mouth that colors hers.

"Did Patterson catch you?"

"I'm . . . I'm a coward," she mutters. "*My favor* . . . I was maybe too operatic of a term. I was always going to use you as a tool, okay. You know that now, too. The favor was accent to scare you . . . but it was real to me, deep down. *Oh my God* . . . I feel so stupid." I clock wet eyes. "Yes, I was running out of time and I snuck my favor when you were asleep . . ."

"Whoa . . ."

"I've been wondering since I turned eighteen what it would be like."

The doc and nurse are wide-eyed as they go about their checklist in a corner of this fairly big room, pretending not to hear.

I pretend it doesn't affect me. "It's . . . okay."

"No, it's technically a battery."

"I forgive you."

"I doubt that. I'll send the Assistant Attorney General when you're feeling better. Good day, *Mr. Cornish* . . . I-I think . . . um . . . you have more visitors now that you're awake."

My eyes follow her out. The folk in scrubs are tending to me without saying a word—the doc seems especially nervous, like they have Mighty Joe Young chained up and sedated instead of me—so I have to prompt him.

In a no bedside manner-having-monotone that beats mine, the doc says, "You're very lucky. The bullet missed your left kidney, exited without hitting your spine. Barring infection . . . you should have normal activity soon . . . full recovery by Thanksgiving, a month away."

He pauses, oddly . . .

"I-I don't like hospitals, man," I tell him. "That you pumped me full of . . . well . . . opioids . . . that's that just the half of it."

"W-Well, the social worker from the . . . ahh . . . Correctional Treatment Facility is coming to discuss that. Good luck, Mr. Cornish."

Now, finally I get some feeling in my left arm. It's handcuffed to the bed rail. I wasn't hallucinating Patterson's rant, I guess.

The nurse, smiling to make up for this asshole's dismal personality and my predicament, slides the table over in front of me and sets up the iPad.

"Another popsicle?" she asks, with a wink.

"No, ma'am."

"You up for more visitors? Now that you're awake the doctor and the police have authorized a few."

I nod. I slide my finger on the screen as she raises the bed's head, fluffs my pillow.

Esme's all dolled-up of course, looking good, adorned in red. That gray streak's more apparent. I listen, transfixed as Croc waddles into the room tapping his cane, chair probably parked outside.

"The Indestructible Captain Scarlet! Remember we used to watch that marionette shit when we were little?" he says. He notices the cuffs and my blank stare no doubt, at the screen. "Aw, fam'ly. I'm sorry."

"Esme . . . spittin' wisdom for a change."

He cranes his neck to look, then pulls up a chair. "She evil, fine as spider spit though."

"Verna here?"

"*Naaaah*. But she sent them flowers right on the window."

"What'd you get me, besides a mass murder rap?"

"Red Lobster gift card."

It hurts to smile.

Doesn't hurt him, despite the mess, the pain. "Hell man," he's chortling, "wid your fan club out there waiting, the flowers . . . an' I saw her majesty an' her entourage of Elliott Nesses leave . . ."

"Just . . . not too geeked about my life now, man. Can't go on like this. Lost decades, not years. *Decades.* You too."

"What you did was justice. What we did was justice. Damn, I even hear that nigga Mattel thinking about runnin' for mayor? Maybe as a *Republican.* Can you believe that's shit?"

"You saved my life. That's the only decent thing."

He gets that awful, hungry look.

"Murder on folk who have it comin' ain't murder. Not those motherfuckers at the barbershop . . . not Bracht, not the men who hurt Stripe, nor the white preppie boys *and* girl what spoilt your dear sister so many years ago, remember?" He stops to hear Esme's soliloquy. "Kill . . . what's this cray bitch who ruined your life causing you to lunch over?"

"Not so sure anymore. See I always say, if I hadn't met Esmeralda in school, I'd have become the man I was *going* to be."

"A baller, Dickie. No stoppin' you, moe."

"Nah, gee. She says I was tested. She's says the pain on the street and now . . . and the years . . . made me the man I was *supposed* to be. And I can't do this bullshit anymore."

"Go back to cheating husbands and bouncing at clubs?"

"Not even that."

"Listen, moe, lemme get your other girls in here, keep your mind off Vampirella, okay? And I'm sure this chick Bivens is scheming' now to get them cuffs off . . ."

He limps to the door, motions . . . in jumps a squealing, squeaking Katie and I have to keep my free arm up to prevent her from falling onto the bed with me or fouling my IV lines. LaKeisha's reticent and distant as usual, and this time is wearing a surgical mask, as she lost too many dear to her during COVID.

As Katie composes herself she eyes the IV. "What they givin' you, Dick? Better not be nothin' cray . . . they need to check your medical history."

LaKeisha just sighs, says, "Jon Snow, Lord Commander of the Night's Watch."

"Ya know . . . whatever happened to this cat, Snow?"

"Books or film?"

"Both, either."

"He's where he needs to be. Most people wouldn't be happy with the answer. But you aren't most people." She taps the handcuffs. "Are you?"

"Rhetorical question?"

I can see LaKeisha smiling under her mask.

The nurse returns with some meds and Katie interrogates her, then allows my treatment. I take a mouthful of water then ask the nurse to adjust the TV. I don't even know what day it is so I randomly ask for sports.

As she advances the channel we hit some infernal news stations and there's Senator Brom Vitter of Texas, being interviewed in Russell Senate Building lobby. He seems pretty confident about the election and his upcoming legal "annoyance." Rather than comment, he's spinning yarns about Texas A & M football, and driving from "survival training" in the Sonoran Desert of Mexico all the way to Galveston for "Frankie & Annette Beach Blanket Bingo"- themed birthday party over a week ago for his wife, so he had no idea major donor Conrad Voss and his daughter Aidy were in D.C. until they burned up in a warehouse. He's staying in D.C. at his rented house until election night then he's headed to a victory party "over Obamaism." The reporter notes the irony that his house is a block from the Obamas' old spot up in Kalorama, on a bluff overlooking Rock Creek Park . . .

"*Tywin Lannister*," LaKeisha huffs. "With the face of a Targaryen. That's his type. Arrogant . . . so arrogant he can't conceive of how evil he truly is." No clue what she's saying but it seems to fit. Indeed, there in the hospital . . . I'm studying him for the first time. "Did you see the details of the research I did awhile back . . . Verna was preoccupied with her case so she didn't know I was using the SFME Nexis account . . . I put it in a PDF."

"I don't know how to open that stuff Keesh."

"You click on it."

"Yeah. Cut me a break."

"No, I can't. You click on it."

"Okay . . . what was it again . . . stuff on Dean Scholtz, crap the Public Defender didn't have . . . Gatekeepers?"

"Yes, and one interesting item about that man—other than him being an unrepentant racist even by Texas standards. Gallingly worse during COVID. Gatekeepers in Texas do security for his rallies when he introduces Trump. He's been to Bracht's hunting lodge, you know. Several years ago was a regular when I was with Southwestern State Oil and Gas. All in the research . . . you didn't read." She shrinks away from my bedside.

"Keesh . . . I'm sorry, okay? Come here . . ."

She keeps her distance, sways like a shy kid as she speaks. "The one thing he *didn't* do that our Orange Jesus never called him on, nor the others, was attack Biden about his son

Hunter, you know, various conspiracy theories, but the under-lying reality was the Biden's son's addiction."

"Not following you."

"Like you, m'lord . . . Vitter's son Randy hot dosed White . . . he was homeless for a time, in Austin. Unlike you, he didn't make it."

Now Katie's standing there listening, hands on her hips. "Let him rest, Keeshy."

"I'm okay . . . and what, Vitter doesn't attack anyone regarding addiction? That's rare for his crowd."

"He doesn't support more money for addicts or rehab but he is just very quiet about it—at a time when these MAGA crowd insist on loud, vicious orthodoxy, and they savage any Republican who backs off. Even those who themselves have been pill poppers or alcoholics. Yet he gets a pass."

Now I'm checking this dude's vampirically pale skin and scary eyes and overly ambitious Texas accent and I thinking why does this man get to cut Dean loose, so sanctimoniously, for shooting two boys, when he's typically happy that other whiteboys and brute cops have run fade on protesters, unarmed brothers?

Clickity-clackity, there in my dome, injured and addled in the hospital . . . "Sonoran Desert? With that skin?"

"He's apparently a fitness freak. Ex-military."

The reporters chase Vitter out of the Russell Building with security and Capitol Police laboring to form a lane for the dude to a waiting SUV. From out of an open rear window on the driver's side two hounds with narrow wolfish features snarl. They calm instantly with the sight of their daddy . . .

An off-camera voice shouts *"Senator you got two dogs now? Does this mean the District and all cities run by liberal Democrats a dangerous place, as indicated by that massacre a day ago in a poor section of town? There are rumors that was not the random lawlessness you've highlighted violence but actually drug related. "*

"Well now let's move on to bigger issues. If we control the White House and Senate again we shall propound a comprehensive urban pacification bill. Until then, let's let local law enforcement handle things."

I'll be a sumbitch . . .

. . . and while the bigger dog starts cutting up again, he pets the slightly smaller one, cooing, *"You happy to see your big brother home again?"*

"Whatchew'all should be schemin' about," Katie interrupts, "is gettin' a hacksaw up in this mug for those handcuffs, *ha!*"

Matter of fact. "Keesh," I whisper. "I gotta get outta here."

"I don't understand," she whispers back.

"You will, baby, you will. Is there a jake out there?"

"Three in fact."

"This is the Deputy Attorney General's personal number I'm writing here. Personal, as in her crib down at Navy Yard, right? I want you and Katie to call it. Tell whoever's there Dickie's about to do something stupid again. *Ave Maria.*"

CHAPTER TWENTY-THREE
Against Medical Advice

PATTERSON'S RIGHT ABOUT ONE THING—PISSING WASN'T a party before this wound, but in the last two days it's become *unpleasant*, and I can't walk or steady my ass on the head without this four-legged cane. There's a jake waiting to lock me back onto the bed I approach in my bathrobe and gown; a male nursing assistant takes my breakfast tray away. At least the IV tubes are out.

Suddenly there's a ruckus outside as I edge onto the bed. In walks the young Indian resident . . . or rather he's backpedaling, arguing . . . as is an older white female doc in a skirt and white coat. Who are they arguing with?

Well, well . . .

"Good morning, Detective Abalos, Detective Goins."

The jake in room exchange whispers with them. "No problem, Sarge," he says to Monica.

No handcuffs for me. The older female doc's now on the phone. Ordering up a wheelchair.

"Mr. Cornish, I have a federal detainer warrant here so we are compelled to deliver you to federal custody, namely a secure ward under Shore Patrol Guard at Bethesda Naval Hospital where you are to remain until you recover. Acting Chief Patterson is being served with a copy at the Daly Building."

I guess Bivens created her own Hail Mary. Two minute drill. But no one called a play and usually I'm part of the audible, I'm not it's designer.

"I don't have any clothes, even a pair of draws."

Goins asks for a pair of scrubs, tee shirt and such that will fit me and that's highly unlikely . . . the nursing assistants scramble as the docs discuss my meds, antibiotics.

"You realize the pain management regimen is tricky for . . . someone like him," the resident points out.

"I've hurt worse."

Okay, yeah it hurts a lot—slipping out of the gown into a tee shirt and scrub bottoms that are high-water on me. Goins gets me a George Washington University zip up hoodie and the these chicks literally convoy me to the elevator, then out to 25th Street and a waiting unmarked, running lights flashing.

I must be the sight, all six-three of me with this damn cane.

Away we zoom. Against medical advice, at least from the good folks at GWU.

Thing is, I'm noticing we aren't headed into the Park, or toward Georgetown, to drive up Wisconsin. Been awhile since I've even been close to Bethesda and certainly the sprawling Naval Hospital near NIH yet driving toward the Mall isn't the way.

"Ladies," I speak up, my back feeling like it's on fire. "Is this for real, or is this a snatch and you gonna sweat me for what happened over in Ward Seven?"

Monica's driving; the pretty sister, Goins, turns over the front seat and grins, says, "It's for real. And not exactly a snatch. And we are not exactly . . . ungrateful to certain parties for putting a lot of bad people out of commission in that house."

"It was still a bad thing . . ."

A two-way radio call comes in and Goins takes it acknowl-edges. It sounds like someone from Patterson's office and things are jumping. I can hear Patterson screaming something about the D.C. Attorney General issuing an opinion letter just about me. Yeah, we're a small city with our own "attorney gen-eral" but don't tell the local pols how grandiose that sounds.

"Did he really think he could hold me without the Feds concurring?"

Monica shushes me as Goins does some tapdance then signs-off. "We could get fired, lose our pensions for this. For you. He'll get over it. He *wants* to get over it."

Goins tosses a large paper bag over the seat. "Your groupies let us into your place. Those are your clothes, shoes. You have twenty-four hours. That's it."

"For what?"

She shrugs. Monica says, "The Chief would say, to stir some shit . . ."

"Nothing from Bivens. No plan, no ideas . . . just pop my stitches?"

I settle back and think maybe I should ride out the apoca-lypse in the hospital . . . access to goodies there. Invite Katie and LaKeisha. Toast a failed life with Verna, toast surren-dering to Esme.

Or yeah—go out like Croc. Run up on a U.S. Senator and stick a Mossberg under his chin? Hey, that method worked with Bracht, right? Or maybe he'll do himself, like Antonelli, after he spills what I think he'll spill.

But who am I? Nothing. Even if I spill, who'll believe me . . . just more circumstantial evidence and inferences, as the chickenhawk prattles on about. I'm just Foghorn Leghorn. A homeless bum, drunk . . . addict . . . lunatic. Lurch. Herman Munster.

The man I could be. No, there's only one play here.

"Just the shoes. Is there a jacket? Gimme a jacket . . ."

"What are you doing?" Goins asks. "Look at your hair . . . you need a shave . . . you gonna look crazier than you look now."

"Uh-huh. Take me up to Seventh and Florida, fast. Try not to look like Twelve. I need something. Got some cash?"

Monica's busting a hard left and we are zooming up 11th Street, Northwest, running lights and sirens in effect.

She's got $33 on her, Goins another $41.

I'm rearranging my hospital gear and a few clothes right there in the back.

"Y'all young ladies keep your eyes forward. I know I'm an attractive older man but we are all about business, right?"

I hear giggles and I'm glad because I can tell all three of us are too tense.

Monica cuts the lights and siren way down before Rhode Island and we drive over to Peach's domain and they dump me off. Goins of all people seems to take a shine to me and instead of Cornish or Mr. Cornish smiles her very pretty smile and says "Hey *Pops* . . . you be careful. Don't rupture any sutures. You aren't gonna tell us what you're up to, are you?"

"No."

"Ok then. We're taking the long, long way up to Bethesda. The Beltway."

"Then we're going to lose you in the men's room in Five Guys. You were hungry."

"Cool."

Hey, it's no less inspired a plan than what I got going.

It's colder out here. So she's not sunning herself in the same spot I left her. Her minions still got the Halloween shit up in the shop window; no one's going in but the usual condition of loud talk and loitering maintains itself outside. She me looking a bit more familiar than the gumshoe costumes I try to wear and note the limp, the real winces, the hospital cane.

Peach is in the back with one legit customer, some bearded whiteboy who has migraines and needs the watered down gummies she's got, and she can't be too sure if he's po-po. Real po-po's down the street, I whisper when I see her. And tell her I got cash-money and I want some Tina. Smokable, in blunt form with a little weed as the conductor. Old school red-blooded American Tina, like Dean got hooked on. In other words, no White.

"Welcome back, I guess?" she shrugs and she disappears with Monica and Goins' money, comes back, puts three in my hand. "Don't forget . . . you gonna fix my lover-man, right?"

I nod. "Need a favor. Got your phone? I mean, that *other* phone. The one you didn't tell the City about I bet, now that . . . what . . . you finally got your THC license?"

She bobs her head. "Whatchew lunchin' fo', man? Come on!"

"Gonna be an expensive call, too. Forgot when I saw you before—you taking Spanish lessons online?"

"Increase my clientele."

"In Manzanillo?"

Her face goes all loose, and I can see eyes get squinty.

"Nigga, you come in here all busted up and I hear things 'bout you and Twelve an' the Feds . . . you snitchin', you wired?"

I smile.

"You know me. And you want me to fix your man Kenny, right? Now take some take deafness lessons the next five minutes, then show me out the back. Twelve's in a blue Buick sedan on S Street . . ."

And after I pray to the Archangel Michael to pardon my flirtation with Lucifer, I'm waddling toward down Florida Avenue, west, as Peach's folk roll down to S Street to bumrush and occupy Monica and Goins' time. Can't let them fuck with me now.

Through the bustle, elbows, nasty looks . . . inhaling the fumes, letting the grime and curb filth stain those scrub bottoms . . . coming by where me and Esme and Mr. Fred and Miz Eva used to squat . . . I'm slowly getting the spoor. On myself.

Funny I thought I was moving up in the world. Now, I'm back on the street, doddering by that spot we lay our heads and it's now a movie theatre, luxury bar . . . yet after COVID no one goes because of the Youngs out on the prowl . . . and a few folk passed out by the light poles, on at the bus stop right there, covered in zombie sores.

Me and my town, full circle.

Given my pained gait, I figure it'll take three hours to go another mile and a half. I stop farther up Florida and panhandle for a jumbo slice. The Iranian dude in there first threatens me, then takes pity when I tell him I'm a veteran and babble how to fix the sputtering light over the is Coke machine with some Elmers glue and some paper clips. Sauce and crumbs tumbling on my jacket helps with the verisimilitude.

It's the large Sprite with ice that helps the most. I drink greedily, let the sugar infect me, move on. And as I do, even in-costume I look less and less like some big surly black activist, come to prod and protest, or big surly black criminal come to rob and terrorize and otherwise breach the peace and sully privilege.

The test comes when an MPD blue and white unit slows, then blows right by me.

A Park Police unit likewise stops at the light at Florida and Connecticut. The jakes in it just eye me. Finally, the driver rolls down the window and tells me to get in a shelter, it's getting cold tonight. "Bums" have been rolled close to here. My dirty ass isn't welcome to sleep anywhere near Dupont Circle. Then they, too, zoom off. Guess I'm ready.

Exhausted, I watch the sun dip, all orange and purple. Feel the wind pick up. Aw, like it was yesterday. So I sit my ass down on a steamy street grate, except this one's twisted almost into a Möbius strip to prevent campers from camping.

I wait.

I think to myself, yeah, the mirror's my only weapon. Hope it works. But Mother Mary, that hospital bed really wasn't so bad, was it . . .

CHAPTER TWENTY-FOUR

Mirror

THEY SAID GOVERNMENT DIDN'T MATTER BACK in the day. If so than why did the robber barons of the North . . . of Manhattan and Pittsburgh and Boston and the Main Line . . . and the old Confederates who made peace with a new order, all build grand mansions of brick and stone over here in styles that escape me—Georgian, Victorian, whatever, where the foreign embassies begin to sprout up, and Rock Creek Park forms a ravine that cleaves the city?

Old school activists and street pundits say it divides the city spiritually as well as physically. Never been a barrier to me. Just easier for cops and rent-a-cops and maids and butlers to shoo me away or throw shit on me; easier to spot me if I housed something useful from the recyling can, or busted a back window to help myself anything I could sell from a laundry room or a garage. In this jont you were merely farther from the sanctuary of the hood where folks supposedly didn't care about garbage or panhandling; puddles of dog piss was okay but a spritz of human piss, nah son.

And so now it's dark out and I'm in the cut in Kalorama, almost to Ashmead Place Northwest, and only blondes jogging or walking little lap dogs clock me singing to myself. Chuck Brown, Moody's Mood . . . *Here I go, Here I go* . . . Not as cover, but to calm my ass. Getting an occasion nervous stare, yet no jakes or mace are coming my way.

That's the house. The same one I imprinted in my dome; whitewashed limestone and a gray slate roof, massive chimneys, giant picture windows . . . and sure enough an SUV's parked on Ashmead as sentinel.

It's not Feds doing protective detail stuff. Their profile never changes. Seen it for years out on the street, scavenging the trash of pols and famous people, trust me. A car around the corner, D.C. plates—one person on her phone. That's the Fed. Maybe an MPD unit will come by, relieve her. I'm betting she'll be gone soon and the Feds likely looking for me specificly once everyone else figures I'm on the loose and they hip her what's up.

This SUV has Texas tags, two crackers in it looking fresh from the type of places where my dad used to drink with the other jarhead sergeants—the white ones he was trying so hard to ingratiate—in the front seat, carrying on, laughing at something.

There . . . the side door to the mansion onto Ashmead opens and out comes the Vitter in a hoodie and sweatpants— two dogs leashed. Two Malinois. He greets the bodyguards, and they all laugh again like the world's going to be a better place for them, and off he goes.

I give him a head start, then hit the SUV.

A few dollars for the Metrobus, or food . . .

. . . and they never stop laughing. Give me five bucks, though. Tell me something stupid like "crack is whack." Tell me to get the fuck out of the neighborhood.

Achingly, I head in the opposite direction as Vitter, knowing I can hit the back of the house, on the Belmont side. The fancy side of Obamas and Ivankas and Jareds. They're all gone now, ceding the alleys to me, and these places always have gardens, walled in, as if we're in Europe.

Check.

The SUV drives off. Cooking with gas! I return to the rear of the house, find spot along a colonnade marking the garden's boundary. The entry'd be a pergola blocked by a locked gate. A rusted lock at that. I wait as a car passes the alley, then see how well my cane does on that lock. Not much effort at all.

I linger until I see the lights go on in the rear window, illuminating a large kitchen. Mrs. Vitter must still be in Galveston, enjoying the surf . . .

. . . and enter, sticking to the shadows. I lay on a cold bench by the small wading pool and a hedge of wilting blooms. I light one of the blunts. Can't inhale, won't inhale . . . and even the taste in my mouth's dangerous. I blow a cloud, cough. Kick over a clay pot.

Floodlights pop, and out he comes leveling a pistol, the dogs in kitchen so anxious to kill me they are literally crying.

"I'm so . . . so sorry sir . . . I-I'm tired . . . so cold."

"I could have killed you, fella!"

Can only raise one arm; the cane's in the other and I make sure he sees some hint of bloody bandages.

"Now git!"

"I-I can't sir. Can hardly walk. Feet swollen . . ." All true. See? "I'm bad . . . bad off. Just want to sleep . . ."

"Junkie scum . . ." I hear, and as he moves into a cross-beam of light I swear this motherfucker's part albino he's so pale. Or he's an extra from one of these World War II movies, the kind you see popping out from the hatch of a panzer in a black uniform, Iron Cross award dangling from his throat. Guess he was blond once, now gray, almost a monkish bowl cut. Blue eyes but just the garden variety blue, not Linda Figgis' Disney character purple-blue. Older than me but yeah, cut but for a little paunch.

The blunt get doused in the grass. I feign shame.

"What's that? You aren't on the fentanyl?"

"N-No sir . . . shit scares me."

He chuckles. "It should. What's your poison?"

"T-Tina in weed, sir. A Torpedo roll."

He thumbs the hammer back on this thing that's big enough to be a .45. "Should I put you out of your misery, big boy?"

"I-I'm just hungry, sleepy, sir."

"We'll let my animals decide." He thumbs the hammer closed.

Oh shit. Fifty-fifty chance. And even then . . .

"Stay put big boy." Now he's backing up to that glass door to the kitchen. He opens it and out comes the bigger dog, barking, snarling, like a rocket. He whistles and it halts. And then . . . it begins to whine.

I lower myself to the wet turf. Hold out my hand. "Hey there . . . Good boy . . . good boy . . ."

"Hell you doin' you sumbitch?"

"Good boy . . ."

The dog's tail starts to wag . . . it moves toward me, cautiously, despite Vitter's commands.

What's your real name, pup? It ain't Woody. On loan . . .

The dog switches up, lunges but I tuck up my nuts and hold fast, it stops short of me, barks like it's fussing, then jumps away, as if it just hazed me and I passed and it's celebrating. Yeah, you remember me, boy. I kept Oso from shooting you, probably messing up the plan and pissing off Aidy even more.

"I'll be goddamned," Vitter mutters. "Never seen Ty do that. Well his sister's not gonna be as agreeable. I'll give you a piece of poundcake my staffer made me, send you off. Don't like it when taxpayers' gotta foot the bill for your weakness but there's no other alternative is 'round here."

"Kindness. No one cares anymore, sir . . . everyone thinks I'm on that Tranq shit."

"Really? You must have me confused with the limo liberals like here, or in Austin who preach one thing, *spit on you* . . . in the same breath. We practice Christian charity at College Station . . ."

After a cursory frisk no doubt for a blade, he's inside and makes me stand outside by the door on this slate patio. Both dogs watch me from the glassed-in kitchen. Ty's sitting, still a bit confused; the sister's vigilant, growling but he seems to be chilling her out.

In the time it takes to slice some poundcake I'm on my back, wheezing, trembling on that cold-ass slate, moist with slug trails and the dogs are going crazy. Hurting for real, no doubt, but I whisper as he's hanging over me, "My sugar . . . *my sugar*, sir . . . ain't got no meds . . ."

I feel his hand around my ankle and I'm in the warm kitchen . . . two wolfish heads above me. I hears something about, him "dropping me if I make a move and the dogs ripping me a new one."

"Take it . . . take it," I beg as I offer the second blunt. "Can't deal with this. Can't sir. Lawd, no . . ." And I luck out he takes it, shoves it his sweatpants pocket. The .45's nowhere to be seen . . .

"You gonna be a special project big boy," he says as he props me against a lower cabinet face. "But you outta here soon. I got some candy or some juice." He shoos the dogs behind a foldable barrier leading to another room. Malinois can probably jump that, easy, so I got to play this real live . . .

The cane's behind me, under my ass. I pull it out slowly as he returns, starts to kneel.

"Nah help me up, please." I offer my arm, start pushing with the cane.

"Huh?" Yet almost by reflex he grabs my arm.

I ask him, "So no one helped Randy, like you're helping me?"

His mouth's wide as trout's on a hook. "Hell you say?"

He shoves me away and dogs start to get circle and grunt.

I swing onto a chair. "And he's Ty. Not Woody?" I point the cane at his chest. "Let's talk."

"Who are you?"

"I'm helpless—a pathetic wretch you dragged into your kitchen. Unhoused. A fiend. Bleeding, even . . . see? I mean . . . go get your pistol. Being a Texan I'm surprised you let out of your sight but I bet you got six in the kitchen somewhere unless being inside the Beltway what—two terms that's twelve years—made you soft?"

"You got five seconds before I jump over and push that barrier down and my dogs gitchew."

"This city's a cancer right? Two ways to kill cancer. Cut it out—can't do that. It's the capital, no matter how much people like you want to bleed it out . . . when you're on its tit, that's the irony."

"Get to the point, boy."

"See this gray hair, wrinkles, scars . . . my eyes. No boy. Years of streetwise. Streetwise that says the way is chemo. Keep the decent shit like the monuments, huh? Then bomb the rest with chemistry. Apache . . ."

"Wait. I've . . . I've seen you. Yep. My Lord, I've seen you . . . the PI?" He's been a cold customer, but now his Ivory soap

face melts . . . cheeks flush, eyes flash. "Un-huh! *The nigger PI?*
Voss and Aidy . . . *Voss and Aidy!* Oh, you're in the shit now! My
boys'll back after midnight . . ."

Those Malinois are ready to jump that thing until I shout,
"And then what? How do you explain me!"

Whoa it's like a bucket of ice hit him. "Ty! Millie! *Shut-up!*"

"It's okay, Ty . . . Ty's a good boy. Millie's a good girl . . ." I
look to him. "A U.S. Senator . . . you gonna bumrush me till
they get back? Put a bullet in my head. How you gonna explain
my corpse, you the face of Making America Great Again." I
shake the cane at him. "I'm material witness now for DOJ. I'm
the nightmare. In your kitchen. The kitchen of a fentanyl
trafficker . . ."

"You . . . *you* . . ."

"And I can be made non-material. Flor, ole Flor . . . she was
ready to cut a deal before she geeked and shot my ass."

He backs to the counter under a bank of china shelves. "I
am a respected leader. I don't know what your sick mind is—"

"I'm not wired, man," I say, cutting him off. "You checked
me. I mean, I was when Flor died, sort of. But without me to
connect all the dots, to tell everyone I was just a pawn,
coerced . . ."

"G-Go on."

"Here are my cards, man. Yeah, it was me at that shoot-out
over in Northeast, in that house Flor's son's owned . . . the
one your party's now running commercials about but you
are disowning. Everybody knows you were a friend of Jaime
Bracht's. You have the drug enforcement intel, shit like that,
at your fingers, damn . . . it must have been real juicy before
Biden took over and shut it off. You shuck and jive about the
border yet take advantage of the chaos. You get real quiet

about trafficking despite your son's death. People either battle the shit that took things they loved away, or embrace it, right?"

"So you're a shrink?"

"I had to read people and things to stay alive. So don't clown me. Had to be you Voss was fronting. Had to be you Voss was talking to on the burner before he got . . . burned."

His jaw tightens. I hold the mirror closer.

"God's truth it was seeing the dog on TV that pushed it, a hunned, Senator."

He grins. "Why didn't you just come to me."

"Because I couldn't have gotten within ten feet of you. Because in this *form* . . . my . . . real self I guess—no one notices me. You even let me into this house. And yeah, I'm bleeding, real live, man."

Maybe a second . . . now two is going by and I swear it's like five minutes of silence. I don't even hear the dogs fussing. Those prosaic blue eyes take their toll, though. After a day of killing myself to be myself, I'm the one breaking first . . .

"Okay . . . here's what I want. I fucked things for you and the Colima people. Now, in a perverted way, that's a decent *curriculum vitae* for fixing things, re-upping, keeping Colima happy."

"What's Colima?"

"I said don't clown me."

"So . . . you become . . . a distributor of certain goods."

I nod.

"What did Flor tell you?"

"Not much. Only met her twice. Danielle Diggs tortured me a pool cue though. I think I'm a little better adjusted than her, and I won't fuck your messenger boys and bag men."

"You won't huh?"

"Kill . . . nah."

Vitter reaches with a sinewy yet pale arm behind his body, yanks a drawer open and out comes yet another gun, looks like a .32 "You were right about being prepared." The barking's getting to him. "I said . . . shut-up! Crates, *now!*"

Millie whines and complies. She disappears and I hear metal clanking against metal. Ty looks behind into that room, then looks at me, Vitter, whines again.

"You really think this was gonna work? You as stupid as Ben Ortiz and cocksure dumbfuck careless as that Ivy League sot Dean Scholtz. Voss too. Thinking you too good to get your hands dirty."

"You don't."

"I do it right. New order is coming. Glad to see you wanna be a pet rather than spare ribs but the pig poke gate's already closed. You're stuck."

"All you motherfuckers must think you're on Mt. Olympus or some shit, huh? Like you wrapped in red, white and blue and nothing can fuck with you? I'm no expert Vitter but I know the street. The street-whys, and if you the *bichote*, and you fuck up and can't re-up, you think these people are going to just be courted like your fund managers and shareholders when they get new juicy promises? Voss is gone. Flor—the shot caller, the guarantor, is gone. You think a bunch of fat millionaires and rednecks'll form a human shield when these Mexicans come here wanting to know why the whole jont's fucked . . . why? Because you all made it *political*. There's D.C., the street. There's D.C., the monuments and politics. Never the twain shall meet, asshole."

"Now you're rude being, nigger. We're going to wait for my boys. There are millions of folks out there who'll believe whatever we tell them to believe because they want to, *they have to*. And that's the street-whys, you follow?"

He motions me toward another hallway, away from the lean and swirling dogs. It's a grand dining room . . . damn table's longer than my apartment, on one wall is a huge mirror, embossed and inlaid. I look terrible. Like I'm ready to die. I can sense he refuses to search himself I that thing even when he sees me behold myself. He's got the bead on me. He can pump a couple rounds and drop my fresh from the hospital, true zombie ass right there. His neighbors might even buy a story that it's Netflix or his bodyguards on Playstation.

Yet still . . . he won't look.

Suddenly, the dogs erupt in howls and snarls.

It's either a shadow or ghost or nothing?

No . . . not nothing. A man, in a baseball cap. I see his reflection in the big mirror. I hear a PFFT and the mirror cracks into a diamond spiderweb pattern. It's almost beautiful . . .

"*What?*" Vitter yells.

Then the right side of Vitter's head explodes in a red and gray plume.

Another man enters behind him, stands over his body. His in a black rain slicker. His head's shaved yet is mottled and not a shiny cue ball smooth.

"*Sí . . . jefe . . . Esto está hecho?* I repeat it, hurriedly.

He just stares back, mute. I see his dark eyes. Nothing else, and the dude in the ball cap flanking me . . . who took the kill shot . . . he's motioning with his head.

"*Los perros . . . m' estan molestando,*" he whispers.

"No . . . *por favor*. He's not good to them. Especially the male. Leave them alive."

"And the bodyguards? If they federales, we kill you too."

"No. They consider you . . . *bad hombres*. Do what you want."
The talking one in the cap comes over to me. I hand him
the other blunt. I don't feel anything, except . . . that I'm just
Croc now. The dude lights it, takes some puffs to fire it up; the
mute one takes a few then holds one big one and tests my
puke reflex, numbed by years on the street, by blowing into
the dead mouth and lungs of Senator Brom Vitter.

They pull me out of the house and put me in the back of a
shiny black Benz and tell me to sit until the bodyguards
return. Woe be to any Young who tries to jack this ride.

The thick-necked crackers indeed return maybe an hour
later, with sixpacks and two pizza boxes.

At least I can still hear Ty and Millie barking inside.
Malinoises are psycho I guess, but they aren't suicidal. When
the assassins return I'm apologizing to Ty for getting all of the
humans he knew killed. We roar across the Park.

In sight of the Cathedral at Woodley, baseball cap urges me
to drink a bottle of Mescal on the back seat. It'll calm me
down, he thinks.

"I'm fine. What now?"

Baseball cap hands me some wipes and tells me to wipe my
prints clean in the back, toss bottle out the window.

"*El Pescedor*," the dude says as the mute, scary one sets the
navi for places unknown, "He want to know if you want to
be *bichote*?"

"You could kill me, I know who y'all are . . . otherwise
nothing stopping me from going to the news media, FBI about
Vitter and Voss, Flor and these *putas* who want to come back
to the White House . . . *el Presidente*, huh?"

The bald, mute one finally turns around, and in the street
lights' glow I see he's still got Vitter's blood on his damn

mouth. "You won't do it," he adds in perfect English. "*El Pescedor*, he knows that is not part of the *street*. Just don't prove him wrong. Now I am going to contact the TV networks and *Washington Post* with a new story. This man here is going contact the police as to where they can get you. In the church. You sought sanctuary. You are sinner. You are in ill health."

"That's Episcopal. I'm Catholic."

Baldy with the scary eyes genuflects. Unlocks the back door. "Now get the fuck out. We'll be watching."

CHAPTER TWENTY-FIVE

The Rub

THE UBER DROPS ME ON ST. Jude's side, off I Street, Southeast. I can see folks' cars in line for their vehicle inspections and the there's a line of humans, breaths puffing like smokestacks into the gray sky, at the DCFD hook and ladder station for free canned goods. Verna and Brother Karl Maria must be happy the firefighters are stepping things up as neither the church nor the SFME has got enough turkeys to serve everyone over here. I recall those days.

Well, those days seem long departed when the security guard sees me in my topcoat, a new suit . . . now I have two. I kneel for a novena in the chapel and head to the SFME side. Kneel? More like keep my ass cheeks on the bench, push up with this cheap cane they gave me until I can walk normally. Whatever "normally" or "normal" still means.

Verna's standing there in a purple knit dress, like big turtle-neck and she's got a sweet brooch, leaves and pumpkins to celebrate the day. She tells Katie and one of the counselors to see if they are ready, as we got to call another Uber to get us uptown, and it's all on my dime.

While we wait, I guess I break down first.

"You look great."

"So do you. You're alive. And . . . I'm thankful . . . today . . . you aren't the hero. Or are you? What are you?"

"Just me. Still figuring that out."

"And your two other women?"

"Throwing shade, or truly trying to be funny? Not cool."

"Asking. Just . . . asking."

"When I get back here, for dinner. I'll spill. After we eat, you, Katie, Keesh. Over sweet potato pie."

"Katie eats pumpkin." She looks over her shoulder. "Here they come."

Katie's flanked by Artemesia Sellers' children. She holds their hands, they eagerly clasp her's.

They look . . . amazing. Reborn, if you are lucky enough to be a kid reborn as a kid. He's in a navy blazer, collared shirt, jeans, sneakers. Nice high-top curly fade on his head! She's in a red jumper and tights, jeans jacket, brown leather sandals. Wonderful little gold ribbons in her braids.

"Ain't nobody scared of big ole Mr. Cornish, right?" Katie asks.

They shake their heads.

"Okay then," I say. "Ready? Be brave."

"Are you hurt?" the little girl asks me.

"Yes, in many places."

"But not as bad as Ar't'ur?"

"That's why I'm here, sweetie."

I call up the car and it scoops us up. I don't think these kids have ridden in a clean sedan driven by someone smiling before. We get up to Medstar in no time as few people are on the streets headed to eats and treats.

Everything's going fine until we get up to the 5th floor. For me, I'm queasy nobody's fixed the window Dean leaped from. Just plywood. I try not look after we pass that set of suites.

For them, the adults, noises, smells, equipment . . . moans is beginning to frighten them. The girl's grip on my arm is like a vice and it's hard to walk with the cane. The boy's now trying to turn tail and head for the elevator.

Gets worse when we enter the unit, and they got to put on caps, gowns, masks, gloves, shoe covers all oversized for their little bodies. No matter I got my gear on too.

"Mama say he dead," the boy says, glum.

"He jus' meat," his sister adds in a whisper.

The nurse and a technician guide the kids closer to the bed, and they are distracted by the tubes, the machines and the sounds they emit. They almost have to be prompted to look . . . a Arthur. Head swollen frightfully, linebacker body thin and frail.

Eyes open, lazily pupils following sounds.

The screeches, the cries, fill the unit. I mean, people are coming by, craning their necks from the nurses' stations. They want to climb on top of him like a human bounce palace but the railings prevent it.

I wish I could laugh, even smile.

"So it's been what, two or three days?" I ask the doctor.

"Three." She looks me up and down. "You look very familiar. Your name again?"

"I'm too old for the NBA."

"Yeah . . . but . . . anyway, this young man. Amazing. Crazy times we live in. Crazy!"

"Any word on brain damage?"

"It could be profound. We'll know more by next week. But he responds to faces, sounds. If we didn't think this would help we wouldn't have authorized it. Who's paying for the rest of the care if the city and the federal government are only picking up a portion? I mean—that's the rumor."

"Don't worry about that. This is a brave kid. What he did . . . it set a lot in motion. He could have sat back and let a bad life happen, let things up . . . and re-up."

She doesn't get it. Don't expect anyone will fully understand. Crazy times, yes.

We return to SFME and have a Thanksgiving dinner on paper plates and it's the best food I've ever tasted. We toast Arthur Sellers with ginger ale and lemonade. I excuse myself for the lil' gents' room and the very low urinals in that kids' wing of the shelter. I can almost taste the sweet potato pie and ice cream and I'm thankful for a full stream of piss that doesn't rock my world. I wash up and push open the door, smiling. Finally. Mother Mary, I'm smiling!

Until I see who greets me. There's a dour white dude in a spy-looking trenchcoat at my eye level. But Bivens is below me, looking up, wrapped in a cobalt blue smooth boiled wool coat, brass buttons glinting, shining. Her hands are in her pockets.

"Dickie."

"Who let you in?"

"That's not nice. It's a holiday."

"We're having turkey. Are you the lame duck?"

"That's even meaner. Yet I'm much happier with the circumstances. Mine at least. On my way to dinner at the White House. It'll be one for the ages, for me. But um . . . I had to stop here."

"What? Kill, just no more bullshit."

She takes a deep breath, like she's about to jump into a pool's deep end. "Esmeralda Rubio. She's dead."

It's like someone turned down a dial in my ears, then shot it way up. I hug the cinderblock wall festooned with children's stick figure artwork. "In . . . Mexico?"

"She was under guard at a beach condo near Vera Cruz." I'm clenching my eyelids as she speaks. "Federal police found her in the shower . . . fully clothed. Hypo in her. A hot dose. Fentanyl. Like what—"

"Stop . . . *stop.*" Now I'm crouching to the chickenhawk's height as I finally open my eyes. They are dry as the Sonoran desert. "She'd been clean over twenty years. No OD . . ."

"Of course not."

"Stamp. Yeah. There's the *rub.*"

"We fought once over what that meant."

"Oh, it's . . . a reminder. To me. Not to smile too much or be too thankful. To look over my shoulder. Message received."

"Would you like to . . ."

"What?"

"We missed Homecoming. My jinx. The Bison are MEAC champs and are going to a bowl game, nevertheless. Can you imagine that, a bowl? Life goes on. Would you like to go with me?"

"Real live?"

"Uh-huh."

"*N-No.* And you spring *this* after what you just told me? Is there anything else?"

Yeah, this is P-out. For good . . .

"Yes, I'm in awe. That's all."

"Don't be. *Please.* Don't be now, don't be at eighteen. Come on."

"You're paying for Arthur Sellers with rest of Bracht's money, aren't you?" She pauses when she hears Verna calling for me. "You're sponsoring those two younger kids. That boy—the baby that started all of this . . . Esmeralda tried to help in her own way . . . he's growing up happy. How could we not be in awe?"

I draw close and the escort gets tense, mean. She calms him as I whisper, "You know goddamn well."

"Happy Thanksgiving Dickie. I have a spare stadium ticket and plane ticket two days after Christmas. I'm an honorary guest at the alumni tailgate jam, along with the VP . . . imagine my sorors' faces. Quite the send-off. You can pretend it's a fourth quarter Hail Mary . . ."

It's so very damp and pea-soup foggy now . . . warmer at midnight than it was at dinner and that's weather in the D-M-V. Most regular people are still nursing the *-itis* or in bed after putting another Thanksgiving in the books among family and friends. Maybe tomorrow I'll stop by the Soldiers and Sailors Home, Daddy. Maybe you'll do an Arthur Sellers and we'll grab a vanilla pudding in the cafeteria, catch up on things.

Yet for now, I'm alone but for some rats staring at me from a dumpster, and pathetic white man in a stringy brown beard offering his last deck of Xanax so he can grab stuffing and gravy. Despite the limited company, I move down the pavement slowly . . . careful not to let my shoes make any scuffing sound.

All around are tents of various materials—some actual tents housed from outdoor stores, some homemade jobs sewn together on a wish and prayer from tarp and rags. Nothing besting me from my scavenging days, as if I should be prideful. In all, I hear the coughs and moans, the snores. This spot, under the freeway not half a mile from St. Jude's and SFME, is the last camp uninfected by the Tranq . . .

. . . and so in this last tent, a combo of pup tent and refrigerator packing boxes, I see a glow within, backlighting limbs.

I hear a girl, not a woman, weeping.

"Bitch shut up. It ain't goin' hurt. Put some spit on it."

I tear the flap open.

"Shit . . . *dayum!*" Kenny yells. He's got his pants and drawers around his ankles. He's got that long knife in one hand that short stubby thing in the other. "Dickie . . . *aw* Hell . . . is that you? You ain't goin' snitch on me ta Peach, is you?"

"Nah, moe. In fact, Peach wanted me to fix you."

"Aw . . . thanks, bruh. I'm good. She jus' company before I git home ta Peach."

"Uh-uh." I lean closer. "Come on out here and let me fix you."

THE END

About the Author

CRITICALLY-ACCLAIMED, AWARD-WINNING author Christopher Chambers is the creator of the Dickie Cornish detective series, including Scavenger, Standalone, and Streetwhys. His short fiction has appeared in numerous award-winning anthologies. He's been nominated for a PEN/Malamud and is an accomplished pulp and graphic novel collaborative author. He sits on the Bouchercon World Mystery Writers Convention Board and is a judge for the Mystery Writers of America Edgars Awards. He lives in Washington, D.C. with his wife and German Shepherd, Max.

RECENT AND FORTHCOMING BOOKS FROM THREE ROOMS PRESS

FICTION

Lucy Jane Bledsoe
No Stopping Us Now

Rishab Borah
The Door to Inferna

Meagan Brothers
Weird Girl and What's His Name

Christopher Chambers
Scavenger
Standalone
StreetWhys

Ebele Chizea
Aquarian Dawn

Ron Dakron
Hello Devilfish!

Ron Dakron
Hello Devilfish!

Robert Duncan
Loudmouth

Amanda Eisenberg
People Are Talking

Michael T. Fournier
Hidden Wheel
Swing State

Kate Gale
Under a Neon Sun

Aaron Hamburger
Nirvana Is Here

William Least Heat-Moon
Celestial Mechanics

Aimee Herman
Everything Grows

Kelly Ann Jacobson
Tink and Wendy
Robin and Her Misfits
Lies of the Toymaker

Jethro K. Lieberman
Everything Is Jake

Eamon Loingsigh
Light of the Diddicoy
Exile on Bridge Street

John Marshall
The Greenfather

Alvin Orloff
Vulgarian Rhapsody

Micki Janae
Of Blood and Lightning

Aram Saroyan
Still Night in L.A.

Robert Silverberg
The Face of the Waters

Stephen Spotte
Animal Wrongs

Richard Vetere
The Writers Afterlife
Champagne and Cocaine

Jessamyn Violet
Secret Rules to Being a Rockstar

Julia Watts
Quiver
Needlework
Lovesick Blossoms

Gina Yates
Narcissus Nobody

MEMOIR & BIOGRAPHY

Nassrine Azimi and Michel Wasserman
Last Boat to Yokohama: The Life and Legacy of Beate Sirota Gordon

William S. Burroughs & Allen Ginsberg
Don't Hide the Madness:
William S. Burroughs in Conversation with Allen Ginsberg
edited by Steven Taylor

James Carr
BAD: The Autobiography of James Carr

Judy Gumbo
Yippie Girl: Exploits in Protest and Defeating the FBI

Judith Malina
Full Moon Stages: Personal Notes from 50 Years of The Living Theatre

Phil Marcade
Punk Avenue: Inside the New York City Underground, 1972–1982

Jillian Marshall
Japanthem: Counter-Cultural Experiences; Cross-Cultural Remixes

Alvin Orloff
Disasterama! Adventures in the Queer Underground 1977–1997

Nicca Ray
Ray by Ray: A Daughter's Take on the Legend of Nicholas Ray

Stephen Spotte
My Watery Self:
Memoirs of a Marine Scientist

Christina Vo & Nghia M. Vo
My Vietnam, Your Vietnam
Vietnamese translation: *Việt Nam Của Con, Việt Nam Của Cha*

PHOTOGRAPHY-MEMOIR

Mike Watt
On & Off Bass

SHORT STORY ANTHOLOGIES

SINGLE AUTHOR

Alien Archives: Stories
by Robert Silverberg

First-Person Singularities: Stories
by Robert Silverberg

Tales from the Eternal Café: Stories
by Janet Hamill, intro by Patti Smith

Time and Time Again:
Sixteen Trips in Time
by Robert Silverberg

The Unvarnished Gary Phillips:
A Mondo Pulp Collection
by Gary Phillips

Voyagers: Twelve Journeys in Space and Time
by Robert Silverberg

MULTI-AUTHOR

The Colors of April
edited by Quan Manh Ha & Cab Tran

Crime + Music: Nineteen Stories of Music-Themed Noir
edited by Jim Fusilli

Dark City Lights: New York Stories
edited by Lawrence Block

The Faking of the President: Twenty Stories of White House Noir
edited by Peter Carlaftes

Florida Happens:
Bouchercon 2018 Anthology
edited by Greg Herren

Have a NYC I, II & III:
New York Short Stories;
edited by Peter Carlaftes & Kat Georges

No Body, No Crime: Twenty-two Tales of Taylor Swift-Inspired Noir
edited by Alex Segura & Joe Clifford

Songs of My Selfie:
An Anthology of Millennial Stories
edited by Constance Renfrow

The Obama Inheritance:
15 Stories of Conspiracy Noir
edited by Gary Phillips

This Way to the End Times:
Classic & New Stories of the Apocalypse
edited by Robert Silverberg

DADA

Maintenant: A Journal of Contemporary Dada Writing & Art
(annual, since 2008)

MIXED MEDIA

John S. Paul
Sign Language: A Painter's Notebook
(photography, poetry and prose)

HUMOR

Peter Carlaftes
A Year on Facebook

FILM & PLAYS

Israel Horovitz
My Old Lady: Complete Stage Play and Screenplay with an Essay on Adaptation

Peter Carlaftes
Triumph For Rent (3 Plays)
Teatrophy (3 More Plays)

Kat Georges
Three Somebodies:
Plays about Notorious Dissidents

TRANSLATIONS

Thomas Bernhard
On Earth and in Hell
(poems of Thomas Bernhard with English translations by Peter Waugh)

Patrizia Gattaceca
Isula d'Anima / Soul Island

César Vallejo | Gerard Malanga
Malanga Chasing Vallejo

George Wallace
EOS: Abductor of Men
(selected poems in Greek & English)

ESSAYS

Richard Katrovas
Raising Girls in Bohemia:
Meditations of an American Father

Vanessa Baden Kelly
Far Away From Close to Home

Erin Wildermuth (editor)
Womentality

POETRY COLLECTIONS

Hala Alyan
Atrium

Peter Carlaftes
DrunkYard Dog
I Fold with the Hand I Was Dealt
Life in the Past Lane

Thomas Fucaloro
It Starts from the Belly and Blooms

Kat Georges
Our Lady of the Hunger
Awe and Other Words Like Wow

Robert Gibbons
Close to the Tree

Israel Horovitz
Heaven and Other Poems

David Lawton
Sharp Blue Stream

Jane LeCroy
Signature Play

Philip Meersman
This Is Belgian Chocolate

Jane Ormerod
Recreational Vehicles on Fire
Welcome to the Museum of Cattle

Lisa Panepinto
On This Borrowed Bike

George Wallace
Poppin' Johnny

Three Rooms Press | New York, NY | Current Catalog: www.threeroomspress.com
Three Rooms Press books are distributed by Publishers Group West: www.pgw.com